Praise for Nathalie Theodore

PRAISE FOR *IF WE PLAY FAIR*

Nathalie Theodore knocks it clean out of the park with this Chicago-to-Maui romance that's equal parts sparkling banter and emotional depth. What begins as a prickly fake relationship between a baseball star with demons and a sharp, ambitious literary agent unfolds into a love story that feels earned, and deeply human.

The enemies-to-lovers tension crackles, but it's the dual POV that is rich with vulnerability, humor, and thoughtful mental health nuance that truly elevates the novel, giving both characters dimension far beyond the genre norm. And then there's Maui: practically a character in its own right. Theodore turns the island into a romantic refuge where walls come down and feelings can't stay benched for long. As a longtime fan, I can say without hesitation that this is Nathalie Theodore's best novel yet.

— Parissa Andideh, Goodreads Reviewer

First off, let me say that I do not frequent the romance genre. I've read three romance novels to date, and they were all written by Nathalie Theodore. What can I say? When you have a talented author for a wife, who continues to literally outdo herself with every book she writes, reading them is a no-brainer.

If We Play Fair is by far Nathalie's best work yet, and that's saying a lot considering the award-winning status of her debut novel!

Nathalie's third novel has all the elements that will keep you wanting more and not wanting to put it down. From the non-stop drama to the witty banter between the two main characters, you'll find yourself saying "just one more page." While the book is fun, it wouldn't be a Nathalie Theodore book if it didn't explore the all-too-real everyday issues (self-doubt and grief) that will surely resonate with the reader. Nathalie does an amazing job exploring these issues through excellent character development, and you'll find yourself immersed in the story and rooting for Holden and Christy.

Given my wife's pattern of constantly raising the bar (and clearing it by a long shot), I cannot wait to see what she has in store for the next book in this series!

— DOMINIQUE THEODORE, GOODREADS REVIEWER

If We Play Fair, the third installment in the Dramatic Hearts Club, was my absolute favorite of the series so far. Christy and Holden were everything in this story of facing your insecurities, dealing with life-altering circumstances, growing into your own, being there for the ones you love, and finding your person when you least expect it. Not to mention, this is Nathalie's spiciest read yet! The growth of both the main and side characters was refreshing, and I loved walking with them through their journeys. Nathalie is a master at incorporating mental health representation in her books, and *If We Play Fair* was no different—it was a story that I've related to even more than any other. This book was a phenomenal follow-up to Books One and Two (with some characters you may recognize along the way)! I'm very excited for the next chapter in the Dramatic Hearts Club universe.

— ELISIA F., GOODREADS REVIEWER

PRAISE FOR *IF MY WISHES CAME TRUE*

I fell in love with *If My Wishes Came True* at first sight, just like Jenna fell for Charlie. In this stellar follow-up to *If The Stars Align* (yes, I went there!) Nathalie Theodore weaves that spark of "meant to be" magic with real, raw moments that hit you right in the heart. This is a beautifully messy, layered journey of two people who have to fight for their happily ever after—and trust me, they deserve every single second, even when they can't quite believe it themselves. Plus, their chemistry lights the page on fire! Fair warning: you'll want to devour this one in a single sitting.

— EMILY COLIN, NEW YORK TIMES BESTSELLING
AUTHOR OF THE MEMORY THIEF

If My Wishes Came True is a worthy sophomore entry to the Dramatic Hearts Club Series! Jenna and Charlie are flawed individuals, and their paths to self-improvement are no different. They are one of the most realistic romance novel couples I've ever read, and I couldn't be happier about it! This story isn't about one person bettering themselves to be with the other–it's about two imperfect people meeting each other where they're at while also working to be better for each other together. I laughed, I cried, I saw pieces of myself reflected in so many of the characters... And it's because Nathalie Theodore understands that people don't want to read a perfect romance about perfect people because they don't exist. I loved *If My Wishes Came True*, and I can't wait to see what comes next!

— ABIGAIL STAPLER, GOODREADS REVIEWER

Nathalie Theodore's latest novel, *If My Wishes Came True*, is a highly anticipated follow-up to her debut, *If The Stars Align*. *If My Wishes Came True* delivers everything I could hope for and more. Once I picked it up, I could not put it down! This is THE ultimate easy-to-read romance novel that I could read over and over again. In this novel, the focus shifts to Jenna, whose quiet charm made a lasting impression in the first book. Her journey is both relatable and aspirational as she stumbles through her past, uncertainty, hope, and the exhilarating, and (sometimes) messy process of falling in love. I was delighted to reunite with familiar faces from the first novel, and see Jenna step in the spotlight to find the happiness she so deserves. Nathalie Theodore has done it again and written another hit!

— PARISSA ANDIDEH, GOODREADS REVIEWER

PRAISE FOR *IF THE STARS ALIGN*
WINNER, 2025 Bronze IPPY Award for Romance

If the Stars Align is a breathtaking exploration of love's power to transform—one raw, honest moment at a time. Theodore's background as a therapist shines here—Dex's struggle with anxiety will resonate with anyone who has ever felt overwhelmed by their own inner demons, and Sunny's perfectionism is all too relatable. Their love story is as authentic as it gets: beautiful, painful, hopeful, and tender. Perfect for fans of Mia Sheridan and Colleen Hoover, this book will claim a place in your heart and stay with you long after you've turned the final page.

— EMILY COLIN, NEW YORK TIMES BESTSELLING
AUTHOR OF THE MEMORY THIEF

I'll be honest, I first bought this book because I was obsessed with the cover but the love story inside is just as beautiful! I cannot get enough of Sunny and Dex!!! The character development is top tier—the author did an amazing job of showing how the protagonists' trauma affected them consciously and subconsciously and how they worked through it to become the versions of themselves that they were always meant to be. The universe always has different plans from what our ego thinks should happen but it all comes out better than imagined once the stars finally align. I can't wait for another book by this author!!

— EMILY MATOS, GOODREADS REVIEWER

Nathalie Theodore enters the romance novel genre with quite a splash! I absolutely LOVED *If the Stars Align*! It is so captivating, well-written, emotion provoking and has such well-developed characters that it is impossible to put down. Theodore takes us on quite the rollercoaster journey as she brilliantly portrays both Sunny and Dex's inner dialogues. She diligently captures both the flaws and beauty of the characters, and portrays such realistic accounts of the world of law, mental health, family dynamics, complicated friendships, and of course, true love. I can't wait for the next book to come out. I have a feeling Nathalie Theodore will be the next big name in romance novel authors!

— SARAH IMBERMAN, GOODREADS REVIEWER

NATHALIE THEODORE

To every woman whose body has been critiqued instead of cherished.
You were never the problem.

CHAPTER 1

Christy

SEPTEMBER 2012

I'm never reading another romance novel again.

With an exasperated sigh, I toss the unpublished manuscript to the opposite end of my window seat, where I always curl up with a good book. This one was no exception. It was heartfelt, smart, and funny. The banter and spice were top-notch. It was everything I could hope for in a love story, both as a literary agent and a lifelong bibliophile.

It was also total bullshit.

There are no men out there like dreamy Edison Ford, who biked across the country *during an apocalypse* to save his one true love, Iris, from certain death.

Just ask my blind date, Trevor, who couldn't be bothered to text me an excuse for standing me up last night.

Instead, he left me waiting at the bar of my favorite sushi restaurant like a hopeful idiot, turning my head each time the door swung open. Would it have killed him to shoot me a message saying he was sick? Swamped at work? Make up a reason, Trevor! That's what white lies are for. And before you say, *Well, maybe he had a family emergency, or something*—he didn't. We were set up by his cousin Ashley, a friend of mine from college, so I called her this morning to see if she'd heard from him. Apparently, he was at a karaoke bar with friends. She knew this because he'd posted several videos on Instagram last night, doing his best impression of Johnny Cash. In an effort to console me, Ashley assured me he sounded a little pitchy.

The sting hasn't worn off yet. And it doesn't help that I spent all day reading about the most perfect man to walk the apocalyptic Earth. Edison Ford would never be such an ill-mannered prick. He knows how to treat a woman.

Boy, does he know.

My pulse quickens as my mind darts back to Chapter Nineteen of this book I'm trying *not* to be obsessed with. The last thing I need is to add a romance writer to my client list right now, when I've never been more jaded about love.

But...fuck if that chapter wasn't the hottest thing I've ever read.

I stare at the manuscript sitting on the other end of the window seat. My cheeks flush, as if Edison himself were flirting with me.

A hint of a smile tugs at my lips, and I look away from the spiralbound book, playing hard to get. But who am I kidding? That scene on the beach, under the stars, is going to live rent-free in my mind forever.

"Fuck it," I say, under my breath.

Excitement ripples through me as I give in to temptation. I'm practically giddy when the crisp pages are in my hands again, and I'm flipping to the part where the spice is off-the-charts. I put on *Rebellious*—a wildly sexy song by pop icon Lola Piper, and the perfect soundtrack for a forbidden tryst. Then I settle back into the coziness of the reading nook my sister Jenna, an uber-talented interior designer and artist, created for me, and I heave a happy sigh.

So, maybe I can't swear off romance novels. My favorite ones are written by badass women anyway, so what would be the point? I can't blame this innocent writer for Trevor's transgressions. Empowered women empower women after all, and as a literary agent who just left an esteemed firm to launch her own agency, my dream is to do exactly that.

No, I won't give up on swoony main characters, but I *can* swear off dating...for the time being, at least. To say that my love life is a disaster would imply that I have one, which is far from the case. At thirty years old, I still only have one ex-boyfriend to my name.

Kyle.

We met during our junior year at Columbia University. Our roommates were in love and inseparable, which meant Kyle and I hung out a lot by default. It was a relationship of convenience, more than anything else. I swear, I saw him shrug, like, "Oh, what the hell," before he first kissed me. It was the least romantic beginning you could imagine. I suppose neither of us believed we had other options, though, because we were together for nearly a decade.

When we broke up two years ago, I took the opportunity to reinvent myself. I moved from New York to Chicago. I updated my beige and black capsule wardrobe with bold prints and florals. I picked a signature color, red, because I love the way it looks with my auburn hair. Now, I hardly ever leave the house without a crimson lip, even to run errands. I'm trying my best to channel "main character energy" and manifest my own Edison Ford.

But as Karaoke Trevor can attest, it's not going well.

At least I can't complain about my career. I was born to be a boss, and here I am representing the most sought-after author of the season. No sooner did I hang up my shingle than I signed Dr. Penelope Dwyer, a buzzworthy love and relationship expert whose debut self-help book is coming out this winter. The highly anticipated launch is sure to put a spotlight on my brand and, maybe I'm shooting for the moon, but I'm hoping I may even catch Lola Piper's eye. Rumor has it, she's writing a memoir about her rise to fame, and repping her would be a dream come true. Beyond the fact that I'm a loyal fan—or *Pipette*, as we unapologetically call ourselves—I've always felt inspired by Lola's determination. Her work ethic is unrivaled. She's built an unbreakable empire, and to top it all off, she's generous, kind, and a brilliant songwriter. I'm sure her book will be phenomenal.

For now, working with her is a pipe dream, if you'll pardon the pun. Regardless, I'm still thanking my lucky stars for landing Penelope. She's an ideal client, too. Smart, motivated, communicative.

Although, come to think of it, she hasn't returned my last two voicemails, and I have several interview requests I need to run by her. I'm sure she's swamped with edits. After I finish rereading this very sexy chapter of *Edison's Love* (and, let's face it, email the author to offer representation), I'll reach out to Penelope again.

I immerse myself in the beach scene, but right as Edison's about to have his way with Iris, my phone rings. It's Frances, my friend and former coworker at Hanover Literary, who introduced me to the sensational Dr. Dwyer. After Kyle and I broke up, she begged me to see the up-and-coming love guru speak at Soho House. I walked in a skeptic and left feeling more hopeful than I had in years. There are a lot of phonies out there, but Penelope's the real deal and practices what she preaches. The love expert has been happily married to her high school sweetheart for twenty years.

"Hey, you," I answer with a smile. "I just spent the entire day reading exceptionally well-written smut. Don't we have the best job ever?"

"Oh, god," she replies, sounding anxiety-ridden.

"What's wrong?" My tone is sympathetic, but I'm not alarmed. It isn't unusual for Frances to call me in a tizzy. She's the sweetest person I've ever met, and you'd think that moving from Iowa to the Big Apple might've hardened her, but no. It only seems to have made her live in constant fear that someone might yell at her. Poor thing.

"Well, I have some news," my friend says, her voice trembling.

"What is it?"

Even her sigh is shaky. "You're not going to like it."

I blink a few times, but don't spiral. Frances has a tendency to blow things out of proportion. "Just tell me. I'm sure it can't be that bad."

She lets out a noise that's part laugh and part whimper. "It's about Dr. Dwyer."

My breath hitches. "*Penelope?*"

Oh god, I hope she's okay. I figured she was swamped with work this week, but is there some other reason she's gone radio silent?

Frances sounds like she's on the verge of crying. "Her husband, Jason, reached out to me, looking for representation. He's writing a tell-all about Penelope. Well, he hasn't actually written anything yet...except for the title."

I clear my throat, a nervous tic I inherited from my dad. When it comes to business, I exude confidence, even in the odd instance where I have to fake it. The throat-clearing is my only tell, and I hate it. "Well, what's the title?"

Her voice comes out as a petrified squeak. "The Biggest Fraud Who Ever Lived."

Okay. Now, I'm panicked. "Please tell me you're joking."

My friend's words spew out, a mile a minute. "I wish I were. Apparently, Penelope's been cheating on her husband left and right since she's been in the spotlight. He's known for a while, but wanted to talk to a lawyer before confronting her. He served her divorce papers last week and hasn't heard from her since. When he got home from work that day, her things were gone. He thinks she ran off with one of her lovers."

"Are you fucking kidding me?" My voice is shrill. "This is a nightmare!"

The most notable client on my list, the relationship "expert" I've been championing, is a sham. What will this scandal do to my reputation? I've always dreamed of running my own agency. Now I'll be the industry's cautionary tale.

All because of Dr. Penelope *Liar*.

"Please don't hate me," Frances cries. "You have no idea how sorry I am. If I hadn't dragged you to hear her speak, you never would've drunk the Kool-Aid, and you wouldn't be representing her. This is all my fault!"

"Jesus, I'm not mad at *you*," I huff. "I'm mad at that two-timing cheat."

"Oh, thank goodness." She heaves a sigh of relief. "Because you're really scary when you're mad. I never told you this, but... you know the noise-canceling headphones I started bringing to work? I bought them after you reamed out the team at Dunn Street Press for delaying your client's pub date."

A nostalgic grin blooms on my face. "I remember that phone call. I drew a crowd outside my office door."

I do enjoy putting assholes in their place. It's one of the perks of agenting. Kyle once mused that I chose a career that lets me yell because showing anger was frowned upon in the Andersen household. Unless, of course, you were my dad.

Anyway, I have to take Kyle's assessment with a grain of salt. He's a radiologist—what does he know about psychology?

Frances is right, though. Usually, I'm a fierce advocate for my clients and will always step up to the plate for them. But in Penelope's case, that's about to change.

I purse my lips. "Did Jason tell his soon-to-be ex that he's planning to expose her?"

"Yes. He had the process server give her two envelopes. One with the divorce papers, and one with the pitch for his book."

"Thanks, Frances. I'm going to get a head start on damage control."

When we hang up, my eyes are burning, and my throat feels tight. My instinct isn't to cry, though. I have no qualms about crying when I'm sad, but that's not my problem. Right now, white-hot rage is coursing through my veins.

So, I pick up one of the pretty mint-green pillows Jenna chose for my window seat, press it to my mouth, and stifle a scream, instead.

I'm not sure what I'm more upset about. The fact that my hard-earned reputation is on the line...or the fact that I bought into Penelope's bullshit.

I walked into Soho House blindly that night. I knew I was about to hear some pop psychologist wax poetic about relationships, but when I found out the topic was "Dating and Self-Esteem: Learning to Love Yourself First," I had to laugh at the irony. If anyone needed to be there, it was me. When it comes to my job, I'm self-assured almost to the point of arrogance. But when it comes to men, my insecurities always win.

Penelope made me feel seen. She convinced me that I could let go of my baggage and stop blaming myself for things I can't control. For not having the perfect body. Or the prettiest face. For not looking like every guy's fantasy, the way my blonde, green-eyed, perfectly proportioned sister does.

Now it's clear she was only spewing nonsense because that's exactly what a roomful of single women in New York wanted to hear. *Needed* to hear.

Including me.

Face flushed with rage, I stomp to my foyer, not bothering to fix my unkempt hair or change out of my baggy sweats. I grab my signature lipstick from my tote and paint my mouth red. Then I slide into my sneakers and take the elevator to the first floor, giving the doorman a quick wave before I head outside and cross the street to the high-rise where my sister lives with her fiancé, Charlie.

I have my own set of keys because I'm at their place so much. I only use them to get into the lobby, though. I wouldn't dare barge into the lovebirds' apartment without knocking first. Those two are so hot for each other, I'm surprised they haven't burned down the building yet.

I've never had a relationship that came anywhere close to that level of passion. But I'm thrilled Jenna found it. She and Charlie went through hell to get their happy ending, and it's hard not to root for them...even when I'm in a shit mood because my hottest romantic relationship is with a fictional character; the closest I've come to true love is my espresso machine; and now the one thing I've always been able to rely on —my professional reputation—is hanging by a thread.

Along with my sanity.

I pound my fist against the door.

"Hey, sis. Who pissed you off?" Charlie says when he opens it.

Tall, tanned, and toned, he's ridiculously attractive—even considering the fact that Jenna once dated an actual movie star. Dex Oliver, the Oscar-winning actor and mental health advocate, grew up with us in Beachwood, Ohio. He was recently named *People Magazine*'s "Sexiest Man Alive," but I think Charlie could give him a run for his money. Right now, though, my almost brother-in-law looks concerned, and maybe the slightest bit uneasy. I guess Frances was right...I do get scary when I'm mad.

When my sweet sister appears behind him, I try my best to dial back my anger. With her doe eyes and gentle disposition, Jenna gives off a Disney princess vibe—so much so that I sometimes expect to see little birds flitting around her. I don't want to shock her with my potty mouth. She has no idea I curse like a sailor when we're not together.

No one in the Andersen house swore when we were growing up. Not even my grumpy dad. He'd say that cursing was unsophisticated, and his main concern was keeping up with the Joneses at the Beachwood country club. My mom wasn't only miserable in her marriage, but depressed. She never spoke up about it, though, and suffered in silence.

When Jenna's first love died, my sister started experiencing waves of depression, too. She spent years trying to run from her past, but it all caught up with her when she moved to Chicago and met Charlie. Finally, she found the courage to go to therapy, and later convinced our mother to do the same. It's been nearly a year since Mom filed for divorce and joined us in the Windy City. Now the three of us are closer than we've ever been, and Mom and Jenna are happier than I've ever seen them.

As for me, I've always put on a good game face. My family never suspected how much anger I had festering inside me as a kid.

I try my best to keep it that way.

With my sister and soon-to-be brother-in-law standing in front of me, I remind myself to unclench my jaw and take a deep breath. Then I pray I can speak without expletives. It'll be no small feat, considering how motherfucking pissed off I am.

"Penelope Dwyer is a fraud," I say as they follow me to the couch, where I curl up under a blanket and make myself at home.

Charlie takes his place on the opposite end of the sofa, and Jenna sits between us with her hand on my knee. I fill them in on the details, but as soon as I'm done, my phone starts chiming.

I dig my cell out of my tote and glance at the screen. It's the Google Alert I set to tell me when my name appears in the news. It's not unusual for me to get press coverage when I've just struck a deal or when my clients' books make bestseller lists. But not on a random Sunday night.

Fingers trembling, I click on the link titled, "Penelope Dwyer's Husband Speaks Out: *My Wife is Full of Sh*t!*"

My stomach churns as I skim the article:

Jason Dwyer, husband of renowned psychologist and relationship expert Dr. Penelope Dwyer, has filed for divorce, and is blasting his soon-to-be ex-wife on social media. In a video posted to his Instagram account this evening, Jason (who is drinking a beer and appears to be inebriated) alleges that the love guru is not only a serial cheater who's had ongoing affairs throughout their marriage—but a charlatan, too.

*"She's a fraud in every way. She never graduated from Cambridge. All she did was audit a class there for a semester. She isn't a real doctor, either [hiccup]. She got some bullshit certificate from an online coaching program that doesn't exist anymore. I swore I'd take her secrets to the grave...but that was before that f*cking b*tch ripped my heart out."*

Earlier this year, Dr. Dwyer signed a seven-figure deal with Roscoe Press for three self-help titles, including her upcoming release, Loving Authentically. *She is repped by Christy Andersen.*

"What's the matter?" Jenna asks, forehead crinkled.

My head is spinning. All I can do is hand her the phone.

With Charlie looking over her shoulder, my sister examines the page, but her expression remains calm. "This can't be true. The cheating part, sure, but not her credentials. Her husband was drunk, not to mention heartbroken. I'm sure he's lying. There's no way Dr. Dwyer's a fake."

I look into Jenna's big, round eyes, her long lashes fluttering, and I want to believe her. I almost do...

Until my phone chimes in her hand, and her jaw drops.

CHAPTER 2
Christy

I bury my face in my hands. "Oh, god, what now?"

"Um...Dr. Dwyer responded to her husband's video," my sister tells me.

I peek at her through parted fingers. "And?"

Jenna swallows, then hands my phone to Charlie. "Will you read it to her?"

He nods, brows drawn together. "Dr. Penelope Dwyer took to social media this evening to...um..." He scratches his head. "To confirm allegations about her credentials."

My eyes go wide. "She did *what*? Why on earth would she admit to that? Why didn't she at least call me first?"

Charlie continues, his tone even, but his cheeks flushed. It happens whenever he's nervous. That's *his* tell. "In the post, which has garnered a million views and counting, Dr. Dwyer says she started the account as performance art, then realized she had a gift for helping people. She insists she's more than qualified to give mental health advice. 'It's not education that matters, it's intuition,' she says. 'I manifested my own destiny, and so can you. My techniques work, and you'll see that when you buy my book this November 1st.'"

"Geez. What a phony," Jenna mutters to herself. Then she turns to me. "Sorry."

"What does the article say about me?" My name must come up somewhere, since the post triggered my Google Alert. I feel sick waiting for Charlie's answer.

"Only that you're her agent," he replies, but his cheeks flush an even deeper shade of red, which makes my palms sweat.

"That's it? Are you sure?"

He scratches his eyebrow. "You're, uh...also mentioned in the comments."

I grab my phone from his hands and read for myself, unable to hold out another second. What I see makes me queasy:

lisatuck1980

I thought Christy Andersen was a hotshot agent. Turns out she's just an idiot.

tacotuesdale

I submitted a manuscript to Christy Andersen once. Got a form rejection letter. Guess my PhD's too real for her liking.

vmacarena216

You'd think Dr. Liar's agent would have vetted her. Guess she was blinded by dollar signs.

And so on and so forth. It's all I can do not to scream bloody murder, which is fitting, because Dr. Liar just killed my career.

"I have to talk to her," I say, clicking Penelope's name in my phone. But it rings endlessly, and she doesn't answer.

Fuck, fuck, fuck, fuck, fuck!

"No one in the literary world will take me seriously again," I fume. "Right when I've started my own business, and my reputation is more important than ever."

Jenna flips her silky hair. "She's a con artist, Christy. She's been building her brand for years, has fans all around the world, and managed to pull the wool over everyone's eyes. No one will blame you for believing in her."

I shake my head. "I didn't do my due diligence. I bought into the hype and didn't bother to do so much as a background check. Maybe the trolls commenting online are right. Maybe I *was* blinded by dollar signs."

Charlie scoffs. "No way. That's not your style."

My shoulders slump. "You're right, it's not. I actually thought she had something special. I don't know why I'm so eager to blame myself."

"Maybe it's easier than admitting you had no control over the situation," my sister suggests.

A tiny smile plays on my lips, suspecting that my sister's insight comes from her beloved therapist. "Sounds like something Esther might say. But fine. I am a bit of a control freak."

"A bit?" she replies, grimacing.

I swat her playfully, but then a sudden thought makes my heart hammer. "What if people think I was in on Penelope's scheme? As her agent, I have everything to gain from her success. It's one thing to be labeled a fool, but to be viewed as complicit? I'll never live that down."

My sister puts her arm around me. "Let's not even go there. You're spiraling. Should I make you some tea?"

I don't think tea's going to do a damn thing in this

situation, but Jenna looks so desperate to help me, I can't refuse. "Sure. Thanks."

"I'll take care of it," Charlie says, standing.

"Can you add a shot of whiskey?" I plead.

He laughs. "You got it."

When my phone chimes yet again, my chest tightens with existential dread.

"You should probably ignore that," Jenna says, taking my cell and setting it on the coffee table. "I'm sure it can wait."

I whimper. "Actually, forget the tea, Charlie. I'll just have whiskey."

As he leaves the room, I shake my head. "This is unbelievable. I've played by the rules my entire life, and now I'm at the center of a PR scandal?" There go my chances of ever representing Lola Piper.

"Speaking of PR scandals," my sister says, "at least you're having a better day than Holden McBride."

I roll my eyes merely thinking about the obnoxious starting pitcher for the Chicago Starlings. The player I love to hate. He reminds me of a subset of guys I went to Columbia with: entitled East Coast pricks who come from old money.

Holden McBride is as famous for his last name as he is for his career in the Majors. His family owes their wealth to a long history of wise property investments, making him as rich as he is talented and handsome. It's a lethal combination. Holden is a notorious player both on and off the field. The paparazzi are obsessed with him. Whatever city he's playing in, you can be sure to find him out on the town with a different gorgeous woman by his side.

I sigh. "What happened? Did he get dumped by his latest celebutante girlfriend?"

Jenna winces. "No...he got drunk and streaked across Soldier Field during the Bears game this afternoon. Security had to carry him out. Talk about embarrassing."

My forehead creases. "What the heck was he doing at a football game when the Starlings were playing? Even if he wasn't scheduled to pitch, he still should've been at Wrigley."

"The Bears invited him for some cross-sport promotional event with a handful of other Chicago athletes. Apparently he was interviewed before the game, and that went fine. But he must have gotten wasted afterward, because he streaked across the field during halftime. I'm shocked you haven't heard! It's all over the news, and you're such a diehard Starlings fan."

"I was swamped with work." I don't tell her that I spent the entire day in a bubble with my new book boyfriend, Edison. But she's right to be surprised about my cluelessness. Under normal circumstances, I'd be current on all the news about my favorite MLB team.

Like many fair-weather fans, I hopped on the Starlings bandwagon when they came back from a string of devastating losses to win the 2008 World Series. I was living in New York at the time, but now that I live in Chicago, I can call myself a legitimate fan. I'm obsessed with the Starlings and catch every game I can, whether on TV or at Wrigley Field. There's nothing better than a warm summer night at the Friendly Confines, so-called because of the stadium's welcoming atmosphere. It's my happy place.

"Well, Charlie had ESPN on earlier, and they're speculating that Holden may get suspended for the rest of the season," Jenna goes on to say.

"Fuck!" I mutter, unable to control myself.

My sister's eyes go wide. "Where did that come from? I thought you hated Holden McBride."

"I can't stand the guy. But we don't have a shot in hell of making it to the postseason without him."

Holden's our star pitcher, and one of the best in the League. He's smart. Calculating on the mound. He uses subtle manipulations to mindfuck each batter, throwing them off their game. Serving a deadly cutter when you'd swear a slider's coming. Not to mention, he's left-handed, which gives him a significant advantage. Because lefties are less common, hitters get less exposure to them and often have trouble adjusting to their pitches.

He's impressive. I played softball on a rec league for years after college and, not to toot my own horn, but I was named MVP more than once. I've hit many homers without breaking a sweat, but I'd hate to go up against Holden McBride.

Although, I did have this sex dream about him once and, in that case, I didn't mind being up against him one bit. I will never, ever, admit to that, though.

"I think you just like looking at him," my sister teases with uncanny timing.

My cheeks flush. "Do not."

"You should check out the video of him streaking. In case you were wondering, he has a really nice ass."

"I couldn't care less about Holden McBride's ass." I clear my throat. *Damn nervous tic.*

"Liar. He's hot as hell."

Charlie comes back into the living room with my drink— one of his signature Manhattans, judging by the maraschino cherry garnish. "Who's hot as hell?"

"You are," Jenna tells her fiancé, who bends down to kiss her forehead.

I'd hate them if I didn't love them so much.

As they gaze at each other with hearts in their eyes, I lift the cocktail glass to my lips. Of course, right when I'm about to take a much-needed sip, my cell rings. My heart picks up speed, because I know exactly who it is, even before I grab the phone from the coffee table.

Penelope.

"I'm going to take this in the other room," I announce, because I'm fairly certain I'm about to lose my shit, and I don't want Jenna and Charlie to witness it.

"What the actual fuck, Penelope?" I say when I'm out of earshot. The words come out louder than I intend them to. I'm sitting on the floor of Jenna's closet with the doors shut, but still.

"Christy, I thought you'd be pleased," she says with a nonchalance that makes my blood boil.

I grit my teeth. "Pleased? What the hell is there to be pleased about?"

"I took control of the narrative," she says. "Spun the story. I basically did your job for you."

"Oh, is that what you did?" I say, about an octave higher than my normal register. "Because the way I see it, you made me the laughingstock of the literary world."

"Hardly," she says, unfazed. "You'll be the agent behind the bestselling work of creative non-fiction in recent history."

"Creative non-fiction? But we marketed your book as self-help!" My fists are clenched.

"Potato, *potahto*."

I'm seeing red at this point. "How can you be so cavalier

about this? Not only have you jeopardized both our careers, you duped millions of fans into believing they could manifest the love they deserve. How dare you give them hope, then rip it to shreds?"

"You mean, how dare I give *you* hope?"

I clear my throat. "Fuck off."

Penelope's right. She made me believe I could conjure the man of my dreams with a little self-love and a new wardrobe. But I refuse to have an honest conversation about my feelings with a performance artist posing as a therapist.

"That sounds like your wounded ego talking, Christy. Why don't we pause for some alternate nostril breathing?"

"Oh, cut the bullshit, you quack!" I shout, then hang up on her.

When I make my way back to the living room, Jenna and Charlie turn to me, alarmed.

"Everything okay?" my sister asks, then glances at her fiancé. "We, um...well, we think we heard you yelling."

They definitely heard me yelling. They look traumatized.

"I'm fine," I lie. "All I need is a good night's sleep, and I'll wake up refreshed and ready to tackle this fiasco."

Jenna frowns. "Promise?"

"Promise." At least I didn't clear my throat this time. "I'll call you in the morning."

"How about a to-go cup for your drink," Charlie suggests. "I'm sure we have a stack, somewhere..."

In the interest of time, I shake my head. I need to get out of here fast, before my rage reignites. "You guys can drink it. But thanks."

We exchange hugs and goodbyes before I take the elevator to the lobby. I'm not even through the revolving door yet when

I start wishing I'd taken Charlie up on his offer. He makes a mean Manhattan.

Come to think of it...so does O'Reilly's, the neighborhood bar up the street.

Without further thought, I start walking that way, not ready to obsess over this alone in my apartment.

The wood-paneled pub isn't very crowded, which is probably to be expected on a Sunday night. I sit at the end of the bar and, while I wait for the bartender to take my order, I look up at the TV screen overhead. ESPN's replaying the footage of the Starlings' star pitcher streaking across Soldier Field.

Damn. He really does have a nice—

"What a jackass," the man seated next to me says. "Am I right?"

I turn toward him with a smile that drops the moment my eyes meet his.

Because sitting beside me is none other than Holden McBride himself.

CHAPTER 3

Holden

Two minutes ago, I was sitting here watching some fresh-out-of-college sportscaster muse about the uncertain future of my career, when a cool breeze made the hairs on the back of my neck stand up. I swiveled around on my barstool, and this striking redhead was stepping into the pub, wearing a frown that nearly broke my heart. She didn't notice me staring. And even before she sat beside me, I'd decided that, of all the down-on-their-luck assholes drinking alone tonight, the universe had chosen me to put a smile on her face.

Something tells me it won't be hard, considering she's watching me make a fucking fool out of myself on national television.

"What a jackass," I say while her gaze is still fixed on the screen. "Am I right?"

Her pretty red lips curl up, and I swear, it knocks the wind out of me. But as soon as she turns to make eye contact, her grin's gone faster than my hardest pitch.

Dammit. That smile probably doesn't count. I'll have to try again.

"Jackass," she repeats, taking a quick glance back at the TV where, I shit you not, they're replaying the Soldier Field footage in slow motion, with the video zoomed in on my glutes. "That's an interesting choice of words."

I chuckle for the first time in twenty-four hours. "Guess I'll add that to the list of poor decisions I've made today."

"What can I get ya?" The bartender steals her attention from me. He's older, with bushy eyebrows and an almost comical scowl. It's my first time here at O'Reilly's but, if I had to guess, I'd say he's the owner. He's the sole person working here, and he spent the last thirty minutes cleaning the oak bar top with the devotion of a doting father.

"Manhattan, please," she replies.

"Put it on my tab," I tell him, which he acknowledges with no eye contact and an almost undetectable nod. He either doesn't know who I am, or doesn't give a shit, and I like that about him. It's refreshing. The redhead, on the other hand, definitely recognizes me, and I'm not sure that's a good thing. When I turn back to her, she's staring at me, stunned.

"Um...thank you." Her gaze shifts to her grey hoodie and matching joggers. Then she clears her throat and unwinds the elastic band that was keeping her hair piled on top of her head. It looked sexy as hell, but I'm equally mesmerized by the reddish-brown waves falling over her shoulders.

God help me, she's fucking gorgeous. I need to play this cool, though, because she seems nervous. Best case scenario: she's attracted to me. But what if she's uncomfortable for some other reason?

Fuck. I hope she's not a Cardinals fan.

She turns her entire body to face me, willing herself not to look at the TV again, I'm guessing.

I gotta say something about the elephant in the room. "Look, it's no secret that my naked butt is on every screen in here and basically impossible to ignore," I begin with a self-deprecating smirk. "But what do you say we try to have a normal conversation anyway?"

"Sure." She bites her lip and twirls a few fiery strands around her index finger. "You go first."

"Alright. Well...that's a solid drink choice," I say, because it's true, and I have to start somewhere. "Are you from New York?"

She offers me half a smile. "Because I ordered a Manhattan?"

I shake my head. "Because of the way you pronounce it."

"I lived there for ten years." The other corner of her mouth lifts, but I'm pretty sure that grin is for the owner, who hands her the drink.

Looks like I'm 0 for 2. I have my work cut out for me, but I'm up to the challenge. Sure beats sitting here alone and wallowing in my bullshit.

"Holden," I say, extending my hand. I always introduce myself, even though most people know who I am. It's the polite thing to do, if you ask me, although I've met my fair share of celebrities who disagree. Like the big-time actor Grady Brooks, who loves to live up to his "Hollywood Bad Boy" persona. Unfortunately, our social circles overlap, and he is hands-down the most arrogant son-of-a-bitch I've ever met. But that's a story for another day.

"I'm Christy." When her palm meets mine, her cheeks flush, and now I'm pretty damn sure she's into me. The way she's meeting my gaze, her lashes fluttering over warm, golden-brown eyes, I swear, we're having a moment.

Until my cell starts vibrating on the bar.

God fucking dammit. It's my agent, Russell. After the Soldier Field debacle, he brought me to his house and ordered me to "stay put" while he figured out how to handle the shitstorm I'd caused. Drunk and, quite frankly, humiliated, I passed out in his guestroom and slept it off. When I woke up an hour ago, he and his wife had already gone to bed, probably anticipating a sleepless night with their infant son, so I took the opportunity to get out of Dodge. I'm a grown man, for fuck's sake. I don't need a babysitter.

That's how I ended up in this pub, a block away from Russell's house. It's the perfect refuge. I can count on one hand how many people are in here, and they seem far more interested in their beers and tonight's fish and chips special than they are in me.

I ignore the call, trying hard to keep my emotions in check. The last thing I want is for this beautiful woman to hear the ugly thoughts running through my head. Nevertheless, a frustrated breath manages to escape me.

She winces. "Rough day?"

I let out a wry laugh. "You could say that." My attention drifts back to the television overhead, where a different sportscaster is reporting about my incident while struggling to keep a straight face.

After taking a swig of her drink, Christy calls out to the surly owner. "Excuse me, sir...would you mind switching the channel? *Channels*, I guess," she says, eyeing the handful of screens around the room.

His bushy eyebrows draw together as he glances at the one directly overhead, then scolds me with a disapproving sigh.

"He'll be hard-pressed to find a station that isn't broadcasting my bare ass," I tell her when he goes to grab the remote.

Finally, she smiles for me, her freckled cheeks flushing, and it's a good thing I'm sitting down, because her grin makes me woozy. But more importantly: mission accomplished. At least today wasn't a total wash.

"Hey! I was watching that!" a man in a Starlings hat seated in the back of the bar protests when the owner starts flipping through channels.

The grump with the remote nods in my direction. "Blame him."

"Way to throw me under the bus, pal," I mutter.

Now, I have to offer the angry fan a sheepish apology so he'll let it go, but I'll be outing myself to the handful of people in here. I'm about to turn around and accept my fate when Christy intervenes.

"You can blame me," she tells the patron. "I mean, I'm not staunchly opposed to nudity on TV, but this feels a little exploitative, wouldn't you say?"

Damn. She's quick on her feet. I already found her incredibly sexy, but now...

The guy grunts, and she turns back to me with a victorious smile on those sultry lips.

"Well played," I say, unable to tear my eyes away from her mouth. "Thanks for that."

"I figured you've probably gotten enough shit for the stunt you pulled today." She takes a sip of her drink. "If you don't mind me asking...what was that all about, anyway? Let me guess. Penance for giving up that grand slam to the Dodgers last week?"

I throw my head back and laugh. She's a ballbuster, and I like it. "Nah. That's just baseball. Shit happens."

Her eyes narrow. "Yeah...but not to you."

My gut tightens from the blow. She's right. My shoulder was fucking killing me during that game. It's not the first time I've broken our lead doctor's cardinal rule: Don't Pitch Through the Pain. But it's the only time my obstinance has resulted in a completely avoidable loss. I'm praying that was a one-off, so I don't have to admit that regular resting and icing hasn't been cutting it these days.

I'm searching for a witty comeback that won't incriminate me, but it's hard when I feel like she can see right through me. Luckily, I'm saved by her ringing phone.

"Lying, cheating scumbag," she mutters at the screen, then sets the phone face down on the bar.

My heart sinks. "Boyfriend troubles?"

"I don't have a boyfriend." She eyes me carefully for a reaction, and I don't hold back. When I smile, so does she. "That was my client. Well, former client, now."

"What kind of work do you do?"

She rolls her eyes. "I'd tell you, but I'm not in the mood to get riled up again."

"Your call," I say, although the thought of her riled up kinda turns me on. "We can talk about baseball, then. You seem familiar with my stats... Are you a fan?"

She raises an eyebrow. "Of yours, or the team?"

I chuckle into my glass of whiskey before taking a sip. "Well, if you gotta ask, I guess I have my answer." My fucking phone's vibrating again. I ignore it.

"You're the best pitcher in the League, and you know it," she says, rolling her eyes as she brings the Manhattan to her lips.

I *am* great...when my goddamn shoulder's not acting up. The last thing I need is to suck at pitching right now, when I'm trying to convince the MLB not to suspend me. But when I plead my case...when I explain that this wasn't some drunken prank, that I'm *grieving*—

"But your reputation off the field precedes you," she goes on. "And I bet you know that, too."

I nod. "So, you think I'm an asshole. Or a clown." My tone is lighthearted, hiding how much that last word stings. I've been the butt of the joke at every McBride family function since I turned down a Harvard education to sign with the Starlings. Imagine how much worse it'll be, now that my actual *butt* is the butt of every joke.

"I don't know you, Holden," Christy says after a drawn-out sip. "I only know what the media wants me to."

"Which is?"

"That you're a..." She clears her throat. "I don't know. *A man about town.*"

I tilt my head, considering her answer. "I've been called worse."

"I suppose the parties and appearances come with the territory. You're a McBride, after all." She lifts the maraschino cherry from her drink by its stem, then lowers it into her mouth.

Holy. Hell. I have to look away to temper my body's response before it becomes obvious.

Then my cell vibrates a third time, and my jaw clenches so hard my temples ache. "Wanna know a secret?"

"Absolutely." Her pretty eyes gleam with curiosity.

I lean in and tuck a few beautiful auburn waves behind her ear, so I can whisper there. She smells fucking intoxicating. Sweet, like birthday cake. When my fingers fall to her waist, she rests the side of her head against mine and, I'm typically not a sap, but I'm pretty sure my goddamn heart flutters. I catch her chest heaving out of the corner of my eye, and I wonder if it's because of my touch. I wonder how she'd react if I kissed the soft skin only an inch from my lips, but she's waiting for my confession, so I tell her. "I fucking hate my last name...and everything that comes along with it."

I don't know why I say it. It's the truth, but I've never uttered the words to anyone, much less a woman I just met. I think it was an excuse to get close to her—in more ways than one. Yes, I'd love to take this feisty redhead home to my bed. But I really like talking to her, too.

I should be careful, though. For all I know, she could be a journalist. She never told me what she does for a living.

Before she can respond, her phone starts chiming with text notifications.

"Great. Now my client's messaging me nonstop. I should really silence this damn thing." She turns it over, glances at the screen, then knocks back the rest of her Manhattan.

"How about another drink?" I suggest, grateful for the interruption, as I was pretty damn close to airing my family's dirty laundry to a stranger. "Maybe a shot this time?"

"Tequila sounds good." She throws the phone in her bag. "But I'm buying. Care to join me? Looks like you're about done with your whiskey."

I don't think a woman has offered to buy me a drink since I became a household name. It takes me several seconds to get over the shock.

"Thanks, but I'm nursing this one. I've had quite enough for today," I say with an eye on the TV screen. There I am again, running like the wind in my birthday suit, this time on a celebrity news show. I guess Mr. Sunshine gave up on finding another source of entertainment. Can't blame him.

"That's fair," she says, watching the replay and stifling a giggle that makes my heart skip a beat. It's the first time since I was escorted out of the stadium that I don't regret what I did.

"Two shots of tequila, please," she says to the owner, whose mouth turns up ever so slightly. Of course he would smile at Christy. Can't blame him for that either.

"Two?" I ask her as he pours.

"Don't worry—they're both for me." She purses her lips, presumably thinking about her work crisis.

I try to get her mind off it. "Wanna take another guess?"

She looks at me questioningly.

"Why I streaked across the field."

"Hmm." She licks salt off the rim of one shot glass, swallows the tequila, then bites into a lime wedge. I find myself wishing that lime wedge were my bottom lip. "You lost a bet?"

"That's close." I look into my whiskey glass and swirl around what's left. "I lost *someone*, actually."

Her breath hitches. "Oh, no. I'm so sorry."

I nod. "My grandmother. She is—*was*—the only person in my family who supported me playing baseball. Now she's gone and, well..." I blink back emotion. "They say grief can manifest in surprising ways. That's what Google tells me, at least."

I consider stopping there, but Christy's leaning toward me, hanging on my every word and, well...I want to tell her more. But I don't need anyone else overhearing my sob story. The owner is busy reorganizing liquor bottles, so I shift my gaze to the only other person at the bar. He's been playing Angry Birds on his phone with laser focus since I got here. Satisfied that no one else is listening, I continue.

"I never should have gone to that football game today. I got the call about my grandma right as I was walking into Soldier Field, and I must've been in shock. I was about to be interviewed for this Chicago Sports promo, so I figured I'd do my best to get through it and process the news later." I heave a sigh. "Well, you can guess how that turned out. After the interview, I got shitfaced and started wandering around the stadium. Made friends with some fraternity bros, and one of them dared me to streak across the field."

I shake my head. "I'm lucky I didn't get arrested. But now I've gone and created a PR nightmare for myself, and potentially killed my goddamn career."

I'm staring into my whiskey glass again when an alarm sounds in my head, signaling that I've overshared. Actually, it's my fucking phone vibrating a fourth time, but never mind. I don't know what it is about this woman that makes me want to pour my heart out. But when I turn her way, her honey-colored eyes are full of sympathy, and her frown is sincere. She's so real. There's no pretense. She's the opposite of most women I meet who, let's face it, are more interested in my family name or my Starlings' jersey than anything else.

"For what it's worth, I think you're going to recover from this," she says with a determined nod. "There's no way anyone could hear your side of the story and not give you the benefit of the doubt."

Christy's eyes dart to her second shot, which she downs even faster than the first. "Also, if it makes you feel any better, you're not the only one whose career is holding on by a thread."

My brows rise. "You wanna talk about it? I don't care if you get riled up."

Something shifts when I say the words. Where she looked stressed before, now she looks resolved. Passionate. Angry.

"I have spent my entire life yearning for the day I could work for myself," she begins, freckled cheeks reddening. "Not having to answer to my boss, or my professors, or my demanding fucking father, whom I hate, by the way. So you're not alone in loathing your name, because being Michael Andersen's daughter blows. But I finally made it to the point in my life where I make my own rules, and what happens? The first client I sign turns out to be a fraud, who's hellbent on destroying her reputation and taking me down with her."

I want to give her a hug. Would it be weird if I gave her a hug? Too much, too soon?

Before I can decide, she motions to the owner. "Excuse me? I'm sorry, I didn't catch your name."

"Arnold," he says, with a bigger attempt at a grin this time.

"One more tequila shot, please, Arnold. Thank you."

"Thanks, Arnie," I tell my new friend. "Can I call you Arnie?"

He glares at me. "No."

Christy shoots the tequila like it's water, then glances at the celebrity news show on TV, which has miraculously moved on from me. But my relief is short-lived, because the next story is about Lola.

Lola Piper. My best friend Nate's sister, whom I've known my entire life.

"Rising star Emmy Mason is speaking out about the end of her friendship with Lola Piper," the reporter announces over a montage of photographs of the two singers. *"Just as Piper's*

latest single, Black and Blue, *debuted this week to critical acclaim, Mason took to Instagram, alleging that she wrote the lyrics of the heartbreak ballad herself, for a collaboration album that Piper later backed out on. Piper's reps have not responded to the allegation, but a source close to the pop icon insists that there's no truth to Mason's statement, and that Piper is not only devastated…but taking a break from the spotlight to recover from the betrayal in private."*

Emmy Mason is full of shit. I was with Lola the night she came up with *Black and Blue.* Unfortunately, I know exactly who inspired the song, too. A sorry excuse for a man, who ripped her heart to shreds.

"I don't believe it for a second," a drunk woman behind us yells toward the television. "That song is *all* Lola."

Christy and I both turn her way and nod in agreement. Not the smartest move on my part, because as soon as the lady sees me, her eyes light up.

"Hey! Aren't you—"

Christy shakes her head. "Nope. Not him. But they really do look alike, don't they?"

When we're both facing the bar again, we trade mischievous smiles. "Think she bought it?" I ask.

Before my partner in crime can answer, the woman starts belting out a Lola Piper song that's playing in the background of the ongoing news coverage.

"Never mind," I tell Christy. "I'm not worried anymore."

She laughs, then turns her attention back to the TV. "Poor Lola," she sighs. "But you know what? This isn't the first time some opportunistic jerk has taken advantage of her, and she's always handled it with dignity and confidence, and supreme *badassness,* and managed to come out on top. She's my idol.

This makes me want to work with her even more." Christy frowns again. That same heartbreaking frown she wore when she first walked in. "Not that I stand a chance, now. Even if I weren't mired in my own scandal, Lola's gone off the grid."

My forehead creases. "Wait a minute. You want to work with Lola Piper?"

I knew the universe brought this redheaded angel here for a reason. Of course, I have no clue what she does for a living, but I'd be happy to talk to Lola and see if it's a service she needs. And I'm about to tell Christy as much when my motherfucking phone vibrates a seventh time. It's the last straw.

"I'm sorry, my agent's hounding me," I tell her. "Let me get him off my back."

I pick up the call. "Look, Russell, I'm sure you have the best of intentions, but I'm not some fucking kid you need to babysit. I slept it off, I'm good now."

He goes off about me being in a bar, because he can hear the televisions blaring in the background. I'm so goddamn pissed, I cut him off. "Are you kidding me? I will do whatever the hell I please. This is my life, and you work for me. Not the other way around. And don't pretend to give a shit about me, when it's clear you're only worried about your own ass." I hang up before he, too, can question my choice of words.

Regretting my outburst, I prop my elbows on the bar and rest my forehead in my hands. "I'm sorry you had to hear that, Christy. I can get a little hotheaded sometimes. It's something I need to work on. I just...I fucking hate agents, you know? It's like, who the fuck do you think you are, telling me what I can and cannot do? They're such arrogant, self-absorbed pricks."

When I turn to her, she's flushed a deeper shade of crimson than I thought possible. Her nostrils are flared. She sweeps her gorgeous hair off her neck and coils it back on top of her head, looking like she's ready for a fight. Did my display of anger really offend her that much? What could I have said that—

"I guess I never told you what I do for work." Her eyes are shooting daggers at me. "I'm a literary agent."

Well, shit.

"Christy, I—"

She stands from her barstool. "I can't believe I almost let you fool me, Holden McBride. I knew you were an asshole before I even met you. If you weren't such a great goddamn pitcher, I'd sell my soul to see you traded to St. Louis. You fucking suck, and I can't believe I fell for your Misunderstood Rich Boy act. I bet you can't get enough of your galas, and your VIP lists, and your...your *supermodel* girlfriends," she adds with an eyeroll and a huff. "Well, keep living the dream, you prick."

All I can think is...no woman has ever told me off before.

Most seem preoccupied with what they can get from me; whether it's season tickets, or an expensive meal at a Michelin-starred restaurant, or even a one-night stand they can tell their friends about. That's one reason I keep the real Holden McBride under lock and key. But Christy's unlike any girl I've met. I guess that's why I opened up to her in the first place. And why I care what she thinks of me.

"You want to know what my dream is?" I tell her. "My dream is to start an athletic program for kids with behavior issues. I was inspired by Dex Oliver, actually." The actor suffered from panic disorder for years before getting help, then created the Dramatic Hearts Academy to support youth mental health through the dramatic arts. It's been such a huge success that he developed an offshoot of the program for adults, called the Dramatic Hearts Club.

"Nice try," she scoffs. "I'm not falling for that either. Do you really expect me to believe you didn't come up with that on the fly, when there's an autographed picture of Dex right there?"

Christy points to the wall behind the bar where, sure enough... *Goddammit.* I had no idea that was there.

She digs into her bag and pulls out some cash, which she smacks onto the bar. "It was great to meet you, Holden McBride. Have a nice life." She gives me a frosty glare that sends chills down my spine. My red-hot vixen is now an ice queen.

With an apologetic smile, she turns to the owner. "See you, Arnie."

The curmudgeon is beaming now.

"Oh, so *she* gets to call you Arnie," I point out, sounding like a whiny little punk, I'll admit. Doesn't matter, though, because he ignores me.

"Bye, darlin'," he tells Christy with flushed cheeks and a fucking twinkle in his eye.

I watch, dejected, as the only woman I've ever dared to be myself with storms out of the pub. I won't make that mistake again.

When I swivel in my seat, I'm face-to-face with good old Arnold. I narrow my gaze at him. "Flirt."

"You never stood a chance," he grumbles with a wistful eye still on the door. "She's way outta your league."

He's right. "You know what? I think I'll have a shot of tequila, after all."

CHAPTER 4
Christy

As I make the short walk home from O'Reilly's, my pulse is racing, not to mention my mind.

Amid my frenzied worries about Dr. Liar and the hex she put on my career, are two even more prominent thoughts.

Number one: I *hate* Holden McBride.

Number two: I'm more attracted to him than I've ever been to any man in my life.

Everyone knows the Starlings' pitcher is hot. That's not front-page news. But sitting mere inches away from that criminally gorgeous face and iconic physique had an effect on me I wasn't prepared for.

Blue-gray eyes I could stare at for hours. Sandy brown hair, tinged by the sun. The perfect amount of stubble covering his deliciously defined jawline. So tall and strong, I wanted to climb him like a tree. He's even sexier than how I picture Edison Ford. And, trust me, that's not the liquor talking.

Meanwhile, there I was, self-conscious as hell in my Sunday

sweats, unwashed hair a total mess and, yet, the way Holden looked at me made me feel...pretty. Beautiful, even.

I bet that flirt makes every woman feel like they're special.

I'm such a fool. I thought this was my meet-cute. The moment where I finally get my own love story, with a leading man who makes my knees weak. Who would make my legs shake like no one else has, I bet. But surely my soulmate wouldn't even think about badmouthing agents.

His asinine comment about my profession was triggering, especially after learning that my biggest client is a fraud. But it wasn't only that. It was the fact that I thought my luck was changing. Just like I was duped by Penelope Fucking Dwyer, I let Holden McBride give me hope. And then I got the rug pulled out from under me. Who am I kidding? He probably looks at every woman the way he looked at me.

It's my own damn fault for being so gullible. From now on, I'll have to be more discerning when it comes to my taste in both clients *and* men.

I make it the two blocks back to my apartment building, chug some water, brush my teeth, and get in bed wearing the same sweats, because why the hell not. I don't even bother fishing my phone out of my tote. I haven't looked at my cell since I silenced it at the bar, and I have no desire to read another online troll's opinion of my character, or prediction about my fate.

When I wake up the next morning, it's nearly eleven, and I have a splitting headache. I get out of bed, make myself fried eggs with toast and coffee, and continue to avoid all electronic devices. I know I'll have to face reality eventually, but if I check messages before I get some food and caffeine in me, the result will not be pretty. At least a full stomach might give me a fighting chance at controlling my temper.

I'm only midway through my cup of French roast, though, when there's a frantic knocking at my door.

The urgency jolts my heart. For a second, I fantasize that it's Holden McBride, desperate to apologize for offending me. Then I berate myself for feeling hopeful again, when I should know better by now.

I look through the peephole as the relentless rapping continues. It's Jenna.

"Oh, thank god you're okay," she says, throwing her arms around me the moment I open the door.

My sister isn't typically the anxious type, so I'm not sure why she's so worked up. Then I remember that I'd promised to call her this morning, and it's nearly noon. I guess it's not surprising she's concerned, given that I'm normally an early riser, and—oh, yeah—my career's imploding.

"I'm so sorry," I tell her. "After I left your place, I went to O'Reilly's to drown my sorrows, then I slept in. Why didn't you use your key, if you were so worried? I wouldn't have been mad."

Jenna flushes pink. "Well...I wasn't sure you'd be alone."

As she walks past me to sit on my couch, my forehead crinkles. "Who would I be with? You know very well that my sex life has been woefully nonexistent these days." Unless you count my vibrator, which I'm surprised hasn't died from overuse.

She raises an eyebrow when I sit beside her. "So...you're not secretly dating Holden McBride?"

"I'm sorry, what did you just say?!" Absurd inquiry aside, how does she even know I was at the same bar as him last night?

I wrack my brain, wondering if it's possible I texted her at some point, between the whiskey, and the tequila, and the moment Holden whispered to me, his lips grazing my ear. I get goosebumps just thinking about it.

But no. If I'd texted my sister and told her I was drinking with the Major League pitcher who'd just streaked across Soldier Field, I would remember. I may have knocked back a few shots on top of that Manhattan, but I can hold my liquor. I was buzzed, not sloppy drunk.

"Have you even looked at your phone today?" Jenna's brows knit in an unsettling combination of concern and fear.

My gut clenches, wondering what fresh hell is waiting for me on the other side of this conversation. "No, I haven't. Penelope kept texting me links to her bogus online meditations last night, so I silenced my phone and haven't picked it up since." I clear my throat. "Um...why? What's going on? And how did you know I met Holden McBride?"

My sister blinks her long lashes while pursing her lips. I have a feeling she'd rather have her wisdom teeth pulled than answer me...and Jenna *hates* going to the dentist.

"Let me just show you." She pulls her cell out of her purse, and I watch with mounting dread as she opens up YouTube, then presses play.

"I can't believe I almost let you fool me, Holden McBride. I knew you were an asshole before I even met you. If you weren't such a great goddamn pitcher, I'd sell my soul to see you—"

"Oh my god!" I pause the video, feeling sick to my stomach. There I am in my gray goddamn sweatsuit, telling off the Major League's hottest player.

"Someone at O'Reilly's must have recorded you on their

phone," my sister says. "Judging by the angle you were filmed from, they were sitting behind you."

I grit my teeth. It had to have been the drunk woman yelling in support of Lola Piper. After all, she did recognize Holden when we turned to give her nods of approval. How dare she do this to a fellow Pipette? Where's the solidarity, for fuck's sake?

"How did you find this?" My mind is spinning.

Jenna rests her hand on my forearm. "After last night's mess with Dr. Dwyer, I set my own Google Alert for you. I wanted to make sure I'd get all the breaking news right away, so I can support you."

My eyes tear up. "Well, that's sweet." I really do have the best big sister.

But...*shit*. If Jenna got a Google Alert, that means my name is attached to this video. When my expression shifts to confusion, she explains. "A friend of Mom's from Beachwood recognized you and said as much in the comments. Maureen from Book Club? Doesn't ring a bell. For what it's worth, though, she thinks you're a badass. And it seems like the journalists and bloggers who've picked up the story do, too."

I stifle a scream. Andersen women don't curse in public, let alone berate a high-profile athlete. "Has Mom seen this?"

Jenna shakes her head. "I don't think so. You know Mom's not really active online. I figured I'd hold off on calling her until I knew you were okay. But I did hear from Sam this morning. She's been trying to get a hold of you since last night. First, because she heard the news about Dr. Dwyer. And now, because she thinks you're, um, *screwing* Holden McBride—her words—and she has a million inappropriate questions. You know Sam."

I manage a laugh. Sam is my closest friend in Chicago, apart from my sister. I met her through Jenna, but they couldn't be more opposite. Where Jenna is sweet and demure, Sam is wild and unfiltered. No man has been able to lock her down yet, which makes her the perfect pal for a night on the town. Although I love my sister to pieces, I have to admit...being myself feels easier around Sam. I don't think there's anything I could say or do that would shock her. Case in point: she sees a video of me telling off an MLB player, and her only concern is getting sex details from me. Not my out-of-control temper and anger issues.

I wonder what Jenna thinks about seeing me red-faced and spewing profanities. What if my anger scares her off? I can't bear the thought of losing the friendship that's bloomed between us since I moved to Chicago. My sister and I weren't close growing up, and I blame that on our dad. The dean of Beachwood's elite private school, he invested all his time in me, the "smart one," not Jenna, the "pretty one." But now that we're grown and realize what a jerk our father is, my sister and I are closer than ever. What if that changes, now that my rage is no longer a shameful secret? Now that it's on YouTube, for all the world to see?

Oh, god. "How many views has this thing gotten?"

Jenna refreshes her browser. "Close to a million."

FUCK!!!

I let out a wry laugh. "It's like the time your interior design video went viral. But way less flattering."

A couple of years ago, a client posted a video of Jenna explaining her creative process. The next morning, she was an Internet sensation, owing to both her bombshell looks and talent. And when the one and only Lola Piper shared the video on her own social media account, Jenna had the world in the palm of her hand. My sister got an international pop icon's attention without even seeking it. That's the difference between her and me.

"Well, I think you look hot," Jenna says.

"Thank you." She's so thoughtful, always going out of her way to boost my self-esteem. She knows it's an issue for me. A knot forms in my stomach when I realize there are probably thousands of strangers discussing my appearance in the comments section, and I bet most of what they're saying is harsh. I'm not the supermodel type Holden McBride is usually seen around town with.

For the sake of my mental health, I can't let myself read their remarks. I've been through this before with Kyle, who was hypercritical of my body, even when I was marathon-training with him, and the fittest I'd ever been in my life. I can't go down this road again.

Besides, I should be less worried about whether I look hot in the video, and more worried about coming across unhinged. If any potential clients weren't already turned off by the Penelope Dwyer scandal, this could be the final nail in the coffin of my career. All thanks to Holden McBride, who clearly brings out the worst in me.

Just when I thought I couldn't loathe him more.

And, on that note...why the hell do my sister and Sam both think I'm sleeping with him?

When I ask Jenna as much, she scrolls up to the title of the video. "Holden McBride's Date Rips Him a New One."

I roll my eyes. "Perfect."

"According to PiperFan4Ever, who posted the video, you and Holden were looking pretty cozy at the bar before you started yelling at him."

Yeah, well, PiperFan4Ever can suck it.

"But I see it in your body language, too," my sister continues. "Both you *and* Holden. I mean, you were standing between his legs. Your mouths were mere inches away. You were reaming him out, but he couldn't take his eyes off you. It looked like you were about to have incredible make-up sex. Or hate sex. One of the two."

I scoff. "Oh my god. That's ridiculous." But the thought of having *any* kind of sex with Holden, be it sweet or savage, makes me tingle. I cross my legs, willing my lady parts to chill the fuck out.

"And when you walked away? He seemed...heartbroken."

My rising eyebrows betray me. "Really? He did?"

Jenna nods and hands me her phone with a tentative grin. I skip to the end of the video, where Holden watches me leave, looking like a sad puppy.

I shake my head. I will not let this player fool me again. "It's all part of his act. Trust me. Last night only confirmed what I already knew. He's an arrogant asshole. Maybe we hit it off at first, but then his agent called, and Holden was a total dick."

"Well, that's too bad, because it sure seemed like you had chemistry. I was hoping you could tell me if his naked body looks as good from the front as it does from behind."

I entertain my sister with a laugh...all the while wondering if I'll ever be able to forget the thrill of Holden's eyes on me. Or if any man will ever look at me that way again. I wish I weren't so convinced of the answer.

"I'm going to grab my phone and see if there are any other fun updates waiting for me," I tell Jenna, hoping the sarcasm in my tone masks my sadness. I dread going through my voicemails and texts, but I need an excuse to go to my bedroom and gather myself.

I've never felt confident in my ability to attract men. There are oodles of women out there who are prettier than I am. Thinner than I am. The only thing that ever set me apart is my successful career. Now, I don't even have that.

The tote bag that's been housing my cell phone for the past twelve hours is taunting me from the armchair by the window. I walk over to it like I'm walking the plank. I'm not sure if my self-esteem can take another hit.

And certainly not a knockdown, drag-out punch. But as irony would have it, that's exactly what I get. Because the first thing I see are five missed calls from an unknown number with a Manhattan area code—and I know in my bones who they must be from. The man I used to share a cell phone plan with when we lived together. The man who must've gotten a new number after we broke up.

Dr. Kyle Walton. The man who made me feel like nothing.

I throw my phone onto the chair and start sobbing.

CHAPTER 5

Holden

I wake up the following morning to the sound of my phone ringing. Not surprisingly, it's my agent. I'm tempted to ignore him and go back to sleep, but when he calls six times in half as many minutes, I figure I should probably answer. My phone's been on "Do Not Disturb" since I was escorted out of Soldier Field yesterday, but Russell is one of the few contacts on my "Favorites" list whose calls can still come through.

Although he's far from my favorite right now. If he'd just given me a little space last night, I wouldn't have lost my cool, and maybe Christy would've stayed. Gotten to know me the way I wanted her to. Kissed me the way I craved. Maybe she'd be in my bed right now, her eyes fluttering open and a smile tugging at her lips.

Instead, she fucking hates me.

I can't pin this all on Russell, though. He was just doing his job. Truth is, I know damn well he cares about me. He's been my agent for the last five years, and I consider him a friend, to boot. He's been stressed lately, with the new baby and the lack of sleep. Leave it to me to make his life a million times harder.

I shouldn't have yelled at him like that. And don't even ask me why I told Christy I hate agents, because it's not true. Not anymore, at least. I did have a shitty experience with my last one, but Russell's a great guy.

I should apologize. Russell knows my temper gets the best of me sometimes and I say shit I don't mean. But that doesn't excuse my bad behavior.

By the time I've come to this conclusion, Russell's sixth call has gone to voicemail. Not surprisingly, though, the seventh follows right on its heels.

"Hey, Russell. I—"

"Why the ever-loving hell aren't you answering your phone?" His words come out in an aggressive whisper.

I can't help but smile. "Let me guess...you're nap trapped."

I'd never heard this term before Russell became a dad to baby Theo, but it's fairly self-explanatory. Lucky for me, my agent can't yell with a sleeping infant on his chest.

"You know it," he says, his tone warmer. I picture him grinning like the proud father he is. "Not sure how much time I have before he wakes up, so, here's the deal... You went viral."

"No shit. My pasty ass was on every TV in the pub," I whisper back. I'm not sure if the baby can hear me, but better safe than sorry. "And speaking of last night, I want to apologize for losing my temper on the phone."

"We're good."

Well, that was easy. Russell's a laidback guy, all things considered, but I was expecting a little more resistance since I was such a dick to him.

"But Holden—I'm not talking about the Soldier Field

debacle. Someone posted a video of your date cursing you out at the bar. It's already trending on YouTube."

"What the fuck?" I say louder than I intended to.

Theo whimpers. *Oops.*

"Dude!" his dad scolds me under his breath.

"Sorry, man," I murmur. "I'm shocked, that's all. First the Bears game, and now this? You must want to wring my neck."

"Are you kidding? Your date-gone-wrong is the best press you've gotten in weeks."

"Huh? How is getting my ass handed to me by a beautiful woman good press?" I can't wait to be able to use the word "ass" again without feeling like I'm setting myself up to be a punchline.

"Because you had it coming, McBride. You've been acting like a real dickwad lately, and people are sick of it."

I run a hand through my hair. "Damn. Tell me how you really feel. And aren't we supposed to be watching our language in front of your son?"

"He's three weeks old. He doesn't understand a fucking word we're saying. All I care about is that he stays asleep so my wife can get some rest."

"How is Shelley, by the way?"

"A goddamn rockstar. She labored over thirty hours to bring our kid into this world. I already knew she was amazing, but now? I fucking worship the ground she walks on."

I nod, a wistful smile on my face. "That's awesome. I'm happy for you guys."

"Thanks, man."

I don't begrudge Russell one bit, but my goddamn soul aches for how much I want a life like that. A woman I'm crazy about. A kid or two I can teach to play ball. A family who, by some fucking miracle, accepts me for who I am. Apart from my grandma, that kind of love seems impossible to come by. God knows my latest shenanigans will only make it harder to find.

"Alright, back to business," Russell quietly redirects. "I think you're well aware that the public's opinion of you has taken a nosedive. You were on thin ice long before the Bears game. The late nights out partying. Paparazzi snapping pics of you, always with some barely dressed woman on your arm—"

I roll my eyes. "No one was barely dressed."

"Their clothes didn't cover shit. Baseball games are a family affair, bro. There are little kids in the stands who look up to you. But no parent's gonna buy their child a McBride jersey if your reputation for screwing a different groupie every night overshadows your pitching. And getting drunk and naked at a football game doesn't help your cause."

"Jesus Christ," I mutter. "First of all, just because I'm seen with a woman doesn't mean I'm screwing her. Maybe in my twenties, sure, but I'm thirty-six. That's not where my head's at anymore."

"Does your dick know that?"

I snort. "Very funny. And as for the Bears game—"

"Look, I'm not trying to be a jerk. Your grandmother died, I get it. I can give you the benefit of the doubt because I know that, underneath your bullshit, you're a good guy... Always looking out for the rookies. Keeping track of staff members' birthdays and buying them ice cream cakes. Helping my sister land her dream job."

"Remind me why I did that again? I mean, Elisia's the best physical therapist we have, don't get me wrong. But she's divulging all my secrets. I never should have asked her to come up with the inscription for her supervisor's cake."

I'm joking, of course. Although, there's more than a grain of truth there. I'm the only McBride who doesn't desperately seek validation for every good deed or act of charity. If that makes me the black sheep, then so be it.

And then there's the fact that Elisia's the only person on staff who has any inkling that my shoulder's been acting up. As long as the pain doesn't interfere with my game, I know my secret's safe. But if it does...I'm screwed. Not to mention the fact that her brother won't be happy with either of us.

Russell huffs a quiet laugh. "If you want to be the unsung hero, that's your call. But keep in mind that your fans don't get to see that side of you. All they know is what the media shows them. Optics matter."

I flinch. That's exactly what Christy said.

"Now, you can get away with a lot of shit because you're a good-looking guy," he continues. "But there's a fine line between being an eligible bachelor and an asshole. I'm afraid you crossed it at Soldier Field."

I heave a sigh. "And you think this video of me getting told off by a gorgeous girl is gonna help?"

"Nope. But dating her will."

I spit out a laugh. "Are you out of your mind? You heard what she said at the bar. She can't stand me."

"Well, you're going to need to turn up that McBride charm, my friend. Because the Internet loves her."

Can't blame them.

"This is how you change your image," Russell goes on. "You date the spitfire who'll keep you in check. Who's hot, yet relatable. And fully fucking clothed, I might add."

I run a hand through my hair. "Trust me, I'd love nothing more. But it's never gonna happen."

"I'm afraid I'm going to need you to put in a little more effort than that. Because your career and reputation depends on this. I talked to the Starlings' PR department this morning."

My gut clenches. "And?"

"For now, they're just issuing a statement saying they're aware of the incident at Soldier Field and are looking into it. But you'll have to explain yourself to the investigations department. Make it clear that you were grieving a loss..."

His pause leads me to think he's skeptical. "You don't think they'll understand?"

"I don't know, man. These decisions tend to hinge on public perception. Since your image is shaky, I think things could go either way."

"So, I either win over the woman who hates me...or my career goes up in flames? That's a little dramatic, isn't it?"

"Holden, let's face facts. You're getting up there in years for a pitcher. Getting suspended for streaking isn't how you want people to remember the end of your career. Particularly when that suspension is all but guaranteed to eliminate the Starlings from the postseason."

He's right. And he doesn't even know about the shoulder issues that could force me into retirement sooner than later. My contract is up this year, and if I'm injured, the likelihood that I'll get an extension isn't great. I'll become a free agent, and what team will want a thirty-six-year-old pitcher with a bum shoulder? This could very well be my last season. I need to consider what I want my legacy to be.

I rub my temples. "What do you want me to do, Russ? I can't force the woman to date me."

"Then ask her very nicely to fake it until this all blows over. Make it worth her while. A YouTuber mentioned her name in the comments, so I did a little research, and it turns out Christy Andersen's dealing with a PR scandal of her own. Did she tell you she's a literary agent?"

"That rings a bell." *If only she'd mentioned it sooner.*

"Well, it looks like she's a damn good one. Graduated from Columbia *summa cum laude...*"

Summa cum laude? Arnie was right. She is way out of my league.

"... Kicked ass at her last agency," Russell goes on. "Then she branched out on her own and signed the one and only Penelope Dwyer."

"Shit. That quack is Christy's client?" No wonder she was so upset last night.

"Yeah. Not great for her image. But a romance with a pro baseball player—whether it's real or not—might be just the thing she needs to take the focus off her Penelope problems."

I scratch my forehead. "Or, people find out we're faking it, and now she looks like a liar herself. Someone who could be complicit in her client's deception."

"Well, you better be *very fucking convincing*, then," he says, raising his voice a little for emphasis. It's enough to wake Theo, who starts wailing. "Shit. I gotta go. Just promise me you'll call Christy. Any chance you got her number before you pissed her off?"

"Unfortunately, no."

"It's fine," he yells over his son's cries. "I'll text you the work number I found on her website. I'm willing to bet it routes to her personal cell. Most solo agents go out of their way to be accessible, especially when they're first starting out. Call her now! And keep me posted!"

When he hangs up, I bury my head in my hands. Christy's

never going to go for this, especially when there's not much in it for her. Sure, fake-dating me might make some strangers on the Internet happy, but is that what she cares about? I doubt it, unless those people are potential clients. Christy cares about her business. Last night she told me she'd always dreamed of being her own boss. Then the first big author she signed turned out to be full of shit. I feel awful for her.

That's when it hits me. I do have something Christy wants. Access to Lola Piper.

I pick up my phone again, eager to hear Lola's take on this fake-dating scheme. I've been asking her for advice about girls since we were kids at the same Manhattan private school. She may be four years younger than me, but she's always been wise beyond her years. Not to mention, smart as fuck. She and her brother Nate, who was in my class, were admitted on scholarship. They weren't poor by any means, they just weren't part of the stuffy New York "elite," like everyone else I knew and couldn't stand. That's why Nate and I became fast friends. And Lola's always been like a little sister to me. Despite being the most famous pop star on the planet now, she's still as down-to-earth as ever.

But right as I'm about to dial her number, I get an incoming call from another "favorite" I'm not eager to hear from.

Margot McBride. My mother.

I can't imagine what she wants. She already left me four voicemails yesterday telling me that she and Dad are livid about my Soldier Field stunt, and I'm no longer welcome at the upcoming "McBride Family Forum." It's a week-long vacation at our estate in Maui that my mom orchestrated under the guise of discussing my grandmother's will. Apparently, Grandma

Evelyn left the bulk of her money to the McBride Family Foundation, with some conditions in place for how it's spent.

Obviously, it would've been easier for our family to meet on the East Coast, where nearly every McBride lives, except me. Mom just wanted an excuse to escape their Park Avenue penthouse while the floors are being redone. My grandmother's death couldn't have come at a better time, as far as Margot's concerned. And before you call me an asshole, my mom isn't grieving. Grandma Evelyn was her mother-in-law, and let's just say, they weren't cut from the same cloth. If you ask me, the biggest difference between them is that Evelyn married a McBride for love, while Margot married one for money.

"Holden, dear," she says the moment I put her on speaker.

I shake my head. "You're going with 'dear' now? That's quite a leap from what you called me in your voicemails yesterday."

Her laugh is fake, as always. "Well, you can't really blame me, can you darling? Besides, that's all in the past now. I'm calling with good news."

"Did you finally get off the waitlist for that outrageously expensive designer handbag?" I say, trying to sound like my interest is sincere. Pretty sure I'm not successful.

She scoffs. "No. And please don't remind me."

"Sorry. Didn't mean to pour salt in the wound." I roll my eyes. "So, what's up?"

"Your father and I have had a change of heart. We'd like you to come to the Forum, after all."

Too bad, because that's the last fucking place I want to be. Especially now, when there's no shortage of material my family can use to make jokes at my expense. I was actually relieved when I found out I'd been banned.

Plus, there's no reason I need to be there to discuss Grandma's will. We've been through this before, when my grandfather passed away. The lawyers will make sure everything's divvied up according to my grandmother's conditions, and then we'll all get a check. Don't see why I need to fly to Maui for that.

I'm about to lie and say I can't make it because I'm pitching. Mom doesn't know my schedule, anyway. But before I get the words out, she goes on.

"We saw the *second* video of you that went viral yesterday, and we were intrigued by your dream of starting an athletic program for children in need. No doubt your grandmother would've loved to support you, since she was such a sports *fanatic—*"

My mother's tone is so full of disdain, she may as well be saying "drug addict."

"—but your brother and sister should be given an opportunity to compete for the money as well. It just wouldn't be fair, otherwise."

My forehead creases. "I'm sorry, I'm not following. We're competing for our inheritance?"

"Yes!" she huffs. "Didn't you read my email with the revised itinerary for Maui?"

"I don't know, Mom. Did you send that before or after you left the angry voicemails threatening to cut ties with me for good?"

I don't think she'd actually follow through. But not a whole lot would change if she did. I'd need to make other plans for Christmas. That's about it.

She exhales but otherwise ignores me, which is par for the course. "Let me get you up to speed. Evelyn left a large sum to the family foundation, with the stipulation that it be used to fund a charitable initiative run by one of her grandchildren. You, Wesley, and Abigail will each put together a proposal to present to the board, and whoever gets the majority vote wins."

"So you're telling me that, if we lose, we get nothing?"

"It's what your grandmother wanted, dear."

I grit my teeth. "Do Wes and Abby even want to compete? I haven't heard either of them mention any passion projects they're dying to get off the ground."

Not that they'd tell me if they did have something in mind. We're not close at all. Abby and I had a falling-out years ago and, unfortunately, never recovered. Now she's busy being a mom to my nine-year-old niece and seven-year-old nephew. Unlike our own mother, Abby's the type who shows up to every single one of her kids' games, always with enough Gatorade and orange slices to fuel both teams. I know this because she goes out of her way to post about her generosity on Instagram, but still.

Wes, on the other hand, is a fucking tool who never thinks about anyone but himself. I highly doubt he's been brainstorming about how he can use his privilege to help those less fortunate.

My mother's reply is curt. "They went to Ivy League schools, Holden. I'm sure they'll have no problem coming up with something."

Nice. She never misses the opportunity to remind me that I gave up a Harvard education.

"So you'll come, then? It'll be such fun," she says, once again making it clear that this so-called "Forum" is nothing more than a vacation for her.

My jaw clenches. I'd rather streak across Soldier Field again than participate in this fucking thing. But the problem is...I really need the money.

I told Christy that I hate being a McBride last night, but I didn't tell her why. It's because every McBride I know, with the exception of my grandma, is obsessed with money. Amassing it. Spending it. Flaunting it. Donating it in exchange for good press.

It disgusts me, which is why I never had the desire to study finance or business at an Ivy League school, like so many McBrides who came before me. Like Wes and Abby, who now have the skills to grow the family fortune after Dad's gone.

All I ever wanted was to play baseball. So that's what I did. The field was the only place I could be myself, so I escaped there as often as possible. As often as Grandma would take me. If anything, I thought my passion for baseball might make me a good sports medicine doctor. I never dreamed I'd get so good that I'd end up a Major League player. Making Major League money.

As soon as I'd earned enough to buy a home, I started donating to various charities. Always anonymously, because I knew what would happen otherwise. My generosity would be another notch in the belt for the McBride family to boast about.

I live comfortably, don't get me wrong. But my savings account doesn't hold anywhere near the amount I'd need to start the athletic program I've dreamed about. I was an idiot, thinking I could rely on my grandmother's money to fund it. Now I'm kicking myself for not setting aside more of my own.

Well, it's not like I can turn back time, so I guess I'm shit out of luck.

"I'll be there," I tell my mom.

The McBride Family Circus, as it may as well be called, starts on Thursday. I'm pitching tomorrow, then I'm off for five days, so the timing works well. I shouldn't have trouble getting the Starlings to excuse my absence for an urgent personal matter. I won't stay in Maui the whole week, but I sure as hell hope it doesn't take that long to convince the board that my sports program is a better idea than whatever my brother and sister pull out of their asses.

My mom claps on the other end of the line. "Wonderful! Oh, and one more thing, dear..."

Jesus Christ. What else could she possibly need from me? "Yes?"

"The Internet loves that redhead from the bar, and goodness knows you could use as much positive press as you can get. Convince her to forgive you, and bring her along, won't you? It shouldn't be hard to persuade her...I mean, you *are* a McBride. Alright, dear. See you in Maui."

She hangs up.

Fuck my fucking life.

I look at my phone screen. I have more missed calls and texts than I care to count. But there's only one person I want to talk to right now.

She picks up on the first ring. "I've been worried about you."

"I've been worried about *you*," I tell her.

Lola heaves a sigh. "Looks like we're both going through shitty times. I'm so sorry about your grandma... Nate told me. He says the memorial will take place over the holidays?"

I manage a wistful smile. "Yeah. It was her favorite time of year. We'll get together at the house in Connecticut, like we always do. She wants us to celebrate her life, not wallow in sorrow over her death."

"She was a special woman. She deserves to be celebrated. Just make sure you give yourself space to grieve, too. Otherwise—"

"I'll end up streaking across Soldier Field during a nationally televised football game?"

"I had a feeling that's why you did it." My friend is quiet, and I can almost see the sadness in her eyes. "Want to come to the cabin and hide from the world with me?"

"How long are you staying?"

"I don't know... Forever?"

My nostrils flare. "I'm sorry about Emmy. Why the fuck would she say she wrote *Black and Blue*?"

"I made the mistake of telling her which guy the song was about." Lola's voice is tinged with regret. "Apparently he was dating her, too, around the same time. I had no idea, but she blames me for him ghosting her."

"Jesus Christ. I never understood what you saw in that guy, Lo. He has no redeeming qualities."

"Listen, I understand why you don't like him. He acts like an ass most of the time because he's damaged, but underneath it all, he has a good heart."

I scoff. "Doubtful."

Lola sighs. "Let's talk about the fierce redhead who told you off at the bar, instead. I'm a fan."

"Me, too," I confess.

A laugh escapes her. "I could tell by the way you were looking at her. So, how do you get her back?"

I smile. "Funny you should ask."

CHAPTER 6
Christy

An hour after I discover the missed calls that could only be from Kyle, I'm still crying my heart out. My sweet sister tries every trick in her playbook to console me. She leads me to the window seat, fluffs my pillows, and covers me with my coziest blanket. She brings me herbal tea, and a fruit salad that's almost too pretty to eat. Then, she rubs my back while giving me a well-meaning pep talk that sounds a lot like a Disney song.

"Someday," Jenna says, "your prince will come. I just know it."

I'm half-expecting a full orchestral accompaniment to burst through my Bose speakers like magic, but my phone rings instead. It's in Jenna's charge now, tucked in the back pocket of her jeans. She examines the screen, and her doe eyes go wide. When I ask if it's the same Manhattan number again, her pouty lips turn down, and my sobs become even more dramatic.

After even a healthy pour of whiskey and Lola Piper's most empowering album, *Irreverent*, don't soothe me, Jenna calls for backup. When she goes to my foyer to use her phone, I assume she's talking to our mom. My gut instinct is to wipe my tears and pull myself together. If Mom comes over, I'm not sure she could handle seeing me this way. She suffered from a low hum of depression most of her life, although Jenna and I didn't know to call it that. What we did know was that our mother often seemed "checked out," and we couldn't rely on her to notice when we were hurting. Much less comfort us.

I have to keep reminding myself that things have changed. Mom started seeing a psychiatrist two years ago and was finally diagnosed. The combination of therapy and anti-depressants has worked wonders for her. I suppose it's possible she could help Jenna get me out of this funk. It's just never happened before.

When there's a knock on my door twenty minutes later, though, it isn't Ingrid Andersen.

It's my friend, Sam.

I'm still seated by the window, swaddled in my throw blanket, when she takes a peek at me, nods hello, then grabs Jenna by the arm and pulls her into my kitchen. They're conversing in hushed tones, but I still make out most of what they're saying. After Jenna rattles off a list of unsuccessful efforts she's made to calm me, Sam weighs in.

"Are we even sure Kyle's the one who's been calling? I mean, New York's a big city. It could be anyone."

"That's what I told Christy, but she says she knows in her gut it's him."

Sam releases a deep sigh. "Well, it's a good thing you called, because I'm an expert on wallowing. When Sunny and I were in college, she broke down like this over Dex several times."

The Sunny in question is megastar Dex Oliver's wife. They were childhood best friends first, then became lovers in early adulthood. If you saw the way they look at each other, you'd know right away they were meant to be. Unfortunately, it took Sunny and Dex ten fucking years to figure that out. In the meantime, Dex dated Jenna in high school, then had a dalliance with her again after Sunny got engaged to another man. But it all worked out in the end. The pair have been happily married for over three years now. They have a beautiful nineteen-month-old daughter named Stella, and recently announced that baby number two is on the way.

"At least in Sunny's case, I could understand where she was coming from," Sam continues. "I mean, Dex may as well have been sculpted by Michaelangelo...but *Kyle Walton*? I've seen pictures, and the guy looks like a fucking breadstick. Not to mention, he can't screw for shit. How could your sister possibly be hung up on him?"

A belly laugh escapes me, but I'm still crying, so I sound hysterical. Sam and Jenna step out of the kitchen, looking alarmed, and make their way over to me.

"I'm not hung up on Kyle," I explain through sniffles as they sit on either side of me. "If I never saw that jerk again, it would be too soon. But all of these calls from him have me falling apart, because I know exactly what he wants to say." I wipe my eyes with my sleeve. "That I made a fool out of myself in that video. That he was right to think I have anger issues. That he barely recognized me because I've put on so much weight. That my career is over, and I'm a big, fat, fucking failure." I pull at the hem of my sweatshirt, keenly aware of the squish where my six-pack abs used to be. "Literally."

My sister looks at me with glistening eyes. "None of those things are true, Christy. And I'm not just saying that because I love you. Kyle messed with your head."

Sam's nostrils flare. "That asshat better hope he never meets me, because the first thing I'll do is sucker punch him in the balls. You are absolutely stunning. And, I know we've all been thinking this, so I'm just going to go ahead and say it: you have the best tits out of the three of us."

"We most certainly have *not* all been thinking that," I say without missing a beat. Sam's candor caught me off guard when we first met, but I'm used to it now. One of the things I love about her is how comfortable she is talking about anything related to sex and sexuality. Plus, she's always telling her female friends how hot we are. If you didn't know her, you'd probably think she was hitting on us, but Sam's as boy-crazy as they come. The unfiltered compliments are her way of hyping us up. I just wish I could believe her.

"Well, it's true," Sam urges, as though reading my mind. She peers over at Jenna, who gives an enthusiastic nod. "You have a bodacious bod, and your career's on fire. Penelope Dwyer is a minor bump on the road to better things. And, as for anger issues, can Kyle blame you? He was giving you mediocre dick for eight whole years!"

When I chuckle again, Jenna smiles. "I knew a dose of Sam was what you needed."

"Happy to provide the comic relief," Sam says with a wink at me. "But seriously, we need to talk about your self-esteem again. Or better yet, read the comments on that video of you and McHottie! I'm guessing you haven't seen them yet, because if you had, your confidence would be through the roof."

My forehead creases. "What? Why? What are people saying?"

Sam leans forward to catch my sister's attention. "You haven't taken a peek either?"

Jenna shakes her head. "My own experience going viral taught me that I'd rather not know what's going through the minds of guys with screennames like *collegebro69*."

Our friend clicks her tongue in disapproval, then scoots closer to put her arm around me. "Well, allow me to fill you in. The people of YouTube have spoken, and they fucking adore you, Christy Andersen. As they should."

I sit up a little straighter, a smile creeping onto my lips. "Really?"

Sam nods. "Where's your phone?"

Jenna pulls it from her back pocket and hands it to me, but the screen is dark, and I can't power it on. "The battery's dead," I tell them. "I'm going to go charge it."

I unswaddle myself and head to my bedroom to plug in my cell. Then I take a few deep breaths in an attempt to decompress. Luckily, I don't mind Sam and Jenna seeing me this way. Besides, I may be a mess, but I'm a sad mess—not an angry one. Society doesn't bat an eye at a crying woman. Watch any romantic comedy, and you'll see the heroine bawling over a man. No big deal. Even tears over a work crisis aren't uncommon. But it's not often that the leading lady is raging on the big screen, for any reason. If anything, frustration materializes as an exaggerated eyeroll, or a snarky comeback. Not the Hulk-like rage that bubbles under the surface of my skin. The kind of wrath that terrifies me, because I'm never confident I can control it. So, while I certainly don't enjoy crying my eyes out, it feels a hell of a lot more acceptable than being mad.

I leave my room, about to return to my sister and Sam, when there's a knock at my door.

Who the fuck could that be?

I shuffle over to the foyer in my bedroom slippers and look through the peephole. Before I can think better of it, I gasp.

"Christy?" Holden McBride's voice is buttery smooth and sexy, even muffled by the door.

"Shit!" I exclaim under my breath.

"I heard that," he says, sounding amused.

"Fuck," I mutter, not bothering to adjust my volume.

"Are you about done cursing? 'Cause I need to talk to you, and it's time-sensitive. Also...your doorman George accompanied me up here, so there's no one manning the front desk."

As I'm rolling my eyes, footsteps approach behind me. When I turn around, Jenna and Sam mime their questions, pointing to the door, then shrugging with their palms turned upward.

I heave a sigh and turn the knob, since I have no other choice. George has a job to do, and I don't want to keep him from it. Even if that means I have to come face-to-face with my nemesis.

When I open the door, my sister squeals. I look back, and she's squeezing our friend's hand, the other palm on her heart, as giddy as if Holden were here to propose to me. Sam's got her eyes on all six feet, four inches of the star pitcher, nodding with a mischievous smile, as if to say, "If you're here to bed Christy, I approve."

"Are you okay?" Holden asks when I turn to him. The concern in his eyes seems genuine.

"I'm fine." I swallow my anger, not wanting to make a scene in front of the doorman, whose gaze on Holden is full of reproach. "I appreciate you bringing him upstairs, George. My phone died."

The doorman's arms are crossed over his puffed-up chest, and I'm pretty sure his wide stance is meant to be intimidating. But seeing as George is nearly a foot shorter than Holden and much rounder, the idea that he poses any threat to the Major Leaguer is more than a little funny. I stifle a smile.

"So, we're all good?" George barks. "I wasn't sure if I should let him in after the stunt he pulled at Soldier Field yesterday. I mean, I'm a Cardinals fan, so I'm biased, but you have to admit it was kinda sketchy." Then he turns to the ball player. "No offense."

Holden scratches his eyebrow. "None taken."

"Yes, we're all good. Thanks again," I tell George with a grin. But as soon as he steps into the elevator, my good humor disappears along with him.

My hands fly to my hips. "What are you doing here, Holden? And how do you even know where I live?"

Still standing in the hallway, he looks down, his expression sheepish. "After you left O'Reilly's last night...well, I ordered a tequila shot to ease the sting of your abrupt departure—"

"*Abrupt* departure? You told me you hated agents. Said we're all 'self-absorbed pieces of shit,' I believe."

He shrugs. "Pretty sure I said 'pricks,' but that's beside the point. Because it isn't true."

I squint at him, my tone icy. "Then, why did you say it?"

"Sometimes I say shit I don't mean, Christy," he replies with a frost in his voice that matches mine.

I scoff. "Cool story, bro."

"Anyway," he says after an exasperated sigh, "I took the shot, and then it occurred to me how late it was, and...I just wanted to make sure you got home okay."

My forehead wrinkles. "So, you followed me. Like a stalker."

"Aww! That's so sweet," Jenna coos, inching closer to me. "Thanks for looking out for my sister."

The baller sees an opportunity and runs with it. He steps forward into the doorframe, hoping for a more sympathetic audience in Jenna and Sam.

"Hey, there. I hope I'm not interrupting anything," he says, oozing charm. "Rehearsal for a new *Charlie's Angels* adaptation, maybe?" He nods toward each of our manes: auburn, blonde, and brunette.

While Jenna giggles and Sam snorts, I glare at him. "Missed your calling as a comedian, I see."

He barely acknowledges me with a smirk before his gaze returns to the smiling faces behind me. "I'm Holden, by the way."

"Almost didn't recognize you with clothes on," Sam teases, which prompts my sister to elbow her.

"I'm Jenna, and this is Sam," she redirects. "Why don't you come in?" She practically leaps toward the door to open it wider for him. *Traitor.* Ever the romantic, her cheeks are flushed with excitement, and I know exactly what she's thinking. That this is the beginning of some sappy love story that Holden McBride and I will tell our grandchildren someday.

Yeah, right.

As he makes his way past me into my apartment, I can't help but notice how intoxicating he smells. Last night, at the bar, I caught a whiff of vanilla and salt on his skin when he whispered in my ear. It was subtle, but enough to make me want to jump his bones. I suspect it was his pheromones casting their spell on me. Now, I detect the same sultry scent, layered with cologne. And unlike the T-shirt and jeans he was wearing at O'Reilly's, he's dressed in slacks that hug his perfectly toned ass, and a polo with sleeves that cut off right at his delicious biceps.

My heart picks up speed. Holden McBride looks good enough to eat. Is it possible he cleaned up like this to impress me? Maybe he did it to torture me. Either way, it's working. I want to sink my teeth into his muscle. Just like that scene in *Edison's Love*, where Iris bites her beau's arm in the throes of passion.

She's so fucking lucky Edison Ford's not a jerk. *Ugh.*

After I close the door, I catch my reflection in the front hall mirror, and horror hits me like a shockwave.

I look like a complete train wreck.

Half my hair has fallen out of the bun it was wrapped in. My eyes are puffy, and the mascara I never washed off my face last night is streaked down my cheeks. My nose is red, and I'm wearing the same fucking sweats Holden saw me in yesterday. But now, there's a huge stain on my shirt, where I must have spilled tea. Possibly whiskey.

I look deranged. No wonder Holden seemed so concerned when I opened the door.

I wipe away rogue mascara with the backs of my hands and pull my hair into a high ponytail. It's an improvement, but when I turn to see how gorgeous the trio behind me looks in comparison, I wish I could crawl under a rock. They could easily be posing for a magazine cover. First there's Holden, whose impressive arms are folded under his swoonworthy pecs. Then there's Sam, the dark-haired beauty in vintage clothes, whose swagger rivals the two-time MVP beside her. Finally, my bombshell sister stands with perfect posture and hands on hips, a pose reminiscent of her high school days as head cheerleader.

Suddenly, I want them all out of my apartment, so I can stuff my face with Oreos. But I'll need to get this conversation over with first. "So, what can I do for you, Holden?"

"I'm sorry for showing up like this," he begins. "I tried calling the phone number on your website half a dozen times, but there was no answer."

My sister's eyes light up. "Do you have a Manhattan area code, by any chance?"

When he nods, Jenna and Sam exchange vindicated looks.

I offer them a half-hearted shrug.

Maybe it should have occurred to me that Holden was the one calling. We may not have discussed him living in New York, but I know very well that he's from there. His family is a staple of Manhattan. And yes, we did both go viral, but why would I ever be so bold as to think that the MLB's most eligible bachelor was the man behind the unknown number? Between that and the prospect of Kyle calling to criticize me, the latter seemed much more plausible.

"Christy thought those calls were from her ex, who's a total dipshit," Sam explains to Holden. "He would only ever have sex with her on Fridays. Can you blame her for not wanting to talk to the guy?"

"Oh my god, Sam!" My jaw drops. I guess she still has the ability to shock me, after all.

Jenna gives our friend a disapproving glare. "Remind me again why I invited you here?"

Holden laughs into his fist.

"I was just giving some context, so he didn't think you were deliberately ignoring him," Sam tells me under her breath.

"I'm pretty sure the fact that he's my ex is enough context," I quip back.

"Agree to disagree?" She smiles with that mischievous glint in her eye that makes you want to be her partner in crime, not her adversary. It's impossible to stay mad at her when she's so fucking funny. And I'm sure she believes she's being helpful.

Now, the pitcher turns to me, intrigued. "Why only Fridays?"

My shoulders slump. But before Sam decides to answer on my behalf, I explain. "He was a stickler for routine, okay?"

Holden looks perplexed as he processes my answer.

"Can we please move on?" I beg.

He unfurrows his brow. "Absolutely. I was actually hoping we could talk for a few minutes. I was going to suggest in private, but I get the sense there isn't much you keep from these two."

He's right. Jenna and Sam know all my secrets...except the real reason Kyle and I broke up.

I guess it was unreasonable of me to think my ex was calling today. For as much as I despise him, he probably wants nothing to do with me either.

"It's fine," I tell Holden. "Whatever you have to say to me, you can say in front of them."

"Literally anything," Sam chimes in. "I have no boundaries."

"I was beginning to get that impression," Holden tells her.

"This one's more straitlaced," Sam goes on with a nod toward my sister, "but she can cover her ears."

Jenna's gleeful laugh is over the top, and I bet she's convinced that Holden's here to ask for my hand in marriage. "Why don't we sit and make ourselves comfortable?" she suggests. "Christy's having a rough day, so I can play hostess. Can I get you something to drink, Holden?"

Thankfully he declines, because I'm really not in the mood for a tea party. I lead the way to the living room, where Jenna and Sam plop down on the couch, while Holden and I choose armchairs opposite each other. Once everyone is seated, he fixes his gaze on me.

"I have a proposition for you, Christy." His seductive tone makes my knees weak.

"Excellent," Sam purrs. "Do tell."

"My agent called me this morning," he begins.

I smirk. "Oh, good! The one you hate, right?"

His nostrils flare. "I'll have you know that the first thing I did was apologize to him."

"Great job! Want a pat on the back?" I roll my eyes.

"Why do I feel like I need popcorn for this?" Sam whispers to Jenna.

Holden's gaze travels to the ceiling, as though he's summoning the strength to deal with me. "Let me just cut to the chase. My reputation's in the toilet, and my agent thinks you're the only person who can help."

A wry laugh escapes me. "That's absurd! Why me?"

He drags a hand down his face. "Because a million people on YouTube think you're the woman I need to put me in my place."

"Oh my gosh!" my sister tells Sam under her breath. "I just watched a romcom exactly like this. He's going to ask her to fake-date him!"

"That's my favorite trope!" Sam whispers back.

I turn to see my sister and our friend huddled together, sharing a movie theater box of M&M's.

"Where did you get that?" I ask Jenna, my forehead creasing.

Her cheeks flush as she finishes chewing. "It was in my purse. Charlie and I went to a matinee yesterday."

Well...I may be experiencing my very own personal hell, but at least my sister and best friend are entertained.

I turn back to Holden. "You're not actually suggesting we pretend to be a couple, are you?"

"I don't know, Red. We could date for real, but seeing as you told me I fucking suck last night, I doubt love is in the cards for us."

Out of the corner of my eye, I see Sam nod before she speaks. "I like him."

My eyes veer back to Holden. "How long would we have to keep up this charade?"

"Just until the Soldier Field thing blows over. Four to six weeks, tops. We go to a few events together, engage in some good-natured verbal sparring for the world to hear, and when the paps photograph us holding hands, suddenly I'm likable again."

I huff out a breath. "And what am *I* getting out of this, exactly? Because if you think you can tempt me with a check, you're wrong. I don't need your old money, Mr. McBride. Or your new money. I've saved up plenty of my own."

It's the first time I see a genuine smile on Holden's face since he got here. But before I blink, it's gone. "Well, you don't have to worry about me giving you cash, because the thought never crossed my mind. Unlike the rest of the McBrides, I don't make a habit of paying people off."

"So, what's in it for me, then? Besides the pleasure of your company." I cross my arms.

His lip quirks up, but his grin is roguish this time. "No one said anything about pleasure."

On the couch, our audience of two tries to hold back giggles. But my body has an entirely different reaction to his last word—not to mention the sensual way it rolled off his tongue.

My cheeks heat. "Seriously, Holden. Now's not a great time in my career to risk looking like a liar. If the only benefit for me is the Internet's short-lived praise, then I'm going to have to pass."

He leans back in his chair, looking far too comfortable. "I had a feeling you might say that. Which is why I came up with an offer I doubt you'll be able to refuse."

"What do you think it is?" Jenna whispers to Sam.

"Shhh. Let's listen."

"Last night, you mentioned how much you'd love to work with Lola Piper," Holden continues. "And if you hadn't stomped away, I would have told you that I know her. Well."

"Bullshit."

"I had a feeling you might say that, too." Holden's grin is smug as he pulls his cell out of his pocket. He unlocks it, then slides it across the coffee table in my direction.

When I take the phone in my hands, I see a shared photo album called "The Three Musketeers." And the creator is "LP."

Lola Piper.

In it are pictures of the pop star long before she became famous—riding her bike, playing hopscotch, eating ice cream—with her older brother Nate, whom I recognize from some of Lola's social media posts. And right alongside them, in every photo, is the one and only Holden McBride, whose blue-gray eyes I'd recognize anywhere. The last photograph was taken more recently, after Lola became famous, because her hair is dyed the bubblegum pink color she's known for. But she isn't wearing one of the sequined leotards or gossamer gowns she performs in, nor is she in one of the couture dresses she's usually spotted in around town. She, Nate, and Holden are in ugly Christmas sweaters, drinking eggnog.

"Oh my god, oh my god, oh my god!" Jenna's now seated on the arm of my chair, and I can practically hear her Lola-loving heart race. "He really does know her!"

Holden nods, his gaze on me. "Help me out, and I'll give you Lola's number. I talked to her before I came over, and she's on board. I told her you're one of the best literary agents in the business, and she was sympathetic about the whole Penelope Dwyer mess."

My breath hitches, and all I can do is stare at him, slack-jawed. Is this really happening? The hottest pitcher in the MLB, who brings out the absolute worst in me (but whom I'm alarmingly attracted to), wants me to pretend I'm dating him in exchange for the opportunity to rep one of the most talented artists of our generation?!

I clear my throat. "I, um...I'm going to need a few minutes to talk this through with my associates."

Jenna and Sam take my cue and follow me into the bedroom.

"What is there to talk about?" Jenna asks, adrenaline rendering her eyes wider than I've ever seen them. "Working with Lola would be your biggest dream come true!"

"But Holden's such an arrogant prick!" I counter. "I am *not* my best self when I'm around him. You saw how bitchy I was out there! I loathe the guy."

"But do you loathe the bulge in his pants?" Sam deadpans.

"Be serious!" I retort.

"I am being serious! It's a valid question. And if you tell me you didn't notice his package, you're lying. I mean, talk about a baseball bat. I bet you could see that thing from outer space."

Sam's right. I definitely noticed.

"Oh my gosh, this is so exciting!" Jenna's on the verge of hyperventilating—and apparently blocking out my exchange with Sam. "You're going to marry Holden McBride, I just know it!"

Sam rolls her eyes. "Cool your jets, lady. I know you're balls deep in wedding planning, but not every meet-cute ends in marriage. Sometimes it just leads to good, old-fashioned fucking." She shifts her gaze to me. "Should we book you an appointment for a bikini wax?"

I shake my head, ignoring her. "Okay. Say I agree to fake-date Holden McBride. What if I'm not convincing? You know how my confidence plummets when it comes to men."

"Well, if you hate him as much as you say you do, what's there to be self-conscious about?" Jenna teases.

Ten bucks says she's planning my bachelorette party in her head.

"Do you want my two cents?" Sam asks me.

"Not really."

Naturally, she goes on anyway. "Have sex with him ASAP. Because nothing says 'fake-dating' like two people who've never played hide the sausage. You've read your fair share of romance novels. Tell me I'm wrong."

Jenna gives an exasperated sigh while also fighting a smile. "Thank you, Sam. She'll be sure to keep that in mind."

I turn to my sister. "You really think I should do this?"

She nods. "Potential love interest aside, you deserve a shot at repping Lola Piper. And she deserves an agent she can trust. I bet that's high on her list of priorities, especially after being betrayed by someone she thought was a friend. I guess you two have that in common."

I roll my eyes. "Yeah. Emmy Mason and Penelope Dwyer can kick rocks."

But Jenna has a point. I do think Lola Piper and I would make a great team. Now more than ever.

I walk back into the living room with Jenna and Sam close on my heels. As I approach Holden, he stands from his chair, towering over my 5'6" frame.

"Holden McBride," I say, reaching out my hand. "You've got yourself a deal."

His smile is victorious. "Excellent." And when our palms meet, the warmth of his skin sends a jolt straight to my heart.

It's going to be an interesting four to six weeks.

"Well, I'd better get going. I have dozens of angry messages from MLB execs that I need to respond to, but I'll be in touch. Can I use the contact info on your website?"

I shrug as we walk to the door, Sam and Jenna following right behind us. "Sure."

"Great," he says. I'll email you the itinerary."

My brows knit together. "Itinerary?"

He nods. "Our first event is on Thursday. In Maui."

"Um, I'm sorry," I sputter. "Did you say, *Maui*?"

He runs a hand through his hair. "We have property on the island."

"*We*...as in, your family?" I clear my throat. Twice.

His tone is nonchalant. "Yup. We're meeting there to discuss my grandmother's will."

My jaw drops. "So, you're telling me that we're traveling to Maui together *this* week...and sharing a room, I assume?"

He laughs. "Well, we won't convince anyone we're dating if we're in separate quarters, now will we."

"And I have to pretend to be your girlfriend in front of your *entire* family who, from what you've told me, sound like they've all got giant sticks up their asses?!"

"Trust me, you have nothing to worry about. You've already won them over. My mom saw the viral video and insisted I bring you. She's not my biggest fan either, so you'll be in good company."

My nostrils flare. "Holden...did you purposely wait until after I agreed to this charade to tell me about your family meeting?"

He cocks his head to the side. "Based on your little rant last night, I figured the McBrides are not my biggest selling point."

I gasp. "You little shit!"

Holden smirks. "You wanna renege? You're so fucking feisty, I didn't peg you for a scaredy-cat. But if you really don't think you can pull this off..."

I clench my fists and take a step closer to him. "If anyone should be scared, it's you, McBride. Because now, I know that you don't play fair—which means I don't have to, either. So, keep that in mind when we're putting on a show for the paparazzi. 'Cause I would hate to accidentally tell them what a reprehensible dickhead you are!"

"Good luck getting Lola's number if you pull a stunt like that," he sneers.

"Good luck recovering your image without me," I snap back.

Holden inches forward, closing the gap between us. His gorgeous goddamn eyes pierce through me. "You wanna play dirty, Red? Well, game on."

Then he opens the door and lets it slam shut behind him.

I turn and lean against it, the boldness fading from my features and leaving sheer angst in its wake. Sam and Jenna stare at me, open-mouthed.

"I am going to be so screwed," I tell them.

Sam's lips quirk up. "If the sexual tension I just witnessed is any indication? Um, *yeah* you are."

CHAPTER 7

Holden

I am so completely and utterly fucked.

Since I left Christy Andersen's apartment forty-eight hours ago, I've barely thought about anything but her. No woman's ever gotten under my skin like this. No woman's ever made me feel this down bad before. And no other woman's ever made me wonder if she's my archenemy or the girl of my dreams. I'll admit, she's played a starring role in my subconscious these past few nights of sleep. Sometimes she's attacking me with that sharp tongue of hers, and sometimes she's using her mouth in far more pleasurable ways.

One thing's for sure: I want to kiss her. I want to do a lot of things to her, but I can't let my mind go there right now, because she's about to get in the car that's taking us to the airport. Starting tonight, we'll be sharing a bedroom for the rest of the week, and I wouldn't blame her for backing out of our deal if I greet her with a raging hard-on.

The second Christy exits her apartment building with two suitcases, the driver reaches for his door handle.

"I've got it, thanks," I tell him as I step out of the car.

She's scowling and, if I had to guess, still upset about the bait and switch I pulled when I told her about the trip to Maui. But Jesus, does she look stunning. The sight of her gorgeous hair in the sunlight is enough to make my heart beat faster. As she gets closer, my palms start to sweat. She's wearing jeans that show off her curves and a white knit top that makes her look like a goddamn angel. A pissed-off angel, but still. By the time she's standing in front of me, I'm as jittery as I was on my first day as a starting pitcher.

I was a kid back then—barely twenty—and desperate to prove two things. First, that I belonged in the Majors. And second, that I wasn't the entitled asshole people assume I am because of my last name.

I had a rocky start that afternoon. I let my nerves get the better of me and allowed five runs in the first two innings. When my coach met me on the mound, I was sure he was going to take me out. Instead, he gave me advice that changed my career and, for better or worse, molded my reputation. He said, "Holden, if there's ever a time to be a cocky son of a bitch, it's now."

Whenever I feel nervous, I remind myself of that. So, I approach the furrow-browed beauty with an easy grin, tuck her hair behind her ear, and whisper with an air of complete confidence, "Will you kiss me?"

Her cheeks flush a deep shade of pink. "Already? Why? Is someone watching us?" She clears her throat, then looks around before her gaze lands back on mine.

I fight a smile. I have no good reason to ask for this kiss except that I've been thinking about it nonstop since she walked through the door of O'Reilly's. Of course, I won't tell her that. If she knows how much power she has over me, I'll lose any leverage I have in this arrangement of ours. So, I come up with an excuse that will appeal to her business acumen instead.

"If we're going to convince anyone we're dating, we'll have to lock lips at some point," I begin. "Better to do it now, on our terms, than worry about a potentially awkward first kiss in front of my family."

She nods, but her forehead remains creased. "You're right."

I have to admit, I'm surprised when Christy inches closer. I half-expected her to roll her eyes and push past me in a huff. I think that's why I asked *her* to kiss *me*—because I figured she'd feel more comfortable taking the lead. But as soon as she slides her arms around my neck and balances on her tiptoes to reach me, she freezes.

"You do it," she pleads under her breath.

"Yes, ma'am." She certainly doesn't have to ask me twice.

I wrap one arm around her waist and bring my other palm to her cheek. I let my mouth softly land on hers. And when she parts her lips for me, our tongues touch, and she lets out this sexy little moan. It's barely audible, but still enough to drive me insane. I thread my fingers through her auburn waves, and she presses her hot-as-fuck body against me, and the outside world begins to fade. I'm honestly grateful when her doorman George interrupts us with a passive-aggressive cough. The last thing I need right now is to get charged with public indecency.

"Can I help with your luggage, Ms. Andersen?" George asks, his eyes fixed on me with disdain, like a disapproving father. I know he's trying to be intimidating, but it's more heartwarming than anything else. I like that he's protective of Christy. And given my questionable reputation, he has every right to think I'm a jackass.

"We're fine, George, thank you," I say with a good-natured

wave of my hand. In response, the doorman makes a V with his fingers and points at his own eyes, then mine, as if to say, "I'm watching you."

He and Arnie would get along well.

Christy, who's facing away from George, is oblivious to the interaction. Her cheeks are bright red, and she looks shell-shocked.

Shit. Is it possible she didn't like the kiss? Was that moan I thought I heard a figment of my imagination? As far as making out goes, I've never gotten any complaints (quite the opposite). But I guess there's a first time for everything.

She finger-combs her waves where I tousled them, then nods toward the car. "I suppose we should get going."

"Ready when you are." I pray my tone is relaxed enough to conceal the fact that I'm second-guessing my kissing skills. "Let me get your bags."

"I'll grab the smaller one. It's heavy."

I scoff. "You really think I can't handle it? Do I need to flex for you, Red?"

She rolls her eyes, but it's the smile she's biting that catches my interest. Though I hate to admit it, I'm desperate for a clue that she's attracted to me. I'm telling myself it's because she's less likely to screw me over if we're screwing. What I worry about is that, deep down, I'm hoping she'll actually fall for me. But Christy Andersen is Ivy League educated, ambitious, and the perfect mix of beautiful and sexy that you don't see every day. I should know better than to think a woman like her would want me for more than just sex. She probably thinks I'm a meathead.

Maybe if you'd gone to Harvard, you'd have a better chance with her, dear, I imagine my mother saying.

"Fine, Hercules." Christy shrugs. "Take both suitcases. But don't say I didn't warn you."

I bend down with a smirk on my face and grab her luggage. Obviously, I can manage just fine. But she wasn't lying—the smaller one is heavier than I expected.

"What did you pack in here? Bricks?" I look at her out of the corner of my eye. "You're not planning to kill me and dump my body in the ocean, are you?"

When she laughs, her whole face lights up, and it's like a dopamine hit to my brain. "Why would I want to kill you, Holden?"

I carry her bags to the back of the car and pop the trunk. "Because you hate me, remember? Or did that kiss give you amnesia?"

She raises an eyebrow. "You wish."

She's right. I do.

I scratch my forehead. "You have to admit, it wasn't a bad kiss." Yes, I'm fishing for compliments. I guess that intoxicating laugh of hers emboldened me.

"I've had better." Christy clears her throat again. I catch her doing it every now and then, and I think it means she's nervous. If I'm lucky, it's because she's lying through her teeth.

"Oh, yeah?" I challenge her. "Don't tell me that TGI Friday was a better kisser than me."

"TGI..." Her features shift from perplexed to amused. "Oh. You're talking about my ex in Manhattan."

I nod. "The guy who'd only fuck you on—"

"Fridays, yes. Trust me, I remember." She heaves a sigh. "That's a clever nickname. When did you come up with it?"

"About thirty seconds after I promised you we'd move on to another topic. I've been dying to test it out ever since."

"What an exciting day for you," she teases.

"It would be, if it weren't for this bullshit family gathering looming over me." I glance at my watch. "Alright, I'd better get these bags in the trunk. I'll let you know if I need your help," I deadpan.

She chuckles. "Make fun of me all you want. But the Starlings need you in tip-top shape to make it to the postseason. I'm just looking out for the team. We wouldn't want you to get sidelined with a shoulder injury from lifting my suitcase."

Christy's joking, of course. But she has no idea how likely that scenario is. The mere thought of it fills me with dread. So, although I laugh it off, when I load the trunk, I switch to using my right arm, so I don't further fuck up my left.

"You never did tell me what you packed in here," I say, hoping she doesn't notice my sleight of hand.

She looks down at her shoes. "Books, mostly."

I half-smile as I close the trunk. "We'll barely be gone a week, and you need an entire suitcase full of reading material? I guess I shouldn't be surprised. You *are* a literary agent." Smiling, I open the car door, and she slips inside.

"Why don't you just use an e-reader?" I ask once I'm seated next to her. "Not a fan?"

She scrunches her nose. "I know I'm in the minority, but I hate them. I actually prefer when authors send me hard copies of their manuscripts. Part of the joy of reading is holding the book in my hands. I love everything about it. How soft and smooth the paper is. That little *whoosh* sound when you turn a page. The final, satisfying smack when you shut the book after reading the last sentence."

"I bet you go to libraries just for the smell," I tease. When the driver pulls away from the curb, I put up the partition between us for privacy.

"Don't get me started." Christy lets out a wistful sigh. "I actually used to dream about getting married at the New York Public Library."

"Used to?"

She shrugs. "I gave up the fantasy when I moved to Chicago. But it was a silly idea to begin with. It costs a fortune to have a wedding there...and even if I had the money, it's hard to justify spending it all on one party. Although I'm sure the library would look stunning all dressed up for a special occasion."

I happen to know she's right. My grandmother was a devoted patron of the New York Public Library, and I always took her to their annual gala. I used to love to watch her face light up the moment she walked through the brass doors, into Astor Hall.

I wonder if Christy gave up her dream of getting married there because it was tied to that moron, TGI Friday. I don't know the guy, obviously, but he had Christy in his bed and turned her down, so he's got to be the dumbest fucking man on the planet.

When we're stopped at a red light, I reach for a bottle of water from the fully stocked bar in the back of the car, because the thought of Christy's ex leaves a bad taste in my mouth. I'm about to offer her a drink, too, when her phone rings.

"It's my mom," she says with a smile. "I should take this. I told her about our arrangement, but don't worry, she won't tell anyone. She likes you. She saw the Soldier Field video, and she's a big fan of your, um...assets."

"Like mother, like daughter?" I ask, but Christy only rolls her eyes as she picks up the phone.

"Hey, Mom! Where've you been these past few days? I'm not used to playing phone tag with you." Christy's eyes go wide, then her jaw drops. "Wait a minute...did I just hear a man's voice in the background? Oh my god, are you *dating* someone?"

As Christy listens, her gaze softens. "Just an old friend? Hmm. I'm not sure I buy that." She grins at me and shakes her head, as though I were privy to the other side of this conversation. It's adorable. I should probably look away and let her talk to her mother in peace, but I can't take my fucking eyes off her.

Christy smiles into the phone. "Oh, you want to talk about *me* now? I wonder why," she teases. "Okay, well...Penelope Dwyer officially lost her book deal, and I fired her yesterday. Even though I'm horrified by her lack of scruples, it still sucked."

She nods while her mom says something encouraging, I'm assuming. Then she steals a glance at me, and her face flushes almost as pink as when we kissed. "Yes, Mom," she whispers.

Christy gives me a sheepish smile, and it's all I can do not to bring my lips to hers again.

"I can't really answer that right now," she murmurs. Then she uses her pretty, manicured fingers to block my view of her mouth. Of course, I can hear her anyway. "Because he's sitting right next to me."

The fact that she's talking to her mom about me does things to my ego that I probably need to keep in check. But I'll worry about that later. For now, I use the opportunity to insert myself into their conversation, because, why not.

"Did you send your mom the itinerary?" I ask. "Does she have any concerns? If you want me to talk to her, just say the word. I'm great with mothers." After a moment of consideration, I frown. "Except for my own."

Her lips quirk up, and she glances out the window as we merge onto the expressway. "Do you want to talk to him, Mom?"

A few seconds later, Christy hands me her phone.

I feel victorious. *Shit*. Considering this is a fake-dating scheme, I'm far too eager to impress this woman and her mother. Nevertheless, I pour on the charm. "Good morning, Mrs. Andersen."

Her laugh is just as sweet as her daughter's. "Please, call me Ingrid."

"Hi, Ingrid. I know you're probably concerned about Christy traveling with a man she barely knows—"

"Oh, I'm not worried at all, honey. You're Holden McBride! Everyone knows who you are. I just want Christy to have fun. You know what they say about all work and no play. That girl's been a workhorse since she was born. I never had to worry about her when she was a kid, because her nose was always in a book. You know the type."

I laugh, thinking about that suitcase. "I have an idea."

Beside me, Christy's gaze turns anxious. "Is she telling you my life story?"

I shake my head, but my grin does nothing to dispel her fear.

Ingrid goes on. "I thought things might change when she started dating Kyle in college..."

Christy gasps. "Did I just hear her say *Kyle*?"

I attempt a more vehement head shake this time, but Christy's unconvinced and chews her bottom lip.

"...But the man was dull as dishwater," her mom goes on.

"So I've heard." I chuckle.

Christy attempts to snatch the phone from me, but I switch it to my other ear. Covering the speaker so Ingrid can't hear, I whisper to her daughter. "Your mom's giving me the type of intel I would get if we were really dating. This is good. It'll make our fake relationship more convincing."

Her shoulders slump. "Fine. But just you wait until I get cozy with *your* mom."

I snicker, but the thought of all the demeaning remarks Margot McBride will surely make about me is stomach-churning.

"Anyway, I'm glad you're shaking things up for Christy," Ingrid goes on. "She could use some spontaneity in her life."

"That's my middle name," I say.

She laughs again, all while her daughter appears to be having a mild panic attack beside me, her palm glued to her forehead. I put my free hand on her leg in an effort to calm her. Then I question myself. It feels so natural to touch her like this...but I'm not sure why. Christy and I aren't actually dating, so, am I crossing a line?

She looks at my hand resting on her jeans and just smiles. Her muscles relax under my palm. I like having that effect on her. I like it a lot. I wonder if she would let me ease her tension in other ways. Like with my tongue between her thighs.

"Speaking of spontaneity..." Ingrid goes on, "how much trouble did you get in for Soldier Field?"

I drag a hand down my face. "Probably not as much as I deserve. The MLB's conducting an investigation, which buys me some time before they make a decision. If this thing blows over soon, I should be okay. I pitched well yesterday, so that helps."

Christy nods in quiet agreement, and I can't help but wonder if she caught the game on TV. I'll admit, the idea that she might be watching definitely motivated me last night.

"I'm happy to hear that, honey," her mom replies. "Well, I don't want to take up too much of your time. Can I say goodbye to Christy?"

"Of course. It was nice talking to you, Ingrid. I hope we can chat again soon."

"Likewise."

After I hand Christy her phone, she scolds her mom for oversharing. But it's good-natured, and whatever Ingrid says in response seems to put her daughter at ease.

Still, her freckled cheeks flush when she hangs up. "I'm never letting you speak to my mom again."

"Good luck, because I'm pretty sure Ingrid and I are best friends now." You think I'm joking, but that conversation was infinitely more pleasant than any interaction I've had with Margot McBride. I don't remember a single time she's called me "honey" that wasn't laced with condescension.

Christy lets out a wistful laugh. "It's funny. I never imagined my mom would be so chatty with you. She wasn't like that growing up. She suffered from depression for years...but now that she's being treated for it, she's so much more social and vibrant. It still takes me by surprise. I feel like I don't know her very well yet."

My hand's still on Christy's thigh, so I give her a gentle squeeze. "You'll get there."

She nods and looks down at her lap. "I think she has a

boyfriend. She's been impossible to reach lately, which isn't like her. And when we do talk, she seems so giddy. But every time I ask if she's dating someone, she denies it."

"Maybe it's early, and she's still feeling things out," I offer. "I'm sure she'll tell you when she's ready."

"She'll probably tell you first," Christy jokes, taking her gaze outside the car window. Worry floods her features as we exit the expressway toward O'Hare International Airport. "Oh my god, we're almost there."

"You okay?" A part of me feels guilty for asking her to put on this charade with me. The other part is really fucking happy. I'm playing with fire, and I know it. Right now, I don't care.

"Just nervous." She blows out a breath. "This is where it begins. For the next four to six weeks, the world will be watching us. Watching *me*. I'm not used to that."

"It sucks," I say as we pull up to the curb.

A beautiful, earnest laugh escapes her. "Good to know. Well...here goes nothing." She unbuckles, then reaches for the door handle, but I stop her.

"Maybe we should kiss again first." I know I'm pushing my luck, but I can't get enough of this woman.

She gives a solemn nod. "A little more practice before we face the masses?"

"Yeah." I unbuckle my own seatbelt. "That, and another chance for me to prove myself—since you claim you've had better kisses."

She smirks. "Why do you need my validation, Holden? Don't you get enough from the throngs of women who fall at your feet every day?"

I shrug. "I guess I'm just competitive. I wouldn't be where I am in my career if I didn't strive to be the best."

"And that applies to kissing, too?" she says with a half-smile.

I let my gaze wander from her eyes, to her mouth, and further down her body. "It applies to everything I do."

Her chest heaves. "You're such a flirt."

"I'm not like this with everyone, Red. You can ask the throngs of women, if you want."

"I'll pass."

"On the women, or the kiss?"

She fights a grin. "What do you think?"

"I think I need to hear you say it." I fix my gaze on hers.

She swallows, then looks at the partition separating us from the front seat. "The driver can't see us, right? Or hear us?"

"Nope."

"And um..." She glances through the rear window. "What about the fact that we're blocking traffic?"

I tuck a strand of hair behind her ear. "You need to get out of your head, Christy. Live in the moment."

"That's never been my strong suit." She lets out an airy breath.

I think about what Ingrid told me on the phone. "Maybe I can help with that."

"Good luck," Christy replies with a wry grin. "Now, about the car..."

I suppress a laugh. "The driver will move if he has to. But he won't disturb us. It's one of the perks of this exorbitantly expensive car service my mom booked for no other reason than to impress you, I think."

Her eyes go wide. "Margot McBride is trying to impress *me*?"

"I told you, she's a fan." I fix my gaze on her mouth, which is still perfectly red despite our last lip-lock. "So...what'll it be?"

Her expression softens along with her tone. "You can kiss me."

"Good." I take my palm to her cheek and let my gaze linger on her pretty brown eyes. Eventually, she shuts them, then leans into me, taking the lead. It's a good thing she can't see me, because her small gesture has me smiling like an idiot.

I meet Christy's lips, hoping to elicit that sexy little moan I'm sure I heard. I get one as soon as my tongue finds hers, and I feel vindicated. The next thing I know, her fingers are moving over my shoulders and into my hair. Her nails on my scalp drive me crazy and, when I take my kisses to her collarbone, I can't help noticing how gorgeous her breasts look in that V-neck top...or how dangerously close they are to my mouth. Resisting temptation, I nip at her earlobe instead, then suck the sweet skin below it. Christy lets out this delicious sigh that tells me everything I need to know. There's no way in hell she's not enjoying this.

My fingers skim the hem of her sweater, then slip underneath the soft threads to find her even softer skin. But when my hand grazes her stomach, her muscles tense. "I think that's enough practice for now," she says.

"Everything okay?" I inch back to give her some space, worried I made her uncomfortable. She seemed as excited by that kiss as I was, until my fingers found the flesh above her waistband. Did my touch turn her off?

What she says next does nothing to alleviate my concern. "I think we need ground rules."

I nod, though my ego's more than a little bruised. "Of course. What did you have in mind?"

"Um..." She heaves a sigh. "We only touch each other over our clothes. So we don't get carried away."

"Understood," I say, even though I couldn't be more confused. Did she stop because she didn't like the feel of my hands on her body...or because she liked it too much? I wish I knew. Christy's harder to read than an ump on an off-day. In this case, I have to work even harder not to take her mixed signals personally. "What else have you got?"

She purses her lips. "I think that's all for now."

"I trust you'll update me if anything else comes to mind? My attorney can draft a contract if your list gets too long," I deadpan.

Her cheeks flush. "I'll keep you posted."

"Excellent," I say, without giving away how dejected I am. I nod toward the world waiting for us outside the confines of this car. "Then, I guess it's showtime. How do you feel?"

"Better, actually."

Talk about mixed signals. There's a twinkle in her eye that makes me think she may have enjoyed kissing me after all. Still, she doesn't say it.

Being the gentleman I am, I decide to help her out. "Thanks to that kiss, right?"

She heaves an exasperated sigh. "Holden, I'm pretty sure I'm here to deflate your ego. Not pad it."

"Well, you're doing a hell of a job," I admit, although she probably thinks I'm joking. "In any case, I'm glad you're feeling confident, because I have it on good authority that we're going to get swarmed by paparazzi in the airport."

Her gaze narrows. "Are you serious?"

I nod. "My agent tipped them off."

Her tone is icy for the first time since I left her apartment the other day. "So, you've known about this all along and decided to tell me sixty seconds before we get out of the car?"

"I thought I'd spare you the anxiety on the ride over." I shrug. "You said yourself that you have a habit of overthinking things."

"And *you* have a habit of blindsiding me with news I won't like when I can't do anything about it," she huffs. "I can't believe I almost forgot how incorrigible you are, even after you tricked me into coming to Maui. You're a total mindfuck, Holden. It's one of the things I dislike most about you."

I dissect her words and focus on the one small win, like a sentimental fool. "We've graduated from hate to dislike? I'll take it."

She looks up through the skylight, her eyes laced with frustration, which I'm hoping is at least partly sexual. "I guess kissing you really did give me amnesia," she says.

I'm full-on glowing now. "Because it was the best kiss you've ever had?"

Christy groans, throwing her hands in the air. "It was a decent kiss, okay? Are you happy?"

"Not yet. But I can work with that."

CHAPTER 8
Christy

As soon as we get through O'Hare airport security, I tell Holden I'm going to freshen up, which is partially true. The paparazzi are likely to pounce at any moment, so it wouldn't hurt to look in the mirror and make sure my lipstick isn't smudged. But there's another reason I race to the ladies' room. Thankfully, there's no line, and the furthest stall is empty. I seek refuge there and whip out my cell.

My hands are shaking, but when Sam picks up on the first ring, I breathe a sigh of relief. "Oh my god," are the only words I can muster.

"Tell me everything," she says with a smile in her voice. "You screwed him already, didn't you. Please tell me you rode him in the backseat of the car."

"Nearly," I say on an exhale.

She stifles a squeal. "Are you serious?"

"Not exactly. But we did kiss."

"And?"

"And...it was fucking amazing, Sam."

"Attagirl."

"I got so carried away, it was like time stopped, and we were the only two people on the planet. I've never felt that way before. But afterward, he spent the entire car ride trying to get me to admit what a great kisser he is, when he knew damn well how much I enjoyed it. I couldn't even stop myself from moaning into his mouth, and he still needs to hear me say how incredible it was?" And given how skilled he is, I'm sure he'd rate me average at best. Why the hell would I admit that he rocked my world when I know he'd never say it back? "What a cocky asshole. He infuriates me!"

Sam snickers. "You want to fuck him, though."

I close my eyes. "So much."

"Well, it sounds like he's game."

"He's a notorious player. He's probably always game." I'm careful not to say his name in case anyone overhears me. What kind of fake girlfriend would I be if I blew our cover on Day One? "He doesn't want *me*, Sam. I just happen to be the warm body sharing his bed this week."

"How dare you talk about my friend that way?" she scolds me. "He should be so lucky to date a badass babe like you."

"That's sweet of you to say...but it's also a load of crap." I sigh. "You've seen the types of women he's usually linked to. Models, actresses, heiresses..."

"So what? Those are the types of women he meets at VIP parties and charity events. Besides, if he actually liked any of them, he'd probably keep 'em around for more than a week. They're just flings, if anything."

"Well, flings or not, those women are on magazine covers."

"Exactly. Which means what you're seeing has been airbrushed by professionals who are paid to make flaws disappear."

"Don't patronize me, Sam. They're still as close to perfect as it gets." My eyes sting, and I fan them to keep my tears from falling. "But that's not all I'm worried about. When we were kissing, he touched my stomach...and I freaked out. I was afraid he'd be turned off by my lack of muscle tone. Then I proceeded to make this ridiculous rule that we can only touch each other over clothes. Now he probably thinks I'm a prude. And a terrible lay."

"Who could blame him," my friend teases. "Well, the fun thing about rules is that they're made to be broken. So forget about the other women, forget about your abs, *stop spiraling*, and have some fun. With his cock."

"Jesus, Sam."

"You knew what you were getting into when you called me, babe. If you wanted coddling, you would've dialed your sister."

I laugh. "You have a point."

"Fifteen minutes, guys," she yells out of nowhere.

My brow furrows. "Where are you?"

"In class," she says, as if I should know that. Sam's a philosophy professor at Northwestern University. And she's right, I did have her schedule memorized last year, because we often met for lunch on days she wasn't teaching. I guess I'm a smidge distracted by the fact that my most promising client turned out to be a fraud, and now I'm fake-dating a Major League pitcher for a shot at working with the world's biggest pop star.

I bring a palm to my forehead. "So, you're telling me there's a room full of college kids listening to our conversation?"

"No need to worry," Sam assures me. "I gave them a pop quiz because I figured you'd call. Besides, it's not like you're on speaker. They can only hear my side of the convo, and they're used to my shenanigans. And before you panic about anonymity, I was careful not to say your name, or the bachelor in question's. I could be talking to my mom for all my students know."

"You'd tell your mom to have fun with someone's cock?" I counter. "Wait. Don't answer that."

Sam laughs.

"You must be really fucking good at your job if you haven't gotten fired yet." I'm joking, of course. Sam is brilliant and was recently awarded a coveted research grant. I think it's safe to say that tenure's in her future.

"These kiddos would never snitch. They love me."

"They'd be crazy not to," I answer with a smile. "So...I just need to chill out? Go with the flow? Drink ashwagandha tea, like you're always trying to get me to do?"

"I'm telling you, the tea works. Why do you think I'm so mellow?"

"My money's on your pot brownies."

She chuckles. "Actually...I've stopped indulging in that variety of brownie."

My eyebrows rise. "Really? What will your eighty-year-old neighbor say? She's addicted to those things."

"Oh, I still bake them for her. They're good for her glaucoma. But as for me...I've decided to make some lifestyle changes."

"Oh yeah?" My forehead creases. "Is everything okay?"

"Yes, I promise. I'll dish when you get back from your trip. But it's nothing bad, so don't worry," Sam insists.

"Alright," I say, but I wish I could press further. My mind flits to the idea that Sam might be pregnant—but I can't imagine her being so nonchalant about it. She's thirty-two and has no interest in settling down. I know that applies to marriage, and I've always assumed it meant she didn't want kids, either. An accidental pregnancy would probably have her pretty shaken up. I dismiss the possibility almost immediately. But I sure am curious to hear more about the impetus for these lifestyle changes.

"You should get back to your man," Sam suggests. "He probably thinks you bailed on him because he dared to slip his fingers beneath your petticoat."

I groan. "I'm mortified."

"You've got this, hot stuff. You know what they say: just listen to your loins."

A laugh bursts from my chest. "I don't think anyone says that."

"Well, they should."

I shake my head. "Love you."

"Love you, too."

I leave the stall, suddenly self-conscious about the fact that I said the word "cock," among other things, in a public restroom. But as I head to the sink, everyone seems too preoccupied with their cumbersome carry-ons, their unruly kids, or their slept-on plane hair to pay me much notice. I reapply my red lipstick, although it's still pretty vibrant considering all the kissing I just did. At least now I can justify splurging for the really good stuff that stays in place.

It's not that I can't afford it. I've just always kept myself on a strict budget. Mom left it to Dad to manage our money growing up, which is on par with trusting Cookie Monster to manage a bakery. Our electricity was shut off a few times due to unpaid bills, but as far as Dad was concerned, driving a brand-new Lexus was worth the minor inconvenience. I learned at an early age that my parents would never be a financial safety net, and that I could only rely on myself to save wisely.

As far as the clothes I bought for this trip to Maui, I got lucky. It's nearly fall here in Chicago and there's a chill in the air, so the beachwear and summer dresses Jenna and I picked out together were on sale. The only items I paid full price for are the white sweater and dark wash jeans I'm wearing.

I give myself a once-over in the mirror. Jenna helped me carefully curate every outfit to highlight my curves. My breasts are the star of the show today. I don't normally wear V-necks, but now I see why my sister insisted I stock up on them. She was also right about how good my ass looks in this designer denim.

It's a rare occasion where I look at my reflection and see someone pretty. There are so many conditions that have to go my way for that to happen. I can't be on the part of my cycle that bloats me, for one thing. My hair has to cooperate, which depends more on the weather than on me—if it's the least bit humid, my waves start to frizz. And my clothes have to fit me to a T. I also need just enough makeup so I don't look washed out. Right now, my skin is glowing, and I'd be willing to bet it's because I just made out with the hottest guy I've ever laid eyes on.

After I work up the nerve to exit the ladies' room, I find him at a nearby coffee stand.

"Good timing," Holden whispers when I'm by his side. "I wasn't sure if you wanted cream or sugar, and that's a problem. You're my girl. I should know these things."

"Oh, um, I take it black. Thank you." When I look up at him, he's wearing a playful grin, and I know this is part of the charade...but damn, is he convincing.

No one's ever called me their *girl* before. Girlfriend, yes.

But my "girl" feels different. A little more possessive, maybe, but in a very sexy way. It reminds me of how the varsity athletes in high school would refer to the pretty cheerleaders they were dating. Girls like my sister, Jenna, who went to a different school, but whose hotness and popularity were renowned.

I was so quiet and mousy back then, the jocks never gave me the time of day, unless they needed help with homework. I used to long for one of them to ask me out on a date. To accompany me to class with his arm resting on my shoulder, or his hand in the back pocket of my jeans, signaling that I was his. Now, here I am, over a decade later, and I finally get the experience...but it's fake.

That's what's on my mind when camera shutters start clicking behind me. I bring my cup to my lips and sneak a glance at Holden out of the corner of my eye. He looks as calm and confident as he does on the mound. Meanwhile, every muscle in my body tenses.

After I've taken a quick sip of coffee, he puts one hand on my waist and tilts up my chin with the other, so that my gaze is fixed on him. Once again, I'm stunned by how spectacularly good-looking he is. So tall. So fit. So sexy. He's the guy I wanted to walk me to class in high school, but a million times hotter, and also famous. When he leans down to whisper in my ear, my nipples harden.

"I hope I'm not breaking any rules by touching your chin," he teases. "But rest assured, it's just for the cameras."

My heart sinks for no good reason. Of course this is all for show. My brain is well aware of that. It's my misguided breasts that need reminding.

When he pulls away, he winks, and I'd be annoyed if I weren't so embarrassed. He definitely thinks I'm a prude.

Whatever high I felt when I checked myself out in the bathroom mirror is gone, but that's no surprise. It's never long before I start feeling like mousy teenaged Christy again.

"Hey, McBride! Over here!" one of the paparazzi yells, trying to get a better photo.

I watch as my fake beau nods in the photographer's direction. His acknowledgment results in a flurry of shutter clicks, followed by a ripple effect of requests to turn his head varying degrees. He's used to this, obviously, but I'm so far outside my comfort zone, I may as well be standing here naked. I've never felt as self-conscious as I have with a dozen lenses pointed at me. At my body. I have no idea what my best angle is for photographs, or if I even have one. And is it true what they say about the camera adding ten pounds?

I turn around for a break from the flashing lights and grab a creamer I don't want from the coffee stand, just for an excuse to linger with my back to the crowd. Then I realize I'm only setting myself up for them to take photos of my ass.

Why the hell did I ever agree to this? It's a nightmare.

"Look this way, Red," one of the photographers calls to me. The entitlement in his tone gets under my skin, and anger stirs in my chest. Who the fuck does he think he is, addressing me that way? There's only one cocky asshole who can call me that, and it's only because he's so infuriatingly hot.

I whip around, feeling less like a timid teenager and more like the boss babe I am when I'm working. Relief floods me as I'm reunited with my agent alter ego. It's perfect timing for the transformation, too, because we're faced with a larger audience now. Over a dozen travelers and counting, many of them in Starlings fan gear, form a half circle around the paparazzi, eager to get their own pictures of Holden.

"Red! Over here!" The offending pap waves to get my attention, and the smug look on his face adds fuel to the spark he ignited.

Maybe that's how I get through this—with the fiery disposition that's a hallmark of my agenting. What is my arrangement with Holden if not a business agreement, anyway? If we play this game to win, both of our careers will benefit. I need to use every advantage I have, and right now, my unreserved confidence as a literary agent would certainly come in handy.

"Sorry, pal. This is the only man who gets to call me 'Red.'" I lean into Holden's side, and he snakes his arm around my shoulder, which makes me tingle in places that have no business tingling right now.

Another voice bellows from the crowd. "Hey, McBride. Any plans to streak again? Or was it a one-time thing?"

Holden turns, and I follow those captivating blue-gray eyes to see an actual cameraman filming us. "I think I'm good for now," he says with a lighthearted chuckle.

"How much trouble did you get in for that?" the cameraman probes further.

"Uh..." Holden scratches his temple. "To be determined."

"Who is that?" I ask my faux boyfriend under my breath.

"TMZ," he says, matter-of-factly.

"Oh. Cool," I say, through gritted teeth.

"Careful," the entitled pap warns TMZ Guy, while nodding in my direction. "She's a feisty one."

"Oh yeah?" I huff. "Would you be calling me feisty if I were a man? Or is it just because I'm a woman who dares to speak out of turn?"

The females in the crowd whoop and holler with

enthusiasm, while the pap rolls his eyes, looking for solidarity from the cameraman. "See what I mean?"

"Hey, Christy," TMZ Guy asks, seemingly undeterred. I'm shocked he knows my name, but I guess that's what happens when you go viral for yelling at Holden McBride. "How do you feel about your boyfriend's streaking stunt?"

"Do you think he'll get suspended?" A second cameraman, presumably from some other entertainment news show, appears out of nowhere.

Egged on by the reporters' brassy behavior, the growing crowd begins to chime in with invasive questions of their own.

"Christy! How did Holden win you back?"

"What's he like in bed?"

"Holden, did your mom freak out when she saw your ass on tv?"

"What will you do if this is the end of your baseball career?"

The goddamn nerve of these people. I shouldn't be surprised that we're in the middle of this shitstorm, given that Holden's agent tipped off the media, but these questions are outrageous. Holden McBride may be a public figure, but does that waive his right to privacy? Does it preclude him from being treated with respect? My blood boils as I'm reminded of an author I represented back in New York, and her similar experience with the press.

Fiona Price, the environmentalist and disinherited daughter of a Fortune 500 CEO, had publicly denounced her father for refusing to implement a sustainability plan she'd developed to reduce the company's carbon footprint. While her book had nothing to do with her family, and everything to do with the groundbreaking research she'd done as a college kid at MIT, the reporters who flocked to her launch party missed the memo.

They asked Fiona every inappropriate question under the sun, not only about her family feud, but also about men she'd been romantically linked to.

Their audacity triggered my inner "Mama Bear." At twenty-six, I was only a year older than Fiona, but that didn't stop me from feeling a fierce need to take care of her. Maybe that comes from years of worrying about my mom's mental health. When Jenna started to experience symptoms of depression after her first love died, my role as the "strong one" was solidified. Anyway, by the time I was done scolding the reporters at Fiona's book launch, they left the event with their tails between their legs.

"Just ignore them," Holden says, probably noticing my jaw tighten as we continue to get bombarded with tactless inquiries.

"The hell with that," I mutter under my breath. Then I face the crowd around us. "Mr. McBride will not be taking any more asinine questions about the Soldier Field incident. It's under investigation, which I'm sure you've heard, seeing as the Starlings' PR team made an announcement two days ago, and it's still the talk of every morning news show. You should know better than to ask us about it."

"What are you, his lawyer or something?" the obnoxious pap asks.

I smirk at him. "I'm an agent. Literary, specifically. But I think I speak for all agents when I say we don't know how to separate work and pleasure." I get a few laughs from the peanut gallery, which I hate to admit, feels good.

"For the record, I'm a big fan of agents," Holden tells our audience, but when I meet his gaze, his mischievous grin is on me. "Definitely don't hate them. You can quote me on that."

"Smooth," I say with a wry smile. "But I'm not letting you off the hook that easy."

"Wouldn't expect anything less from you, Red." There's a cocksure gleam in his eye, now that I've granted him exclusive rights to that nickname. He's oozing arrogance, as usual, but his expression is a mix of flirtatious and intimate that sets my loins on fire. If I listened to them like Sam suggested, I'd be begging him to screw me right here in this airport terminal. It's not the first time I've had to take her advice with a grain of salt.

So, instead of mauling him, I turn back to address our spectators. "Well, as much as my boyfriend enjoys flexing for photographs, we have a flight to catch."

I sling my carry-on over my shoulder, grateful that Holden insisted on checking our other bags. I joked it was because he isn't strong enough to put my heavy suitcase in the overhead bin, of course, but it's nice that we don't have to roll our luggage through this crowd. The quicker we get out of here, the better. I take his hand before cutting through the sea of cameras. "If you'll excuse us."

When I look up at him, he's smiling. "This way," he nods, directing me toward our gate. On the walk over, he's stopped five or six times, mostly by families with young children who want his autograph. And, likely because of the young fans, no one asks about the Soldier Field incident, which is a welcome change.

I have to say, it's a bit shocking how sweet he is with the kids. Not that I think he'd be a jerk, but he's much more down-to-earth than I've ever seen him. He kneels to meet their gazes. Gives them fist bumps and high-fives. He asks them if they play baseball, and what their favorite position is. Then he thoroughly answers their questions about how to throw different pitches. It makes me wonder if he wants to settle down someday and have a family. It also ignites my fucking loins again.

The autographs slow us down, so eventually we have to pick up our pace. The walk to the gate seems endless. "I'm surprised your mom didn't book a private jet," I tease, still floored by the idea that she hired a driver to impress me.

Holden smirks. "Oh, believe me, she tried."

My jaw drops. "No way. Really?"

He nods. "I hate flying private, and she knows that. It reminds me of the family trips we took when I was a kid. They weren't about seeing the world or experiencing different cultures, or, god forbid, having fun. They were about business deals, photo ops, and shopping sprees."

"Hmm." I tilt my head. "That's one way of looking at it."

"You probably think I sound like a spoiled brat," he guesses. "That I should be grateful for my family's wealth, and that many people can't afford to travel abroad, period, so I should shut the fuck up?"

I fight a self-satisfied smile. "*My* family couldn't afford to travel abroad. Period."

"Shit," he says. "You're serious?"

"Yes," I answer. "My dad was dean of the elite private school in Beachwood. He made a decent income, but he spent it all on himself. Country club membership, luxury car, Rolex. Anything to impress his stuffy colleagues. There was never enough left for us to go on vacation. Maybe I seem worldly to you, but it's probably thanks to all the books I've read. I've never been outside the country. And this is my first time traveling outside the continental US."

By the time we finally make it to our gate, everyone has already boarded, so we show our passes and step through to the jet bridge before Holden replies.

"That explains why you didn't travel as a kid, but what about as an adult?" He shrugs. "You're a successful literary agent. I imagine you could go abroad if you wanted to."

"Well, Kyle and I were together for most of my twenties, and…" I hesitate, not wanting to go into too much detail about the man who, as Jenna put it, "messed with my head."

"He was 'dull as dishwater'?" Holden suggests.

The corners of my eyes crinkle in amusement. "Did my mom tell you that?"

"Yup."

"Of course she did," I say with a chuckle. "She says the same thing about my dad, and she's not wrong on either count. I wish I'd realized sooner how similar they are. They hardly ever smile. They have no sense of humor or zest for life. Kyle traveled abroad once a year with his grandparents, but he never looked forward to it. It was an obligation more than anything else."

"Sounds like you picked a real winner, Red," he teases.

I roll my eyes. "Don't get me started. I can't blame Kyle for everything, though. I could have traveled on my own if I'd wanted to. But given my dad's reckless spending habits, I've always erred on the side of saving my money for a rainy day. If my business goes under, my parents sure as hell won't be able to help me."

We're at the end of the jet bridge and about to board the plane, when Holden gives my arm a gentle squeeze, then turns me toward him. "I'm sorry, Christy. Really." He lets out a sigh. "I guess I do need you to put me in my place."

"That's why I'm here."

He nods with a furrowed brow as we board. A flight attendant with a beautiful pink plumeria behind her ear greets us with an "Aloha, Mr. McBride and Ms. Andersen," then walks us to our seats. When we're sitting, she gives us a warm smile. "Can I get you champagne? Something to eat?"

I look over to Holden. "I'm fine with my coffee."

He nods in agreement, then turns to the flight attendant. "Maybe later. Thank you."

After she leaves, I look in every direction. We're the last people on the plane, but somehow, the first-class cabin is empty. "How are we the only ones up here?"

Holden closes his eyes and lets out a deep exhale. "Margot McBride, that's how."

I pause with my cup in midair and turn to him. "Are you telling me she booked the entire first-class cabin because you wouldn't agree to a private jet? Isn't that a little passive-aggressive?"

He lets out a wry laugh. "Little doesn't begin to describe it. If passive aggression were an Olympic sport, my mom would medal."

"So, we have all of this space, just for us? It seems like such a waste." If I had more money than God, I'd donate the excess to those in need rather than buy an entire first-class cabin for no good reason. But maybe that's just me.

"I don't disagree," Holden says.

I raise an eyebrow at him. "Then why did you let your mom book our flights? Or the luxury car service, for that matter? Are travel arrangements too plebeian a task for Holden McBride?"

"You're cute when you mock me, you know that?"

"If you think you can distract me with compliments, think again," I say. But damn if I'm not a little distracted now.

He heaves a sigh. "My mom's travel agent made the arrangements, alright? That's just the way it's always been."

I'm sure it has. His family probably employs a small army to handle the mundane chores of daily life. For someone who hates being a McBride, Holden sure seems comfortable taking advantage of the perks. And whatever his parents' employees don't manage for him, I bet the Starlings' staff handles. Case in point, the sports agent who's managing his PR crisis right now. Must be nice.

"It doesn't have to be that way," I counter. "You *are* capable of doing things for yourself, you know. You're a big boy."

"Oh, you have no idea," he says with a devilish smile.

I scoff. "You're wearing gray sweatpants, Holden. Everyone in this airport has an idea."

"Not everyone, Christy. Just the redheads who happen to be looking."

Fuck! He didn't really catch me checking out his package, did he?

I clear my throat. "Well, aren't you a master of using humor to avoid uncomfortable conversations."

"I think you're the one who's uncomfortable," he says with a knowing grin that makes my cheeks blazing hot.

I cross my arms over my chest. "At least I know how to make my own travel reservations."

He smirks. "You're something else."

And you're starting to remind me of my father.

My dad doesn't have the first clue how to take care of himself. When my mom left him, he had to move in with my grandma, because he can't make anything more sophisticated than a peanut butter sandwich, and I'd be willing to bet he doesn't know how to do laundry. And rather than learn how to stand on his own two feet, he went on dates five nights a week until he found a girlfriend to take him in.

Ugh.

Just what I need. Another man in my life who gives off Michael Andersen vibes. Wasn't Kyle enough? Where is Edison Ford when I need him?

My eyes dart to my carry-on. Of course, I brought *Edison's Love* with me as a comfort read. I also still want to reach out to the author, Haley Quinlan, to offer her representation. I wonder what the chances are she'd want to work with me, given the professional scandal I'm embroiled in.

Thanks a lot, Dr. Liar. Not only did she knowingly put my career in jeopardy, she's done nothing to help clear my name. Would it kill her to make a statement via social media about her angelic literary agent, Christy Andersen, who had no idea she signed a fraud, despite conducting her due diligence? I doubt anyone would believe Penelope, but she could have at least tried. Now my only recourse is to fake-date this manchild.

It's a good thing I only have to put up with Holden for the next six weeks or so. The more convincing our fake relationship is, the sooner his image will be restored, which means I could be done with this charade even before then.

I reach into my tote bag for my cell phone, put the camera in selfie mode, then turn to Holden. "Kiss my cheek."

His eyes widen. "I didn't think you'd want to commemorate the moment I called you out for picturing what's under my sweatpants, but whatever floats your boat."

The smug look on his face drives me crazy, and I have to

stifle a scream. "I'm sure you believe the whole world revolves around your dick, but—*news flash*—I'm just doing my job. The sooner we fix your reputation, the better for both of us, right?" I angle the camera toward us. "Now, be a good boy and kiss me, so I can post this on Instagram."

CHAPTER 9

Holden

Christy Andersen is throwing me off my game.

See, I'm not used to women resisting my charms. I know how that sounds, but hear me out. I come from a prominent family. I'm a professional athlete. I'm objectively good-looking, or so I'm told. Repeatedly.

Fuck, I do sound like an asshole. But I swear this woman's attracted to me, so why is she resisting so hard? Why is she hellbent on getting our deal over and done with? I mean, I know I should be, too. My reputation and career are on the line, and if I don't have my career, who am I? That question makes me sick to my stomach, which is why I generally avoid it. Needless to say, the stakes are huge, but for some reason, getting this ice queen to warm up to me seems equally important.

True, I'm not used to women playing hard to get. But there's more to it than that. Every now and then, Christy offers me a glimpse of what's beneath the hard exterior. When she took pity on me at the bar and asked Arnie to find a channel that wasn't airing my bare ass. When she was on the phone with her mom and beamed at me like we were sharing a private joke.

When she molded her body to mine while we were kissing. Even the way she fiercely defended me in front of those reporters. Her words may have been scathing, but the gesture behind them was sweet. Not to mention hot. She was protecting me. And I don't think it was an act. She could have ignored the reporters, like I told her to, and not said a thing.

Every time I feel like I'm winning her over, though, she gets frosty again. I know she thinks I'm an entitled prick, and I'm doing a very poor job of proving otherwise. Let me tell you, I sure didn't enjoy explaining why I sat back and let my mother make our travel arrangements. That was fucking humbling. But would you believe me if I said no one's ever called me out on that before? Most women I meet are thrilled to experience the perks of old money. I don't think they give a shit who ordered the Rolls Royce, as long as they get to ride in it.

Not Christy. The more unimpressed she is by my family's wealth, the more I like her. The problem is, I can't change where I came from. And if she thinks I reek of privilege now, it'll only get worse when I take her to the McBrides' opulent Maui estate.

For now, at least, I get to enjoy her head on my shoulder as she sleeps. After she took that selfie of us to post on Instagram, she had us go through a laundry list of get-to-know-you questions she conjured in an effort to make our fake relationship as convincing as possible. I was in favor of getting to know each other more organically in casual conversation, but she vetoed that idea off the bat. She was all business. At least now she knows my favorite movie is *Rookie of the Year*, in case anyone quizzes her.

And I'll tell you what I learned about Christy: her mother was right. She's barely had any fun in her entire life. She never skipped class in high school—not even on Senior Ditch Day, which she spent studying in the library. She never stayed out all night partying in college. Never mind anything more daring, like skinny-dipping. None of these questions were on her inventory, of course, but I told her she wasn't the only one who'd prepared a list. Mine just wasn't on paper. Anyway, she refused to answer the rest because they were all sexual in nature.

Minus my unwelcome interruptions, her survey took over two hours to get through, and by the time our in-flight meal came, her eyelids were heavy. As soon as she finished her poke bowl, she dozed off.

Now we hit a patch of choppy air, and she stirs with a furrowed brow. I take her hand and give it a gentle squeeze, and her features relax. I want to kiss the top of her head so badly. She smells like dessert again, and I've never had a sweet tooth, but damn do I crave her.

The next wave of turbulence is bumpier, and Christy wakes with a start.

"We're okay," I say, meeting her concerned gaze. "The pilot said it'll be smooth sailing after the next few minutes."

She shakes her head. "It's not just that... I had the worst dream." She pulls her hand from mine and touches the side of her cheek that's pink from leaning on me. "Was I sleeping on your shoulder?"

"Don't worry, it's fine. Good for optics, right?"

She looks around the empty cabin.

"The flight attendant came through several times," I lie. The first-class cabin crew are pretty good at gauging when passengers would prefer to be left alone. But I don't want Christy to feel embarrassed. "Anyway, what was your dream about?"

"Your mom."

I grimace. "So it was a nightmare, then. What happened? Did she kill you with fake kindness and backhanded compliments?"

"Worse. She told me she didn't buy our relationship, and that no one else would either. She said both our careers were going to go up in flames."

"She would never say that, Red." I tilt my head. "She absolutely would *think* it, but she'd never say it. She'd much rather fuel your paranoia with heavy sighs and subtle eyerolls."

Speaking of eyerolls, Christy's isn't subtle. "Be serious, Holden. My subconscious Margot McBride has a point. I'm not the type of woman you're typically with, so who's going to believe we're a couple? I mean, didn't you once have a relationship with an actual princess?"

"That was very short-lived." I shrug. "She wanted me to move abroad, and I would've had to give up baseball. It was never going to work."

She blinks at me a few times as she processes my answer. "Well, I'm not rich, and I'm not royalty. It's one thing to fake a relationship in front of the paparazzi for five minutes, but won't your family see right through our act once they get to know me?"

"Honestly, I don't think so, Christy. My family's so fucking self-absorbed, they can barely see past their own noses. Or nose-jobs, depending on who we're talking about."

She snort-laughs, and it's adorable. "That was pretty funny," she says, "I'll give you that. But I still don't feel better. You said yourself that you don't get along with your family. So what if they find out we're faking and tell the press to tarnish your already-shaky reputation? Or mine?"

I shake my head. "If I go down, the McBride name goes down with me. Trust me, my mom would sooner swear off Botox than let that happen. Maintaining the family's longstanding prestige is the only fucking thing she cares about."

"If you're sure..." Christy bites her lip, still anxious.

I hate that I'm causing her stress. But maybe there's a way around it. "You know what? I think we should tell my family the truth," I suggest. "Being honest will take the pressure off. My parents will just be grateful that you're helping me clean up my image. They won't care that our relationship is fake."

Even my real relationships aren't of interest to them, unless there's some financial benefit they can take advantage of. Once, they urged me to go after the daughter of a banking magnate, in hopes they could parlay the connection into more favorable loans. They didn't give a shit that I had no interest in her. Why would they start caring about my happiness now, when they never have before?

Christy heaves a sigh of relief. "Really? We can do that?"

"Of course. Anything to make this easier on you. I know I'm asking a lot."

"Thank you, Holden." She smiles, and the tension in her features fades. "When will we let your family in on our secret?"

"We'll do it tomorrow, at breakfast. That's our first family event." I heave a sigh. "The first of too many."

She winces. "Yeah, I saw the itinerary. So, let me get this straight...you and your siblings have to compete for your inheritance? That sounds pretty cutthroat."

"Tell me about it." I smirk. "It was my mom's idea, of course. Grandma Evelyn would never want to pit Abby, Wes, and me against each other. And she'd never play favorites, either. That's why she kept the language in her will broad. All it says is that the money's supposed to fund a charitable initiative run by *one* of her grandchildren. I'm pretty sure she meant for that grandchild to be me."

"What makes you say that?"

"She knew about the sports program for kids I want to develop." I half-smile. "You know, my long-held dream I told you about at the bar?"

Christy's eyes go wide. "Oh, no. You mean, the one I accused you of making up on the fly?"

"Right after you called me an asshole," I add, enjoying the flush on her face as I tease her.

"Turns out I'm the asshole. I'm sorry, Holden." Her shoulders slump. "But...I do have a way of making it up to you, if you're interested."

I raise an eyebrow, my gaze falling down the length of her body. "Oh, I'm *very* interested, Red."

Christy elbows me. "Get your mind out of the gutter, McBride. You said you want to model your sports program after Dex Oliver's Dramatic Hearts Academy, right? Well, my sister dated him in high school, and they're still friends, if you need an introduction."

"I appreciate that," I say with a grin. "But Lola already made the connection. I sent Dex a copy of my proposal, and he said he'd review it and be in touch soon."

She nods. "Ah yes, Lola. I forgot she dated Dex, too."

"Yeah, briefly. For her sake, I wish it had worked out between them." I rake a hand through my hair. "He seems like a good guy, and Lola's taste in men is usually abysmal at best."

"Well, Dex was holding out for his soulmate. I don't think any other woman ever stood a chance," Christy tells me. "As for Lola, she definitely does seem to have a thing for bad boys."

"Don't get me started." I drag a hand down my stubble. "Since she was in middle school, she's come crying to me and Nate about guys more times than I can count."

Christy's gaze falls to her lap. "So you and Lola never..."

I'm dying to ask why she's interested in whether I ever hooked up with Lola, but I don't want her to think I'm deflecting, so I tell her the honest truth. "No way. She's like the little sister I never had. When we were kids, I once asked her parents if they'd trade her for Wes."

If only.

The mere thought of my brother makes my muscles tight. The ache travels down my neck and into my bad shoulder. I dig my thumb into the inflamed tissue, trying to get relief. Damn, I hope my physical therapist can help with this pain when I'm back in Chicago. Elisia's the best in the business. If she can't work out these kinks, I'm screwed.

"You okay?" Christy eyes my shoulder with concern.

"Yeah," I lie. "I'm just trying to make sure my arm stays loose. Talking about my family makes me tense. But the good news is, we don't have to see them until tomorrow," I add, eager to change the subject. "Tonight, we're free, so let me know what you want to do, and we'll do it. I know the island like the back of my hand. I'll take you wherever you want to go."

I promised Ingrid Andersen I'd help her daughter have fun this week, and that's what I'm going to do. Whether Christy wants to snorkel, or hike, or just lie on a beach during our unscheduled hours, I'll show her the time of her life. And if she happens to fall for me in the process, so be it.

"Oh." I can practically see her wheels spinning. "I figured since there was nothing on the itinerary, I'd probably catch up on work.

I'm up to my eyeballs in manuscripts. And there's a debut author I want to get an offer out to before someone else snatches her up. She's a romance writer, and the good ones are hot commodities. But feel free to go without me. I'll be fine. I'm assuming there's a kitchen where I can make myself a sandwich, or something?"

I glance down so she can't see the amused look in my eyes. "There's twenty-four seven room service. No menu. You tell them what you want, and they make it for you. But are you really telling me you want to stay in and work on your first night in Maui? Come on, Red. Wouldn't you rather enjoy paradise while you can?"

Her eyes are wide. "Are you kidding me? Spending the night in luxurious accommodations, reading a good book, and eating any food I want, whenever I want it? What could be more enjoyable than that?"

Not hanging out with me, clearly.

I'm feeling pretty damn sorry for myself, but I chuckle anyway. "I guess I forgot who I was talking to. The thing is, it probably wouldn't look great if I'm photographed wandering around the island by myself when we're supposed to be together, so..."

Yeah, I went there. I'm not proud of myself for throwing our agreement in her face, but this woman only seems to have one setting, and it's work mode. Desperate times call for desperate measures, as they say. Plus, if Ingrid knew that her daughter was planning to stay in and read on her first night in paradise, I think she'd support me playing dirty.

Christy's body deflates with disappointment, which does absolutely nothing for my already-bruised ego. "Ugh, you're right," she says. "Well, can we make it a quick dinner, then?

Something casual, like a food truck? We can eat on the beach, and I'll work when we get back."

"You got it."

Fucking hell. If I'm going to show this woman the time of her life, I sure have my work cut out for me.

When our plane lands and we're still taxiing down the runway, Christy turns her cell back on.

"Whoa." Her eyes go wide. "Our selfie has over forty thousand likes, and my Instagram followers tripled."

"Look at you, already benefiting from our business deal. Wanna find out how many followers you'll gain if we post a picture where I'm kissing your neck? Or maybe even a little lower?" My gaze slips to the V of her sweater, and that perfect bit of cleavage that keeps calling to me like a fucking siren song.

"Eyes up here, McBride," she huffs, pointing at her face. "And you don't have to flirt with me when no one's watching, you know."

"Not sure I can help it," I say, my gaze where she wants it.

She flushes a deep shade of pink. "Well, try. We need firm boundaries so things don't get messy."

I run a hand through my hair and—yeah, I'll admit it—I'm flexing my bicep a little. "You know what I think, Red? I think *you* need firm boundaries, because my flirting turns you on, and you don't trust yourself not to act on it."

"That's bullshit."

"Tell that to your nipples."

Christy looks down, gasps, then crosses her arms over her chest. "You leave my nipples out of this! It's chilly in here."

I smirk. "Keep telling yourself that."

"Okay, new rule," she announces, crossing her legs now, too. "We do whatever we need to make our relationship convincing in public, but when we're alone, we stop. I don't want either of us to mistake this for something it isn't."

Her message is clear. She's afraid *I'm* going to mistake this for something it isn't.

"You're the boss," I say in a lighthearted attempt to hide how I really feel about her request.

Not long after, we're walking down the jet bridge leading into Maui's Kahului Airport. I take advantage of the crowd at the gate and grab Christy's hand. She looks at me and gives a brief nod of approval, as if to say, "Right. It's showtime."

You bet your sweet ass it is.

I stop in the middle of a busy walkway and cradle her face in my hands.

"What are you doing?" she whispers, her eyes searching mine for answers.

"I'm playing by the rules," I tell her. Then I lean down and kiss her pretty red lips until we hear whoops and cheers from our audience.

That's all I give her. No hint of tongue. No wandering hands. Just a kiss I'm hoping will leave her wanting more.

When I pull away, her fingers float to her mouth, and she smiles, stunned. Then I grab her hand again, and we keep walking.

Between signing autographs, posing for pictures, and getting our suitcases from baggage claim, it's another thirty minutes before we make it outside. It's midafternoon when we step into the humid Hawaiian air, and the sun is shining in a cloudless sky. It's a perfect eighty degrees.

Christy fans her face with her hand. "It's balmy out here. I'm going to have to take off this sweater."

Seeing as there's no one within earshot, I resist the urge to say anything that might offend her delicate sensibilities. But needless to say, I'm pretty fucking excited that her clothes are coming off.

She puts her tote bag on top of her luggage, then crosses her arms, pulling at the hem of her shirt and lifting it over her head. The whole thing seems to happen in slow motion as she moves her hips while she shimmies out of it, her chest bouncing.

No flirting, my ass. This must be payback for the gray sweatpants I wore on purpose. Tit for tat, I guess.

Under her sweater is a V-neck tank that I'm frankly jealous of, because it gets to hug her curves so tight.

"Much better," she says, flipping her gorgeous red hair. "Oh, and would you mind putting sunscreen on my back? It doesn't take much for me to burn."

She pulls a tube out of her tote bag and hands it to me.

Of course, I opt to give her shit rather than comply with the simple task. "Well, I would...but I don't want to break our contract. What was that rule again? No touching bare skin? It's a little vague, don't you think? We should probably amend it."

She closes her eyes and takes a deep breath. "Just do it, okay? The rules don't apply when it's a question of sun safety."

"I'll try to remember that," I tease as she turns around, moving her hair over her shoulder for me.

I rub the lotion into her skin, taking my time to press my thumb into any little knots of tension I come across. Her muscles relax under my touch, just like when I had my hand on her thigh on the ride to O'Hare. I take the small win and smile. But I can't help but wonder, again, what bothered her so much about my fingers moving under her shirt to touch her waist.

With her facing away from me, I'm ballsy enough to ask. "What was that about, earlier? In the car. When I grazed your stomach, you flinched."

The muscles I'd just loosened up are taut again. "I'm just ticklish, that's all."

"I don't buy that."

Her shoulders rise as she inhales. "Not everyone's as confident in their skin as you are, Holden. I wouldn't streak if you paid me a million dollars." She turns around, grabs the tube from me, and puts it back in her tote. "Shall we?"

I nod, accepting her answer because I can tell it's a touchy subject. Then I lead her to our car, which is waiting at the curb. Yes, it's another luxury car with a driver my mother paid for— and I don't know what to make of the fact that Christy doesn't give me a hard time about it now. When I glance at her, she's busy looking at the sky. I almost forgot it's her first time on the island. She must be so eager to see the surrounding tropical paradise that verbal sparring isn't at the forefront of her mind. I doubt my reprieve will last long. But I don't mind Christy's biting wit. In fact, it ranks high on the list of things about her that I find sexy as hell.

"Palm trees," she says with an air of amazement that makes me want to show her the entire world.

While she looks all around with wonder, I gaze at her the same way. "Is this your first time seeing them?"

She nods. "Jenna lived in LA for a few years, but I never visited her there." Her grin fades. "We weren't close back then. We only saw each other in Beachwood, on holidays."

My chest tightens, thinking of my own strained relationship

with my sister Abby, and the role I played in getting us here. "What brought you closer? If you don't mind my asking."

"Well, Jenna had been dealing with a major loss...and I didn't know how to help her. Or, I guess I wasn't the right person to help her. Eventually, she found an amazing therapist, and it's been life-changing. We're the closest we've ever been. Jenna's the one who urged me to move to Chicago."

"I'm happy for you," I say, enjoying the delight in her eyes. At the same time, I'm silently thanking Jenna for bringing her sister to the Windy City.

It's a different ride than the one we took to the airport. No kissing this time, which I'll admit is a bummer. Instead, Christy looks out the window and asks me all about the island. Some questions I can answer, like where my favorite beach is. Others, I have to pass on to our driver Ana, a native, who tells us all about Maui's history. As soon as I put down the glass divider so we can talk to her, I take Christy's hand in mine. She doesn't give me a nod of approval this time, but our fingers stay intertwined for the rest of the drive.

As we near the estate, I experience its magic through her wide eyes. From the road, the stone walls on opposite ends of the wrought-iron gate are unremarkable. They were designed to keep passersby from being too curious about the property. But once we're inside, driving down the winding palm-lined lane to the main house, Christy's gasp doesn't surprise me.

If this isn't paradise, I don't know what is. We're surrounded by lush tropical plants as far as the eye can see. Plumeria perfumes the air, and native monkeypod trees stretch over fifty feet high, their branches forming a canopy that shields the estate from the blazing sun. Christy can only see the main house from here, but at eighteen thousand square feet, it's enough to make her jaw drop. She hasn't even laid eyes on the private beach, the dock where my parents keep the yacht, the tennis court, the fitness center, or the multiple pools available to serve any whim—whether it's swimming laps or watching the sun set over the ocean. All in all, we're looking at a ten-acre oceanfront private resort with a full-time staff, and every amenity you could possibly think of.

"Are we the first ones here?" Christy asks when Ana drops us off at the main house.

I nod. "The rest of the family took the private jet from New York. They won't arrive until late tonight."

She grabs the handle of her suitcase full of books and eyes the vast, wraparound porch with an eager grin. My guess is she's imagining herself reading in one of the wicker armchairs. "Well...lead the way."

"We're actually not staying in the main house," I tell her.

"Oh. Where are we staying?"

"It's called the, uh..." I drag a hand down my chin, trying to hold back my smile. "The Honeymoon Bungalow."

She clears her throat. "The what?"

Of course I didn't have to tell Christy we call it that, but then I wouldn't get to see her cheeks flush at the idea of sharing the estate's most romantic quarters with me.

"The McBrides have a longstanding tradition of honeymooning on the island," I explain. "Originally, there was only the main house. But when my parents got married, my grandparents were living here. They'd moved from New York because they were tired of the frigid winters. Anyway, Grandma Evelyn had the bungalow built to give my parents privacy on their honeymoon."

Christy raises an eyebrow. "And we're staying there because..."

I chuckle. "It's where I always stay. It's closest to the path that leads to the beach, and I like swimming in the ocean."

Maybe it's in my head, but the saltwater seems to help the inflammation in my shoulder. But that's not the only reason I prefer the bungalow. I prefer it because it's the furthest residence from the main house. And the further I am from my family, the fewer opportunities they have to take cheap shots at me.

"Okay," she says with an easygoing shrug that takes me by surprise. "Lead me to the bungalow, I guess."

Although it's a beautiful ten-minute walk on a path punctuated by koi ponds and orchid arches, I don't want to carry our luggage that far for my shoulder's sake. Instead, I drive us there in one of the golf carts we keep at the main house, for whenever we need to zip around the estate.

There's a tropical garden in front of the bungalow that shields it from the main path for total privacy. When we walk into the love nest, I watch Christy as her eyes slowly roam over its vaulted wood ceiling, across the airy single room we'll be sharing and, more significantly, to the king-sized, four-poster canopy bed. Other than a small but luxurious bathroom and a sleek kitchenette, that's about all the interior has to offer. It makes sense, given it was designed for newlyweds.

On the ocean-facing side, floor-to-ceiling sliding glass doors lead to an outdoor living space—or lanai, as it's called on the island. It's a haven of relaxation. Plush couches, potted palms, a coffee table, a hammock. And just off the lanai is an intimate heated spa pool that overlooks the ocean. After Christy soaks it all in, she brings her palm to her heart.

"Holden, this is so beautiful," she says, and I swear, she's glowing.

"I'm glad you like it." That's an understatement. The way this island lights her up intoxicates me.

She turns her gaze back inside. "I'm going to shower and change before we leave, okay?"

"Make yourself at home."

While she's in the bathroom, I have to work hard not to think about the fact that she's naked and wet on the other side of the wall. Desperate for a distraction, I take time unpacking my suitcase, then put on shorts and a T-shirt for the quick, casual dinner she had in mind.

The last thing I'm expecting is for her to emerge thirty minutes later wearing this sexy white dress that's like a shot of adrenaline to my heart. Her gorgeous, long hair is pinned back on one side, while loose waves fall over her other shoulder. And the way she's looking at me with those pretty brown eyes makes me feel unsteady.

"Holden," she says. "I want to renegotiate our contract."

CHAPTER 10
Christy

Holden's face lights up like a kid's on Christmas morning. "I knew you'd come around."

He closes the gap between us with one eager step and kisses me with a fervor that's like nothing I've ever experienced. It's lustful, and hungry, and the type of kiss I've only read about in romance novels. I'm so stunned that I forget what I wanted to tell him and get caught up in the heat of the moment. In the way our mouths meet like there's a magnetic pull between us. In the way I feel him smile when our tongues touch, and the way my own lips curl to match his. In the way he pulls me close, and suddenly I feel like I'm floating.

Oh, wait—I *am* floating.

Somewhere within the realm of this kiss, Holden lifted me off the ground. And as for how my legs ended up wrapped around his waist, well...they must have a mind of their own. By the time I come back to my senses, he's carrying me to the mammoth bed in the middle of the room.

"Holden!" I cry out, breathless.

He groans into my neck. "God, I love the way my name sounds rolling off your tongue."

"No, Holden...wait," I say when we're mere inches from the bed.

He stops in his tracks, still holding me tight as my feet find the floor. "What's wrong, baby?"

No one's ever called me "baby" before. I never thought I'd *want* anyone to call me "baby." But the sexy rasp in Holden's voice is like an aphrodisiac, making me crave more of him. Now it's all I can do not to fall back onto the sprawling bed and take him down with me. I have to grab the closest bedpost to keep myself upright.

My heart's racing as I run my fingers through my hair, then smooth out my dress, which hiked up considerably when my legs were clasped around him. Go figure. "When I said I wanted to renegotiate our contract, I wasn't talking about the, um, physical aspects of our arrangement."

He unwinds his arms from my hips, then scratches his forehead as he widens the space between us. "Is that right?" His smile is not only smug but justified, given how willingly I gave in to his kiss. "I thought you were finally ready to admit we have chemistry, Red. Pretty fucking intense chemistry, if you ask me."

My cheeks flame. "Of course we have chemistry, Holden. You're a gargantuan flirt. I wouldn't be surprised if you had chemistry with a brick wall."

"I'm sorry, I didn't hear anything you said after you called me 'gargantuan.'" His smirk reminds me how fucking annoying he can be.

I heave a sigh. "See? *This* is why we need ground rules. Because your over-the-top flirtation makes it impossible to take you seriously. Much less get to know who you are under the overtly sexual exterior."

"You gotta admit, you enjoy the exterior," he replies, seemingly unfazed.

I roll my eyes, making it clear how frustrated I am. But when the color in his face deepens the slightest bit, I wonder if my words actually got through to him.

Maybe Holden isn't being a jackass for shits and giggles. Maybe his notorious shenanigans are a byproduct of "growing up McBride."

The thought first struck me after my shower, when I was looking for a hairdryer in one of the vanity drawers and found an old photograph of him and his family. I studied it for a while, trying to figure out the story behind it. Considering I read books for a living, it's probably no surprise that I look for stories everywhere. And the tale this picture told broke my heart.

Spring was in full bloom, and judging by the balloons in the garden, the McBrides were celebrating a special occasion. Everyone was dressed in their Sunday best—except Holden. He must have been nine or ten. Grandma Evelyn had just brought him home from his baseball game, and he was still in his uniform, covered in dirt, the way a Little Leaguer should be. He'd probably hit a line drive to the outfield and slid headfirst into home plate. I bet he was on cloud nine, until he joined the party late, and no one cared about his grand slam. Least of all his mom, who didn't want him to ruin the family picture (by looking like a normal kid, I might add). I imagine she suggested, in her passive aggressive way, that he sit this one out. But Grandma wouldn't hear of it. Proud, protective, and fiercely loyal, she took Holden's hand, and they joined the rest of the family. Grandma stood proud with a defiant glint in her eye.

And next to her, Holden was crying, his left hand balled into a fist. Maybe he wished he could throw a punch. Or maybe he just wanted to pitch.

When I put the photo back where I found it, I had to hold back my own tears. That's the moment I decided that, for the sake of the miserable little boy in that picture, I would give Holden the benefit of the doubt.

"Listen," I say. "I owe you an apology. You offered to show me around the island tonight, and I blew you off in favor of work. That was shitty of me, and I'm sorry."

He plays it off with a shrug. "No big deal."

"Yes, it is. Since the night we met, I haven't been my best self. The Penelope scandal turned my world upside down, and I can get a little...*catty*, for lack of a better word, when I'm stressed." My smile is sheepish. "I've even been known to lash out a time or two, if you can believe it."

"You? Lash out?" He chuckles. "Never."

"I've made a lot of assumptions about you, and that's not fair," I go on. "Just because everyone knows who you are, doesn't mean they actually *know* you. Myself included. I'd like to change that."

Holden raises an eyebrow at me, intrigued.

"That's what I meant by renegotiating our contract. Just because we're faking a relationship doesn't mean we can't get properly acquainted. Yes, we're lying to the world, but let's at least be genuine with each other. If there's one thing I hate, it's believing I know someone, only to find out they're not the person I thought they were. That's why I was so triggered by Penelope's bait and switch."

And don't get me started on Kyle's.

Holden's nod is sympathetic. "You don't have to twist my

arm to get me to spend quality time with you, Red. What did you have in mind?"

I smile. "I'd like you to show me your favorite spots on the island. We have less than a week here, and I want to make the most of it. Starting tonight." I look down at the dress I chose in anticipation of an evening out with him. It's a white, midi-length sundress with a corset top that cinches my waist, and a full skirt that hides my imperfections.

"So, I guess all that work you were planning to catch up on can wait?" he teases.

I shrug. "What's the point of being your own boss if you never take advantage of the flexibility, right?"

Although I shouldn't wait much longer to make an offer to Haley Quinlan, the author of *Edison's Love*. I bet she'll have a long list of agents dying to represent her. Including Colin Finch. He worked with me at Hanover Literary before he moved to London, where he now runs one of the most prestigious agencies in the UK. As far as my job goes, he's the closest thing I have to a nemesis. He has impeccable taste and seeks out all the same authors I do. If I had a nickel for every time a potential client was torn between the two of us, well...I'd still be nowhere near as rich as the McBrides. But I could probably buy myself a candy bar.

I wonder how likely Haley would be to choose me over Colin, now that my reputation's been sullied? The thought makes me feel sick, so I push it out of my mind, for now.

"Holden, I've been in a rut for longer than I care to admit, and I want you to help me break out of it," I go on. "I just have one condition."

Smiling, he drags a hand over his stubble. "Of course you do."

"I need you to be *real* with me. I want to see what's underneath the shameless flirtation and lame innuendos," I joke.

"Ouch," he says, feigning injury with an exaggerated wince. "Can't say anyone's called my come-ons lame before."

When he settles his eyes on mine, his expression shifts to something that looks a heck of a lot like adoration. It makes my skin flush and my stomach tie up in knots. I don't know the feeling of being adored firsthand. But his gaze reminds me of the way Charlie looks at my sister.

I have to remind myself that this is all part of Holden's charm. He's a ladies' man for a reason. He makes every woman feel this way.

"Well, there's a first time for everything," I say, breaking eye contact and looking down at my feet. "So...what do you say? Can you be real with me?"

He runs a thumb over his bottom lip as he considers my question. For a few seconds, I'm convinced he's going to turn me down. Finally, he grins.

"You've got yourself a deal, Red."

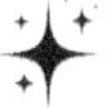

Holden changes again, into khaki pants and a short-sleeved linen shirt that better matches my aesthetic. He looks sexy as hell. Afterward, he picks a Range Rover from the main house's six-car garage and tells me we're going to the best sushi spot on the island. It's a short drive, and we talk about baseball nearly the whole time. He tells me his favorite player is Ken Griffey Jr., who's known for his beautiful swing. Holden insists his own swing, in comparison, is "shit." When he was a kid, he spent the better part of a year trying to replicate the former outfielder's fluid motion, but never came close. Eventually, Holden gave up and tried his hand at pitching. The rest is history. And though he didn't quite follow in Ken Griffey Jr.'s footsteps, he honored his favorite player by picking the same jersey number: twenty-four.

The way his face lights up when he talks about his career makes it clear how much the sport means to him. And I have to say, it's the first time I've heard him speak about something with such genuine enthusiasm. No posturing, no pretense. It's a good look for him.

I'm fascinated by Holden's origin story and have at least a dozen more questions for him, but before I know it, he pulls into a parking lot.

"This is it," he says, nodding directly in front of us. I follow his gaze, stunned.

I'm not quite sure what I was expecting. Valet parking, at the very least. An opulent exterior dripping with Swarovski crystals, maybe. Or, at the other end of the spectrum, an elusive celebrity hotspot hidden inside an unmarked warehouse. The kind of place you can only gain admission to with a password or a special key.

The last thing I anticipated was for Holden to take me to a strip mall for sushi...but here we are. Nestled in a row of shops and eateries, this place looks like it could be in Beachwood, Ohio. The storefront has a fun, friendly vibe. Overhead, the name of the restaurant glows in a cartoonish font, and there's pop music playing through outdoor speakers.

I fucking love it.

The owner greets Holden with a beaming smile when we

walk in, and the two exchange one of those bro hugs that starts with a handshake and ends with a pat on the back.

"Are you okay to sit at the bar?" Holden asks me. "It's where we first met, after all."

He slips his arm around my waist for the first time since we kissed in the bungalow, and I'm reminded that we're performing now. I take a quick glance around and see several pairs of eyes on us.

I guess I should give them something to watch. I mean, that *is* part of my job description as Holden's fake girlfriend. And when it comes to work, I always go above and beyond.

"Well, aren't you a romantic at heart?" I stand on my tiptoes because, even in heels, I can barely reach his cheek. When I plant my lips there, he tightens his grip on me. In the distance, a cell phone camera flashes. Then another.

We follow the owner to our seats at the bar. While we peruse the menu, Holden takes my hand and holds it in his lap, absentmindedly circling his thumb over mine. If there's one thing I know about this man I just met, it's that he's fueled by physical touch. His hands gravitate toward my body at any opportunity, and I've never felt more desired.

Kyle rarely touched me outside of sex. And even then, he never grabbed me like he couldn't get enough of me. He never kissed me like he couldn't wait to fuck me. Meanwhile, in a matter of days, a veritable stranger has checked both of those boxes, and more.

As I sit next to Holden and bask in the attention his fingers are paying to mine, I feel my boundaries begin to fade. But if we have sex and it's as good as I imagine, will I get attached to him? If so, I'll be setting myself up for heartache. I mean, I may not despise Holden the way I did three days ago, but he's still a manchild. Even assuming he wants me—which I still find hard to believe—I could never be with someone like him long-term. So, if we sleep together, it has to stay casual.

"What are you thinking, Red?"

Shit.

I look up from our intertwined hands to see Holden's gaze fixed on the menu. Phew. He's talking about food. He has no idea I spent the last several minutes contemplating whether to hook up with him in our giant bungalow bed that practically demands sex.

"I'm an adventurous eater," I reply with flushed cheeks. "Let's start with your favorites and go from there."

After Holden puts in our order, he pulls his phone out of his back pocket and scrolls through messages. "My agent says we're getting great press."

"That's good to hear," I reply, despite knowing that, the more convincing we are, the sooner this arrangement comes to an end. It's a double-edged sword. But if being convincing means I get to lean in and kiss him right now, I guess I'm willing to take the risk.

I keep the kiss short and sweet because we're in public, but when I pull away, Holden whispers in my ear.

"This honesty clause in our contract...it goes both ways, I assume?"

I clear my throat, fearing what happens when I say yes. Will he ask me why I keep kissing him tonight? Will he want to know what's *really* been on my mind since we got to the restaurant?

Eventually, I have to answer him. "It's only fair."

"Good," he says. "Just checking."

He leaves it at that.

It's the most romantic date I've ever had—real or otherwise. The sushi is out-of-this-world, melt-in-your-mouth delicious. And when Holden feeds me the last pieces of sashimi with his chopsticks, I nearly swoon. The drinks I order are fruity, and tropical, and strong. Before we leave the restaurant, Holden pulls a fresh orchid out of my rum punch and puts it behind my left ear. He tells me that, in Hawaiian culture, this means I'm spoken for.

I know it's all part of the act. But the more cocktails I have, the easier it is for me to forget. It's a dangerous game we're playing.

After dinner, Holden drives us back to the estate, and we walk to the private beach near our bungalow. The first thing I see when we step onto the sand is a lavish daybed with wispy white curtains, glowing under a canopy of string lights. I stop dead in my tracks, stunned by the beauty of it all.

"Don't worry, I'll be on my best behavior," Holden says. My heart sinks. In keeping with our contract, he's kept his hands off me since we left our audience at the restaurant. It's the opposite of what I want right now.

When we sit, he grabs a bottle of chilled champagne from an elegant standing wine chiller.

"Where did that come from?" I ask, baffled. "Did you order it before we left the restaurant?"

He shakes his head, his expression bordering on sheepish. "The staff here are amazing. They bend over backward to anticipate our needs. There's a lot that goes on behind the scenes to make it appear seamless."

I take in the vast ocean view in front of me and soak up the sound of the crashing waves. "This isn't just seamless, Holden. It's magic. I feel like I'm in a fairytale."

"Do you hate it?" His forehead is creased as he waits for my answer.

"Not even a little bit." I sigh. "I just can't get used to it, that's all."

Holden's silent as he pours our champagne.

"What should we toast to?" I ask him.

"To making the most of your time here." When we clink glasses, the mischievous glint in his eyes thrills me, despite myself. I was starting to think I wouldn't see it again tonight.

I take a sip of liquid courage. "Did you have something particular in mind?"

Holden drains his glass in one large gulp, then nods toward the ocean. "Let's go skinny-dipping."

I laugh. "Not a chance."

"Come on, Red. You're thirty years old and haven't done a rebellious thing in your life. Isn't it about time you had some fun?"

"What's so fun about swimming without clothes on?" I shrug. "I don't see the appeal."

"It feels good as hell, for one thing," Holden tells me.

I smirk. "I think you just like being naked."

"I do," he says without hesitation.

"Well...I don't." My gaze falls to my champagne flute, and I take another sip.

"The ocean doesn't care what you look like, Christy," he says. "And as for me...I'd be lying if I said I wasn't curious. But I'll close my eyes."

"Liar." My cheeks flush.

"Scout's Honor," he says, holding up three fingers.

I roll my eyes. "Oh, well, in *that* case..."

"Look," he says, smiling. "This isn't about me sneaking a peek, okay? You asked me to be real with you, so I'm telling the truth." He refills his glass and tops mine off. "The first time I went skinny-dipping was on this island. It was my fifteenth birthday, and my parents fucking forgot, because they were too busy wooing a restaurateur and his wife, in hopes of convincing them to lease from us."

"Hmm. That sounds a lot like the plot of *Sixteen Candles*," I tease.

"Yeah, well...I wish I could say I'm bullshitting, but I'm not." He swallows another gulp. "If my grandma had been here, she would've baked a pineapple upside-down cake, like she always did for our birthdays. But my grandfather was recovering from knee surgery, so they stayed back in New York."

My heart aches for young Holden again. "I'm sorry. As dysfunctional as my parents were, they remembered every birthday. I would've been so upset if they'd forgotten."

"I was *pissed*. I sprinted here from the main house, stripped off my clothes, and ran into the ocean. And, I know it was only temporary, but for a handful of glorious minutes, I didn't care about anything."

"That sounds nice," I admit.

"That's why I want you to try it," he replies. "I want you to experience how freeing it is to let go of what's weighing you down, and let the saltwater keep you afloat. I think you'd enjoy it."

I nod and down the rest of my champagne, staring out at the placid water. "Okay."

His eyes light up with genuine excitement. It's endearing. "You mean it?"

"Yes. But you first," I direct him.

He finishes his drink and sets down the glass. Then, without hesitation, he stands and starts unbuttoning his shirt. He's facing away from me, and as I savor the last of my own bubbly, I admire his broad shoulders, his muscular arms, and the lines of his back, tapering down to his waist. When he unzips his shorts, I tear my eyes away out of respect for his privacy, although it's pretty clear he doesn't give a shit. And why would he? From what I've seen so far, his body is nothing short of perfect.

When the water's at waist level, Holden calls out to me. "Your turn, Red. I won't face you until you're ready."

I never planned to take off all my clothes. But I do strip down to my underwear. I also take the orchid from behind my ear and set it on top of my dress, so it doesn't get lost in the ocean. Then I swim out to him, and when the water's covering my strapless bra, I tell him he can turn around.

"How does it feel?" He's looking only into my eyes.

I smile. "The water's so warm. I wasn't expecting that."

The underwire of my bra is digging into my skin, and I want to rip it off and toss it into the Pacific, but I'm not brave enough.

I don't know why I decide to fess up. Maybe it's all the drinks I've had tonight. But I did promise to be honest with Holden.

"I'm cheating," I admit.

He tilts his head. "What do you mean?"

I swim closer to him and wrap my arms around his neck,

which lifts me out of the water just enough for him to see my bra.

"It's okay," he says, brushing hair out of my face. "Baby steps."

His words are so soothing, every muscle in my body relaxes. And when his hands land soft-as-ever on my bare waist, I don't flinch.

"Is this okay?" he asks me.

"Yes."

"What about this?" He kisses my cheek.

I nod. "We're in public, right?"

"Definitely."

Who cares that there's no one in sight.

The moment our lips meet, my legs wrap around him again, like in the bungalow, and his arms fold across my back. He holds me tight against his beautiful, glistening chest, and we kiss slowly and sensually, the warm water supporting our embrace. Now, I'm weightless and free, my mind focused only on how incredible his touch feels at every point of contact.

He pulls back and gazes at every inch of me within his view. When his eyes come back to mine, he says, "You're so fucking beautiful, Christy."

If I didn't know any better, I'd think there was an anchor tied to my waist. But this sinking feeling isn't new. It's a decade's worth of heavy baggage, pulling me under the surface.

I hate myself for being so insecure. Is my sister right? Did Kyle really fuck with my head and make it impossible for me to see my body as anything other than flawed? When I look at my reflection, am I seeing my true self? Or is my brain distorting the image like a funhouse mirror?

And, if so, how do I undo the damage? Is it even possible?

Holden's brow furrows at my silence. "Baby, you know you're gorgeous, right?"

I look away, but it doesn't help. I burst into tears and bury my face in his neck.

His hand moves up to cradle my head, and he delivers a few sweet kisses onto my hair. "Tell me what's wrong."

Can I tell him that, between the eight years I spent with Kyle, and the five one-night stands I've had, no man has ever called me beautiful before tonight? That it feels impossible to believe—especially coming from the most attractive man I've ever met?

I shake my head. "I wish I could. But it's not that easy."

He nods, then kisses my forehead, his hand cupping my face. "Let's go get some sleep."

There's no awkwardness on our first night in the bungalow. When we're both showered and changed, we take opposite ends of the king-sized bed. I wear a sports bra underneath my modest pajama set. He fluffs my pillows for me, then turns off the light.

"Goodnight, Red."

"Goodnight, Holden."

In the darkness, he reaches for my hand.

CHAPTER 11

Holden

I wake up to the glow of early morning sun streaming through the windows. It's just enough light to see Christy sleeping beside me, curled up and hugging the largest of her three pillows. I wish her arms were around me instead. But she's closer to the middle of the bed than where she started, at least. I'll take it.

Sound asleep, her features are so sweet and angelic, you'd never guess what a spitfire she is. Almond-shaped eyes that turn up a little at the corners, making every glance of hers sultry. That smattering of freckles over the apples of her cheeks and her button nose. The Cupid's bow that makes me want to kiss her when she smiles.

Everything about her pulls at my heartstrings. She looks so peaceful now, but the way she cried in my arms last night tells me how much pain she's carrying. I have a feeling I know exactly which uptight dickwad is to blame for this...and my distaste for him grows by the second. I wonder what it would take to undo the harm he caused.

As I'm daydreaming about all the ways I can make Christy

feel beautiful, my cell buzzes on the nightstand. I pick it up to see a new text message. And speaking of uptight dickwads, it's from my brother.

WES

Hope you're planning on wearing clothes to breakfast, big bro.

I roll my eyes. I bet he has an entire arsenal of wisecracks about my naked run across Soldier Field. He couldn't even wait a fucking hour until he sees me to give me grief.

ME

And miss an opportunity to remind you how small your dick is compared to mine? Never.

With an exasperated sigh, I fling my phone onto an armchair across the room. Great—now I'm in a shit mood, and the day's barely begun. It'll only get worse when I take Christy to the main house, and my parents start in on me, too.

When I was a kid and they'd piss me off like this, I'd go to the park and practice pitching. I'd throw the ball as hard as I could, imagining I was aiming at them. I can't do that now, of course, since I'm resting my goddamn shoulder. A swim would probably help calm my nerves before facing everyone, but I don't want to leave Christy here alone after how upset she was last night.

Before our dip in the ocean, we'd been having a great time. I know I was, at least. It was the best date of my life. Real or otherwise. That brain of hers fascinates me. She's so quick-witted. So well-read. So sweet, under the layers of feisty. I love the whole package.

Did I just say *love*? I'm pretty sure I meant *like*. In my thirty-six years on this earth, I've never been in love. Being on the road so much doesn't make it easy to maintain a relationship. But it's not just that. A lot of the guys on the team are married or have serious girlfriends. They aren't McBrides, though. Most women I go out with are pretty obvious about the fact that they're looking for a golden ticket to the upper echelon. They pick the most lavish restaurants for our dates. Order the most expensive dishes on the menu. Flat-out ask me to buy them gifts, or take them on vacation, when I barely know them. I've had the same rotten luck with women since my first girlfriend, back in high school. After a while, a guy can't help but get jaded.

Christy's nothing like them, which probably explains why I'm feeling things for her I've never felt before. That, and the fact that she happens to be the most beautiful woman I've ever seen. And I've seen a lot of pretty girls in my life. But there's something about Christy that sets her apart. She has this rare, timeless beauty, like an Old Hollywood movie star. The fact that she doesn't know it, because her shit-for-brains ex didn't appreciate her, pisses me off. TGI Friday better pray we never end up in the same room.

Blood boiling again, I stalk out to the lanai. Similar to the champagne on the beach last night, a fresh pot of Kona coffee and a tropical fruit tray await—like "magic," as Christy would say. I pour myself a cup and watch the sunlit waves as I attempt to mentally prepare myself for the days to come. I'm no closer to making that happen when Christy steps onto the lanai.

She's wearing a cream-colored linen sundress with green palm fronds on it that are the perfect contrast to her red lips and hair. My heart skips a beat when I notice the orchid I gave her at dinner is back behind her left ear. If only this angel were truly mine. She's breathtaking. I've spent the past thirty minutes staring at the most stunning ocean view, but it's got nothing on the woman standing in front of me.

"Good morning," she says with a sudden furrow in her brow that makes me wonder if she's as stressed about spending the day with my family as I am.

She sits in her own chair instead of next to me on the loveseat. I try not to read too much into this, but fail miserably. I was already tense after my tool of a brother texted me, but the angst in Christy's eyes sends me into a tailspin. "You okay, Red?"

I hope she's not embarrassed about last night. She was vulnerable with me...and I liked it. I hated that she was sad, don't get me wrong. But the fact that she was comfortable crying on my shoulder felt significant. Christy doesn't strike me as the type to wear her heart on her sleeve. She's always had to fend for herself, which means she probably doesn't feel safe with most people. She didn't feel safe with her parents, who barely supported her financially, not to mention emotionally. And she sure as fuck didn't feel safe with Kyle. Three of the most important people in her life neglected her needs. So for her to melt into my arms made me feel...I don't know.

Fuck it, I do know. It made me feel special. Like, maybe there's a shot in hell that, one day, she'd give me her heart.

But what if it was the alcohol that made her emotional? What if she regrets opening up to me, or kissing me, or this ridiculous fake dating scheme? What if she wants to leave the island, go back to her normal life, and pretend she never met me?

Christy shakes her head. "No. I'm not okay."

Shit.

She heaves a sigh. "Between the Penelope Dwyer scandal and the hard launch of our relationship, my name's been in the press a lot, which isn't surprising. But this morning I took some time to read through some of the comments about us, and..." She looks down at her lap.

"What are people saying?" I shift to the edge of the loveseat I wish she were sharing with me.

"Most of the feedback is positive, like your agent said. But there's a small subset of trolls who think I'm dating you because I need good publicity to counteract the threat Dr. Liar poses to my brand." Her cheeks flush. "They think I'm a fraud, too, Holden. Just like I feared."

Goddammit. If this scheme doesn't work in Christy's favor, and her career is ruined because I roped her into my mess, I will never forgive myself.

"Haters are gonna hate, Red. It's what they do. But as long as they're the minority, I don't think we need to worry too much." I pronounce the words in a calm, steady tone, hoping she can't tell that I'm on the verge of freaking the fuck out. To make matters worse, as my gut turns into a pit of dread, my phone buzzes again.

I knew Wes wouldn't let me get the last word about his dick. I glare at his message.

WES

Too bad that extra inch doesn't make up for your pea-sized brain.

I clench my left fist, wishing there were a baseball in my hand I could hurl at him. When my nails are digging so far into my palm that I nearly break skin, I stop and look up, hoping Christy didn't notice. Thankfully she's staring out at the water.

My phone fucking vibrates again, and I'm tempted to chuck it into the Pacific rather than read another message from my brother. Against my better judgment, I open his text.

WES

> By the way, big bro, I can't wait to go up against you for Grandma's cash. I put together a slide deck, an appendix, and 3D prototypes for good measure. You know, things I learned in grad school. But don't worry. I'm sure your high school education prepared you to make a decent posterboard. Just don't skimp on the glitter.

"Holden, we're still planning to tell your family that we're faking our relationship, right?" Christy asks. "This morning, at breakfast?"

Her voice barely penetrates my racing thoughts about Wes's jabs at my intelligence. These are only the latest in a collection of insults so large, I could fill a scrapbook. And if you think I had it coming for that cheap shot about his dick, well, he's the one who made us measure ten years ago, and now he has to live with the consequences. My bragging rights were earned fair and square.

Anyway, given the rage coursing through my veins, my response to Christy's question is more curt than I'd like. "Yeah. It'll be fine."

But will it *actually* be fine? When I suggested we let my family in on our scheme, I'd barely seen or talked to Wes in nearly a year. I guess it's true what they say: out of sight, out of mind. Sometimes I forget what a shitty human he is...but now that he's going out of his way to remind me, do I really want to trust him with a secret this big? Sure, he wouldn't want to drag the McBride name through the mud any more than the rest of my family. But if there were a way he could sabotage me without making himself look bad, he'd do it in a heartbeat. The guy's hated me almost as long as I can remember.

You wouldn't think Wes would have such a giant fucking chip on his shoulder, considering he's far and away our mom's favorite kid. He was born on Christmas Day, which might explain why she considers him God's gift to mankind. He's also the baby of the family—two years younger than me, and four years younger than Abby. I never cared too much that Wes got all the attention from Mom, but Abby sure as hell did. He stole her title of "Golden Child," and I don't think she's ever forgiven him.

I, on the other hand, wanted to have a close relationship with my brother. When he was five, he took an interest in my baseball equipment, so I decided to teach him. I thought it would be something cool for us to bond over. Turns out, it tore us apart. The kid tried his hardest, but he just wasn't athletic. His hand-eye coordination was shit. He wasn't particularly fast, or agile. Maybe he would've improved with age or practice, who knows. But he was such a sore loser, he didn't give himself the chance to find out. He never picked up a baseball bat again and decided to hate me instead.

The fact that our dad gave Wes such a hard time about his lack of athleticism doomed our already-tense relationship. It didn't help that my brother had a passion for baking, and preferred spending afternoons in the kitchen with our personal chef to playing ball with me. Needless to say, Dad didn't approve of Wes's choice.

Back then, my father encouraged my talent only insofar as it would help my college applications stand out. When I got into Harvard and chose to sign with the Starlings instead, he fucking gave up on me. Sure, he'll brag about my arm when he's trying to woo a potential business partner. But as far as actual pride goes, forget it. And even though Wes met our dad's academic expectations and then some—graduating from Harvard at the top of his class, then going on to get an MBA from Wharton—somehow, that wasn't enough to satisfy our father.

If he could combine the two of us into a single son who was a remarkable athlete *and* an academic, maybe he'd be proud. But as it stands, we're both disappointments. And even though I get no more love from him than Wes does, my brother still manages to blame me for Dad's lack of approval.

"Are you sure you want to tell your family the truth, Holden? You don't sound convinced."

I run a hand through my hair, exasperated by the whole fucking situation. By the shitstorm I've found myself in because I don't know how to grieve the most important person in my life. By the fact that her loss was immeasurable because the other McBrides could give two shits about me. Most of all, by the valid fear in Christy's eyes, and the way the future of her hard-earned career now hinges on my coldhearted family finding a sufficient personal stake in this scheme to be willing to play along. Because heaven forbid my well-being could ever be reason enough.

Rage builds in my chest, and my words spew out before I can filter myself. "Jesus, Red. Yes, I'm sure. Let's just go to breakfast and get this fucking thing over with, so we can move on with our lives."

Her expression shifts from anxious to stunned before her gaze hardens. When she speaks, her tone is icy. "Great idea. My patience for moody assholes ran out years ago, so the sooner we wrap this up, the better."

She marches back inside the bungalow before I can say sorry. Not that I could pull off a sincere apology at the moment, even if I tried. I'm not proud, but the way I'm behaving right now is *classic* Holden McBride. When I'm pissed off, I get tunnel vision. I can't see beyond my rage and end up saying dumb shit I don't mean. I'm having the adult male equivalent of a toddler tantrum, I guess—just like at the bar, when I told Christy I hated agents. The worst part is, when I'm upset like this, I can't articulate my feelings until I've had a chance to cool off.

The best I could do, if Christy would let me, is take her in my arms and hold her until she softens under my grip. Until she understands what I'm not capable of saying right now. That I'm triggered by my family. That they bring out the worst in me. That moving on with my life is the last thing I want if it means I never get to see her again.

But when I follow her inside, her body language tells me to stay far away. She's seated on the edge of the bed...legs crossed, arms folded over her chest, shoulders hunched. She's protecting her heart. From me.

I can't stand it.

"Ready to go?" She doesn't look me in the eye.

Well, at least I don't have to agonize over whether or not to tell my family we're faking our relationship. There's no chance Christy could pretend to like me right now.

I nod, and we leave the bungalow in excruciating silence. I decide to drive us to the main house in a golf cart, to spare her the awkwardness of a ten-minute walk through paradise with a man she despises. A man whose mood swings remind her of her father. Of her insufferable ex.

Fuck.

To add insult to injury, when we arrive, Wes is sitting on the front porch. He probably couldn't wait to show me how much muscle he's put on since we saw each other last Christmas.

Considering all the shit Dad gave him as a kid for not being as athletically inclined as me, maybe it's no surprise my brother has a giant chip on his shoulder. It kills him that I'm a pro athlete, when sports are the one thing he doesn't excel at. His only recourse is to make sure he's so muscular that the media doesn't peg him as Holden McBride's scrawny little brother. The guy's more ripped than I am. All he does besides work is lift weights, and I don't think he's eaten bread since the nineties. It's a shame, considering he has a passion for food, and even spent the whole summer before fifth grade making sourdough with our nanny. To this day, I still think about his olive loaf. It was fucking delicious.

"Good to see you, brother," he says, pulling me in for a hug that makes my skin crawl.

"Likewise," I growl in his ear. He pulls away from me, beaming.

He's putting on a show for Christy, because nothing pleases him more than letting my girlfriends know he's the golden boy of the family, in case they're looking to upgrade. Shockingly, no woman I've been with has taken him up on his offer.

"And you must be Christy." He holds out his hand, and when their palms meet, a wave of nausea hits me. I look away, my gaze landing on the orchid behind her ear, and all I can think is, *She's mine. No other man should be touching her.*

I'm aware it's an irrational thought. I've known the woman less than a week. We aren't really dating, and I have no right to feel jealous. Still, I wrap a possessive arm around her waist. "Let's get you inside so you can meet the rest of the family."

As I lead Christy away from my snake of a brother, I turn my head and catch him checking out her ass. Then he winks at me.

Fucker.

When we step into the house, Christy takes an audible breath. I forget how stunning it is the first time you see it. The entryway looks like the lobby of a five-star hotel. Marble floors, high ceilings. An airy, open design that gives way to stunning tropical views in every direction. There's a koi pond in the center of the foyer, and Christy flits over to it with an awestruck smile on her face.

Jesus Christ, I love her.

Like *her. Holy hell, what is happening to me?*

My nine-year-old niece Maisie, and seven-year-old nephew Matt, run in from the dining room, their mouths covered in jelly. "Uncle Holden! Uncle Holden!"

I squat down to their level and pull them in for a bear hug. I fucking adore these kids. It breaks my heart that I rarely see them more than once a year, over the holidays. If only their mom and I were closer.

"We watched you pitch on Tuesday," Matt says, looking at me like I'm a goddamn superhero. Relief floods me. At least there are two people in this house who like me.

"Oh, yeah? What'd you think? Did I do okay?"

"You were pretty good," Matt says with an adorable, sheepish shrug.

"Can we play baseball with you?" Maisie asks, tugging at my shirtsleeve.

"Of course! But I better warm up first, if I'm going up against you two sluggers."

My niece and nephew giggle, and my heart swells.

"Maisie! Matt!" Abby yells from faraway. "No sticky fingers in the living room! Come back and wash your hands!"

The kids' eyes go wide before they run, laughing and shrieking, in the opposite direction of their mom. A few seconds later, Abby appears, jogging after them.

"Hey, guys," she calls out with a nod toward me and Christy as she follows the sound of her kids' footsteps.

That's it. That's all she says. Then she's gone.

I guess I shouldn't be surprised. Abby tends to do her own thing at family gatherings. Whether it's chasing after her kids to avoid an awkward exchange with her estranged brother, or skipping Thanksgiving dinner to draft a "time-sensitive" email to her book club, she manages to keep herself busy enough that we hardly see her. And as for her husband, well, I doubt he's here. Wyatt's crazy about Abby, but he cannot fucking stand my parents. He's a cool guy. I like him.

Finally, I hear the *click clack* of absurdly expensive high heels heading our way. Christy steps back from the koi pond and stands right by my side, her arm brushing mine, closer than she's been all morning. She's wide-eyed and still, like a doe in the forest, sensing a predator nearby. She's not wrong.

Margot McBride comes into view, wearing a floral dress she probably bought straight off the runway at New York Fashion Week. Somehow, she looks five years younger than the last time I saw her. Either she has the most skilled plastic surgeon on the planet, or she made a deal with the devil. I'd place my money on the latter.

"Hello, dear." She leans in to kiss my cheek, enveloping me in a cloud of the custom fragrance she orders from a master perfumer in Paris—for a measly ten thousand euros per ounce.

"And you must be Christine," she says, bringing her palms together like the gracious hostess she pretends to be.

"Christina, actually." She clears her throat. "But everyone calls me Christy."

My mom's brow twitches, which is probably as close to a furrow as she can get, given all the Botox. "Oh, what a pity. *Christine* suits you so well." She reaches for Christy's hand. "Anyway, it's a pleasure to meet you, dear."

"Thank you so much for having me, Mrs. McBride."

My heart rate picks up when my mom eyes Christy head to toe.

"My word, aren't you voluptuous?" Margot says. "And that hair? You're a real-life Jessica Rabbit."

Christy flushes. "Oh. Well, thank you."

I heave a sigh. I wish Mom didn't feel compelled to comment on the appearance of every woman she meets but, compared to what I've witnessed in the past, this interaction was pretty benign. It was also enlightening. I had a massive crush on Jessica Rabbit when I was a kid. No wonder I'm so out-of-my-mind attracted to Christy.

"That reminds me," Margot goes on. "I didn't get a chance to ask Holden if you have any food restrictions, so we can alert the chef. You're not on any special diets, are you, Christine?"

"It's *Christy*, Mom," I say through gritted teeth. She chooses not to hear me.

Christy's polite as ever. "Don't worry, Mrs. McBride. I'm not on any special diets."

My mother's gaze travels down the length of Christy's body again. "I didn't think so, dear."

I'm mortified.

I feel Christy shift uncomfortably beside me, and I want to

apologize for my ill-mannered mother's behavior, but my dad walks in from the lanai, fresh off a business call, I'm sure. He's still wearing his Bluetooth earpiece.

"Dad," I say, greeting him with a nod.

Julian McBride glares at me. "I see you decided to wear clothes today."

Behind me, Wes snickers.

I ignore them both, which feels like it takes Herculean strength. "Dad, this is Christy."

Unsmiling, he reaches for her hand. "Christina Andersen. High school valedictorian. Phi Beta Kappa. Graduated from Columbia *summa cum laude*. Impressive."

Jesus. He sounds like a fucking robot.

"She's not here for a job interview, you know," I tell my father.

"Don't mind Holden, Dad," Wes chimes in. "He's probably just confused by all those fancy academic words. Need me to explain what Phi Beta Kappa is, big bro?"

I pinch the bridge of my nose, hoping it'll stifle the urge to punch him. "I'm good, Wesley. Thank you."

"Let me know if you change your mind." Wes steps forward so he's within Christy's line of sight. "I was Phi Beta Kappa, too. At Harvard."

"Congratulations," Christy says with an almost undetectable hint of sarcasm. I crack a smile for the first time since we set foot in this house.

"Must be slim pickings in Chicago if a Phi Beta Kappa can't find someone more suitable to date than a ballplayer," my old man grumbles.

"I'm still not convinced this isn't some kind of PR stunt," Wes adds.

"Oh, come now," my mom scolds her husband and younger son. "Their relationship isn't so far-fetched. I mean, every woman needs a diversion now and then, isn't that right, Christine?" Mom winks at her. "I'm sure this isn't meant to be long term. She'll have her fun and be on her way, just like the others."

Christy turns to me, looking shell-shocked.

"Charming, aren't they?" I say under my breath. "Well, I guess now's as good a time as any to tell them..."

My mom's brow attempts to crease again. "Tell us what?"

"It *is* a PR stunt!" Wes pumps his fist in the air with a victorious grin. "I knew you could never land an intellectual like her."

I open my mouth, ready to concede, when Christy wraps her arms around my waist. I meet her gaze, and she gives me a smile so sweet that, for a glorious split second, I forget my family's here.

"Holden and I didn't just meet at the bar last Sunday," she says with so much conviction, I almost believe her myself. "We've been dating in secret for months. We wanted to find our footing as a couple first, before we went public. But the truth is...we're head over heels in love." Her eyes narrow on my mom. "And I'm not going anywhere."

CHAPTER 12

Christy

Margot McBride's lips curve upward an almost undetectable amount. Still, I don't miss the little sneer that flashes across her professionally sculpted features like a lightning bolt.

I smile at her through clenched teeth. *That's right, lady. You're officially on my shit list.*

Even before she insulted Holden, I knew this woman would be trouble. She refuses to call me by my name, for one thing. And, trust me, her subtle digs about my weight didn't go unnoticed. I bet she'll be monitoring everything I consume in her presence, just like Kyle used to do. I'll be lucky if I make it through this week without my food issues resurfacing.

"Well, there you have it," Holden jumps in before his family can respond to our declaration of love. "Christy and I are in it for the long haul. Now, if you'll excuse us, I need her help adjusting the tape on my shoulder. I did it myself this morning, and it feels a little wonky. We'll join you in the dining room when we're done."

Julian McBride scowls. "Why anyone would knowingly subject their body to years of debilitating strain is beyond me."

"Thanks for weighing in, Dad." Holden's response is rushed as he takes my hand and leads me across the pristine marble tiles of the mansion's grand entrance, down an equally majestic hallway featuring a *floor-to-ceiling aquarium wall* that I'm desperate to get a better look at, if my fake boyfriend's pace were not so hurried.

Finally, he opens a door at the end of the hall and pulls me inside a gorgeous, spa-like bathroom. Constructed of black lava stone and a glimmering wood I suspect is native to Hawaii, it's a haven of tranquility—complete with subtle orchid and palm frond accents, and even a trickling fountain built into a rugged rock wall. It's all so stunning, I can't stop my eyes from roaming over the space. So when Holden picks me up and sets me down on the sparkling quartzite countertop, I'm startled, to say the least.

"What are you—" I begin to ask, when he cups my face in his warm palms and kisses me with an intensity that makes my heart pound and my stomach flutter. With his mouth on mine, I forget all about our rocky start this morning. Never mind our contract.

If it's not the best kiss I've ever had, it's certainly in the top two. Regardless, Holden wins. He's only competing against himself, at this point. Our first kiss far surpassed any I've ever experienced, and I can't imagine another man besting him. So, as our lips brush against each other's and our tongues intertwine, I'm both thrilled and devastated, knowing the days I get to enjoy Holden's kisses are numbered.

When he pulls away, his eyes are smiling.

So are mine. "Um, what was *that* for?"

He drags a hand over his stubble. "The way you showed up for me out there? It really turned me on. I just had to get you alone. But...we're technically still in public, right? Seeing as my family's only a fastball away."

I giggle. "Pitcher humor. I like it."

"Thought you might." He takes a step closer. "So, about that kiss...we're still playing fair, don't you agree?"

He adjusts the orchid behind my left ear. I wore it again this morning because I like the feeling of being spoken for, even if it's make-believe. I agreed to play pretend, after all. Should I be alarmed that it's starting to feel like I'm playing with fire? My boundaries get hazier by the minute. Especially after how sweet Holden was with me last night. He's the first man whose shoulder I've cried on. Dad and Kyle were averse to big emotional displays.

"It doesn't feel like we're breaking any rules." My cheeks warm from lying. "So, your shoulder's okay, then?"

"It's fine." He rubs a knuckle over his brow. "Now, level with me, Red. Why'd you go rogue and tell my family we're together? I thought you were too stressed to play this game in front of them."

My blood boils again as I replay the McBride clan's belittling comments about a man who'll go down in history as one of the best pitchers the League has ever seen. The truth is, I barely kept it together out there. I hated the way they were treating Holden, and my protective instincts went into overdrive. It was all I could do not to tell his family to go fuck themselves.

"Well, they really didn't leave me much choice. My god,

Holden, they are…" I heave an exasperated sigh. "Well, they're atrocious. For lack of a better word."

I can think of dozens of better words, to be honest. But it's probably best I leave it at that.

A genuine laugh escapes him, and he looks happier than he has all morning.

That's when it dawns on me how stressed he must have been when he woke up today, knowing what he was in for. So, I take his hand. "They're the reason you snapped at me this morning, aren't they."

He nods, looking down at my lap before his eyes flit back to mine. "I'm so sorry."

"I understand." I give his fingers a gentle squeeze before I let go.

Holden grips the countertop on either side of me, his gaze fixed on mine. He's so close, I wonder if he can feel my heart hammering. "I want to amend our contract, Christy. But first, I have a few questions."

"Okay." My voice is a near-whisper, and my palms are sweaty.

"Remember when you promised you'd be real with me?" Holden raises an eyebrow.

Oh god, here we go. It's truth time. "Yes, I remember."

"Good. I want to make sure we're on the same page." His blue-gray eyes smolder at me, sexy and hypnotic. "Are you attracted to me, Red?"

By instinct, I roll my eyes. "Have you ever met a woman who isn't attracted to you?"

He stifles a laugh. "You're not answering the question, baby. But I think I know why, so let me try this again."

He takes both my hands in his and steps back an inch, giving me a little more room to breathe. My shoulders relax within seconds. It's not the first time he's had this effect on me. Somehow, he's more attuned to my body than I am. He seems to always know what I need. I have to work hard not to think about how that would translate if I let him have his way with me.

"Last night, I asked if you knew how beautiful you are, and you cried," he reminds me.

My eyes well up again, but I don't bury my face in his neck this time. I'm too curious to hear what he's going to say next.

"You don't have to tell me why...but I have a strong suspicion his name starts with a T and ends in Friday."

I sputter a tearful laugh.

"That dipshit didn't treat you right, and now you have no idea how gorgeous you are." He balls his left hand into a fist. Just like he did as a kid, in that old family photo. "I can't stand the idea of you going through life like that. That's why I want to change our agreement. I want to help undo the harm he caused you. I want to show you how stunning I think you are." He half-smiles. "Do you have any idea what you do to me, Christy? My dick's been hard since the day I met you."

I smirk. "Yeah, well, I'm sure your—"

He presses his index finger to my lips while he speaks. "And before you say anything self-deprecating... No, I don't have a permanent hard-on for every woman I meet."

Well, then. I guess Holden can read my mind as well as my body. "Fine."

"I want you to know what it feels like to be with a man who's hungry for you, baby. That's what you deserve. But I need to make sure you want me." He brings his hands to my waist. "Be honest with me."

This feels like a dream. A fantasy. The island. The estate. The impossibly handsome ballplayer who's desperate to have sex with me. None of it seems real. Not even the sound of my voice, when I answer him. "Yes, Holden. I want you."

It's the first time in my life that I'm giving into my body over my brain. My mind is convinced I'm making a terrible mistake. I hear her screaming that nothing good can come of this. That I'll end up heartbroken, because our fake relationship has an expiration date.

I can't fall for him. We're not a good match. He's a manchild, and a hothead. There's a million reasons this decision is disastrous.

My loins could not care less. They're choosing lust. Passion. A sexy adventure I'll look back on with a smile, when I'm old and gray.

"Perfect," he says on a deep exhale. "New rules start now."

My breath catches as he starts kissing my neck and kneading my hips with his fingers. "Holden! You *cannot* fuck me here— your family's right down the hall!"

"I wouldn't dream of it, Red." He looks back up at me with a devious grin. "I say we have about ten minutes before they get suspicious, and there's no way I'm letting our first time happen when we're on the clock. But I still want to make you come. You'll just have to be quiet. Can you do that for me, baby?"

I swallow. "Yes."

"Excellent." He runs his hand up my thigh. "Now be a good girl and spread your legs."

I do as I'm told, wrapping my thighs around him and

wondering if I'm about to wake up in the bungalow with a racing heart and damp underwear. But the warmth of his fingers when he pushes my satin bikini briefs to the side and finds my clit feels better than anything I could ever dream up.

"You're so wet for me," he says, looking pleased.

"You want the truth?" I pant. "I've been wet for you since the night we met."

Even before, if you count that sex dream I had after his epic performance in Game 7 of the 2008 World Series.

"I knew it," he says with a victorious smile before he crashes his mouth to mine again. He kisses me slowly and sensually, matching the rhythm of his fingers as he works absolute magic between my thighs. He's a Major League pitcher, after all. Of course he's skilled with his hands.

Wild with desire, I take his bottom lip between my teeth and bite, which elicits a low growl from his throat. "So feisty, Christy. I love it." Then he slides a finger carefully inside me. It's only now that I register how huge his hands are.

"Oh my god," I gasp, trying my best to stay quiet as pleasure floods my body.

"So fucking tight, baby," he groans.

I writhe against his hand as he pumps one finger inside me, then two, all while keeping his thumb pressed against my clit. I'm close to unraveling when he kneels between my legs.

"Lift your hips for me. I want to see how pretty you are."

I comply, and the smile in his eyes turns to wonder when he slips off my panties. "I knew you'd be fucking gorgeous. And I'm about to worship you like the goddess you are," he promises, right before he kisses my inner thighs.

"We're going to be late," I whisper, unsure if I actually give a damn, or if the concern is more of an automatic response. A remnant of the former Christy Andersen, pre-Holden McBride.

"This won't take long," he says.

His mouth lands on me, and he starts exploring me with his tongue, lapping me up in almost torturous slow motion. Then he glides around my clit in gentle circles that drive me utterly insane. I express my pleasure in hushed sighs, but when he cranks up the speed and pressure, swiping the tip of his tongue back and forth, I moan louder than I intend.

Holden pulls back, smiling. "I can only make you come if you're quiet, baby. Okay?"

"Okay," I whimper, my chest heaving.

"Good girl." He gets back to work, licking me with expert flicks as I run my fingers through his hair, trying my best not to yell out his name. True to his word, I come hard and fast against his mouth. My legs shake, thighs closing in around his head while he finishes me off. Afterward, I release my grip from his hair and my limbs go limp as I try to catch my breath.

He stands and tucks a strand of hair behind my right ear, looking proud of himself. "How do you feel?"

"How do I—" I let out an airy laugh. "I feel incredible." I kiss his cheek, then wipe the sheen from his lips. I'm about to reach for a tissue from an exquisite holder made of lava stone, when he stops me.

"Don't waste that, baby. You're too delicious."

I watch, a bit mesmerized, as he takes my thumb in his mouth and licks it clean. Maybe his enthusiasm is so sexy because it's foreign to me. Kyle went down on me regularly, but I'm sure he only did it because he couldn't last long enough inside me to make me come. Yes, we both got off, but there was nothing passionate about it. Our sex life was transactional. The second I climaxed, he was off to the bathroom, where he'd spend several minutes gargling with mouthwash and brushing his teeth. I think it's safe to say that eating me out didn't turn him on.

Meanwhile, Holden's dick is hard as a rock. I feel it, pressed against me. "When do I get to reciprocate?" I ask. "I feel badly leaving you in this condition."

He laughs. "I appreciate the sentiment, but this isn't about me, Red. We're working on *your* confidence. I'm already cocky as fuck."

I bite my lip, glancing at the enormous bulge in his pants. "You most certainly are."

"You really want to play with it, don't you." Holden looks amused when I tear my eyes away from his package and gaze back up at him.

"I do," I admit.

He presses his lips against my ear. "Don't worry, baby. I'll let you enjoy it later. When we're in the bungalow, and there's no one around to hear you scream. Sound good?"

He steps back and I nod, flushed. His words excite me so much, I want to reach for his zipper right here and now. But his despicable family is expecting us.

I slide off the countertop, turn toward the mirror, and finger-comb my mussed-up hair. "I guess we can't avoid breakfast much longer. I just need a minute to freshen up."

"Of course. I'll wait in the hall, so we can enter the lion's den together." He heaves a sigh, and the playfulness fades from his features. Then his gaze travels south. "Well, at least my cock's not hard anymore."

I respond with a sympathetic smile before he leaves. When

he closes the door behind him, my heart starts pounding all over again.

I cannot believe Holden McBride just made me come.

I clean myself up, but before I join him in the hall, I feel my phone vibrate in my purse. I pull it out and see a new text message.

SAM

Have you fucked him yet???

I swear, she has a sixth sense for when her friends are having orgasms. I'm beaming as I type my reply.

ME

He just went down on me. I've never come that fast in my life. He also called me a "good girl," Sam. I felt like the heroine in a romance novel.

Holden may not be as even-keeled as my favorite fictional hero, but when it comes to sex, his confidence and swagger scream "Edison Ford." It's like Holden's making my wildest fantasies come true. Just thinking about it makes me tingle.

My phone vibrates again.

SAM

I can die happy now.

I giggle and put my cell back in my purse. I had a feeling I'd be getting an eager text from Sam this morning, but I'm surprised I haven't heard from Jenna yet. Or my mom. The three of us have a group chat, and I texted last night to let them know I landed safely. They replied immediately and told me to have a wonderful trip, but I figured I'd get some follow-up messages after my first night sharing a bed with Holden. I guess the day's still young. Jenna's probably busy with wedding plans. Or having steamy sex with Charlie. And as for my mom...well, I'm still not convinced she isn't dating someone.

I meet Holden in the hall, and we walk hand in hand to the dining room, which opens onto a lanai with an ocean view so stunning, it looks like a postcard. Mr. and Mrs. McBride sit at opposite ends of an elegant, polished wood table, with Wes seated at his mother's side. Abby and her children are nowhere to be found, but I suspect they've already eaten, judging by Maisie and Matt's jammy little faces when they ran out to hug Holden. It was an adorable encounter. He's so darn good with kids, I may have swooned a little.

But I am *not* here to fall in love. I'm here to save my career, help Holden salvage his reputation...and have mind-blowing sex. The end.

I follow my faux boyfriend, who picks the only two seats that aren't next to a family member. I assume this is a strategic decision, and silently thank my lucky stars that I'm not rubbing elbows with any McBride other than Holden. Clearly, I don't mind rubbing up against him, but I can't think about that right now, while Margot's eyeing me over her coffee cup.

Instead, I focus on the extravagant spread on the table. There are bowls of tropical fruit arranged so beautifully, they look like works of art. Trays of smoked salmon folded into gorgeous rosettes. Platters of buttery croissants and cakey muffins that smell like they were just pulled out of the oven. And on each plate, a printed menu on elegant cardstock, featuring a mouthwatering selection of hot dishes made to order.

It's enough food for ten hungry families, and the McBrides

hardly qualify as one, seeing as they're barely eating. Mrs. McBride has an uneaten omelet on her plate. Her husband is reading the newspaper while sipping a Bloody Mary. Wes is drinking something that makes me shudder, because it reminds me of the chalky protein shakes Kyle used to make us for breakfast when we were marathon-training. Those were the days I used to go to bed with a growling stomach every night and dream of cupcakes, and potato chips, and all the other foods my ex refused to have in our home, because *he* wouldn't be able to resist temptation. That's the reason he gave me, at least.

"Holden, dear, you must try the omelet. It's divine," Margot says, though she still hasn't taken a bite of her own.

"It couldn't be better than what I ate this morning," her son replies, his hand finding my bare knee under the table. I sip from my glass of water to conceal my smile. Unfortunately, there's not much I can do to hide my flushed cheeks.

Julian McBride doesn't look up from his newspaper. "You must be referring to the papaya. It's abundant this time of year."

"Yup. The papaya." Holden's fingers travel upward, caressing my thigh. "Sweetest thing I ever tasted."

I have to hold my breath to keep from laughing. Wes is scrolling on his phone, oblivious, but Margot's eyes are burning holes right through me. Somehow, I manage to keep a straight face.

Holden and I both heed his mother's advice and order the omelet which, I won't hesitate to say, is the most delicious plate of eggs I've had in my life. So delicious, in fact, that I'm *almost* unbothered by her endless rant about the "incompetents" who are redoing the floors of their Manhattan penthouse.

Sadly, I eat nothing more. I'm dying to try a pastry or two

(or three), but I can't be the only one to indulge. I'm already the only person in this room who doesn't look like a fitness model. First there's Holden, the professional athlete. Then Wes, who looks like Holden on steroids. Even Mr. McBride is ripped for a man his age. And his wife looks like she does Pilates all day long. What would she say if I stuffed my face with carbs the way I want to? I hate that I care. But I do.

After breakfast, Holden turns down an invitation to go kayaking, in favor of playing baseball with his niece and nephew. Abby's on the phone with her husband when Maisie and Matt ask her if they can go, and all she does is nod in their direction, then thank Holden with a wave. Her expression, however, is stone-faced. He hasn't said much to me about his relationship with Abby, but I think it's safe to say it's strained. Yesterday, when I was telling him that Jenna and I became close only recently, he seemed intrigued. My guess is, he wishes he and Abby could patch things up, too.

In any case, Holden invites me to join him and the kids, and I couldn't be more grateful for the reprieve from the rest of his family. I'm also lowkey geeking out over the fact that *the* Holden McBride is going to pitch to me. I'm intimidated, of course, but excited.

First, he drives the four of us to the estate's fitness center, so he can pick up baseball gear. I don't know why I'm picturing a large room with a few treadmills and some free weights, like the workout facilities you see in hotels. This fitness center looks like a resort in and of itself—the type of luxury wellness retreat you read about in travel magazines.

In addition to the eight studios featuring equipment for activities ranging from yoga to kickboxing, there's a fully stocked locker room, where Holden says I'll find athleticwear to change into. Right away, my mind starts spinning, imagining that every outfit will be Margot McBride-sized. Maybe Holden catches the worry on my face, because he assures me I'll have plenty of options to choose from.

He's right, of course. I find a cute pair of athletic shorts that fit me well, a sports bra that's not even a smidge too tight, and a tank to wear over it. Afterward, I pull my hair back into a ponytail, throw on some socks, and slip into a brand-new pair of New Balance sneakers. I can't help but wonder how this works. Will we come back later so I can return the clothes? Or do I keep them, while one of these stealthy staff members I keep hearing about replaces the items overnight, like some sort of Athleisure Fairy? I wish I knew. I'll admit, I'm too embarrassed to ask. Holden's world is so foreign to me.

When I come out of the locker room, he's fitting Maisie and Matt with Starlings baseball caps that have their uncle's signature scrawled across the brim in black marker. The kids are beaming as they admire themselves in the mirror.

"Where's my autographed hat?" I joke.

Holden's eyes widen as they travel over the length of my body. When his gaze meets mine again, he nods his approval, giving me butterflies. "Wasn't sure you'd want one, Red. When we met at the bar, I got the sense you weren't my biggest fan."

My cheeks heat. "I guess I changed my mind."

"I can't imagine why." His grin is flirtatious as he opens a closet full of Starlings gear and takes out two more hats. He puts one on backward and looks so damn sexy, I have to anchor my hand on the wall to steady myself. Then he pulls a Sharpie from his pocket and signs the other one for me before placing it on my head.

My smile is as wide as his niece and nephew's. "Thank you."

He winks at me in his backward baseball cap, and my nipples harden.

We head back to the car, and I help him strap the kids into their booster seats. Afterward, we load the baseball equipment into the trunk together. "By the way, you look hot as fuck in those little shorts," he whispers in my ear. Then he grabs my ass.

Holden drives us to a baseball field about twenty minutes from the estate. On our way, he tells me about all the times his grandmother used to take him there.

"Grandma Evelyn played softball when she was a kid." His eyes are on the road, but his gaze is wistful. "She was really good, too. She actually got recruited to play professional baseball when she was twenty. But the day before her first practice, she met my grandpa. It was love at first sight. So she quit the team, and they got hitched three months later."

"That's so sweet," I say. "Although it's too bad she gave up baseball. Did she really have to quit the team?"

Holden frowns. "Unfortunately, there weren't any women's leagues on the East Coast. Grandma Evelyn was born and raised in South Bend, Indiana, and that's where she was recruited. My grandfather was in town on business, swept her off her feet, and she moved to New York soon after. She said she knew it was the right choice, and she never looked back."

"Wait," I tell him, my brow furrowing. "Was this during World War II?"

He nods. "It was 1943. Women's sports had become more popular, since the men were off fighting. That's how the All-American Girls Professional Baseball League was born. That's the league that recruited my grandma. Have you heard of it?"

"Are you kidding? *A League of Their Own* is my favorite

movie!" I exclaim. "Wow, Holden. Your grandma sounds like the coolest woman ever."

"She was." He smiles, but after several seconds, his forehead creases. "Is that really your favorite movie, Red? How did I miss that? I could have sworn we covered movies on the very thorough list of get-to-know-you questions you drafted for our flight here."

I laugh. "*I* asked *you* about your favorite movie. But you wouldn't stick to the script." I look back at the kids, who are both sound asleep. Exhausted from making their mom chase after them all morning, I bet. "You only asked me naughty questions, remember?"

We're at a red light, and he gives me a quick, sultry glance. "I remember you refusing to answer them."

My cheeks warm. "I think you'll get your answers sooner or later."

He takes my hand and kisses it.

When we get to the field, I let him play with Maisie and Matt on their own first, while I cheer from the bleachers. I know Holden doesn't get to see them often, and I want to make sure they have plenty of quality time together. It's clear how much he loves them. He's so goddamn sweet with them, I feel like my ovaries are about to explode.

An hour later, the kids are hungry, so they join me on the bleachers to eat the snacks they chose from the fitness center's pantry. That's when Holden calls to me from the pitcher's mound. "You're up to bat, Red."

I bite my lip, smiling, and grab one of the bats Holden brought for me, then walk to home plate with a racing heart. He went easy on the kids, of course, and he'll probably do the same for me. Still, I'm nervous.

"Have you played before?" he asks.

I tilt my head. "I've dabbled."

I don't tell him I played softball on a recreational league with Kyle for years. And I definitely don't tell him I was named MVP three times. That was a lifetime ago. It's been ages since I've swung a bat, and I very well might suck now.

"Alright, baby. Let's see what you've got. Name your pitch. You want a curveball? Slider? Fastball?"

I want to impress him—that's what I want. "Surprise me."

His eyebrows rise, amused. And when he pitches a slow, predictable fastball right over the plate, my muscle memory kicks in and I fucking crush it.

"Holy shit," he says, eyeing my line drive. "That's a home run."

Maisie and Matt are jumping up and down, cheering for me from the bleachers and spilling Goldfish crackers everywhere.

My laugh is one of pure joy. As soon as it escapes, I realize that kind of belly laugh is something I haven't had enough of in my life.

"You've been holding out on me," Holden says, shaking his head in awe.

"I played on a rec league in Manhattan," I admit. "I was pretty good, I guess."

"Pretty good? Your swing is beautiful. Reminds me of Ken Griffey Jr."

I beam at him. "That's your favorite player."

Holden winks at me. "I might have a new one now."

The four of us play together for another hour or so, then we take the tired kiddos back to the main house, where lunch is being served on the lanai. The rest of the family's already eaten, so Holden and I enjoy our seared scallops side by side in a blissful moment of privacy. Between savored bites and stolen kisses, he grills me about my softball skills.

The rest of the day is free of family time, since Mr. McBride couldn't resist setting up business meetings with a few real estate bigwigs while in Maui. When Holden and I get back to the bungalow, the awareness that we're finally alone sets in. It's just me and him, and the ocean air.

And the magnificent bed in the middle of our room.

"What do you want to do now?" he asks me.

CHAPTER 13

Holden

Christy's gaze shifts down to her clothes. To the tank top and shorts she looks sexy as hell in. The ones I'm dying to rip off her hot-as-fuck body.

"I'm just going to, um...change into something a little more comfortable." Her beautiful, freckled cheeks are pink as she pulls at the hem of her shirt. "And I should probably take a quick shower. It was hot out there on the baseball field."

She's right. I'm covered in dirt and sweat, myself. Getting clean just wasn't at the forefront of my mind. But as much as I want Christy, what I want even more is for her to feel comfortable with me. So, I nod. "Good call. I'll get cleaned up, too. I can use the outdoor shower by the spa pool."

She lets out a deep breath. "Great. I'll meet you back here." Her gaze travels to the bed, then to me, her skin still flushed with nervous excitement. I wonder if a kiss will help put her at ease. It'll remind her what we have to look forward to: a bungalow all to ourselves, and hours to explore the physical chemistry even Christy can't deny.

I take her face in my hands and lightly press my mouth to hers. She makes this adorable little sound that's halfway between a moan and a sigh. She's happy. When I step back, her eyes are still closed, and she's smiling.

"Thank you for that," she says, looking much more relaxed.

Mission accomplished.

She heads to the bathroom, and I make my way to the outdoor shower. I lather up and rinse off, then linger a little, so the warm water can loosen my tight shoulder. It's not like I threw any hard pitches today while playing with Christy and the kids. But even though I limited myself to gentle tosses, I probably shouldn't have thrown for as long as I did. We were having so much fun, though. And Christy surprised the hell out of me with those beautiful swings...

My grandmother would have liked her.

Fuck.

Now, I know I'm screwed. If I'm sitting here wishing she could have met Christy, my heart is on the line. I never introduced a single woman to Grandma Evelyn. Unless you count my high school girlfriend, who came over daily to spend time with me and my family. I thought it was because she loved me, but I was wrong. She only loved stealing my mother's jewelry.

That relationship fucked me up. I'll be the first to admit I have trust issues. It's hard to let people in when you're always wondering if they have ulterior motives.

That fear's never crossed my mind with Christy. From the moment we met at the bar, I couldn't help baring my soul to this woman.

But I don't see this ending well for me. Christy Andersen

isn't going to seriously fall for a ballplayer, is she? No, she'll probably marry a renowned professor of Comparative Literature, or a Pulitzer Prize-winning novelist. Or a doctor, like that piece of shit, Kyle. Someone with an advanced degree, no doubt. Not a man whose academic career ended with high school.

Unless...

If the sex is so damn good she can't bear to let me go, could I actually stand a chance?

I better bring my A game. If sex is all I have to offer this woman, I need to knock her goddamn socks off.

Christy's still in the bathroom when I finish showering, so I throw on a pair of shorts and stretch my shoulder on the lanai, just in case I overdid it on the baseball field today. While I'm at it, I work on my lower body, too. I can't rock Christy's world if my hips are tight.

Maybe I should do a quick round of sun salutations. Yoga's good for tight hips.

I wish I had a foam roller here. There's one at the fitness center, but...

Jesus. Am I nervous? I've never been nervous to fuck in my entire life.

Nervous to pitch, yes. But I guess my coach's advice still applies: *Holden, if there's ever a time to be a cocky son of a bitch, it's now.*

I take a deep breath and pull my waistband away from my abs so I can look down my shorts. There's no way she won't be impressed by my dick. "You've got this, bro," I say to it.

"Holden?"

I look up to see Christy standing in the doorway, and my eyes go wide. "Wow."

She's so goddamn beautiful. Long, wet hair. A steamy glow on her skin, from the shower. Her signature red lipstick, freshly applied. And to top it off, she's wearing lingerie. A cream-colored, satin slip dress that's a hell of a lot skimpier than the pajamas she slept in last night.

"Thanks," she says, looking down and tucking a wet strand behind her ear. When her gaze meets mine again, there's an amused look on her face. "Were you just...talking to your penis?"

I shrug, grinning. "What? You've never spoken to your vulva before?"

Christy's laugh puts me at ease. She's so adorable, I can't help but scoop her up and kiss her. And my eagerness to throw her onto the bed far outweighs the little voice in my head that says I shouldn't lift her because of my shoulder. Was that a twinge I just felt?

I don't know. I don't care.

The most beautiful woman I've ever laid eyes on is wrapping her legs around my waist. She's kissing me back, eager and hungry. And I'm pretty sure she's not wearing underwear.

"Can I take you to bed, baby?" I whisper.

She nods, smiling, then presses her mouth back to mine.

Inside the bungalow, it's dark. Christy turned off all the lights. Closed every blind and drew every curtain shut.

I think back to yesterday, in the car, when I touched her bare stomach, and she flinched. She said, "Not everyone's as confident in their skin as you are, Holden."

I think back to last night, in the ocean, when she left on her bra and panties. She said she didn't enjoy being naked. And before we swam to shore, she asked if I could get out of the water first and grab her a towel.

She's terrified of me seeing her body.

Man, I hate that fucker, Kyle. I can't imagine what he said to make this beautiful woman so self-conscious. Every inch of her I've seen is gorgeous, and I'm willing to bet the rest is, too.

Her curves drive me fucking crazy. I'm dying to slip her out of her lingerie and see what's underneath. Put those full, perky tits in my mouth, and suck on her rock-hard nipples. Work my way down, and kiss the soft flesh between her belly button and pelvis. Flip her onto her stomach, and press my lips to every inch of skin, from the back of her neck, down to that plump, sexy ass. Maybe take a bite, while I'm down there. Kyle wasn't up to the task of adoring Christy's body, but I am. It'll be the easiest thing I ever do.

She has to be comfortable being naked with me first, though. My gut tells me that, tonight, she'd rather keep on her lingerie. Of course, I'll check with her first, to be sure.

I set her on the bed, and she pulls me on top of her. While we kiss, I let her take the lead. She's passionate, running her fingers through my hair, up and down my back, and over my bare shoulders. Her touch is electric, sparking a primal hunger in me, and it takes every ounce of restraint I have not to act on my urges. If I did, her legs would be hooked over my shoulders right now, and I'd be fucking her six ways from Sunday.

But my needs are not the priority, Christy's are. So, while taking things slow in bed is not my typical MO...today, it'll have to be.

"You look incredible," I say, smoothing my hand over her satin-covered breast, instead of grabbing it the way I'm desperate to. When my fingers travel south to her belly, I feel her muscles tighten the slightest bit. She doesn't flinch like yesterday, though. That's progress.

Now, I need to find out if she'll let me undress her. I have to be subtle, though. I don't want to pressure her into anything she's not ready for. "Did you pack this knowing you wanted to wear it for me, baby?"

In the dark, I barely make out her sheepish smile. "My sister threw it in my bag, while I wasn't looking. I found it last night, with a note that said, 'Just in case.'"

"Please thank her on my behalf." My fingers travel across her hips to grip her ass. "You're so damn sexy in this little dress, I can't decide if I wanna fuck you with it on or off. What do you think?"

She clears her throat before she answers. "Um...dress *on* sounds pretty hot, actually."

I nod. "I think so, too, baby."

I'm not lying. Yes, I've fantasized about motorboating her bare tits countless times—but, that can wait. I'm just happy to be here. I've wanted Christy since I first laid eyes on her at the bar. I'll take whatever she's willing to give.

With the decision made to keep her clothes on, Christy's body softens under me. Her face, too. She looks so goddamn relieved, it breaks my heart.

If nothing else comes of this arrangement with Christy, I hope I can at least boost her confidence. Even if she rejects me in the end, it would be worth it.

I kiss her pretty lips, then move down, cupping her breasts to give me ample access to her cleavage. When I nip and suck at the skin there, she moans her approval, so I linger, tugging at her flesh a little harder. The idea that I might leave a hickey makes me grin. Like the orchid behind her ear, it lets the world know she's mine.

Eventually I shift my attention to her nipples, which are a

lot less shy than their owner. Standing at attention, they're begging to be noticed, so I suck them through the thin layer of Christy's lingerie. It drives her fucking wild. Her sighs get louder, and her legs open wider, and I take the invitation to eat her out again. She didn't get my best work at the main house this morning, given the concerns about time and noise level, so I don't hold back now. I bury my face in her sweet little pussy and lick her until she's gushing. Until her whole body shudders with pleasure, and she melts onto the mattress with a joyful laugh, after screaming my name.

Hell yeah. I am so fucking good at this.

"Oh my god, Holden. You are so fucking good at that."

I know, baby. "I'm glad you enjoyed yourself."

Another giggle escapes her. As she works to catch her breath, I wipe my mouth on the back of my hand and lie down next to her. While she recovers, her fingers skate up and down my arm. This time her touch is soothing. More tender than the way you'd touch a one-night stand—which is all I've been since my last relationship fizzled two years ago. It's only now that I realize how much I've missed this kind of affection. Even if Christy were to decide this is as far as she's ready to go with me today, I'd fall asleep a happy man.

But when Christy moves to kneel beside me, her gaze on the erection pitching a tent below my waistband, I have no objections. And I have a feeling I'm about to get a lot happier.

"Take off your shorts, please," she says.

"Such a good girl, asking so nicely." I raise an eyebrow. "Are you ready to see how hard you make me?"

She nods, biting a smile.

Here we go.

I slide off my shorts and toss them to the side. Then I lie

back down, my cock pointing straight to the ceiling, and I watch her reaction.

"Whoa."

It's huge. I know.

She covers her upturned lips with her palm, and her wide eyes ping-pong between my dick and my face before she speaks. "Well...I'm not supposed to be stroking your ego, so I guess I'll stroke *this* instead."

I laugh. "Do what you need to do, baby."

I lace my fingers behind my head and enjoy the sensation of her hand moving up and down my shaft. But then she starts incorporating her mouth...massaging my dick head with her tongue, and—

Holy fucking shit. This woman knows what she's doing.

I wasn't expecting that, given her lackluster sex life with Kyle. I thought I'd have to teach her a thing or two. I guess Christy's full of surprises. I'm still getting over the shock of seeing her beautiful swing on the baseball field.

God, that was hot. The way she gripped the baseball bat... *Fuck*. Now I'm even more turned on. And her pretty mouth feels so goddamn good, I swear I'm about to—

No, no, no. I *cannot* let myself come from a two-minute blowjob. I don't care how incredible it is. I'm a grown man, not a teenager.

Just breathe, dude. Think about baseball. Lord, I hope the Brewers lose today. That'll put us back in first place. Their new starting pitcher has a pretty fucking good curveball. And he pitched a no-hitter last night. Show-off. He can't be older than twenty-two, twenty-three. Bet his shoulder's loose as fuck. Must be nice. And, speaking of nice—

"Jesus, baby," I pant. "You really enjoy sucking, don't you."

"Mmm," she moans, which makes my cock throb. Thankfully, she stops blowing me right before I hit the point of no return. "And *you* really enjoy my mouth on you, don't you," she says with the same fiery confidence that, up until now, I thought she reserved for telling me off. Her feistiness was a turn-on, even then. But now that she's had her pretty lips around my dick? *Holy shit.*

I run my fingers through my hair as I exhale. "That's an understatement, Red."

"Good." She looks pleased. "Can you get a condom? I want to see what else you enjoy."

"Yes, ma'am." I grab one from my wallet on the nightstand. When it's on, she straddles me. I would've guessed she'd want *me* to be on top, at least to start. Once again, Christy defies expectations.

I can't take my eyes off her gorgeous face as she sinks down onto my cock. I see the pleasure on her lips. In her fluttering lashes. But when I'm in all the way, her breath hitches.

"Are you okay, baby? Is it too much?"

Christy shakes her head, her lids shut. "You feel amazing, Holden."

Maybe it's a good thing she can't see how wide I'm grinning.

Once she settles onto me, she starts riding me like a pro. I let her control the pace because she's tight as fuck, and I'm a little worried about hurting her. But her moans tell me she's just fine. Probably because she's dripping wet. I watch, mesmerized, as she glides back and forth on my dick, swallowing every inch of me. With each roll of her hips, my pleasure increases tenfold. If I last more than five minutes, it'll be a miracle.

When Christy starts moving faster, I force myself to think about baseball again.

Eventually, I make it back from the brink, but I need to figure out how to stay here long enough for her to come. Focusing on her pleasure instead of mine seems to help. Yes, she's rocking my world, but she's also having a hell of a good time, herself. I see it in the curl of her lips. The arch of her back. The unbridled way she's flipping her hair. She looks so wild and beautiful, I'm desperate to kiss her. I sit up, so I can.

Now that we're face-to-face, Christy wraps her arms and legs around me. Being in this position with her is on another level. It's hot, and intimate, and opens her up to me completely.

"Oh my god," she gasps. "You're hitting me so deep."

"Does it feel good, baby?"

"I love it."

"I love having you on top of me."

One thing's for sure: this woman may be shy when it comes to her physical appearance, but when it comes to fucking, she's the most self-assured I've seen her. Just when I thought I couldn't be more obsessed, Christy proves herself to be a sex goddess.

We find a rhythm, her luscious hips meeting my thrusts as we kiss. I can tell she's close to climaxing when she whimpers and bites her bottom lip.

"That's right. Come on my cock like a good girl." My voice is low and hoarse as I try to keep my own orgasm at bay. It's not easy when her gorgeous cleavage is bouncing in my face.

She heaves a sigh. "God, I love when you call me that."

"I know you do," I whisper as I tighten my grip on her glorious ass.

Now she's riding me so hard that a satin strap falls from her shoulder, nearly exposing one of her tits. I start to fix it for her, but she stops me.

"It's okay," she says.

"You sure?"

"Yes," she pants.

"I wanna suck your nipple while you come," I say between ragged breaths. "I think you'd like it." I sweep the hair back from her beautiful, flushed face. "But only if you're comfortable."

She looks into my eyes. "I'm comfortable."

"Promise?"

"I promise."

I pull at the fabric just enough to reveal one exceptionally beautiful breast. "So fucking perfect."

When she smiles, I start sucking, and it doesn't take long for her to orgasm. The way her muscles pulse and tighten around me drives me over the edge, and I come right along with her.

I'm just relieved I lasted long enough to get her off.

That was the best goddamn sex of my life. No contest.

Afterward, we lie next to each other, panting.

"Holden? Can I tell you something?"

I turn to face her. "Of course."

"That was the first time I've ever..." She clears her throat, and her eyes dart away for a second before landing back on mine. "That was the first time I've ever come during sex. Well, during penetration. You know what I mean."

What I know is, I haven't been this happy since the Starlings won the 2008 World Series.

"I think so," I tease her, "but, just to be clear...you're saying I'm the best sex of your life, right?"

She rolls her eyes, but her lips curve upward. Meanwhile, I'm silently thanking my dick.

Well done, player. Way to pull through.

"The others complained that I was too tight. Can you believe it? And they were nowhere near as big as you." She laughs. "Anyway, most of them didn't last very long."

Yeah, no shit. Poor fuckers. I almost became one of them.

Regardless, I plaster an incredulous look on my face. "Really, baby? Well, I think you're perfect. So...I guess you were just sleeping with the wrong guys."

Let that sink in, Red.

"Thank you, Holden."

"For the orgasm?" I crack a smile.

She shakes her head. "For the compliments. For making me feel so good about myself."

"I mean every word." My gaze is fixed on hers. "I hope you know that."

"I think I do..." She lets out a deep sigh. "I just have some trust issues I'm still grappling with."

Once again, I bet I know who's to blame. It sucks when you open yourself up to someone who doesn't deserve it. I remember the feeling well.

"But I've come a long way," she goes on. "Mending my relationships with Jenna and my mom has helped a lot. The three of us are so close now, we tell each other everything. Maybe even too much." She laughs. "It feels incredible knowing they're in my corner, though. I haven't always had that kind of emotional support in my life. I mean, my dad hasn't reached out to me once since Penelope Dwyer showed her true colors. And he's well aware that I represented her. He used to brag about it all the time on Facebook."

My heart aches for her. Dysfunctional relationships with my parents and siblings aside, I enjoyed decades' worth of love and support from my grandmother. Plus, I've always had the Pipers to lean on. Nate, Lola, and their parents are like family to me. In fact, had I not been summoned to Maui, Nate was planning to fly out to Chicago this week, so I didn't have to tackle my grief and bad press alone. It's comforting to know I have support when the shit hits the fan.

I'd like to be that support for Christy.

I take her hand. "Well, I'm in your corner now, too."

She blinks at me a few times before smiling. "Thank you."

She's flustered. It's too much, too soon, and I know it. We're not really dating. We just had amazing sex, yes, but I'm sure she only sees this as a casual fling. Something she'll look back on one day, when she's married to that Pulitzer Prize-winning author.

The thought of her with another man makes me feel sick. All I want is to wrap my arms around this woman, pull her close, and never let go. It's not an option, I know. But we could at least spend the rest of the day in bed. Holding each other. Shooting the shit.

Who the hell am I right now? Holden McBride doesn't cuddle. He doesn't do pillow talk. And he definitely doesn't get jealous.

Not until today, I guess. It's a good thing I just gave Christy the best sex of her life, but I have to keep it up—no pun intended. If I'm going to impress this woman with my sexual prowess, I need to be consistent. Maybe we should do it again after I've recovered. I bet I'll last a lot longer, since I already came.

I run my fingers through her pretty hair. "So, um...what do

you want to do next? Have a snack, then go for Round Two, maybe?"

Please say yes.

"Actually," Christy begins, "I've been meaning to reach out to this romance writer I want to represent...Haley Quinlan. I read her manuscript cover to cover on Sunday and fell in love with it. Then my career went off the rails, and I delayed making the offer, because I was scared she'd reject me. Last night, I had this nightmare that she picked my rival over me."

What the fuck? I offer her another mind-blowing orgasm, and she wants to do *work* instead? If I weren't so damn cocksure, I'd be offended.

Shit. I think I'm offended.

"Anyone who rejects you is out of their mind," I say with a furrowed brow and a fragile ego. Because, if it wasn't already obvious how *gone* I am for this woman, well...

Good thing she's oblivious to my pining.

"I hope you're right," she responds. "Maybe I'm on a high from the orgasms you gave me, but I'm ready to get in touch with her. I'm feeling more confident than I have in a long time."

I think back to what I told myself an hour ago: *If nothing else comes of this arrangement with Christy, I hope I can at least boost her confidence. Even if she rejects me in the end, it would be worth it.*

Well, that was before I slept with her.

So I'm a baseball player, not an academic. Who says we can't end up together? Our physical connection is like nothing I've ever experienced. And she all but said she feels the same. A week ago, I would have told you I didn't believe in soulmates. Today? I'm not sure that's true.

Do I still want to undo the damage TGI Friday caused? Of course. But not so another man can reap the benefits. Fuck that.

The only reason Christy's still single is because she has no idea how amazing she is. If I do my job right, she'll never doubt her worth again. She'll walk into her next relationship with an open heart, ready to be loved.

And I'll be damned if it isn't by me.

CHAPTER 14

Christy

It doesn't take me long to draft my offer of representation to Haley Quinlan. I'm on such a high from the best sex of my life that gushing about a romantic hero feels easy.

Edison Ford is charming, and funny, and *cocky*, to be sure, but he has the goods to back it up. He's athletic, strong, and commanding... And it's a good thing, too, because he's fighting for love during an apocalypse. His body is his livelihood. It's his lethal weapon, when he needs it to be. With his opponents, he's unyielding, but when it comes to Iris...man, does he bend to her will. When she needs him to be gentle, he is. When she wants him to take control, he does. When the world is crumbling, he makes her feel safe. And the best part is, she doesn't even have to ask. If she could, she would, but the baggage she carries from her past is too heavy. That doesn't scare off Edison. Because he knows her. He reads her like she's his favorite novel, and it is *so* fucking sexy.

Wait a minute.

Now that I think about it, Edison Ford seems familiar. But

I'm sure I've never come across a romance hero remotely like him.

Huh. It must be because the novel's been on my mind all week. I even had a few dreams about it, since I was so nervous to send Haley the offer letter.

That was before I slept with Holden. Now, I'm a changed woman. Let's face it, it's tough to be anxious when you're having earth-shattering orgasms.

That man is *so* damn good in bed. And don't get me started on how sexy he is. Everyone knows about his handsome face and chiseled ass, but the rest of his body? *Fuck. Me. (Yes, he did! I can hardly believe it.)* Broad shoulders. Perfect pecs. The strongest arms I've ever seen. Legs too, for that matter. Washboard abs, and this sexy trail of golden-brown hair leading to a penis so spectacular, I almost cried tears of joy when I first saw it.

I know I need to temper my excitement, but you have to understand, I have been waiting my entire adult life to have good sex. When Kyle and I broke up, I went searching for it. After eight years of chronic disappointment, I was desperate to see what else was out there. Unfortunately, one after the other, every cock I took for a test-drive succumbed to the same fate as Kyle's.

The problem wasn't them, it was me. My anatomy, to be exact. I was too tight for a guy to last any substantial amount of time, and I would never have satisfying sex. Or so I thought...until Holden. Before him, my best sexual experience was with a guy I met at a hotel bar in downtown Chicago. He was in town for his friend's bachelor party. We hit it off, and I went back to his room. Long story short, he was so embarrassed by his performance, he went down on me until the sun came up. It was fun, I won't lie. But it wasn't what I was craving.

And then there's Holden, with his magnificent dick, who fucks me for as long as I need, and tells me I'm perfect. I think I finally believe he's attracted to me. He's gone out of his way to prove it. So I'm leaning into this. I'm having not just good, but stellar sex, and I deserve it. Even if it's only temporary.

After I email the offer letter, Holden suggests we celebrate by going to a luau at a nearby resort. He says it'll be good publicity, since lots of tourists will be there taking videos.

"You're not going to make me yell at you so we go viral again, are you?" I tease as he's choosing something to wear from the closet. I'm already dressed and lounging on the bed.

He only winks at me.

I'm about to ask him to elaborate on what that wink means, when my phone chimes. It's a text from Jenna—finally.

While Holden gets dressed, I read her message.

JENNA

Did you find the gift I hid in your suitcase?
And, more importantly, did you wear it??

Cheeks flushed, I giggle. This is the kind of relationship I always dreamed about having with my sister. The kind where we'd talk about guys, and sex, and love. The kind we missed out on for years, because our horrible father pitted us against each other growing up. Jenna was diagnosed with dyslexia as a kid, and he never forgave her for it. From that day forward, he put immense pressure on me to succeed in school, while essentially ignoring my sister.

I'm so grateful we're past that now. Beaming, I write her back.

ME

Yes…and yes!

Jenna's reply is lightning-fast.

JENNA

OMG!! I knew it!! I think I'm going to faint. Was the sex amazing? Like, soulmate-level??

ME

It was incredible. But as for soulmates? Let's not get carried away.

As soon as I hit send, I regret it. So I follow that up with another message.

ME

Just out of curiosity, though…how does one know if they're having soulmate-level sex? Asking for a friend who had the best orgasm of her life today.

Three dots appear, then disappear, and appear once more before my sister answers.

JENNA

Eeeek! I'm so happy for you, Christy!! I don't know how I'll ever calm down. Anyway, I'm sure it's different for every couple. But in my experience with Charlie, it's like he can read my body. What I want, what I need. And the orgasms come so much more easily.

I blink at the screen.

"Ready to go?" Holden asks me.

It's a perfect seventy-five degrees when we arrive at the resort. The luau is on their private beach, and we're greeted by hula dancers who place fresh orchid leis around our necks and hand us Mai Tais. The flower behind my ear is beginning to wilt, so Holden plucks the fresh one from his drink and replaces it. Then he kisses me, and camera phones start flashing.

He doesn't hold back. His tongue is deep in my mouth, his hands are traveling over my hips to grip my ass. It's the kind of kiss that tells the world we're sleeping together.

When he steps back, I'm breathless. "Holden, there are children here." I look around but, to my surprise, I'm wrong. "Or maybe not. Is this luau adults-only?"

He shakes his head. "Technically, no. But this one's more of a fine-dining experience, so you won't see many kids. It caters to honeymooners, mostly." He tucks my hair behind my ear, giving me butterflies. "I thought you might enjoy this more than the family-friendly ones I take Maisie and Matt to."

My heart flutters. I love how invested he is in his relationship with his niece and nephew. If only he were closer with their mom. I'm dying to know what went down between him and Abby, but if she's as shitty as the rest of the family, I'm guessing Holden's right to hold a grudge. I don't want to ask him and risk dredging up old wounds, though.

My fake beau kisses me again.

"So, is this what you want to go viral for?" I ask after another passionate lip-lock. "I can see the headline already: *Holden McBride and Date Enjoy PDA-Filled Luau in Maui.*"

"Could be worse, right?" There's a twinkle in his eye. "But you're not just my date, anymore. You're my girlfriend."

"Aww! So sweet!" Two young women, one blonde and one brunette, gush over us. Over Holden, actually. I can't blame them. They ask for a selfie, and he's so gracious and accommodating. The blonde requests a minute to fix her makeup, and Holden offers to hold her purse while she applies lipstick. And when the brunette doesn't like the first take because there's a strand of hair in her face, Holden takes five more pictures, making sure there's at least one photo both women approve of.

He really is dreamy. Ugh.

This is just a fling, Christy.

We sit for dinner at peak sunset. The sky is a fiery mix of pink, purple, and orange that takes my breath away. When night falls, and we're under a canopy of stars, hula dancers take the stage. The main course is one I will never forget. Fresh grilled mahi mahi, served with passion fruit butter, and a fluffy coconut rice that's to die for. I enjoy it so much, Holden feeds me the last forkfuls of his meal. His gesture is so cute and sweet that, under any other circumstances, I would gag. The way I do, sometimes, when Jenna and Charlie get lovey-dovey around me. But none of this is real. It's a fantasy. Take the way Holden's looking at me right now, like he's utterly smitten. I know it's just for show.

But damn if he's not convincing.

So much so, that I can't help wondering what's on his mind. Emboldened by my second Mai Tai, I ask him.

He whispers in my ear. "I can't stop thinking about how good you feel."

I flush, smiling. "Oh."

"About how wild you are. How sexy. About that one perfect tit you let me see."

"Holden," I breathe out. "You're going to make me wet my seat."

"Well, I'm hard as a rock, so now we're even." When he leans back in his chair, his blue-gray eyes are full of mischief.

I cross my legs, trying to shut down what's happening between them. It doesn't help. It might be making things worse, actually. I want to suggest we head back to our bungalow bed, but just as I press my lips to his ear, the emcee requests the crowd's attention.

"We have a special guest here tonight," he says. "Anyone here a Chicago Starlings fan?"

All eyes are on us as the guests clap and cheer. I turn crimson, but Holden's just smiling, unfazed. He's used to this.

"Come on up, MVP," the emcee continues. "And bring your pretty lady with you."

I suck in a breath. "What? Why me?"

"This'll be fun, Red." He squeezes my hand. "Trust me."

"Ladies and gentlemen, we have a treat for you tonight," the emcee announces as Holden and I make our way to the stage. "Now, typically, a hula dancing contest is not part of our program..."

My eyebrows fly up. "Contest?"

Holden stifles a smile.

"You're more likely to see that at the family-friendly luaus down the road, with the big buffets and the kiddie cocktails," the emcee goes on. "But Mr. McBride here asked for a favor. And seeing as he introduced me to my wife...well, I owe him."

"That's so sweet," I whisper to Holden as the crowd applauds.

He nods with a smile. "She works at the estate. Teaches yoga at the fitness center. I've known him for years and thought they'd be a good match."

"Now, we'll need a few more participants," the emcee goes

on and, right away, a dozen hands fly up. The volunteers are mostly women, no doubt eager to get an up-close glimpse of *the* Holden McBride. But a few men join us onstage as well, patting the famous ballplayer on the back and shaking his hand.

The contest rules are simple. In the first round, the professional dancers take the stage, demonstrating a few basic moves while the live band plays rhythmic Hawaiian melodies, known as *mele*, on drums and ukeleles. Our job is to mirror the choreography as closely as possible. The emcee is our judge, and a tough one, too. Within a minute, he boots half the contestants offstage—including Holden.

"Sorry, ladies. I know you love to see Mr. McBride swivel those hips, but I don't want him to throw out his back before his next game," the emcee jokes.

I almost forgot that Holden's pitching on Monday. Just two more nights in paradise before we travel to Milwaukee, where he'll go head-to-head with the Brewers' new starting pitcher. Whether we fly back here afterward will depend on the outcome of tomorrow's meeting to discuss Grandma Evelyn's will. If things are sorted out by Sunday, there'd be no reason for us to return to the island.

Which means I need to enjoy every minute while I still can.

"Good luck, Red," Holden says, kissing my cheek before he exits the stage.

Round Two is a freestyle contest, where we're encouraged to improvise using any combination of moves we can remember. Once the music starts, I settle my gaze on Holden, who's standing on the sidelines, watching only me. I don't have any background in dance, but with his eyes on my body, moving to the beat of the drums feels effortless. This time, the audience picks the winner, voting with their cheers.

I win by a landslide. And not only because Holden's yelling so loudly.

My face flushes with surprise as my hands float to my heart. I know it's silly, but I'm genuinely happy. While I was dancing, I felt so confident and carefree. Sexy, even. I didn't know I had it in me.

I'm guessing Holden did.

As soon as I'm offstage, he pulls me into his arms and congratulates me.

"What made you ask them to host a dance contest?" I ask, grinning.

"This was the best of both worlds," he explains. "I get to take you to the most romantic luau on the island...and *you* get to win a dance contest, like they host at the kid-friendly ones."

"But...how did you know I would win?" My brow furrows. "Oh, god. The contest wasn't rigged, was it?"

Holden laughs. "No, baby. Believe me." He leans to whisper in my ear. "I knew you'd win because of the way your hips move when you're grinding on my cock. It's the sexiest thing I've ever seen."

My cheeks heat.

"You're a lot more confident in your body than you realize, Red. That's what I wanted to show you."

His words push my desire over the edge. I bite my lip, trying to keep myself from nipping at his. "Can we go back to the bungalow now?"

"Thought you'd never ask."

But no sooner are we in the Range Rover, still parked in the resort's lot, than we start kissing. We're all over each other. Chests heaving, hands roaming.

I've never felt a need like this. Desperate for his touch, I coax his fingers up my dress and into my underwear.

"My god, woman," he groans into my neck as he massages my clit. "You have the wettest pussy I've ever had the pleasure of knowing."

"It's only because she likes you so much," I whisper.

"Well, the feeling is very fucking mutual."

Holden moves his hand to grip my thigh. For a moment he's frozen, taking deep breaths, like he's trying to resist his urges. This ace pitcher, who is unflappable on the mound, is struggling to control himself around *me*. His gorgeous blue-gray eyes are wild, like he wants to eat me alive.

My heart pounds from the thrill of it.

"We can't do this here." His gaze darts around the parking lot and lands on another couple, walking to their car. "Can you wait 'til we get back?"

"Yes." I guess I'll have to.

The estate's just over thirty minutes from here, which isn't ideal. But what other choice do we have? Holden's trying to clean up his image, and the last thing he needs is a sex tape scandal.

To my surprise, he smirks. "Well, I can't."

When he puts the Range Rover in drive and zooms out of the lot, tires screeching, a smile erupts on my face. "Where are you taking me?"

He half-smiles. "Somewhere we won't get caught."

With one hand glued to my thigh, he steers us into the lush, tropical night. I lean back in my seat, savoring the feeling.

This is the girl I wanted to be in high school. The one dating the hot varsity athlete who drives her home during lunch, so they can fuck while her parents are at work. Is it pathetic how much I envied her back then? Maybe. Is it silly how cool I feel right now? Perhaps. I don't care. Holden's healing an old wound. If teenaged Christy had gotten any attention from guys, she probably wouldn't have spent her twenties with a man who acted like he was doing her a favor by dating her.

About two miles from the resort, on a quiet, coastal road, Holden stops at a pull-off overlooking the ocean, then kills the engine. There's no one in sight. Just me, and him, and the waves crashing below us.

He pushes his seat as far back as it'll go. "Come here, baby."

"First things first." When I lift my hips and slide off my underwear, Holden's breath hitches. Then I straddle his lap, and his heart hammers against mine. For several seconds, his gaze roams my face, from my eyes down to my lips, and back again.

"You make me insane, Christy Andersen," he says. "You have, since we met at the bar. But now that I know what you taste like...and what you feel like when you come on my cock, it's all I can think about." He works his fingers into my hair. "You're even better than I imagined."

I cup his face in my palms, and my thumbs graze his stubble. "So are you."

And I don't only mean when it comes to sex. There's so much more to Holden McBride than I gave him credit for. But if I think too hard about the ways he continues to surprise me, I'm afraid I'll—

He presses his mouth to mine with urgency. Then his hands grip my bare ass, kneading my flesh, as his kisses fall to my cleavage. My fingers travel up and down his biceps, then move to unbutton his shirt for unfettered access to his perfect pecs. When my tongue rolls over his nipple, he sucks in a breath.

I look up at him. "Do you like that?"

"Very much."

As my mouth roams over his chest, his fingers find their way to my slit. He circles my opening a few times before sliding into me.

I let out a soft moan, arching my back. His fingers feel so good, especially the way they're hooked and massaging my G-spot. Still, it's not enough. So, I plead with him. "I need you."

"What do you need, baby?" He nips at the top of my breast. "Tell me."

"I need you to fill me completely. The way only *you* can."

Holden shifts forward and grabs his wallet from his back pocket. He pulls out a foil wrapper, rips it open, then hands me the condom.

I unzip his pants and unleash his beautiful dick. Slowly, I unroll the latex, enjoying the way pleasure washes over his face as my fingers move down his shaft. Then I lift my hips and kiss him, using one hand to guide his cock where I want it. I lower myself an inch, then squeeze.

"Holy fuck," he groans. "This is going to be over real quick if you keep playing like that."

I can't help but smile, enjoying the effect I have on him. When I relax my muscles and slide all the way down, he lets out this deep sigh and his eyes flutter shut. I love it.

I start working my hips like I did onstage. My mind travels back to Holden's compliments about the way I move during sex. But it's no surprise how comfortable I am in this position, seeing as Kyle and I both preferred it. He liked me on top because he was always tired from long shifts at the hospital. And

I just liked being in control. I liked deciding how fast, or slow, or deep we went. Because, ultimately, I didn't trust Kyle with my body.

Holden watches me grind, his hands on my waist. "I bet every guy who saw you dance tonight wanted to fuck you," he pants. "But they're shit out of luck, 'cause this pussy is mine."

His possessiveness makes me rabid with desire. I ride him faster, seeking out the same mind-blowing orgasm I had in bed with him this afternoon.

"Let me help you, baby." Gripping my hips, he uses his strength to slide me up and down the length of his cock. He's the one doing all the work now, and he does it with ease. If it were any other man, I'm sure my muscles would tense the moment I relinquished control. I'd worry he'd go too fast and hurt me. The way Kyle did, when we first started sleeping together.

But in this moment with Holden, I'm nothing but turned on. And, with him taking the lead, he's able to thrust even deeper than I thought possible.

"Oh my god!" I whimper.

"I'd ask if you're okay," he pants, "but you've never looked happier."

A laugh escapes me. "Your dick is top-notch, Holden."

"I know it is, baby." His breath is warm in my ear. "And it's yours for as long as you want it."

I'm so close to climaxing, my brain so fuzzy with pleasure, that I don't bother asking what he means by that. He probably doesn't mean anything. People say all sorts of crazy things when they're in the throes of amazing sex.

Holden's lips skate over my collarbone and down to my

cleavage again. "Maybe I should suck your other nipple this time. What do you think?"

Apart from the crumpled pair of undies on the passenger seat, I'm still fully clothed. I don't know if he didn't bother trying to undress me because we're in the car, or because he knows I'm uncomfortable being naked. All I know is, this dress does an amazing job of slimming my waistline. I feel sexy in it. But I'm also desperate for his mouth on my nipple.

To give him access, I take off my strapless bra and throw it next to my underwear. Then I peel away the fabric covering my right breast.

His gaze falls to it. "Just as perfect as the other one."

I grin at him before closing my eyes and riding the wave of my impending orgasm. Coming feels even easier this time, the way he's moving my hips for me. Before I know it, I'm shuddering and shaking, and telling Holden he's the best sex of my life. The minute the words are out of my mouth, he climaxes too. Utterly spent, I rest my head on his shoulder while he's still inside me. He holds me and strokes my back.

It's intimate. And real. And I'm having trouble remembering which part of this relationship is fake.

Back at the bungalow, we take our time getting ready for bed, then crawl under the covers. I'm exhausted, but I know I'll have a hard time falling asleep unless I read for a little while. It's been my routine for years, and I missed it last night. I glance at the suitcase full of books I brought with me.

"Would it bother you if I used my reading light?" I ask Holden with a sheepish smile.

He chuckles. "Of course not. What kind of man would I be if I kept a literary agent from her books?"

Giddiness floods me as I hop out of bed to get my luggage.

I'm too sleepy to start a new novel, so I decide to go for one of my comfort reads. I brought two cozy mysteries, but after all the sex I had today, I'm in the mood for something steamier. *Edison's Love* it is.

"Got anything for me in there?"

I look up from my suitcase, a bit stunned. I hate to judge a book by its cover, but I didn't figure Holden for the reading type. Now, I feel like an ass. "What are you in the mood for?"

He shrugs. "Do you have any classics in that traveling library of yours?"

"How about *The Great Gatsby*? It was my favorite book in high school."

Holden blinks at me.

That's when I realize that particular novel might hit a little too close to home, given it's a critique of high society. "Or, I also have—"

"*The Great Gatsby*'s perfect," he says. "Thanks. It's been a while since I've read it."

When the two of us are in bed together, reading side-by-side, I can't stop myself from smiling. Kyle wasn't a reader, unless you count the well-loved science textbooks he kept from college. He was happy to flip through an astrophysics tome every now and then, but reading fiction was out of the question. I used to dream of the day he'd show the slightest bit of interest in the manuscripts I was reading for work, but it never happened. He couldn't get it up for me, in more ways than one.

And then, there's Holden.

I flip to the sexy beach scene in *Edison's Love*. It's easy to find, since I marked the chapter with so many tabs. When I read it for the first time last weekend, I hadn't had sex in months.

Today, Holden made me come four times. Heart racing with excitement, I re-read every spicy detail of Edison and Iris's oceanside tryst with new eyes.

Then Holden's cell phone vibrates on the nightstand. I glance at the clock. It's midnight.

"Sorry, baby, I gotta take this. It's my agent," he explains before answering. "Hey, man. No, I'm awake. But you're up early. What time is it in Chicago, 6:00 a.m.? Is everything alright with Theo and Shelley?" Holden nods. "Okay, good. Good."

He's quiet for what seems like an eternity, except for a few sighs and uh-huhs. "Fuck," he finally says, then drags a hand down his chin. "Yeah, I know. I know. Alright, man. Thanks for calling."

Holden hangs up the phone and squeezes it until his knuckles turn white. I'm surprised the screen doesn't shatter in his iron grip. When he puts the cell on the nightstand, he still doesn't look at me. He closes his eyes and pinches the bridge of his nose. I hope he doesn't break his bones.

"What's wrong?" I rest my hand on his forearm.

When he turns to me, his jaw is clenched. "I'm not pitching on Monday. The MLB completed their investigation of the Soldier Field incident. They're making me take time off."

My heart sinks. "How long?"

His tone is dejected. "Two weeks."

I'm stunned. "Two weeks? But isn't that—"

"The rest of the season? Yup." He heaves a sigh. "And without me, our odds of making it to the postseason are pretty grim. Not to mention, my contract's up, so if this streaking scandal doesn't blow over soon, I can pretty much kiss my career goodbye."

"I can't believe they suspended you." I shake my head. "I

thought they'd be more understanding, given the circumstances."

He purses his lips. "It's not a formal suspension. They're calling it bereavement leave."

I tilt my head. "Maybe that's not such a bad thing, Holden. You just lost someone very special, and—"

"I know, Red." He exhales. "I know."

His face is flushed, his eyes glassy. I know I'm treading on thin ice, but I don't let it stop me. I hate seeing him this way. "It might help if you talked about it. About her."

He swings his legs over the side of the bed, so his back is turned to me. "I'll be fine. I'm going to go for a swim to clear my head."

Without another word, he gets up and leaves.

When he shuts the door behind him, I feel so alone. So empty. But why? What right do I have to feel this way?

Holden doesn't have to bare his soul to me. He doesn't have to take my advice. He doesn't owe me anything.

That's when I remember what poor, misguided Christy forgot, in the afterglow of that insanely hot car sex...

There's nothing real here. Our relationship is for show.

And Holden just stopped faking it.

Holden

When I wake up the next morning, Christy's asleep on the opposite side of the bed, as far from me as possible. Facing away, with her feet dangling over the edge of the mattress, she looks like she's got a fifty-fifty shot of rolling right onto the hardwood floor. And if anything could make me feel shittier than I already do, that would be it.

I shift closer and slide my arms around her waist. Still sleeping, she lets out a little sigh and lifts her hand to where mine are clasped over her stomach. Then she turns toward me, eyes closed, but smiling. When her lashes flutter open and her gaze meets mine, though, she looks stunned.

"Um, hi." She clears her throat. "Did I oversleep? We're not late for the meeting, are we?"

If only. Being stuck in a conference room with my relatives is bad enough on its own, and that's not even considering the reason I have to be there. With the assistance of our attorney, we'll be reviewing the portion of my grandmother's will that relates to the money she left to the family foundation. Then we'll go over guidelines for the competition between Abby, Wes, and me. It'll be all business without Grandma Evelyn there. She was the heart of our family. She was the light, laughter, and warmth. And now she's gone.

I hold Christy a little tighter, wishing we could spend the day tangled up in these sheets together instead. Wishing I'd stayed and talked to her about my grandma last night. Maybe then she'd have woken up in my arms, instead of six feet away.

"We have plenty of time," I explain. "I just grabbed you because I was afraid you were going to fall off the bed."

"Oh," she says, her freckled cheeks flushing. "Thank you."

For a moment, she lies still, her beautiful brown eyes questioning me. If I actually had the courage to be honest with her, she'd be wondering what kind of moron turns down emotional support from the woman whose heart he's determined to win. A woman he wants, more than anything, to consider him for more than just casual sex.

When she rolls onto her back, I move the arm that's underneath her so I can prop myself up on my elbow. But I keep my other hand on her hip.

"Listen, Red. About last night—"

"Holden, it's fine." Her expression stays neutral. "You don't owe me anything. I'm not your girlfriend."

Fuck. Even though she's right, her words hit me like a punch to the gut. There's no sadness in her tone, no angst. Nothing to lead me to believe she'd like our circumstances to change. Regardless, I want to explain why I left.

"Look, I didn't mean to storm out of here like that. But after my agent called, I felt like crap, and I didn't want to burden you with another fucking tantrum. I had an amazing day with you yesterday, Christy..."

She smiles and the tension in my stomach eases.

"And I wasn't going to ruin it with my shit mood. I'm sure you've noticed that talking about my feelings doesn't come naturally. My family..." I heave a sigh. "Well, we've always swept things under the rug. It's the McBride way, I guess. When I was a kid, if something was eating at me, I'd find a physical outlet. Baseball, running, swimming, whatever. It's the only way I know how to calm down."

She nods, her brow furrowed. I can see her wheels spinning, but I can't begin to guess what she's thinking. It takes her several seconds to respond.

When she does, her expression softens. "To be honest, Holden...I can relate. The McBride way sounds a hell of a lot like the Andersen way. Sometimes, I—" Clearing her throat, she looks down at her hands, which are resting on her stomach.

"Tell me." I take her fingers in mine.

Turning to face me again, she goes on. "Sometimes, I get so angry, I'm afraid I'm going to Hulk out."

"Like the night we met?" I tease.

"Just like that." She huffs a laugh. "I can handle other emotions just fine, but anger was frowned upon the most at my house, so I've always bottled mine up. I'd probably benefit from a physical outlet, myself."

I smile, rubbing my thumb over her soft skin. "I think I might know the perfect release for when you're mad, Red."

Giggling, she rolls her eyes, then skates a finger all the way down my bare chest, toward the waistband of my shorts. "I bet you do."

"I'm not talking about sex. Although...that's an option, too," I say, moving my hand to massage her hipbone. "Whenever you want it."

Her cheeks turn a brighter shade of pink.

I should probably stop laying my cards on the table like this. I keep dropping hints that I'd happily fuck her forever, if given the chance. I'm pretty sure I said something to that effect when she was riding me in the Range Rover last night. But controlling my urges around this woman is next to impossible.

"Good to know." Her eyes are smiling. "So, if you're not talking about sex...what *are* you talking about?"

"Baseball," I tell her. "You have such a powerful swing as it is, I'd be curious to see how far you can hit when you're pissed off."

She bites her lip. "You'd actually want to play baseball with me when I'm mad?"

"Sure. Why not?"

"I don't know, it's just..." She clears her throat. "Do you really think you could handle seeing me that way? At my worst?"

My brow creases with confusion, until I realize what she means. Her lame-as-fuck ex didn't know what to do with her body *or* her temper.

I tuck her pretty hair behind her ear. "I don't think there's any part of you I can't handle."

It's true. I'm not just saying that to get laid. Although, given the effect my words have on Christy, it's safe to say things are heading in that direction.

Take her lips, for example, which are gravitating toward mine, while her hand slides inside my shorts to meet my rigid cock. She grins the moment she makes contact. "Do we have time for this?"

"I think we can swing it," I say, rolling on top of her.

"Was that another baseball pun?" She laughs, and it melts my fucking heart.

"If I say yes, is that a strike against me?"

Her whole face lights up when she giggles this time. "There's no way you're striking out with me, Holden McBride."

Christy's eyes roam over my chest, her fingers tracing a line up my arms and around my shoulders, until her hands are clasped behind my neck. But when her gaze meets mine, her smile is replaced with something more...I don't know. Earnest.

I debate what to say next. Do I tell her that nothing about our relationship is fake to me? Do I ask if there's a chance she feels the same way? But if she doesn't, I risk never seeing this look on her face again. So tender. So real. Openhearted, in a way she hasn't shown me, until now.

She couldn't be more beautiful. My eyes travel across her sweet face, trying to capture every feature. Every freckle. There's only one word that comes to mind, but I can't say it out loud.

Mine. Mine. Mine.

I decide to let my kisses do the talking. Slow, but deep. Gentle, but eager. My hands move up and down the curve of her waist, then under her back, so I can pull her even closer to me. Her fingernails graze my neck and run into my hair and over my scalp. Sometimes our eyes flutter open at the same time, and we smile before our lips meet again.

Time doesn't cross my mind. The world could be burning down around us, and I wouldn't notice. Everything about this woman consumes me. The way she moves, the way she moans, the way she tastes. Her sweet scent, her fiery hair, her soft curves. She's the epitome of feminine. So goddamn sexy.

We kiss for so long that her lips are swollen, and her skin's a little pink from my stubble.

I need her so fucking much.

I thread my fingers through hers, arcing our hands toward the headboard, pinning her down to the bed. "Is this okay?"

She smiles while nodding. "Yes."

This is big. The fact that she's letting me take control—that she trusts me with her body—is meaningful. Even if she is fully clothed.

Christy's still in the tank top and shorts she wore to bed. I forgot to draw the curtains when I got back from my swim last night, and the sun is peeking through the blinds. I don't know how she feels about being naked in this light. Both times we had sex yesterday, it was dark.

"You get to decide if and when your clothes come off," I tell her. "Okay?"

"Okay," she whispers, then bites her lip. "Holden?"

"Yeah?"

"Thank you for..." She swallows. "For being so patient with me."

Patient is probably the last word I'd use to describe myself. Restless, impulsive, irritable, sure. And if you asked the women I've dated, I'm sure they'd have a few choice words to add to the list. The truth is, patience doesn't come easily to me.

Unless I'm with Christy. Everything feels so different with her. *I'm* so different. I'm a much better version of myself. And I don't even have to try.

I'm reminded of something I haven't thought of in years. Something my grandmother told me when I was barely eighteen. I'd just broken up with my high school girlfriend who stole from us—although I never told a soul about her transgressions. I was heartbroken, because I thought we were in love. So, I asked Grandma Evelyn how you know when the real thing comes along. She said, "You'll know it's love when being with that person feels as natural as breathing."

She said, when she met my grandfather, she knew right away he was the one.

"Holden? Is everything okay?" Christy's voice snaps me back to the present.

"Yes, baby." I kiss her forehead. "I'm fine."

I'm just in love with you, that's all.

I press my mouth to her neck, hoping to distract her from asking further questions, when there's a forceful knock at the door. And another. And another, still.

Christy looks alarmed. "Who is that?"

Unfortunately, I have a pretty good idea whose bulging biceps are responsible for the relentless pounding.

"Hey, Holden—open up. It's Wes."

Fuck.

"Hold that thought," I say to Christy as I roll off her to get out of bed. "I'll be right back."

"Come on, big bro," Wes bellows. "I know you're in there."

Jackass.

As I throw on a T-shirt, Christy glances at the clock on the nightstand, then lets out a little gasp. "Oh my god! We only have twenty minutes to get to the main house." Her shoulders slump. "I think we may have missed our window for sex. Raincheck?"

I grin despite my brother's relentless knocking. "Just say the word."

"I guess I'll go get dressed." Christy shifts to sit on the edge of the bed, then raises her fingers to her mouth and smiles. "I can't believe we kissed for that long."

"I can." I give her another quick peck before she heads to

the bathroom. Just in time for me to deal with Wes before he huffs and puffs and blows the entire bungalow down.

"Holden! What the fuck?" he says as soon as I open the door.

"Good morning to you, too, asshole."

His brow is furrowed. "Where's Christy? I need to talk to her."

I scoff. "The hell you do."

"Come on, man. I need to know if she has a very particular type of hydrating face mist that my girlfriend forgot to bring with her."

I raise an eyebrow. "Girlfriend? Since when do you have a girlfriend?"

"Since when do *you*?" he challenges me.

My gut clenches. The last thing I need is for Wes to start asking questions about my fake relationship, no matter how real it feels to me. So I don't belabor the point.

"What is this mist she needs?" I ask on a long exhale. "And why can't you just send one of the staff to buy it for her?"

"Because it's some limited edition artisanal shit they don't sell here, that's why." He rolls his eyes. "But my girlfriend just got off a long flight and insists her skin looks dry, and she won't come to the family meeting until she can fix it."

"She sounds fun," I deadpan.

Wes smirks. "I think you'll like her, actually."

"Why don't you ask Mom? She probably has a fucking pharmacy's worth of mists your girlfriend could try."

"Because the bungalow's closer to our guesthouse, and we're pressed for time," my brother huffs.

I heave a sigh. "Alright, I'll ask Christy. But don't get your hopes up. I've never once seen her use face mist."

Granted we've only shared a bed for two nights, but still. As far as my brother knows, Christy and I have been together for months. God, I wish that were true. Maybe one day.

"Well, Christy's a natural beauty," he says, licking his lips. "And speaking of natural, she's got one hell of a rack. Great ass, too."

I ball my left fist. "If you want your jaw to stay intact, I'd highly recommend you keep my woman's name out of your mouth."

Wes rolls his eyes. "Oh, please. There's no way in hell you could take me in a fight."

"That's funny." I chuckle. "You may be ripped, but you weren't born with my arm, little brother."

He looks away from my gaze. "Fuck off."

"Seems like I struck a nerve." My grin is smug.

"Yeah, well, your arm doesn't mean shit if you're not playing ball," Wes spews. "I heard on ESPN that you won't be pitching for the foreseeable future."

My stomach churns, but I do my best to hide my angst. "They gave me bereavement leave, dickwad. If you cared the slightest bit about Grandma dying, maybe you'd need it, too."

"She lived a good, long life, Holden. And you should be grateful she wasn't here to see you streak across Soldier Field like a fucking idiot." He taunts me with his smile. "Your career's over, man. Face it. They're just calling it 'bereavement leave' to soften the blow."

Rage ignites in my veins, so steaming hot, I start to sweat. "Speaking of blows, I hope that pretty face of yours can hold up to my left hook."

He lets out a wry laugh. "Just like a neanderthal to fight

with fists instead of words. I wouldn't expect any less from a man who never went to college."

It's sad, isn't it? We both know exactly what to say to make the other feel like a worthless piece of shit. I guess we have our dad's unreasonable expectations to thank for that. But at the end of the day, Wes is right about me. And if I punch him, I'll only prove his point. I'll also risk messing up my shoulder even more than it already is. So what can I do, but stand here with my jaw clenched?

My brother crosses his arms over his chest, looking satisfied. "Don't bother Christy about the face mist. I'll go check with Mom. But do tell your girlfriend I said hi."

I take a step toward him, and he starts casually backing away.

"Oh, and if you ever want to swap companions for a night, I would *definitely* be on board," he goes on, continuing to retreat which, to his credit, is a smart decision. "And before you say no, just wait until you see my girlfriend. I have a feeling you'll be interested."

"What a lucky lady," I seethe. "I wonder what she'd think if she knew you were trying to pimp her out. You're disgusting."

"Well, I will say this, brother," he says, wiping his forehead. "She's no luckier than Christy—dating a soon-to-be has-been with no education."

Blind with rage, I lunge toward him just as I hear footsteps behind me.

"Holden?"

I turn toward Christy, my pulse racing.

"Hey, Christy," I barely hear Wes say, because my ears are ringing. "Just stopped by to say hi. I'll see you guys at the main house."

When I turn around, he's gone.

Christy closes the door as I stand there, frozen, then takes my hand. "Are you okay?"

My breaths are shallow. "No."

She takes one step closer to me, then another. Her hands move up my arms, over my shoulders, and around my neck. As my heart hammers, she holds me.

"Hugs are physical outlets, too," she says against my chest.

My eyes burn as I squeeze her tight, kissing the top of her head. She's wearing the orchid behind her left ear again, which makes me happier than it should. I lift her into my arms, despite my shoulder twinge. She wraps her legs around me, and I rest my head in the crook of her neck. My heart beats fast, but I focus on her instead. On her sweet scent, and her fingers stroking my hair. After a minute or two, I relax...and my heart syncs with hers, which is slow and steady.

"Better?" she asks when I set her down.

"Better."

And it's true. Except that I'm falling harder for her by the minute, and I'm scared shitless.

As hard as I try to woo this woman, I still know what I'm up against. Maybe there's a chance Christy's catching feelings for me...but this isn't her real life. She's living out a fantasy on this island. Maui may be a second home to me, but to her, it's a novelty. She's here for one week, under bizarre circumstances, sharing a bed with a professional baseball player she thinks is hot. May as well sleep with him, right? Sure, the sex is amazing, and maybe he's not the asshole she once thought he was. Fine. But that doesn't make him relationship material.

He's a McBride, for fuck's sake. His family sucks. He grew up with a silver spoon in his mouth and doesn't know how to book a goddamn flight. He's a hothead, and moody, and his shoulder is fucked, and his career's most likely over. And if he thinks she would entertain a relationship with him past the terms of their agreement, well, he's dumber than she thought.

"Ready to enter the lion's den?" Christy asks, her frown sympathetic.

I let out a deep breath. "Ready as I'll ever be."

When we get to the main house, breakfast is being served on the lanai. Abby and the kids are nowhere in sight. And neither is Wes, thankfully. I imagine he's still dealing with his high-maintenance girlfriend. That's assuming Wes actually has a girlfriend. I wouldn't put it past him to make up that bullshit face mist story as an excuse to stop by and get under my skin before our family meeting. Wes is competitive as fuck, and I'm sure he wants nothing more than to see me fail at earning Grandma's inheritance. Anything he can do to get in my head, he will.

With Christy's hand in mine, we greet my parents, and I introduce her to the three board members of the family foundation, who will hear proposals from me and my siblings and decide the fate of my grandmother's money.

First, there's my great-uncle Alistair. He's my grandpa's only brother, and something of a black sheep, like me. No, he didn't choose to play ball instead of studying business or finance. He chose to become a *doctor* of all things. The nerve of him, right? His father always said that Alistair's choice to pursue medicine was a blatant rejection of the legacy generations of McBrides worked so hard to build. Even despite Alistair's lengthy career as one of Manhattan's premier cardiologists, and a long history of serving the family's philanthropic interests, his parents always considered him a disappointment.

Next, there's Alistair's granddaughter, Zoe McBride. She's the only child of my uncle Henry, and his first wife, Shannon. At eighteen, this is Zoe's first time serving on the board. I don't know my cousin well at all. Unlike the long line of East Coast McBrides before her, she grew up in California. Her parents split when she was two, and her mom moved from New York to San Francisco, so she could be closer to family. The court awarded Shannon full custody of Zoe, because my uncle Henry traveled too much to offer the kind of stability she needed.

Finally, there's Daniel Jimenez, a tax attorney my family hand-picked to be an impartial member of the board. He's around my age—mid-to-late thirties at most—which makes him relatively young to serve in this position. But he's a handsome, charismatic guy, who's widely regarded as an expert in his field and has been named a "super lawyer" in numerous publications. He's even a regular commentator on CNN, which is how my parents discovered him.

Normally my mom and dad would vote, too, but they recused themselves due to the obvious conflict of interest. No one wants to have to choose between their children, especially when it's so painfully obvious who their least favorite is. Although my mom did encourage me to throw my hat in the ring for Grandma's inheritance, she was probably obligated to under the terms of my grandmother's will. Trust me, if she and my dad had any say in the matter of voting, I'd be cut after the first round.

As for me and my siblings, we take turns sitting on the board. Right now, Abby's serving, but since she's also vying for Grandma's money, she won't be voting either.

After exchanging hellos with everyone, Christy and I help ourselves to the breakfast spread. There's no room for us where the others are sitting, which is more than fine with me. Christy's also relieved and can barely hide the smile on her face. We grab chairs on the opposite end of the lanai and, for several peaceful minutes, I'm able to tune out my family and focus only on her. We talk, and flirt, and even sneak kisses when we think no one's watching. It's a great way to start what I know will be a tough day, and I'm even feeling relaxed when the lanai door slides open and my brother appears.

As I suspected, there's no girlfriend in sight. More and more, I'm starting to think *he's* the one faking a relationship.

Thirty minutes later, we head to one of the conference rooms downstairs to discuss the terms and conditions of the competition for my grandmother's money. The money I desperately need to make my sports program happen, because I've been donating the bulk of my earnings to charity for years. Normally, our family attorney would be here in person to lead the meeting, but he's joining us on a video call from Manhattan because it's his son's bar mitzvah weekend. Abby walks into the room right as we're beginning and takes her seat in silence. A pang of guilt hits me when she doesn't so much as look in my direction. Then a wave of sadness, when I think about how much I'll miss Maisie and Matt when we leave the island. They're with a babysitter now, I assume.

The meeting goes surprisingly smoothly, even despite Wes's laundry list of questions and points of clarification regarding the relevant clauses of Grandma's will. Our attorney is nearly done outlining the guidelines of the competition when the door to the conference room opens behind me.

"Hi, everyone. Sorry I'm late."

Her voice sends a chill down my spine. I don't even have to turn around to know who's walking into the room. I'd recognize that throaty rasp of hers anywhere.

As her heels clack on the tiles, I glance across the table at Wes, whose gaze is already fixed on me. He's been lying in wait. Watching for my reaction. Smug as ever, he stifles a smile. Then he turns away.

"Hey, babe," he says to his girlfriend.

CHAPTER 16

Christy

They call her "The Siren." She's one of the most iconic supermodels of our time, touted as having nearly "perfect" proportions, which she's known for showing off in provocative couture and seductive poses. I was an awkward preteen in middle school when she first rose to fame. She had barely turned eighteen and was on the cover of every magazine. Now in her thirties, she has decades worth of runway shows and photoshoots under her belt, most notably wearing next to nothing as both a Victoria's Secret Angel and Sports Illustrated swimsuit model. She's edgy, unapologetic, and the epitome of "sex sells."

Most people associate Caterina Hart with the wildly controversial men's fragrance ad she did years ago. She was sitting on a bed, completely nude, nipples barely covered by her fingertips. And her legs were spread, with a bottle of the brand's signature scent strategically placed between them. There was no slogan, but the message was clear: "This cologne is a pussy magnet." Eventually, after a significant amount of backlash, the ad was banned.

But that's not what I think of when I see her. As she runway-walks to her seat looking drop-dead gorgeous in tiny silk shorts and a bandeau top that hugs curves that seem impossible given her willowy frame, my mind flits back to a scorching hot afternoon in Manhattan. The air conditioning had given out at Hanover Literary, and the office was stifling, so our boss decided to close up shop at noon. It was Kyle's day off, and I figured he'd just be waking up, so we could get lunch together. Not the doughy bagels piled high with cream cheese that I constantly craved, but he'd definitely go for a salad with dressing on the side.

When I opened the door to the apartment we shared, Kyle was seated at his computer with headphones on, facing away from me, so he didn't hear or see me come in. But I'll never forget the picture of Caterina Hart on his screen. She had this seductive twinkle in her eye and a smirk, almost like she was mocking me. Then there was my boyfriend, with a bottle of *my* lotion, jerking off with groans of pleasure and a level of excitement I had no idea he was capable of.

Stunned, I turned around and left the apartment for the closest coffee shop, where I stayed and worked until it was time for us to go on our evening run. But that entire afternoon, as I sat reading and drinking my iced latte, I couldn't shake Caterina's condescending gaze, which seemed to confirm everything I'd been trying for years not to believe about myself: That I wasn't sexy. That the man who was supposed to love me wasn't attracted to me. That he had more fun fucking his own hand than touching me.

I didn't blame Kyle for my shortcomings. Sure, I was in fantastic shape at the time from constant marathon training and the strict diet he had us both on. But I didn't have The

Siren's tiny waist or thigh gap, so obviously there was room for improvement. That was the day I decided to cut carbs. Kyle was thrilled. But from that afternoon forward, I couldn't see a picture of Caterina Hart without feeling inadequate and wildly jealous. It's juvenile and pathetic, but I've hated her ever since.

Love her or hate her, there's no denying she's stunning, with her espresso-colored hair, and her hazel eyes popping against tanned skin. As she sits, exuding confidence and sensuality from every pore, my insecurities come roaring back, tenfold. I lament the days when I could fit into sample sizes, even if Kyle still didn't find me beautiful.

I know that slim physique wasn't meant for me. If it were, I wouldn't have had to chase it by running fifty miles a week and barely eating. And I know that, while my natural curves aren't Kyle's cup of tea, my body drives some men wild. Including Holden McBride.

I'm also keenly aware that what matters most is that *I* love my figure. And I'm working on it. But it's been a long and bumpy road. The first thing I did after Kyle and I broke up was go to the bodega on our block and buy everything he wouldn't allow in our home. Chips, candy bars, ice cream, cookies. I binge-ate most of it that night, then had a panic attack and forced myself to run ten miles. The next day, I went to The Strand and bought every self-help book I could find on disordered eating and body dysmorphia.

I've made my way through nearly all of them in the past two years and gained a lot of insight. I also met with a nutritionist who helped me make an eating plan, since Kyle's rigid rules fucked with my brain. I stopped running, which I frankly hated, and now I opt for power yoga classes with Jenna, instead.

I eat sweets in moderation, although not without residual guilt and shame.

I don't know why I never went to therapy. For all the times I begged Jenna to seek support after her first love died, you'd think I'd have made myself an appointment in a heartbeat. But no. My reluctance is probably the reason Jenna put off seeing a therapist for so long, too. Our family dynamic was so messy growing up, we became used to taking care of ourselves. To this day, I don't trust others with my feelings.

Plus, my issues aren't *that* bad...are they? For the most part, I'm fine, except for situations where I'm triggered.

Like right now.

Nearly everyone at the table is gaping at Caterina. Wes, of course, is smug as can be, eyeing his gorgeous girlfriend. I guess it's no surprise he's dating a supermodel. He's undeniably attractive, although the way he treats Holden is so ugly, I can barely see past it. Otherwise, Wes looks a lot like his brother, apart from the extra muscle and slightly darker hair.

Next to them, Margot McBride beams at the stunning couple with pride, while her husband gives Caterina a once-over that makes my skin crawl. His octogenarian uncle Alistair gazes at the model with a nostalgic smile, as if thinking, *I remember the days when I could bag a hottie like that.* Then there's Dan Jimenez, who's staring at her, slack-jawed, while Zoe's wide-eyed wonder borders on reverence. On her left is Abby, who looks stunned. I don't know how long Wes has been dating Caterina, but I guess it's news to his sister.

Finally, there's Holden, whose attention isn't on his brother's girlfriend, but on Wes. Holden's glaring at him with a clenched jaw, still upset over this morning's altercation, I assume. I have no idea what Wes said to make his brother so angry, but I didn't want to ask. Once Holden calmed down, I figured it was best he stayed that way, considering we have to endure a hellishly long day with his family.

The McBrides are all business as the terms of the competition for Grandma Evelyn's money are clarified. They don't even bat an eye when the amount of the bequest is announced—a whopping two hundred million dollars. As for me, I almost gasped, but managed to catch myself in time. Ultimately, Alistair, Dan, and Zoe will decide which of the siblings' proposals will best "serve the family's interests" (I believe that's code for, "make them richer") and "uphold the family legacy" (in other words, "make them look good").

In an interesting turn of events, Abby announces that she's decided to pull out of the race, because the time commitment would limit how involved she can be with Maisie and Matt's extracurricular activities. When Holden hears this, he looks down and half-smiles. I doubt Margot McBride made much of an effort to attend his Little League games, and I think he's touched by Abby's dedication. It's sweet. But my heart aches for him, again, wishing he had a better relationship with his sister, especially considering what a loving uncle he is.

Wes is smiling, too, but his fist pump tells me it's only because he likes his odds of winning, with Abby out of the running. Now it's down to the McBride brothers, who will go head-to-head starting this afternoon. But first, per Margot's itinerary, we take a break for swimming and sunbathing at the main house's infinity pool.

I knew this was on today's agenda, so I came prepared. Trying on swimsuits was far and away the most uncomfortable part of my pre-Maui shopping spree with Jenna. Eventually, I found one that I felt moderately comfortable in: a hybrid between a bikini and a one-piece, with sexy cutouts at the waist but, more importantly, a slimming panel of fabric covering my belly. While Jenna insisted I looked like a bombshell, I also bought a sarong to layer over it, missing the days when my thighs were lean and muscular from running.

I was already nervous this morning as it was, knowing I'd be in swimwear in front of Holden and his family. What I did *not* expect was that I'd be wearing a swimsuit anywhere in the same fucking zip code as Victoria's Secret Angel, Caterina Hart.

The thought sends me into a near panic. Cold sweat breaks out on my skin.

Holden takes my hand as we walk to the pool house to change. "You okay, baby?"

That's when I realize my shoulders are up to my ears, and I've been grinding my teeth. "I'm just a little warm," I lie, fanning my face for effect.

"I'll grab you a bottle of water," he says, looking concerned.

"Thank you." My heart swells at his thoughtfulness. He's not bending over backward, by any means, but when you're used to taking care of yourself, the smallest gesture feels grand. When I look up at him and smile, his face softens, but not entirely. I know today's not easy for him.

"How are *you* feeling?" I ask.

He runs his fingers through his hair, exhaling. "I'm...I don't know. All I want is to be alone with you."

There's nothing playful or flirtatious about the way he says it. There's longing in his eyes, just like when we kissed for an hour this morning. It was tender, sweet, passionate. Romantic.

It was real.

Wasn't it? I'm not imagining this connection between us, am I?

"I feel the same way," I tell him. It's the absolute truth. I want to go back to the happy bubble of our bungalow and forget anyone else exists. Especially Caterina Hart.

"Tonight," he says with a wink that gives me butterflies. We've just entered the pool house, which may as well be a luxury spa for how elegant and spacious it is. Sunrays stream in through a skylight overhead, and the scent of plumeria wafts through the space, while tranquil music plays over speakers. The women's changing area is to our right, while the men's is down the hall. Holden kisses me before heading that way.

I'm still standing in the same spot when my phone vibrates. I hope it's Jenna or my mom. Last night, after Holden left, I was upset and had trouble falling asleep, so I called them, but neither answered. It was 7:00 a.m. in Chicago, which is early for Jenna, but my mom should've been awake, so I left her a message. Maybe she'd have called right back if I'd told her the truth:

That I think I'm falling for Holden.

That I've never felt this way about a man before.

That I'm terrified he'll hurt me.

Instead, I only said that I was having a great time, but I missed her and wanted to say hi.

Eventually, I fell asleep, and when I woke up this morning, I had texts from both my mom and sister, saying almost the exact same thing: they missed me too, didn't want to wake me, and would call later. I have to say, it was strange...like they'd coordinated their responses.

Am I being paranoid? Probably. But the closeness I've cultivated with my mom and sister over the past year is so precious to me, sometimes I'm terrified I'll lose it. It doesn't help that Jenna's the spitting image of our mom, while I look like Dad. Sometimes I worry that my sister and mother have a closer bond because they're so similar, although they've never done anything to give my fear any credence.

I know that spending a week in Maui can't break what we have, but it's still hard being so far away from them. I've dreamed of having a supportive family like this my entire life.

My dad, of course, is a lost cause. I never hear from him unless I call him first. I don't know why I bother maintaining our relationship, only to be disappointed time and time again. Jenna gave up on our father years ago. But she has even more reasons to hate him than I do. He never supported her artistic talent and even forbade her from painting after her dyslexia diagnosis, insisting she focus her attention on reading and writing. Jenna worked her ass off to get into one of the top architecture programs in the country, and Dad still wasn't impressed. Meanwhile, Jenna was miserable. Finally, she found the courage to pursue her passion and switch careers. Needless to say, our father has never congratulated her on her success as a painter.

By the time I find my phone at the very bottom of my tote, I miss the call. But when I glance at the screen, I see that it was from Sam. Right away, she sends me a text.

SAM

Um, excuse me…this kiss is so hot, I had to take a cold shower! Get it, girl!!

Below her message is a link, which I click with shaky fingers.

Every time I go viral, I'm filled with dread, wondering what fresh hell awaits me in the comments section. While most of the reactions to my relationship with Holden have been positive, I still worry about the trolls who think I'm only dating him to save my career.

If they only knew how much my heart aches at the thought of parting ways with him when this is over. If they only knew how ambivalent I feel about him connecting me with Lola Piper after all is said and done. Of course I'd love the opportunity to work with her. I just don't want it to be a parting gift Holden gives me when his image is restored and the novelty of... whatever's going on between us, wears off.

But when I press play to watch the video of Holden kissing me at the luau last night, my worries subside—at least for now. There's nothing fake about this lip-lock. The way he's looking at me with Edison Ford-like yearning is undeniable.

I scroll down to the comments, and a wave of giddiness washes over me.

emilyinchicago
They're so cute together!
aurea24starlingsfan
Love them! Hope he comes back to the Starlings next season.
amygetsliterary
So happy for you, Christy. You deserve this after getting conned by Penelope Dwyer.

I smile knowing that, whatever happens between me and Holden, at least I'm helping him get his career back on track. He deserves it. And the fact that my reputation seems to be holding up in the wake of Penelope's deceit is the icing on the cake.

I'm about to throw my phone in my tote when someone's screenname in the comments section catches my eye. The moniker jumps out at me for two reasons. First, because it reminds me of Kyle. And second, because this person posted several comments, all in a row.

manhattanmarathonman
Thought he only dated models. Guess not.
manhattanmarathonman
Maybe he lost a bet.
manhattanmarathonman
I guess that streaking incident really ruined his rep. What a serious downgrade from his last girlfriend.

There's more, but I have to stop, or I might throw up. A sob escapes me.

At the same time, a door creaks open down the hall, and I'm sure it's Holden. I don't want him to see me like this. Blurry-eyed, I run into the women's changing room, praying no one else is in there. Holden and I were the last to leave the conference room because he had messages from his agent he needed to respond to, so I'm hoping everyone's already at the pool.

I run into a dressing room, tears streaming down my face, heart hammering. My first thought is that Kyle himself wrote those nasty comments. But why would he be so cruel? What did I ever do to him, besides give him the benefit of the doubt, over and over again? Yes, I should have broken up with him sooner, but *he* broke my fucking self-esteem. If he was so goddamn miserable, why the fuck didn't he do us both a favor and just leave?

My second thought is that I have to put on a bathing suit right now, when I'm feeling worse than ever about myself. And that Holden will take one look at Caterina in whatever barely-there bikini she's wearing, and he'll wonder why he was ever attracted to me in the first place.

Despite the fact that I'm a nervous wreck, I know I can't stay in this changing room forever. I send Holden a quick text telling him I got delayed because Sam called, and I'll meet him at the pool in a few minutes. Then I slip off my flattering midi dress and wiggle into my swimwear, which somehow feels much more constraining than when I first tried it on. I top it off with the sarong, of course. At least, as a redhead, I can blame my fair skin for being more covered up than anyone else.

When I come out of the dressing room, I'm surprised to see Holden's sister Abby seated at the built in vanity in the corner of the room. She's putting on mascara and makes eye contact with my reflection in the mirror.

Abby looks like what I imagine her mother did, before all the cosmetic enhancements and plastic surgery. Nothing about her is over the top. Her golden-brown hair looks natural, compared to Margot McBride's bleached blonde. She's fresh-faced and glowing, and the laugh lines around her mouth and eyes tell me she's not afraid to be her age. Her linen set is fashionable, but doesn't scream wealth. And the concern in her eyes reminds me of the tender way Holden looks at me.

"Hey," she says. "Is everything okay? I thought I heard sniffling."

That's a gracious description, considering I was sobbing. "I'll be fine," I say, although I'm not sure I believe it. "I just made the mistake of reading comments some troll made about me online."

"People suck." Abby caps her mascara and picks up a tube of brow gel. "Why do you think I'm touching up my makeup to go to the pool? Because if my cousin Zoe posts a photo of us on social media, and I look like shit, I'll never hear the end of it."

My frown is sympathetic. "That's a lot of pressure."

"God knows I don't handle it well." She finishes applying the brow gel and sets the tube back down. "And, on that note, I'm sorry I didn't introduce myself yesterday. I get triggered at family gatherings, and my solution is to ignore everybody." She shrugs. "Anyway, I'm Abby."

Smiling, I meet her outstretched hand. "Christy."

She blots the color on her mouth. "You and Holden seem happy."

"We are," I say, before I have time to overthink my response.

Abby combs her hair. "I've never seen him so affectionate. Holden's not usually one for PDA. If he's kissing you like that in front of a crowd at a luau, he must be smitten."

"Well, the feeling's mutual," I admit.

"Good." Her smile is warm, but wistful. It's not the smile of a woman who dislikes her brother, I'll tell you that. She looks down at her eyeshadow palette. "How's Holden doing? You know...since our grandmother died?"

I wince. "It's been tough on him. But I think spending time with Maisie and Matt is helping. He loves them so much."

I hope I'm not overstepping. But if there's something I can do to mend Holden and Abby's relationship, shouldn't I? Clearly they're both longing to be closer. Just like I used to long to be closer to Jenna.

"I know he does." She heaves a sigh, her eyes glassy. "I feel awful. Holden was so close with Grandma Evelyn, and when I heard he'd streaked across Soldier Field, I knew he had to be taking her death really hard. I wanted to reach out, but—"

Her cell rings on the vanity table.

"Excuse me." When she sits up straighter, it's almost as if she's trying to shake off the heaviness in her heart. Then she grabs her phone and examines the screen. "I'm so sorry, I have to take this."

I nod. "Of course."

She waves goodbye, and I leave the changing room. When I step into the hall, I'm surprised to see Holden waiting for me. But also relieved. Regardless of how angsty I'm feeling, his presence comforts me.

"Hi," I say, smiling as he wraps his arms around my waist. "Didn't you see my text? I didn't mean to make you wait for me."

"I wanted to make sure you were okay." He tilts my chin up, his eyes searching mine. "Were you crying, Red?"

I bite my lip. "Just a little."

"Tell me what's wrong." The worry on his face tugs at my heart. So does the tender way he's stroking my back. I remember Abby's words: *I've never seen him so affectionate.*

I want to be honest with him. But if I tell him I'm upset because some troll made ugly comments about me online, won't he read them?

What a serious downgrade from his last girlfriend.

And when he does, well...that'll be the end of us. Won't it? Try as I might, I can't shake the fear that Holden's infatuation with me won't last. That sooner or later, he'll come to his senses and remember he can do better. It's bad enough that the sexiest woman on the planet is dating his brother. Won't Holden feel like he's falling short? And why would I point him to *manhattanmarathonman*'s comments? So I can further tip the scales against me?

No thanks.

"I'm fine, I promise. I just got a little emotional while the lawyer was reading your grandma's will, that's all. It reminded me of when my own grandmother passed away."

It's true, my maternal grandma is no longer with us. Never mind the fact that she died before I was born.

"I'm so sorry," Holden says, his brows knitting together. "I didn't even think about how this might affect you."

Great. Now he feels terrible for no reason, and I feel terrible for lying. "I'll be fine," I insist. "She passed away a long time ago."

"Well, let me know if you need anything." He kisses me, then takes my hand as we head outside to the pool. "And, by the way, you look hot as fuck."

I wonder if he'll still feel that way after he sees me next to Caterina Hart.

When we make it to the pool, I search for the supermodel, who's sunbathing on a lounge chair next to her boyfriend. As it turns out, she's wearing a fairly modest bikini...at least in comparison to what she's typically photographed in. She still looks impossibly perfect. Holden directs us to the far opposite side of the pool from them, which is understandable, given his disagreement with Wes this morning. It's also fine by me. The farther I am from Caterina, the harder it'll be for anyone to compare our very different bodies.

Next to my lounge chair, on a side table, there's a chilled bottle of water waiting for me, along with a beautiful platter of light bites—smoked salmon tartines, caprese skewers, and the like—which Holden ordered in case I needed a mid-morning pick-me-up. It all looks delicious, but I'm afraid it will bloat me, and I'll be even more uncomfortable in my bathing suit. Maybe I'll wait until just before we leave the pool to indulge.

After we sit, Maisie and Matt appear with a young woman I assume is their babysitter. Abby still hasn't emerged, and when the kids beg Holden to swim with them, I assure him he can go without me, since I have work to catch up on. The truth is, I don't want to take off my sarong to get in the water. But reading has always been my therapy, and I could use a good novel to immerse myself in right now. Anything to clear my mind of *manhattanmarathonman*'s wretched comments.

Twenty minutes later, I'm three chapters into a psychological thriller that already has my heart pumping, when the lounge chair next to me squeaks. I look to my right, expecting to see Holden, but to my surprise, it's The Siren.

"You must be Christy," she says, holding out her hand. "Caterina."

"Nice to meet you." Wow. She's even more striking up close. Legs for days. Perky breasts. Flawless skin. Not to mention, her stomach is toned and flat. She looks airbrushed. I try to block out the memory of my ex pleasuring himself while ogling her insanely hot body.

"I like that shade of red on you," she says, pointing to my mouth.

"Oh, thank you." I grin, pleased that my signature lipstick is supermodel-approved. I wonder if she makes a habit of complimenting women she meets, to put them at ease. If so, it's not a bad strategy.

"So, how long have you been dating Holden?" she asks.

My gut clenches. When I went rogue yesterday and told his

parents we'd been seeing each other in secret for a while, I didn't have a particular timeframe in mind. And Holden and I never discussed it afterward. "About six months," I say, hoping I sound believable.

But shit... What if she asked Holden first, and she's testing me? What if she doesn't believe we're dating, because Holden's banged all of her hot model friends, and she thinks there's no chance in hell I'm his type?

"Cool." Her lip quirks up in a half-smile. "You know, I saw that video of you telling him off at the bar. You're a badass."

My cheeks flush, a bit flattered by Caterina's praise, despite myself. "Hardly. But thanks. How about you and Wes? Have you been dating awhile?"

She shakes her head. "Only two and a half weeks, or so. But the chemistry's intense. We can't keep our hands off each other."

"That's great," I tell her, although I'm not sure it is, given that Wes is such an arrogant fucking prick.

When Caterina doesn't respond, I follow her gaze to the pool. Right there in the center, amid Maisie and Matt's squeals and splashes, is Holden, frozen and looking in this direction.

Wait a minute... Is he staring at Caterina? It's hard to tell, because he's wearing sunglasses.

"I'd better get back to Wes," she says. But when she stands, she falters and sits back down, gripping the edge of her chair.

I gasp. "Are you alright?" She's lucky she didn't wipe out on the concrete and hit her head.

She takes a deep breath and nods. "Just lightheaded. I've been in the air for the last twenty-four hours, traveling from London, and my circadian rhythm is off. Plus, I'm intermittent fasting…my body doesn't know what time it is…and I can't remember the last time I ate."

I reach for the tray of food to the other side of me. "Here, have one of these."

When she looks at the sumptuous appetizers, her nose crinkles. "Thank you, but I can't eat that. I'm doing a photoshoot on Monday, and the dairy will go straight to my gut." Her eyes flash back to Holden, who's getting out of the pool and headed in this direction. "I'm going to go lie down. It was nice to meet you, Christy."

This time, she jets off without incident, right as Holden sits next to me. "Everything okay?" His tone is stern, and I'm not sure I understand why.

"Caterina felt lightheaded, so she's going to lie down," I explain. "Maybe you should send Wes to check on her."

His jaw clenches. "I will."

"By the way, she asked me how long we've been dating," I add. "I told her six months."

A wave of something resembling panic washes over Holden's face. He must be thinking what I'm thinking: Caterina's on to us.

"Did she say anything else? About our relationship?"

"No." I clear my throat. "Why? Do you think she's suspicious?"

Holden shakes his head. "No, baby. Of course not. I just… I'm not sure what her intentions are with my brother, that's all. Something seems off, and I don't trust her."

As he turns to watch her walk away, my heart's still racing, and I don't know why. Is it the thriller I was reading? The fact that Caterina appeared out of nowhere to talk to me, then nearly passed out?

Or is it the way Holden can't tear his eyes off her?

When she disappears from sight, he turns back to me, then nods toward the untouched platter of appetizers. "You didn't eat. Do you want me to get you something else?"

Should I tell him that the moment Caterina looked at the tantalizing little bites with disgust, I vowed not to touch them either? That my old eating issues came rushing back? That he shouldn't be surprised if I give up carbs the rest of this trip?

"No, thanks. I'm not hungry," I lie.

A mouthwatering lunch of bánh mi sandwiches and Vietnamese noodles is served on the lanai. With a heavy heart, I turn it down in favor of a side salad, echoing Caterina's request. Luckily, she seems to have recovered from her lightheadedness. She and Wes are seated across from Margot and Julian, and the two couples are chatting like old friends.

Once again, Holden picks seats as far away from them as possible. At one point, he and his brother make eye contact, and Wes flashes Holden a taunting smile. I fear it's only a matter of time before they come to blows. If I hadn't intervened this morning, they certainly would have.

Holden turns his chair to avoid his brother's gaze, but scowls through most of lunch, until his phone chimes. When he looks at the screen, a weight lifts off him, and he smiles.

"Dex just messaged me," he says. "He read my proposal, and he's on board. If I win the competition, my sports program will be an official offshoot of the Dramatic Hearts Academy. We'll call it Racing Hearts."

"That's incredible news!" I lean in to give him a kiss. "And the timing couldn't be more perfect."

He heaves a sigh. "Tell me about it. Dex doesn't even know that the showdown starts today. I was hoping I'd get his approval before my presentation, because I know the board will see Dex Oliver's attachment to the project as an asset. But I didn't want to rush him for an answer, so I decided not to tell him about the time crunch. I never expected to hear back from him this soon."

"It's like the stars aligned," I say. Holden smiles again and kisses me.

After lunch, we head back to the conference room to kick off the competition for Grandma Evelyn's money. The McBride brothers draw straws because they both want to go first, which I find interesting. Whoever loses by drawing the shorter straw will go tomorrow, which seems like an advantage to me, since they'll see the first presentation and can tweak theirs tonight if necessary. But the brothers are so eager to crush each other, I guess they don't see it that way. In any event, Holden wins.

"Four years ago, shortly after my grandfather died, Grandma Evelyn traveled to Chicago by herself to watch me pitch Game Seven of the World Series," Holden begins, walking around the room with a confident gleam in his eye. He may not be used to presenting to a board, but he's done his fair share of interviews and public speaking as both a Starling and a McBride. He's calm and poised. And so fucking handsome.

I can hardly take my gaze off him, but I do notice Wes roll his eyes and sneer at the mention of the World Series. His inferiority complex is on full display. He'll never be the athlete Holden is, so he takes jabs at his brother's intelligence to make himself feel better. Maybe I was wrong about Holden, and Wes is the manchild. A middle school bully with an MBA.

"She didn't tell me she was coming to the game," Holden goes on about his grandmother. "She just showed up at my doorstep with a suitcase. Of course, I was thrilled to see her. I was *always* thrilled to see her." Standing at the head of the table, he looks down at his shoes and swallows. "But she was eighty-eight years old, and I worried about her flying alone.

"When I asked her why she'd made the trip, she told me she needed baseball because she was angry. She was angry at Grandpa, because they were supposed to surprise me together, and he died before he could hold up his end of the bargain." Holden lets out a wistful laugh, his gaze far away. "She said if she were younger, she would've taken that anger to a baseball field. It's what she did as a kid, when she was mad at her parents for getting a divorce. But she was too old for that now. So she was going to live vicariously through me."

Holden sighs. "I would've done anything to put a smile on that woman's face. She's the reason I am who I am."

Wes barely hides a smirk, but everyone else in the room is invested in Holden's story. Even his parents are grinning and, if I'm not mistaken, they look a bit surprised. It's hard to tell with Margot, because of all the Botox. But Julian's got an eyebrow raised and a half-smile that makes me think he had no idea how charming his son is. I'm sure, like any narcissist, he'll happily take credit for it, though.

"I pitched a complete game that day," Holden continues. "And a shutout, too. I didn't allow a single run in nine innings, and it was all for Evelyn McBride. Now, I know what you're going to say. No one can just *decide* they're going to pitch a complete game." He runs a hand though his hair. "But the truth is, every time I'm on the mound, I decide I'm going to pitch a complete game. That's how competitive I am. Most of the time, it doesn't happen. But that day, it did."

He half-smiles. "Maybe Grandpa had something to do with it. He couldn't take his beloved wife to see me pitch, so he helped me clinch a win. I don't know. I was exhausted, mentally and physically, but I pushed through because I wanted to look into the stands when I got the World Series-winning strike and see Grandma's face light up with that signature grin."

He chuckles, his eyes glistening. "And boy, did she deliver. I'd always known that baseball helped me manage my own feelings, but to see it work for someone else? Someone I love? That was powerful. That's the day I got the idea for Racing Hearts. A safe space for young people to explore team sports as an emotional outlet."

Well, if I wasn't already smitten with Holden McBride, he just sealed the deal.

After outlining his vision for the program, Holden plays a video he put together in support of Racing Hearts, featuring interviews with a handful of his Starlings teammates—a few of whom had difficult childhoods and credit baseball for turning their lives around. It's hard not to be moved by Holden's presentation, and when he's done, the board members are nodding while taking enthusiastic notes, which seems like a good sign.

On our way out of the conference room, I cast a lustful gaze at the tiered tray of tea scones and petit fours no one has touched, and I can't help but wonder why Margot orders these decadent treats when no one eats them. Maybe she's doing it to torture me. I wouldn't put it past her.

When we're back in the bungalow, Holden's so exhausted

from the stress of the day that he collapses onto the bed, taking me with him.

"I'm so proud of you," I say as he holds me in his arms, stroking my hair. "You nailed that presentation."

"Thanks, baby." He sighs. "I guess we'll see what Wes has up his sleeve tomorrow."

In response, my stomach growls.

"You must be starving," he says. "You barely ate lunch. Are you sure you're feeling okay?"

I feel like bursting into tears and devouring a burger, but I don't tell him that. "I'm fine. I think I may have overindulged the past couple of days, so I'm trying to eat lighter, that's all."

He surveys my face, and I know he can see through my bullshit. "Let me order you something. Anything you want."

"A salad with grilled chicken sounds good," I say with a shrug.

"That's it?" He sighs. "Can I ask them to put avocado on it, at least? Maybe walnuts for extra protein?"

I huff a laugh. "Sure."

"Alright. I'm going to pick it up from the kitchen. It'll be faster than waiting for them to bring it here. I'll be back soon." He kisses my forehead.

"Thank you."

After he's gone, I check my email and see a message from Haley Quinlan. My heart hammers as I click on it.

Christy, thank you so much for your kind words about Edison's Love. *I want you to know that this decision didn't come easily, but I've chosen to sign with another agent. I really appreciate—*

I can't read anymore because of the tears in my eyes. I'd be willing to bet anything that she signed with my nemesis, Colin

Finch. Could this day get any fucking worse? My entire *being* is unraveling. My self-esteem? In the tank. The progress I've made with my disordered eating? Gone. My career that I worked so hard for? Decimated.

Sobbing, I call Jenna. I really need to hear her voice right now. By some miracle, she picks up.

"Christy, what's wrong?" she asks when she hears me crying.

I tell her about Haley Quinlan, but nothing else.

"I'm so sorry, babe," she says. "It's her loss—and I mean that. I know this is a tough time for you, but your career will recover. The Internet is obsessed with you and Holden. Pretty soon no one will remember you ever represented Penelope."

"I hope so." My lip quivers.

"Is everything okay, otherwise?"

"Yeah. I just miss you and Mom." I sniffle. "Maybe I'm crazy, but...it kinda feels like you're avoiding me."

Jenna's silent.

My breath hitches. "Oh my god... *Are* you avoiding me?"

"Christy, I, um...I don't know what to say."

"How can you not know what to say?" My head is spinning, and my empty stomach feels sick. "Either you're avoiding me, or you're not."

My sister's so quiet, I barely hear her. "I think it's better if we talk in person when you get back."

A sob almost chokes me. "No, Jenna. If you have something to tell me, do it now. Otherwise I'm going to assume the worst, and I can't deal with the added stress right now."

It takes several seconds for her to respond. "Mom's going to kill me, but...I don't want to keep secrets from you," she begins with a sigh. "Look, this came as a shock to me, and I know it will to you, too. But it doesn't change anything about our relationship and how much I love you, okay?"

"What on Earth are you talking about?" I plead.

"Remember that picture I found in Mom's closet years ago? She was standing next to this blond guy we thought might have been an old boyfriend? He had his arm around her, and they seemed so happy."

"Yeah..." I say, wheels turning.

"Well, his name is Tim Shaker. He was her high school sweetheart. They reconnected recently, and they still have feelings for each other. He's a painter, Christy."

My jaw drops.

Jenna takes a ragged breath. "It turns out he's my biological father. The paternity results came back yesterday."

No, no, no, no, no.

"Christy? Are you there?"

I knew Jenna was about to drop a bomb on me, but I never once imagined this. I thought she might tell me that our mom was sick. Or that Grandma Andersen passed away, not that we're that close. I never once expected she'd tell me we have different dads.

It's like the Universe is giving me the finger. My whole goddamn world is toppling over, one piece at a time, like dominoes.

"Christy, I wanted to tell you earlier. The timing was just so awful. Mom told me she suspected Tim was my dad the same day you found out about Penelope Dwyer. And I thought, why stress you out until after we take the paternity test?"

I'm speechless.

"Christy? Christy, please...say something."

I can see it clear as day: Jenna, and our mom, and Tim

Fucking Shaker will be the happy family unit I always longed for. And I'll be left with Michael Andersen, who doesn't give a shit about me.

"I have to go," I say, my tone hurried. "Holden will be back any minute, and I need to pull myself together. I'll call you later."

But I won't call her later, I know that much.

And instead of pulling myself together, I hang up the phone and scream.

CHAPTER 17

I'm on the stone path that curves through the bungalow's private garden when I hear Christy scream.

Panic floods me, and I bolt through the front door, prepared to do whatever the fuck it takes to protect her. I'll rip a man to shreds with my bare hands, if need be.

But I find Christy sitting on our bed cross-legged, with red-rimmed eyes and a look of sheer embarrassment on her face. That's when I begin to put the pieces together.

She's pissed about something. And that roar I heard was Christy Hulking out. Now she's ashamed.

Despite sprinting to her side in a panic, I'm still holding the to-go bag with the salads I picked up from the kitchen. I place it on the nightstand before sitting next to her. "Talk to me, Red."

"I didn't mean to scare you. I'm sorry," she says as a tear rolls down her face. "If I'd known you were outside, I—"

"What? You would've kept it bottled up inside, like you always do? Because your dad and Kyle couldn't handle it?" I wipe her cheek with my thumb. "I'm not like them, baby. I ran in here because I thought someone was hurting you and I might have to kill them. *That's* why I panicked. But your emotions don't scare me one bit. Now, talk."

My words make her lip quiver with the hint of a smile. But it's fleeting. Soon, her face scrunches, and she buries it in the crook of my neck. I inch closer and wrap my arms around her as she sobs.

"After you left, I checked my email..." she squeaks out, "and I had a message from Haley Quinlan saying she decided to go with another agent."

I squeeze her tighter. "Oh, baby, I'm so sorry."

"And then, I..."

I feel her shaking her head back and forth against my shoulder, like she's trying to clear her mind of a disturbing thought. I stroke her back, trying to calm her down. The way she calmed me earlier, when I was upset. "Tell me, Christy."

She burrows even deeper into me, intent on hiding her tears. I'm fine with that, as long as she keeps talking. I need her to know she's safe with me. And when I say "need," I mean it. The urge is primal, driving me to take care of her in a way I've never taken care of anyone in my life. I don't understand it— but I don't question it, because of how natural it feels. Like my fucked-up shoulder was made for her to cry on.

"I called Jenna, because I thought hearing her voice would make me feel better, but she sounded so weird on the phone. So, I kept prodding, and eventually she told me." She draws in a breath. "My mom reconnected with an ex-boyfriend recently, and it turns out he's Jenna's biological father."

She lets out this wail that tears through my heart. But she grips the bedsheet at the same time, squeezing so hard her knuckles turn white.

"You're angry," I tell her.

She relaxes her hand. "I'm not. I'm sad."

I take her fingers in mine and massage them. "You're both. I know anger when I see it."

She pulls away now, but her eyes meet mine, still teary. "I'm not ready to talk about it yet."

I nod, glancing at the bag of food on the nightstand. "Good call. We'll eat first. I got myself a salad, too. Then we're going outside so you can show me how far you can hit when you're pissed off."

She slumps back onto the pillows. "I'm too tired to play baseball."

"That's because you've barely eaten today." I grab one to-go box out of the bag. It's packaged so artfully, it looks like a present. I unwrap the twine from the recycled cardboard box, freeing decorative rosemary sprigs along with the flatware, which is folded in a linen napkin with an embroidered orchid on it.

"I think I lost my appetite again. Maybe I'm coming down with something." Christy clears her throat, then her eyes dart away from mine, which tells me everything I need to know.

"Cut the bullshit, baby." I take her hand again, hoping she'll turn her gaze back to me. She does, although reluctantly. "Do you wanna know what makes me an effective pitcher?"

Her pretty brown eyes are curious as she nods.

"I'm good at reading body language. Even the smallest shift in stance tells me what a batter's thinking." She looks interested, so I go on. "If they're leaning back, they're expecting a fastball. If they're crowding the plate, they're looking for an inside pitch. I figure out what they're expecting and switch things up to throw them off their game."

As Christy listens, excitement washes over her face, which makes me smile.

"All of that to say, Red…you're a piss-poor liar with half a dozen tells, and I know you're hungry. So, let's eat."

"What? I thought I only had one tell," she pouts.

"Sorry to burst your bubble." I load up her fork with chicken, greens, avocado, nuts, and seeds for a perfect bite, then hold it to her lips. The corners of her mouth turn up as she opens it for me.

I'll feed her the whole damn thing if she wants me to, I'm just relieved she's eating. Now, as for why she's been acting weird about food all day, I suspect it has something to do with the supermodel my brother invited here to taunt me. The one who, with a few choice words, could sabotage my relationship with Christy.

Yes, I know we're not technically a couple. Just this morning, Christy said I don't owe her anything—although I can't say I agree. That's why I want to be honest with her about my history with Cat. Or I *did* want to be honest, until Christy felt the need to starve herself.

Thankfully, our chef makes a mean salad, and after the first few bites, Christy forgets she's "not hungry." She grabs the fork from my hand and continues eating on her own, spearing every last leaf until the container's clean. When she assures me she's full and doesn't want more, I eat the other salad.

Afterward, we change into workout gear. Our baseball equipment's still in the Range Rover from when we played with the kids yesterday, so we grab the car from the main house and head to the same field. I like it because it's typically only used by a Little League team on weekends and is otherwise available. Tonight, Christy and I have the diamond to ourselves.

I take my place on the mound as she settles into her batting stance at home plate. We both have on the Starlings hats I got us from the fitness center yesterday, and I can't help but enjoy the fact that she's wearing my name—even if it is just scrawled on the brim of her cap. I have to stop myself from picturing how gorgeous she'd look in only my jersey and nothing else.

"Alright, Red. Here's the plan," I say, focusing on the task at hand. "You're going to yell out something that pisses you off, and then I'll pitch to you. You smack the hell out of the ball, and we keep going until everything's off your chest. Sound good?"

She bites her lip. "Do I really have to yell?"

Her cheeks are flushed with embarrassment, and I know why. "Look, I get that you're afraid of losing control when you're angry. Afraid of scaring people away."

Her gaze falls to her shoes.

"But I've already seen you Hulk out, and I'm still here," I go on. "There's nothing shameful about your anger, Christy. It's normal. You only *think* it's not because you were raised in a house where you weren't allowed to be mad."

She nods, her eyes glistening. When she speaks, her voice is thin. "Thank you, Holden. I really needed to hear that."

I wink at her.

"Okay, let's do this." She lets out a sigh and shakes off her tears. Looking down at the dirt, she begins. "I'm pissed at my dad for being a self-absorbed piece of shit who never calls me."

Her words are loud enough for me to hear, but she's holding back. When she meets my gaze, I throw her a slow, straight fastball, like the ones she hit yesterday. But she's anxious. I can tell by the death grip she has on the bat. As I suspect, she swings too early and misses.

"Fuck!" she yells.

I nod. "That's right, baby. Be mad. Now, take it out on the ball. But first, you're going to want to loosen those fingers just a bit. Try relaxing your shoulders, too."

Christy takes my direction, and something clicks. She looks more confident this time, and her words are louder. "I'm pissed that my mom and Jenna have been keeping this huge secret from me."

I toss her the same pitch, and this time she smashes it, driving the ball into left field. "That was fucking beautiful," I say when it drops just inside the foul line. I turn back to see her eyes lit up with fiery determination, and I smile. "Let's see what else you've got."

Now there's a little more bite to her tone. "I'm pissed that I've spent my whole life wondering why Jenna's so much prettier than I am, and now I have my answer."

"No," I say, shaking my head. My heart hurts that she believes that. "Baby, you and Jenna are different, but that doesn't mean—"

"I don't need you to counsel me, McBride. Just throw the goddamn ball." She digs her back heel into the dirt.

I choke on a laugh. "Yes, ma'am."

"And no more kid tosses. I'm not Maisie or Matt, I can handle a real fastball," she adds, her brows knit together.

Little does she know, I'm trying to protect my goddamn shoulder, especially since I pitched to her and the kids yesterday. Still, I should be able to throw a little harder and not cause further damage. I hope.

I challenge her with a slightly faster pitch I think she can handle, and she belts it over my head. It's a beautiful line drive to center, and her next several hits are homers as well.

As she continues batting, her shouts get louder:

"I'm pissed that the career I've spent *years* building can collapse in the blink of an eye."

"I'm pissed at the trolls in the comments sections who don't give a shit that they're offending real fucking people with real fucking feelings!"

"I'm pissed at Kyle Fucking Walton for taking me for granted."

"And I'm pissed at myself for letting a man treat me like garbage for eight miserable years...and not having the courage to leave until I caught him *cheating*."

This time she drops the bat and collapses onto her knees. I drop my glove and the ball in my hand, then run over to crouch beside her. When she looks at me, her face is flushed and her eyes are glassy.

"I never told anyone the truth about why I broke up with Kyle," she says. "Not, Jenna, or my mom, or Sam. I was too embarrassed. And so mad at myself. All the signs were there... Suddenly, he was staying out late all the time. When I asked where he'd been, he'd avoid my gaze. He said he was just getting to know the new crop of residents. And he never wanted me to join them. He insisted they'd bore me to tears with their shop talk." She sniffles.

"One evening, I was out with a few friends from work, and I ran into Kyle and his colleagues at a wine bar in the East Village. The second I saw the woman sitting next to him, I was filled with dread. She was exactly his type. Dark hair. Olive skin. Tall and willowy. She was the opposite of me in every way. I should have confronted him that night, but I ignored it."

"Why?" My brow is furrowed.

"Because I didn't think I could do better. Isn't that sad?"

She wipes sweat off her brow. "One week later, I left work early with a headache, and when I got home, he was fucking her on our couch."

Her gaze is far away, like she's reliving the moment. My gut churns for her. At the same time, I'm thinking about how much I'd like to rip Kyle's nuts off.

Then, out of nowhere, Christy chuckles. "And you wanna know the wildest part? It wasn't even a Friday."

We both laugh, and I'm relieved she can find some humor in the situation now. But there's still sadness in her eyes. I reach for her hand and interlace our fingers. "I'm so sorry he broke your heart."

She heaves a sigh. "Kyle broke my self-esteem, not my heart. We did say 'I love you,' but there was never any passion behind it. It was more of a formality. All our friends in relationships were saying it, so we figured we should be saying it too. The truth is...I don't think I've ever been in love."

"Me neither."

Well, until now. But I'm not brave enough to put that card on the table yet.

"So," I go on, "do you feel better after hitting all those home runs?"

She nods. "You were right. I had a lot to get off my chest. I think I definitely put a dent in it."

Her smile is wistful, and I wish I could do more to alleviate her stress. That's when it dawns on me that I can. "Look, I just want you to know that, regardless of how things shake out after our publicity stunt, I'm still going to introduce you to Lola. I don't want you to feel like you have to earn it, because you already have. You're a kickass literary agent, and she'd be lucky to have you."

Christy's face lights up. "Really?"

"Of course."

She wraps her arms around me, tighter than ever before. "Thank you so much, Holden. I appreciate it more than you know."

"It's my pleasure." It's true. Making her happy is the ultimate high. I close my eyes and savor the moment. Christy's soft hair tickling my neck, her breath on my shoulder. Her perfect tits pressed against my chest. Her heart beating against mine.

When she unravels from me, she looks down at her tank top, which is damp and sticking to her skin. Grimacing, she pulls the fabric away from her stomach. "Sorry I'm so sweaty."

I shake my head. "You have nothing to apologize for. You put in work, baby. The way you were swinging that bat? I've never been so turned on in my life."

Her cheeks flush a deeper shade of pink than they already were from the heat. "Is that so?"

"It sure is." I lick my lips. "In fact, I really wanna fuck you right now...all hot and sweaty from playing baseball with me."

She crinkles her nose. "You don't want me to shower first?"

I'm sure Kyle would have insisted on it. His loss. "What's the point of getting clean if we're just going to get dirty again?" I eye the glistening skin on her neck. "Mind if I get a taste?"

Christy tilts her head, offering me access. A smile creeps on her lips as I turn my hat backward, so the brim doesn't get in my way. Then I bring my mouth just below her ear and kiss her. She smells incredible and tastes even better. I flick my tongue across her flesh, enjoying her salty sweetness.

"Mmm," she moans. "Let's get out of here."

I drive us back to the estate in record time without getting a speeding ticket. When we walk through the door to the bungalow, we're practically clawing at each other.

"Hold that thought while I wash my hands," I tell her. "I want to touch you, but I have dirt under my nails from the field."

"What a gentleman." She smiles before kissing me with a fervor that makes my balls ache. Then she pulls away and looks at her own fingers. "I should wash mine, too."

I take her to the bathroom and we lather each other's hands before rinsing and drying them off. After I hang the towel back up, I turn to see Christy looking in the mirror with a furrowed brow.

"Ugh...I'm a mess." She takes off her Starlings hat and re-does her ponytail. "I don't feel very sexy."

"Then you don't see what I see." I move behind her and kiss her neck as she watches our reflection.

"Maybe you're blind," she replies with a wry smile.

My forehead creases with concern. "Baby, don't say that."

She looks down at the soap bubbles popping in the sink. "You may need to cut me some slack today. I had to wear a bathing suit next to a Victoria's Secret model."

God, my heart aches. How the fuck am I supposed to tell her about my past with Cat when she's already feeling so insecure? I can't. Not now.

I turn her to face me. "You're one of a kind, Red. This hair...these freckles. The cupid's bow I love to kiss." I meet her smile with my lips, and my hands move to her ass. "This hot-as-fuck body that I can't stop thinking about."

Christy laces her fingers at the nape of my neck, her expression earnest. "I'm sorry I have so much baggage."

"You don't have to be sorry." I cup her face in my palms and kiss her again and again. "Just try to believe me when I say you're the most beautiful woman I've ever laid eyes on."

Christy fixes her gaze on me for several seconds, like she's trying to read my mind. I decide to help her out. I take her fingers and place them on my chest. "Maybe you have a hard time believing my words...but what about my racing heart? Feel that? This is what happens when you kiss me."

She smiles, her eyes glistening.

I shift her hand south to the rock-hard bulge under my waistband. "And this is what happens every time I think about you. My pitching strategy applies to sex, too. Read my body. It's telling you everything you need to know."

Her gaze falls to my erection, and when she starts to massage me through my shorts, I have to fight the urge to unsheathe my cock and bend her over the vanity. But until she's completely comfortable with me taking control, she gets to be in the driver's seat.

When she looks back up at me, there's resolve in her expression. "Take my clothes off, Holden. All of them."

With her hand still on my bulge, Christy feels my dick throb at the invitation and laughs. I move my hands to the hem of her tank top, then peel it off and toss it aside, leaving her sports bra on, for now. Then I get on my knees and pull down her shorts and panties at the same time. Call me eager. She steps out of them, but folds her arms around her stomach.

I look up at her from where I'm still kneeling on the bathroom tile. "Don't hide from me, baby."

She bites her lip. "I used to have a six-pack, Holden."

"I don't give a flying fuck about a six-pack, Christy." It's the truth.

She giggles, but her eyes are teary, so I go on.

"You like my body because it's strong and solid, right?" After considering my question, she nods. "Well, I like yours because it's supple and soft," I explain. "Opposites attract. That's not so impossible to believe, is it?"

"I guess not." Slowly, she moves her arms away from her belly, which is just as beautiful and feminine as the rest of her.

I kiss the soft skin surrounding her navel. "You're fucking gorgeous."

When I stand, my fingers travel up her arms and shoulders, then land on the straps of her sports bra. "These things are a bitch to take off."

A genuine laugh escapes her, which was my goal. Normally, I keep my thoughts on sports bra removal to myself and hope for the best. But Christy's breaths are shallow, which means she's nervous about being completely naked in front of me. I figured a little comic relief couldn't hurt.

"Do you need my help?" she asks, still smiling.

"How about you tie your hair up, so it doesn't get caught on anything," I suggest.

She coils her pretty red ponytail into a knot on top of her head, which she tucks into her elastic band. It's the same hairstyle she was wearing the night we met. When she stormed out of O'Reilly's, my heart sank. I thought I'd never see her again—but look at us now. She's about to let me see *all* of her. It's a privilege I don't take for granted, knowing this isn't easy for her.

To be honest, I can't imagine what her hang-up is about her breasts. From what I've seen, they're fucking perfect. But after I shimmy the bra over her raised arms, she bites her lip, looking nervous as fuck.

I try to put her at ease. "You want the truth, Red? You have the prettiest tits I've ever seen."

Should I tell her I'm dying to motorboat them?

With a furrowed brow, she turns to look at herself in the mirror. "I feel like you're just being nice."

My cock strains the fabric of my shorts in disagreement. I press it against her bare ass. "Is that *really* what you feel?"

A hint of a smile appears, but she still heaves a sigh.

"Do you want to tell me what you're so worried about?"

Christy nods, but looks back down at the soap bubbles in the sink. Her cheeks flush. "If you're tired of hearing me talk about Kyle…trust me, you're not the only one. I'm sick to death of letting him dictate how I feel about my body. And I'm trying hard to stop. But the reason I'm self-conscious is…" She clears her throat. "He asked me to wear a bra during sex. My breasts are slightly different sizes, and he said it distracted him."

"Jesus Christ," I mutter as I shake my head. "Baby, he's an outlier. I can guarantee you most guys are just happy to see tits…we're not obsessing over insignificant details." I wrap my arms around her. "Not only did I not notice, but I wouldn't give a shit if I did. And I'm definitely not going to stand here like a fucking tool and compare your breasts, when I can have fun with them instead."

Christy watches in the mirror as I slide one hand up to massage her nipple, while the other settles between her thighs. I glide my middle finger in circles over her warm, wet slit. "Already dripping for me. Good girl."

She smiles and starts moving her hips in circles, heightening her enjoyment as I continue to stroke her. I fucking love that about her. She isn't shy about wanting to get off and does whatever she needs to get there. It's sexy as hell.

"This is what you deserve, baby. Mind-blowing sex whenever you want it," I whisper in her ear. "Believe me, if I'd have been lucky enough to have you in my bed for eight years, you would've had a permanent smile on your face from being so well-fucked."

"Oh my god, Holden." She grins as she leans back against my chest and closes her eyes, her hips moving faster. "You always know exactly what to say."

The sweet scent of her hair, combined with her glistening sweat and the sexy sound of her arousal on my fingers makes me rabid for her. Never mind her luscious ass grinding against my cock. I wonder if she's ever made a guy come in his pants. I'd hate to be the first.

"I want you so badly," she says as though reading my mind.

Thank god.

"Oh, yeah?" I meet her gaze in the mirror. "You want me to show you how pretty you look when you're getting good dick?"

Christy nods and whimpers. I take my hands off her body and rush to free myself of my clothes.

"Wait," she says, kneeling to pick up the baseball cap I discarded onto the bathroom tiles. "You look so fucking hot with your hat on backward."

I smile and grab it from her. "Guess I better put it back on, then."

When my hat's in place, I wrap my arms around her again and kiss the nape of her neck, then work my way down her shoulder while kneading her breasts. After kissing the path that leads back up to her ear, I catch her gaze in the mirror. "We look good together, Red," I say, despite myself.

Her response is to reach for my dick, smoothing her thumb back and forth across the head. Is she agreeing with me, or ignoring what I said? I wish I knew. But the next words out of her mouth distract me enough that I stop obsessing over it. "Get a condom," she says.

I grab one from the top drawer of the vanity and put it on, then tease her by rubbing the head of my cock against her opening.

"More," she begs.

I push inside of her, but barely an inch. "How's that?"

She shakes her head in response and grips the edge of the vanity before shifting her hips all the way back to swallow my dick. And swallow it, she does. This is the first time we've fucked in this position, and I'm deeper inside her than ever.

"That's better," she says, pleased with herself. Taking the lead, she shifts forward and back in delicious, slow, sensual movements that have me forgetting my own name. She's so goddamn beautiful with her hair piled on top of her head, her skin flushed pink, and my cock inside her.

I draw her attention to the mirror. "Look at how fucking gorgeous you are, Red. Can you see it now?"

Her gaze is drunk with pleasure, her voice breathless with desire. "I see it."

She continues grinding on me and watches with fascination as my features contort in various expressions of bliss. "See what you do to me?" I pant. "You're the best lay I've ever had. So tight and wet. So eager to fuck."

She nods, a mischievous glint in her eye. "That's me."

"If only you could see the view from here," I tell her, my hand on the small of her back. "I can't stop staring at your perfect pussy, taking all of this dick."

"God, I love your dirty mouth," she says as she starts moving faster, chasing her orgasm.

"I know you do, baby," I tell her. "I know exactly what you like. Your body's an open book to me."

When I meet her gaze again, she's looking at me like I hung the moon, and I'm not sure why. All I know is that I love it.

"Fuck me, Holden," she says, slowing her hips to a stop. "I want you to take over... And don't hold back."

I start thrusting, but slowly. "Are you sure, baby?"

She nods, moaning in approval when I pick up speed. "I want you to fuck my brains out. Just like in the sex dream I had after you won the World Series."

"Jesus, Red," I huff. "If you keep talking like that, I won't last another minute."

"That's okay. I'm almost there myself."

"Good girl. Let me finish you off." My thrusts are fast and rough, which is how I've been wanting to fuck her since I took her clothes off. I grip her waist with one hand while my other finds her clit. "How does this feel?"

"Amazing," she moans.

As I pound her, our eyes stay fixed on each other in the mirror. It's so damn hot. "You take me so well, baby," I say.

When her tight muscles start quivering on my cock, I watch the pleasure flood her features, leaving a blissful smile on her face that's so goddamn beautiful, it makes me come.

Afterward, I turn her around and we kiss for several minutes, unable to get enough of each other, I guess. At least, I hope she can't get enough of me. God knows that's how I feel about her.

"Want to shower together?" I ask her in between kisses.

It feels so good when she says yes without hesitating.

Later that night, I expect to sleep like a baby. But while Christy fades the moment her head hits the pillow, my fucking shoulder starts aching. I shouldn't have pitched again today, even if they were soft throws. Guess what, though? I'll do it again tomorrow if Christy asks me to. I'd do anything it takes to put a smile on her face.

Thirty minutes later, when I'm still awake despite popping ibuprofen, I decide to read for a bit. I can't find *The Great Gatsby*, and I don't want to wake Christy, so I grab the *Edison's Love* manuscript from her nightstand and head out to the lanai. She spoke so highly of it, and I have to admit, I'm curious. When I see that she tabbed nearly an entire chapter and wrote dozens of notes in the margins of each page, I start there, even though it's near the end of the novel.

From the first line of the chapter, I'm hooked. I've never read a romance novel before, but I get the appeal. The pages that Christy tabbed include a sexy beach scene that not only makes my dick hard again, but gives me valuable insight about the woman whose heart I'm trying to win.

I read the chapter twice, then head back to bed at 1:00 a.m. As soon as I'm under the covers, though, the glow of my phone screen captures my attention. I reach for it on the nightstand and see that I just missed a call.

No—wait. I missed *six* calls.

And they're all from Caterina Hart.

CHAPTER 18

Christy

When I sit across from Caterina in the conference room the next morning, I feel silly that I ever carried a grudge against her. It's not *her* fault I caught my boyfriend in a compromising position with her photograph. Kyle deserved the blame. Not for pleasuring himself, but for all the ways he destroyed my self-esteem. Unfortunately, confronting him demanded a level of confidence I didn't possess. So I took my anger out on The Siren instead. I made her the scapegoat, rather than face my dysfunctional relationship.

Of course, hindsight is twenty-twenty. And after having the hottest sex of my life with Holden last night, my vision is rosy.

Our bathroom tryst was the most vulnerable I've been with a man since my first time with Kyle. And damn, did Holden reward me for it. I let him see all of me, and his response was the exact opposite of my ex-boyfriend's. The way Holden watched me in the mirror changed the way I see myself. I've never felt more beautiful in my life. Even this morning, when I was applying my red lipstick, I couldn't stop smiling at my reflection.

And the events leading up to that sizzling hot sex were some of the most intimate I've experienced: Holden comforting me while I cried; feeding me when I refused to eat; listening to me scream on that baseball field. The moments themselves were unromantic, but they were raw and genuine. They were the stuff that real relationships are made of. Now, my hangups about dating him are gone.

True, I'd pegged Holden as a moody manchild. And even worse, I compared him to Kyle and my dad. But he's nothing like them. The way he takes care of me is proof of that. Since I met this man, I've yelled, and sobbed, and unveiled my long list of insecurities, and he hasn't flinched. Not once.

I'm falling in love with him.

And I think he feels the same way.

This morning, I woke up in his arms. When my eyes fluttered open, he was smiling at me. His hands were clasped tight around my waist, like he never wanted to let go.

He kissed my forehead, the tip of my nose, and my lips. Then his brow furrowed with concern, and he asked me how I was feeling. That's when I remembered the bombshell my sister dropped on me yesterday. I reached for my phone on the nightstand and saw that I had several messages from her and my mom. Right away, all the angst I'd felt when Jenna shared the news came flooding back.

My mind raced with childhood memories. The way Dad never supported Jenna's artistic talent. The way he gave up on her when she couldn't meet his high academic standards. The way he pressured me to excel, as if I owed him twice as many achievements because he only had one daughter he could brag about to his country club friends. Not to mention the wedge he drove between me and Jenna because of the ugly way he treated her. The divide my sister and I had to work so hard to mend.

Every spiraling thought led me to the same fear: what if this revelation that Jenna and I have different fathers breaks us again?

Reading the panic on my face, Holden suggested I get some coffee and breakfast in me before responding. I agreed, and he went out to the lanai, put together a tray of food, and brought it back to bed. Then he helped me craft a simple text to my mom and Jenna, telling them I loved them and would call after the McBride family meeting this morning.

This relationship can't be fake. The way Holden treats me speaks volumes. And last night, he proved in no uncertain terms that he's attracted to me. Even now, in the conference room, as I sit a stone's throw away from one of the most gorgeous women on the planet, I feel secure. Caterina Hart isn't a threat to me.

Everyone has taken their seats around the table, except Dan Jimenez. The tax attorney extraordinaire is in Mr. McBride's study, on the phone with CNN. They called just as we were all arriving at the main house, asking for his commentary on a developing news story. Next to me, Holden's jaw is clenched, and his hands are balled up in fists. Despite how sweet he's been with me this morning, I can tell he's anxious.

It's no surprise, given today's agenda. Wes is chomping at the bit to present his proposal to the board. With each passing minute, he glances at his watch and rolls his eyes. I can't imagine he could come up with a better way to honor Grandma Evelyn's legacy than Holden's Racing Hearts proposal. But I'm sure Wes is eager to prove me wrong.

"Christine, dear," Mrs. McBride calls to me from her seat next to Caterina. "Would you like a pastry?"

Holden scowls. "It's *Christy*, Mom."

She ignores him.

I look at the untouched tray of delights on the credenza behind her. Freshly made donuts filled with ube custard and rolled in powdered sugar; flaky pineapple turnovers sprinkled with toasted coconut flakes; and fluffy mango muffins topped with macadamia nut streusel. The heavenly scent of vanilla, butter, and fried dough fills the entire room, impossible to ignore.

As tempted as I am, I can't shake the feeling that Margot McBride is purposely singling me out. *Let's ask the* voluptuous *girl if she wants carbs.*

Her imaginary words hit me like a punch to the gut. Not because I'm shocked that the McBride matriarch would think such a thing. But because of how much I still care. Even after Holden made me feel like a goddess last night.

"I'm fine, thank you." When I clear my throat, Holden takes my hand.

His mom purses her lips. "I just hate to see them go to waste."

My chest tightens. "Why don't you have one?"

"Well, I watch my weight, dear." Margot's smile sends a shiver down my spine.

Holden lets go of my hand and slides his chair back, nostrils flared. My stomach churns, as I'm sure he's about to defend my honor, and I'd rather not be the cause of a McBride family showdown. But just as he's about to speak, his sister's voice fills the air.

"I don't think a tummy tuck counts as watching your weight, Mom," Abby says from her seat next to me.

Holden's brow unfurrows, and he chokes on a laugh as I turn to Abby and smile. Even their dad is amused and chuckles for the first time since I met him.

"Julian!" Margot scolds her husband.

"Sorry to keep everyone waiting," Dan says when he enters the room.

Mr. McBride beams, delighted to be off the hook. "Perfect timing."

Wes is all business. "Great, let's get started." Without further ado, he projects his presentation onto the large pull-down screen on the wall.

What I see makes my jaw drop.

It's a photograph of Caterina Hart, lying naked on a beach. She's on her stomach, with her head resting on folded arms, her bare breasts hardly covered by the sand, and her arched back sloping upward to her perfectly sculpted ass. Below her, in elegant script, is the title of Wes's proposal:

Siren Serum: Your Secret Weapon Against Cellulite.

"What the fuck?" Holden vocalizes my thoughts with perfect accuracy.

His brother smirks. "Sorry, bro. Only board members get to ask questions during the presentation. But don't feel bad. No one here expects an athlete to be familiar with corporate etiquette."

Holden lets out a wry laugh. "You may want to fact-check that with Nike, New Balance, Gatorade, and the other dozen corporations I've partnered with. I assure you they'll disagree."

While Wes's gaze narrows on his brother, my heart swells with pride.

"Well, since Holden can't ask the question, I will," Great-Uncle Alistair barks from the opposite end of the table. "What the fuck, Wesley?"

Wes's eyes go wide, surprised by the attack. It's clear the youngest McBride isn't accustomed to being challenged. He probably expected his great-uncle to drool over the picture of his hot model girlfriend—not foam at the mouth.

"Is this how you honor your late grandmother?" Alistair continues, his tone gruff. "I'll bet dear Evelyn is rolling over in her grave. And may I remind you that the money she bequeathed must fund a *charitable* organization. Like your brother's." The old man winks at Holden.

Wes nods, barely hiding his annoyance with a forced smile. "If you'll allow me to continue with the presentation, I think you'll find that all your questions will be answered."

"Let's hear him out, Alistair," Mrs. McBride says, smiling at Caterina like they're the best of friends. In response, the model squeezes Margot's hand. It's odd. Caterina's barely been dating Wes for three weeks, yet she's so comfortable with his family. Maybe it's a money thing. With her wealth and status, she fits in seamlessly with the McBrides, while I couldn't feel more out of place.

"Thank you, Mom," Wes jumps in over the sound of his great-uncle's disapproving exhale. "Before I get into our business plan, I'm going to let the beauty and brains of our operation tell you about her vision for Siren Serum." He places a hand on his girlfriend's shoulder. "Want to take it away, Cat?"

"Thanks, honey," she says with a beaming smile, then stands, in case anyone forgot how tall and leggy she is. She looks sexy yet professional in a tailored black mini dress paired with an oversized cream blazer and black stilettos. Her hair is sleek and shiny, pulled off her face in a perfect ponytail, so as not to hide her flawless makeup and glowing skin.

"When Wes told me his family was looking to fund a charitable endeavor, I knew in my heart that this collaboration was meant to be," she says, a sultry rasp in her voice that commands the attention of everyone in the room. Julian, Margot, Wes, Zoe, and Dan can barely contain their smiles. Then there are the skeptics: Alistair, Abby, Holden, and me. Of course, the only opinions that matter are those of the board. But with two members on Team Siren and only one on Team Holden, I don't like his odds.

Hopefully, by the end of this presentation, the scale will tip in his favor. Isn't it obvious that Caterina Hart is trying to con the McBrides into funding her cellulite serum side hustle?

"With my star power, and your business acumen," she goes on with an eye on Julian McBride, "the possibilities are endless. Just think of all the Siren-approved health and beauty products we could offer. But for now, a cellulite serum is a great place to start. I mean, I think we can all agree that every woman wants firm thighs." On that last note, I swear, she looks right at me.

Rage stirs in my chest. At least now, I'm not ashamed of it. That batting session with Holden last night was exactly what I needed. Especially when he insisted my anger is normal. He was right. Even now, I'm not the only one who's pissed. Next to me, my boyfriend heaves an agitated sigh and runs his fingers through his hair.

"Siren Serum is the premier cellulite treatment the world has been waiting for," the model continues, ignoring Holden and turning her attention to Alistair, Dan, and Zoe. "What makes it better than the rest? A soon-to-be patented blend of

Brazilian botanicals developed by an herbalist so good, The Siren keeps her on speed dial."

Did she really just refer to herself in the third person? It takes an effort not to roll my eyes.

"Last year, I flew to Rio de Janeiro to shoot for Sports Illustrated. Now, I know this is hard to believe, but..." She bites her lip. "The night before the photoshoot, I noticed a dimple on my thigh." Her hand floats to her heart and she closes her eyes, clearly overwhelmed by the traumatic memory.

"Luckily, my personal assistant saved the day. She'd heard about an esteemed herbalist through the PA grapevine, and let's just say I'm not the only celebrity who has turned to her during a crisis. Thirty minutes later, I had this miracle serum and, I swear, after one application, the dimple was undetectable." Caterina's gaze lands on Dan Jimenez, who's so enamored, I can almost see the hearts in his eyes.

"Of course, no serum can cure cellulite, so I have to apply it daily," the model goes on. "But because it's formulated with Brazilian botanicals, I have peace of mind knowing I'm not putting toxins in my body. Even better, the clean ingredients mean we can market our product to females of all ages."

My eyes go wide.

"I'm sorry, Ms. Hart...are you saying you want to sell your cellulite cream to *children*?" Alistair asks, taking the words out of my mouth.

"It's a serum, not a cream," Caterina corrects with a smile befitting a cover girl. "But yes. Preteens and adolescents are a booming market for skincare products. I think we'd be foolish not to take advantage."

"I'd totally buy it," young Zoe McBride chimes in, gazing at

Caterina with reverence, as though the model were her idol. For all we know, she is.

"Thank you, Zoe. And, finally," Caterina continues before a disgruntled-looking Alistair can follow up, "in keeping with the McBride tradition of philanthropy, 10 percent of sales will go to skin cancer research." She smiles at Dan and Zoe before she sits. "Want to take it from here, Wes?"

Over the next hour, the Wharton School graduate presents a business plan so clear, thorough, and compelling, it's hard not to be impressed. In addition to the stacks of documents supporting the viability of Siren Serum, Wes wows the board with prototypes of the product's packaging, which gives a warm, tropical vibe that's sure to appeal to the masses.

I have to admit, when Wes first projected that photograph of naked Caterina onto the screen, I thought it was game over for them. But by the time the younger McBride brother is done presenting, I'm not so sure. With Wes at the helm of this company, Siren Serum is sure to be a financial success. And since he and Caterina have agreed to be equal partners, the McBrides stand to make a substantial profit. From a business perspective, the proposal is certainly enticing. I can tell from Holden's furrowed brow that he thinks so, too.

Even Alistair's tune has changed. He may not be sold quite yet, but his expression shifted from disgust to intrigue as soon as Wes handed out his appendix of revenue projections. His robust financial analysis is the kind of hard evidence board members love to see in a proposal, and the fact that Holden provided nothing of the sort makes me queasy.

Ugh. I knew he should have opted to go second when he drew the longer straw.

"Well, we have a lot to think about," Alistair announces

with a furrowed brow when Wes starts packing up the prototypes. "Holden, I just got word from the family foundation's administrative assistant that she received the appendix you emailed yesterday, but couldn't open the file. Try sending it again, won't you? We'll need it when we deliberate."

Holden nods. "Of course, Alistair. Thanks for letting me know."

I release a breath, relieved that Holden submitted financials, after all. At least Racing Hearts has a fighting chance now.

"Whichever proposal we choose will have a significant impact on the future of the McBride Family Foundation, and we do not take our responsibility lightly," Alistair continues. "Zoe, Daniel, and I will meet on our own over the next two days, and we'll reconvene as a group on Tuesday to announce our decision."

"May the best man win," Wes says with a sneer in Holden's direction.

After the meeting's adjourned, we skip lunch on the lanai with Holden's family in favor of getting as far the fuck away from them as possible. I've never seen Holden as agitated as he was during Wes and Caterina's presentation, and even as we're on the secluded path back to our bungalow, his brow remains creased and his breaths are shallow.

"I still think you have an excellent shot," I say, squeezing the hand that's interlaced with mine. "How does your financial analysis compare to Wes's?"

Holden smirks. "It doesn't."

"What do you mean?"

"What I mean is..." He stops next to a koi pond and rakes a hand through his hair, his frustration out of place in the serene setting. "I don't fucking have one."

My forehead creases. "But Alistair said—"

"He was throwing me a bone. I guess he hasn't eliminated Racing Hearts from contention yet. But I'm going to have to put something impressive together and..." He heaves a sigh.

"What?"

"I have no idea how to do it." He shakes his head, cheeks flushed with embarrassment. "My brother's right. I don't know shit about business proposals, and it shows. Revenue projections never crossed my mind when I was putting together my presentation. I bet you think I'm a fucking idiot."

"Far from it. I promise." I wrap my arms around his waist and press my head to his chest. The rapid thumping against my ear is proof of how crucial a program like Racing Hearts is. Holden needs to see this through.

"Don't let Wes get in your head," I say when I step back. "Of course, he nailed his presentation. He has an MBA from the best business school in the country. This is his wheelhouse, and it gives him an edge, but your idea is better, Holden. And you know it. It's what your grandmother would've wanted."

Holden's eyes glisten. "I know that, baby. But I won't win this competition on heart alone. At the end of the day, the McBrides are a business. They're not going to pick my program unless there's a sound financial basis for it. And whatever appendix I scramble to put together by tonight is going to be underwhelming at best, because I don't know what the hell I'm doing."

A smile creeps on my lips. "You know who does? My soon-to-be brother-in-law, Charlie. He has an MBA from Dartmouth, and I'm sure he'd be happy to help."

Holden shakes his head. "I don't want to impose."

"It's fine, trust me. Charlie loves a passion project, and he's involved with the Dramatic Hearts Club," I explain. "He and Jenna bought a house in Tuscany, and they're partnering with Dex to renovate it for use as a retreat space. When I tell Charlie about Racing Hearts, I know he'll jump at the chance to support your program."

"Are you sure, Red? I don't feel right dragging you and Charlie into the mess I made for myself. If I'd bothered to Google what goes into a business proposal, I wouldn't need rescuing right now."

"Stop blaming yourself. Live and learn, right? You have teams of people doing things for you on a daily basis, Holden. It's no surprise you didn't think about putting together financials."

The fact that he feels so ashamed is what sets him apart from the likes of Michael Andersen, who can't so much as fry an egg but couldn't care less how that reflects on him.

"You're very gracious." The tension in Holden's face eases when he leans down to kiss me.

My knees go weak. *I'm just in love with you, that's all.*

"Once we get to the bungalow, I'll call my mom and Jenna, then I can set up a time for us to talk to Charlie."

"Thank you, baby."

The relief in Holden's eyes is worth the flutter of nerves in my gut. But if he didn't need Charlie's help, I'd put off calling my mom and sister a little longer. The truth is, I've never dreaded a conversation more in my life.

Will Tim Shaker be the next man to drive a wedge between me and my sister?

I wish I didn't have to find out.

CHAPTER 19
Christy

Ten minutes later, I'm sitting in bed with my phone in my hands, waiting for my sister to answer. Holden's on the lanai after making me promise I'll come out and get him if I need anything. It's the most supported I've ever felt by a man, and I couldn't be more grateful. Especially as I'm about to confess to my family that I'm terrified of losing them.

But when Jenna picks up and tells me that she and Mom are together, and they've been waiting for my call so they can FaceTime me, my shoulders relax a little. And when I see their red-rimmed eyes, their pink noses, and the worry lines on their foreheads, I'm flooded with relief.

They wouldn't be this upset if they didn't love me as much as I love them.

"Christy, honey, I was going to tell you as soon as you got home from Maui. I just didn't want to ruin your trip," my mom says.

"I know you meant well," I tell her.

And I do. It's just that I get triggered when people keep secrets from me. I hate the feeling of having the wool pulled over my eyes. Penelope Dwyer's deception was bad enough, and she was lying to *everyone*. It's even worse when the lie's directed only at me. Like Kyle's infidelity. It's so hard to trust again after a betrayal like that.

And speaking of infidelity...I wonder how my father took the news that Jenna's not his biological daughter. "Did you tell Dad?"

"Yes." Ingrid Andersen takes a breath. "I called him yesterday, and he said he wasn't surprised. That he always suspected. Of course, I always suspected, too. Ever since Jenna was a toddler and picked up a paintbrush. She had such a passion for art, just like Tim."

My sister's looking down at her lap.

"How are *you* feeling about all this?" I ask her. A pang of guilt hits my gut for not checking in with her sooner. The news came as a shock to me, yes. But Jenna's the one who just discovered she has a father she knew nothing about.

She shrugs. "Honestly? I'm relieved. It explains so much. Dad wasn't a great father to either of us, but he flat-out ignored me. It's kind of easier to swallow now that I know I'm not his biological daughter."

My heart aches for her. "He's an asshole, Jenna. He should have loved you, regardless. You're not hard to love."

"Thanks, Christy." She wipes a tear on the back of her hand. "I love you so much. Nothing will ever change that."

I nod, my own eyes glistening. "Ditto."

Our mother's lip quivers. "I'm so sorry for blowing up your lives like this."

Jenna puts a comforting hand on her shoulder. "It's okay. We'll be fine, I promise."

I nod, although I'm not so sure. What happens when it's

Christmas, and Jenna and Mom are celebrating with Tim Shaker, and Dad's holed up with his girlfriend? I'm sure Michael Andersen has all but given up on me, too. I'm not the golden daughter anymore. My career's in jeopardy, and I've done nothing of late for him to brag about to his colleagues. Unless you count publicly making out with Holden McBride. Unfortunately, my dad's a loyal Cincinnati Reds fan.

"Honey, Tim is really eager to meet you, too," Mom says to me as my palms begin to sweat.

My eyebrows rise. "Really?" I don't want to get my hopes up. Maybe she's only saying that because she sees the worry in my eyes.

"Oh, yes," my mom insists, pressing a tissue to her cheek. "He's an avid reader, and he'd love some recommendations, if you're open to it."

"Of course. That sounds nice." I can't help but smile. Knowing that Tim wants me to feel included emboldens me to ask the question that's been weighing heaviest on my mind. I turn my gaze to Jenna. "Have you met him yet?"

She shakes her head. "I want to wait until you're home. I want us to meet him together."

Tears of relief stream down my face as Jenna's answer puts my biggest fear to rest.

"Are you alright?" my sister asks, her forehead creased.

I smile through a sob. "I was just so scared of losing you again. But that's not going to happen, is it."

Jenna shakes her head. "Never. We're sisters, just the same as before. Nothing can change that."

I let out a shaky breath. "Promise?"

She nods. "Promise."

"Jenna's spent all day worrying about you, honey. Believe

me, she's not going anywhere," my mother adds with a reassuring smile.

A laugh escapes me, and I wipe my eyes in an effort to compose myself. Now that my mom and sister have put me at ease, I can admit I'm curious about my mother's first love. "Mom, can you tell me more about Tim? Jenna says he was your high school sweetheart?"

My mother sniffles. "We loved each other very much, but we wanted different things in life. Tim's father died when we were in high school and left him money, so he deferred his college admission to travel. He wanted to see the world...visit all the best art museums. And paint, of course. I wanted a house and a family, so we broke up.

"Then I met Michael, and he was so keen to settle down, I thought he must be the *one*." She heaves a sigh. "He was very charming back then. Swept me off my feet. But once we were engaged, his true colors came out. He'd yell sometimes. Say nasty things. Then he'd show up on my doorstep with flowers. I chalked it up to wedding stress." She tucks a strand of blonde hair behind her ear.

"The night before the wedding, Tim stopped by my parents' house and asked if I would go for a drive with him. The minute I got in the car, he told me he still loved me. He'd heard I was getting married and came to stop me. He'd been selected for a painting apprenticeship in Geneva, Switzerland and wanted me to go with him." My mom shakes her head. "But I was too scared. He had no plans to come back to the US. He wasn't sure when he'd ever want to settle down and start a family. So, I said no."

My smile is mischievous. "And, let me guess...you had a little goodbye romp in the car?"

Jenna nods, biting her lip. Meanwhile my mom's face turns crimson, and she hides behind her palms.

"And it was unprotected, too, in case you hadn't guessed." My sister giggles.

"Rookie move, Mom," I tease.

"Hey!" Jenna objects with a playful grin. "If it weren't for her rookie move, I wouldn't be here."

"Good point," I concede with a smile.

"Well, I *was* a rookie," Mom admits, still flushed. "That was my first time."

"Aww!" Jenna gushes. "You didn't tell me that."

"And now you're back together, after all these years? That's so sweet," I chime in.

"He never got married. He said he knew I'd come around one day." My mother laughs.

"Tim sounds great. I'm happy for you, Mom. And I'm excited to meet him." It's true.

"Thank you, honey," she says. "I love you so much."

"Me, too," Jenna adds.

I blow them a kiss. "Ditto."

I feel worlds better when we're done chatting and, before we hang up, I schedule a call with Charlie to go over financials for Racing Hearts. Then I walk out to the lanai, where Holden has a lunch of lobster Cobb salad waiting for us.

While we eat, I catch him up on the video call with my family, and his sincere smile gives me butterflies. Afterward, he hands me a small, gold gift bag with wisps of pink tissue paper peeking out. Inside is a beautiful purple silk orchid.

"I noticed you like wearing them, so I wanted you to have one to take home as a souvenir." He plucks the real one, which is beginning to wilt, from behind my ear, and replaces it.

My heart hammers from the sweetness of his gesture. Not to mention, the smitten way he's looking at me. "That's so thoughtful, Holden. Thank you."

"I also made a phone call while you were talking to your mom and Jenna," he says. "I was invited to attend the annual gala at the New York Public Library on Monday. I initially declined because, well...I used to take Grandma Evelyn every year, and I didn't think I'd want to go without her. But that was before I met you. What do you say, Red? Will you be my date?"

My breath hitches. The New York Public Library was my happy place when I lived in Manhattan. Does Holden remember me mentioning that I used to dream about getting married there? I doubt it. It was a casual remark I made in passing. But he does know how much I adore books. "I would love to."

"Great. I'll make the travel arrangements. *Myself*," he adds, to emphasize that he won't be letting his mother call the shots this time.

"That's a good look for you," I say, beaming with both pride on his behalf and giddiness on mine. I may not be getting married at the New York Public Library, but I'm just as excited to attend this benefit.

Thankfully, I packed a couple of gala-appropriate dresses, just in case. You never know where a McBride will take you. I just hope Holden isn't making these grand gestures because he's afraid I think less of him after he admitted he needed help with the appendix. The truth is, I found his vulnerability extremely sexy.

To show my gratitude, I kiss him like we don't have to work on his proposal all afternoon. And for a few minutes, I forget we do, until Charlie calls.

My brother-in-law to-be and Holden get along even better than I imagined. Charlie's a baseball aficionado, although he grew up in Denver and is loyal to their MLB team. I've been trying to convert him into a Starlings fan since I moved to Chicago, and I think befriending Holden might seal the deal. Within minutes, the men are making plans for all four of us to get drinks when we're back in the Windy City.

I have to work to hide the giddy smile on my face.

First, Holden McBride gifted me a silk orchid to wear behind my left ear, signaling to the world that I'm his. Then he asked me to be his date to a gala at the most romantic venue in New York. (Say what you want, but I will die on this hill.) And now, he's planning a double date with my sister and her fiancé.

If I wake up and this was all a dream, I'm going to be really fucking pissed.

Three hours and an early dinner on the lanai later, Holden is emailing his appendix to the family foundation's administrative assistant. Not only is it as impressive as you would expect from a Dartmouth graduate, Charlie helped us redefine Racing Hearts as a revenue-generating business to rival Siren Serum in terms of profit. While the sports program will remain a charitable endeavor at its core, the addition of a for-profit component guarantees financial success via premier sports camps, elite coaching packages boasting big-name professional athletes, wellness retreats for adult and corporate clients, and even a sportswear line.

"It's perfect, Holden," I say as soon as he hits send. "Racing Hearts still honors Grandma Evelyn the way you envisioned, but now it satisfies the board's money-lust, too."

"We make a great team, Red. I can't thank you enough."

We're on the lanai, sitting on the loveseat, and he pulls me onto his lap. "Can I take you out to celebrate?"

"How could I say no to that?" I brush my lips against his, and he responds by coaxing his tongue into my mouth for a deep, soulful kiss that makes my heart flutter. "Where are we going?"

He winks at me. "It's a surprise."

A smile blooms on my face as I shift to straddle him. "What should I wear?" When we started working on the appendix together, I changed out of the designer maxi dress I'd been sporting in favor of a tank top and shorts.

"You don't have to dress up...it'll just be us," he says, gripping my ass with a seductive gleam in his eye.

"I'm intrigued." I run my hands over Holden's broad shoulders, and his breaths pick up speed. The heat between us is palpable. His eyes are hungry as they travel from my lips, down my throat, and over my cleavage.

"Let's go before I push those little shorts to the side and take you right here," he says in my ear.

I swallow. "Okay."

Holden leads me down the path to the private beach. It's golden hour, and the sky is breathtaking. It's like Mother Nature struck a match and lit the horizon on fire. I pick up my pace, eager to get a better view from the shore, and Holden follows right behind me.

But as we approach the ocean waves and Holden's surprise comes into view, my steps slow to a halt.

Beside me, Holden's voice is low and soft. I turn to see him reading from a folded piece of paper that must've been in his pocket. His words describe the scene in front of me.

"There's a large, woven picnic blanket spread out on the sand.

Cream-colored, with tassels. And sitting on top is a lone bouquet of wildflowers. Edison wished he could give Iris so much more. Roses. Chilled champagne. A feast. But they'd run out of food. This might be their last night. Together. Alive. When the world is on the precipice, you never know.

"Tomorrow, Edison would forage. He would leave the abandoned shed they called home and cross the hill to No-Man's Land. His return wasn't guaranteed. Edison and Iris both knew this, although neither said it out loud. Tomorrow was a question mark. Tonight would be their vow.

"He wished he could give her so much more. But he gave her all he had. A picnic blanket. Wildflowers. And the sunset."

I turn to Holden, my eyes wet. "You read *Edison's Love?*"

He folds the paper with the lines he copied by hand and puts it back in his pocket. "Not all of it, yet. But I was curious about the chapter you tabbed."

My cheeks blaze, as hot as the fiery sky. "So, you know what happens next."

His eyes burn through me. "Yes."

I take his hand, echoing Iris's words. "Come. Let's watch day fade to night."

Holden and I sit on the blanket, side by side. I reach for the wildflowers and smell them. "I can't believe you did this for me."

He wraps his arm around me as the sky turns a dozen shades of pink and coral. "Is this the part of the book that made you fall for Edison?"

I turn to face Holden, whose eyes are still on the horizon. "I think I fell for him long before this scene."

His lips quirk up. "But this chapter is the only one you

tabbed. Tell me why, Red. I think I know, but I want to hear you say it."

I clear my throat, my heartbeat louder than the ebb and flow of the tide. I follow his gaze and watch as the heavens paint themselves blue.

"Tell me," he urges.

"Iris always needed to be in charge. When it came to her career, her relationships. To sex." I glance down at the wildflowers in my lap. "The beach scene is where she realizes she can die trying to control the uncontrollable, or let go and live. For the first time ever, she surrenders. To Edison."

"How does she surrender?" Holden rasps in the darkness.

The sky is peppered with stars when I turn to meet his gaze. "She lets him have his way with her. She gives him control of her pleasure."

He half-smiles. "You liked that, didn't you."

I nod.

"And what happens next?" He licks his lips, thirsting for my answer.

My heart pounds. "She has the best sex of her life."

He pulls me closer to him, his mouth just millimeters from mine. "Is that what you want, Christy? To give me control of your pleasure?"

Holden's blue-gray eyes are so commanding, I lie down on the blanket, at his mercy. He shifts on top of me, his erection finding the wet warmth between my thighs, even through layers of clothes. I arch into him, ready to be consumed.

"I need to hear you say it, baby."

"Yes."

I have no idea what to expect, but for the first time in my life, the uncertainty thrills me. The wild beat of my heart isn't anxiety, it's anticipation. I got a taste of unbridled Holden last night, when I told him not to hold back. The sex was so primal and intense, I came as hard and fast as he was fucking me. And even though he satisfied my needs and then some, he also left me craving more. More of Holden's wild side.

I think my wishes are about to come true.

The first thing he does is undress me, and it's the fastest my clothes have ever come off. When he strips me down to my panties, he pulls them off with his teeth. Now, all I'm wearing is the purple silk orchid he gifted me. He stops to rake his ravenous eyes from my head to my heels.

"Open your thighs for me, baby."

I do as I'm told.

He kneels in front of me, and his eager gaze lingers between my legs. With a mischievous smile, he grabs the hem of his white T-shirt and yanks it over his head with one hand.

There he is. Holden Fucking McBride. The most gorgeous man I've ever seen. Sun-kissed hair and skin. Rock-hard body. Blue-gray eyes that make me ache for wanting him.

"Look at you, Red. So wet, and I haven't even touched you yet." He lies on his stomach, propped on his elbows, and hooks my knees over his shoulders. "It's a good thing I'm hungry."

His tongue is warm and soft, just like the tropical air on my skin. He tortures me with long, slow strokes that make me drip like a fucking faucet onto the blanket beneath me. No one's ever turned me on like this. Needless to say, I never soaked through the sheets when I was with Kyle.

"Give me your hand, baby," he says. I have no idea what he wants with it, but I trust him.

Holden takes my middle finger and puts it right where I'm

gushing. "Now, be a good girl and rub that on your nipples while I eat you out."

It's nothing I've ever done before. Nothing I'd ever think to do, but my fingertips glide so easily over the slick peaks of my breasts, my pleasure turns up tenfold. Not just where I'm massaging myself, but where Holden is giving me the best head of my life. I close my eyes and enjoy the ride, my back arching more with every flick of his tongue on my clit. And when he slips his fingers inside me as he's still lapping me up, warmth ripples through my body like the ocean waves crashing onto the shore just a few feet away.

"Holden, oh my—" is all I manage to say before my thighs start to shake against his sexy stubble.

Afterward, he plants gentle kisses on my stomach as I stroke his hair. "How did I do?" he asks with a twinkle in his eye, because he knows very fucking well how he did.

"I've had better," I tease, flushed and smiling from the trip to cloud nine he sent me on.

He picks up on my reference to the first time we locked lips. "Oh, yeah? Just like you've had better kisses? Well, I guess I better up my game."

His palms land on either side of my face, and his mouth meets mine. For several sensual minutes, we make out under the moon and stars, our sighs and whispers accompanied by the rushing sound of the tide. I can taste myself on his lips, a sweet reminder that he's mine. It's all so intoxicating. The salt air, the sand, the star pitcher I loved to hate. The one I dreamed about long before we met. The one who's pulling off his shorts and putting on a condom. Who's giving me the most majestic piece of wood I've ever had.

For all the times he's made me come, this still feels surreal.

Holden McBride is fucking me.

And he's so goddamn good. He's on top of me, grinding his hips in slow, sensuous circles. Working his body in ways he couldn't when I was in control. I scold myself for not letting him do this to me sooner. I didn't think I liked this position, but I was wrong. With Holden, it's absolute magic. Every time he grazes my clit, I moan.

"Such a good girl, letting me fuck you like this," he says. "You know what good girls get, Red?"

I shake my head in a haze of pleasure.

"They get good dick."

"The best dick," I say, which prompts him to lift my legs up and over his shoulders. Now, instead of grinding, he pierces me with deep, delicious thrusts that feel dangerous in the best way. Like he could saw me in half if he wanted to.

"Holy shit, Holden," I cry out in ecstasy. "You're better than my favorite vibrator. And that is *really* saying something."

He laughs between thrusts. "Plus I'm always fully charged."

When I giggle, my muscles tighten around him, making his dick throb inside me. He winces with pleasure. "Jesus, baby. No woman's ever made me come just by laughing, but I guess there's a first time for everything."

The earnest way he looks at me tugs so hard at my heart, I have to fight the urge to tell him the truth about how I feel. That I'm falling for him. That I've fallen. That I've never been in love before, but I'm sure this is it. It feels so natural with Holden.

I don't think Kyle and I ever once laughed during sex. And I know we didn't lock eyes like this. He never peppered my face with sweet kisses. We didn't pause to take each other in, like we were the only two people in the world who mattered. If Holden doesn't start thrusting again soon, I have no idea what kind of confession I'll make in the heat of this moment.

"Don't stop," I tell him. "I'll be good, I promise. No more squeezing your dick with my giggles."

He gives me a smoldering smile. "Turn onto your stomach for me, baby."

He pulls out, and I obey, desperate for him to sink his beautiful cock back where it belongs. Eager to find out what he has in store for me. As my exhilarated heart pounds into the blanket underneath us, he lies on top of me, sweeps my hair off my back and kisses slowly down the length of my spine. Each press of his lips on my skin spurs a question in my mind: *What will he do next?*

I'd let him do whatever he wants to me.

He knows my body. He knows me. I don't understand it, but there's no denying it either. This is what Jenna was talking about: soulmate sex.

While Holden kisses every inch of my bare back, he has one hand on my breast and the other between my thighs, never missing an opportunity to pleasure me. The weight of him on top of me presses my pelvis into his warm palm, and I can't resist the urge to grind against his fingers.

"That's it, baby. Make yourself feel good." His words are a breathy whisper on my skin.

"Holden, I want you," I beg. "I need you inside me again."

"How bad do you want it, Red?" he asks, his fingers grazing my G-spot.

"Oh my god," I moan. "I want you more than anything."

"That's not half as much as I want you, baby," he says as he shifts down my body and bites my ass.

Kyle would never, I think to myself with a smile.

Finally, Holden parts my legs with his knee and presses the head of his cock against my slit, coating himself in my wetness. As he takes his first, slow thrust, he threads his hands through mine. I've never been in a more vulnerable position. Lying face down, with six feet, four inches of pure muscle pinning me to the ground. I've also never felt more safe.

"What would I do without this perfect pussy?" he rasps in my ear, echoing my sentiments about his perfect penis and the deliciously full feeling I've only ever had with him.

"Maybe you don't have to find out," I say as his thrusts pick up speed.

"You wanna keep getting this dick, don't you, baby." There's a smile in his voice.

"I do," I whimper, my second orgasm beginning to take shape as his cock stretches my very limits. "You feel fucking amazing, Holden."

"Baby, you're the best pussy I've ever had," he pants, his breath warm on my neck.

His admission makes me giddy. And the best part is, I believe him. "Just wait until you feel me without a condom."

"Jesus, Red," he groans. "Are you gonna let me fuck you raw one day?"

I don't hesitate. "Yes."

My answer makes him feral, and he drives his cock into me, harder and faster. I'm on the edge of orgasm when he coaxes me onto my back so he's on top again. He barely misses a beat. He's so strong, I'm like putty in his hands. It's sexy as fuck.

"Now, be a good girl, and look at me while I make you come." He strokes my hair, smoothing it away from my face. So sweet, tender, and romantic. Three qualities I've never had in a lover until now.

Pleasure bursts inside me like fireworks as my climax melds with Holden's. I cry out his name into the lush, tropical night. In the throes of my orgasm, I sink my teeth into his bicep, like I've been wanting to do since we met. He shudders and groans louder than he ever has.

And then we're a heap of racing hearts, shallow breaths, and salty skin. But instead of rolling off me, Holden kisses me. Again and again and again. He makes my eyes well up. And my heart swell. He makes me feel all sorts of things I've never felt before.

This relationship can't be fake.

Somewhere, I find the courage to say what's on my mind.

"You're not like this with other women, are you," I whisper, my gaze locked on his.

"No, baby." His eyes don't part from mine. "Not even close."

CHAPTER 20

Holden

I'm sitting on the lanai, drinking a cup of Kona coffee while Christy showers. The morning sun is shining bright over a calm blue ocean. The clear skies are a perfect reflection of how fucking happy I am.

This is it. I'm in love. I found her.

"Actually...*I* found her."

My grandmother's voice sails past me on a warm island breeze. But when I look to my left, she's seated right next to me on the wicker loveseat, appearing out of thin air.

"Grandma? What are you..." I search for the right words. "How are you here?"

"I'd explain, but you won't understand." Her smile is ethereal. "And I can't stay long. But I miss you, my sweet boy."

My eyes burn, but I can't cry. If I do, I'm afraid I'll never stop. I can't answer her, either. My words get stuck in my throat.

I miss you more than anything.

She takes my hand in hers, but I can't feel her soft, wrinkled skin. I can only remember what it felt like.

"I knew this would be hard on you, but I didn't think you'd run naked across a football field," she teases.

My cheeks flush. "I'm so sorry, Grandma. I didn't mean to—"

"Oh, hush. I was flattered." She frowns. "And worried. That's why I brought her to you."

"I don't..." I shake my head. "What are you saying?"

A memory forms in my mind. I'm at O'Reilly's pub, seated at the bar, when a cool breeze makes the hairs on the back of my neck stand up. I swivel around on my stool, and this striking redhead is stepping into the pub, wearing a frown that nearly breaks my heart.

"You know exactly who I'm talking about," Grandma says.

My heart pounds. "You...you brought me Christy?"

"Well, you would've met her eventually, of course." There's a twinkle in her eye. "The two of you were meant to be. But I did pull some strings to expedite the process."

I knew she was the one, I say to myself, watching the waves wash over the sand.

Grandma Evelyn must hear my thought. "Just like *I* knew, when I met your grandfather."

"How can I ever thank you?" I turn to study her features, doing my best to memorize them with the time we have left. She's exactly as I want to remember her. Younger and healthier than she was right before she passed away. She's wearing the gold earrings I bought her with my allowance when I was fourteen. They were a Mother's Day gift. Yes, Mother's Day.

"You don't have to thank me." She tilts her head. "It'd be nice if you won that competition, though."

My smile is wistful. "If I do, it'll be thanks to Christy and her sister's fiancé, Charlie. We were a team. They didn't do the work *for* me, they did the work *with* me. I'm not used to feeling so supported, Grandma."

She smiles, and it feels like sunshine on my skin.

"And Christy's so damn smart," I go on. "I was blown away. That brain of hers... I'm falling more and more in love by the minute."

"You deserve her, Holden. And she deserves you." My grandmother's voice sounds farther away, although she's still sitting beside me.

I drag a hand down my face and exhale.

"What's the matter, sweetheart?" Grandma has an amused look in her eye, like she knows what I'm worried about and thinks I'm being silly.

"I'm just..." I look down at my lap. "I'm afraid I'm going to screw this up."

The Siren.

I don't know if the voice in my head is mine or my grandmother's, but when I look next to me, there's no one there.

I wake with a start.

I'm not on the lanai, but in bed, and Christy's sleeping beside me. My heart hammers as my brain processes what just happened.

I didn't see Grandma Evelyn. It was a dream.

But it felt so real. So does the fear of losing Christy.

Last night, the sex was on another level—and not only because she feels so damn good. When she told me she fell for Edison long before the beach scene, I knew she was talking about me. I could hear it in her voice. And she knows I feel the same way about her.

You're not like this with other women, are you, she said.

It wasn't a question, but I answered her anyway. And when I did, her smile was brighter than the stars over our heads. But now that I know Christy has feelings for me, I'm wracked with guilt because I haven't told her the truth about Caterina Hart yet.

That's not her real name, by the way. She was born Cathryn Hartman, but her agent suggested she pick something sexier. It's fitting that she'd have an alter ego, seeing as she's so goddamn two-faced.

Cat's been calling and texting me nonstop, saying we need to talk, but what's the point? She's with Wes now, and I'm with Christy. Why dredge up the past? That's how I see it, anyway, but I doubt Cat agrees. If there's one thing I know about her, she will do anything to get what she wants. And I'm afraid she still wants me. If so, nothing will stop her from sabotaging my relationship with Christy. And the longer I put off telling my girl the truth, the worse it'll be if my ex beats me to it.

But I can't very well tell Christy now. Not when her eyes just fluttered open, and she's giving me the most adoring look I've received in my entire thirty-six years of life.

"Good morning." There's a sweet, sleepy rasp in her voice, and she's never looked more beautiful. It's her confidence. We slept without clothes on last night, which was her idea. This comfortable, carefree side of her is sexy as fuck. The sheet's only covering her from the waist down, and she's relaxed as ever. Except for her nipples, which are standing at attention, beckoning me.

"Morning." My smile matches hers when I move to kiss her.

And so begins an epic day of being naked with Christy. We have nowhere to be until dinner at the main house tonight, right before we take the private jet to New York for the library gala. Until then, there's nothing on the McBride Family Itinerary to keep us from enjoying each other's bodies, so that's what we do for hours. In bed. In our heated spa pool that overlooks the ocean. In the shower. We're not only having sex, although there's no shortage of orgasms for either of us. First, we eat breakfast in bed. Then we work up an appetite for lunch. Afterward, we nap for a while, then skinny-dip in warm water. This time, Christy admits she's a fan. Finally, we rinse each other off and wash each other's hair.

It's all so fucking amazing until 4:00 p.m., when I'm dressing for the first time all day, and I get this snapping pain in my shoulder while putting on a T-shirt.

I wince. "Fuck."

"What's wrong?" Christy abandons her search for a hair tie and stands next to where I'm seated on the edge of the bed.

"I'm fine. My shoulder's just a little tight because I haven't been keeping up with my stretches and workout regimen these past few days."

I'm definitely downplaying the pain, but there's a lot of truth to what I just said. Maybe it wouldn't kill me to hit the gym. "I should probably spend some time at the fitness center," I go on. "Want to keep me company?"

"I do...but this would be a good time for me to stay here and catch up on work." Christy bites her lip. "I mean, I guess I could bring a manuscript to the gym, but if I try to read while you're working out, I'll just end up staring at your hot body the entire time."

I half-smile. "You haven't had enough of me yet?"

She echoes what I said to her last night. "Not even close."

My heart swells, and I kiss her. "Call me if you need anything. I'll probably sit in the steam room for a bit first to loosen up. I should be back in about an hour and a half."

As I make the short walk to the fitness center, I can't stop grinning. I think about the dream I had this morning, but now my worries about Cat take a backseat to my grandmother's confession.

She brought me and Christy together.

Some might call the idea preposterous, but you know what? I believe that Christy Andersen and I were meant to be. It's the only explanation for how I fell so hard and fast.

Yup, everything's going to be fine. Tomorrow, Christy and I will fly to New York for the library gala. I'll show her the time of her life at the venue she once dreamed of getting married in. We'll come back to Maui for a day or two—long enough for me to win this competition, I hope—and then we'll leave again. We'll return to Chicago *together*. As a couple, I mean. And, once we're settled in, I'll tell her about Cat, who will be miles away in Manhattan. The news won't hit Christy as hard when she doesn't have to rub elbows with "The Siren" every day. And I'm sure she'll understand why I didn't tell her sooner.

I have nothing to worry about.

"Holden!"

I've just stepped into the fitness center lobby when that throaty rasp cuts through me like a knife. Cat's coming toward me with a gym bag slung over her shoulder, pink cheeks, and sweat on her brow. She's on her way out, just as I'm on my way in. If I'd left the bungalow two minutes later, I'd have missed her.

"Finally," she huffs. "Can we talk?"

My eyes search the space behind her. "Where's your boyfriend?"

"Taking a nap. We didn't get much sleep last night." She bites a smile. "Why? Are you jealous?"

"Hardly." I roll my eyes. "But it *is* fucked up, Cat. You, dating my brother."

She shrugs, but there's an amused grin playing on her lips. She's enjoying this. "Wes said he texted you and you were cool with it."

I squint. "When? I'm pretty sure I'd remember getting a text from him about you."

Her gaze travels upward as she thinks. "A few weeks ago. It was like, two in the morning? He may have been a little drunk."

I wrack my brain. I do remember him sending me a text, late one night. I think it said something along the lines of, *About to get a taste of what it's like to be you, brother.* I had no fucking clue what he meant and didn't care to respond. "Guess I must have missed it."

Her hands move to her hips, her expression indignant. "Why have you been ignoring my phone calls?"

Down the hall, a staff member comes out of the yoga studio with a cleaning cart. I nod toward the nearby weight room, which is empty. Although it doesn't have a door, it's sectioned off by a partial wall that offers a bit more privacy than our present surroundings.

Cat's smile is victorious.

As she follows me into the studio, my limbs are heavy, weighed down by dread. Having this conversation is the last thing I want to do, but at this point, I don't have much choice except to get it over with as quickly as possible, so I can get back to Christy.

I sit on the closest bench to the entryway, so I can keep an eye out for foot traffic in the hall. Cat takes a seat across from me.

"Look," I begin, not quite meeting her gaze. "We agreed it would be best not to talk to each other anymore."

She shakes her head with a defiant pout. "That was *your* suggestion. I never agreed to it."

I rub my left shoulder, which is starting to ache again from tension. "Well, I don't think there's anything left to say."

"We have *history*, Holden. We dated for three years." Her eyes round. "Does that mean nothing to you?"

"That was high school, Cat. We were kids." My jaw clenches.

Her posture straightens, as if my words were a blow she didn't see coming, and she wants to make sure she's prepared for the next one. "When did you get this cold? We may have been kids, but you were my first...everything. Don't you owe me a little respect?"

Her question is all it takes for me to start seeing red. "*Respect*?" I scoff. "Are you fucking kidding me? Were you respecting *me* when you stole my mom's jewelry?"

Cat's eyebrows fly up for a split second before her signature cool demeanor sets back in. "I don't know what you're talking about."

My nostrils flare. "The hell you don't."

She crosses her legs, her gaze shifting to the floor. "If I remember correctly, your housekeeper stole from Margot."

"You and I both know it wasn't Loretta." I move to the edge of the bench and try to meet her eyes, but she still won't look at me. "You planted that necklace in her purse so she'd take the fall."

She shifts backward an inch. "You can't prove that."

When I don't answer, she finally makes eye contact, so I enlighten her. "There was a security camera in my mom's walk-in closet, Cat. I knew Loretta wouldn't steal from us, so I watched the tape, and there you were, digging through every drawer and taking all the most expensive shit. I was fucking... devastated."

She deflates, her shoulders slumping. "Does your mom know?"

"No." I sigh. "I hid the tape. They blamed Loretta for that, too. I felt like absolute shit. Luckily, there was a kid on my baseball team whose family was looking for a cleaner, so I made the connection. I don't think I would've been able to live with myself, otherwise."

Her voice is so thin, I barely make out the words. "Why did you cover for me?"

"I didn't do it for you, Cat. I did it for me." My chest tightens. "I was fucking embarrassed. I couldn't believe my girlfriend of three years would do that to me. To my family. And I still have the tape, by the way. I kept it all these years to remind me to think twice before I give someone my trust."

"So, that's why you broke up with me... I should've known. One day you were in love with me, and the next day you needed space." Her lip quivers.

Bile rises to my throat. "No, Cat. I was never in love with you. You can't be in love with someone you don't know. You are not the person I thought you were."

"Way to hold a fucking grudge, Holden." Her face reddens. "You said it yourself, that was years ago. We were kids."

I sneer at the irony. "And now, here you are, trying to steal from my family again. And it's not just a few necklaces this time, it's my grandmother's legacy. How dare you, Cat?" My voice shakes. "You know how much she meant to me. You know how bad it fucked me up when she finally told me she was sick."

"Yeah." Her eyes well up. "It fucked you up so bad, you landed in my bed. And cheated on your girlfriend, apparently..." Cat wipes her cheek. "She told me you've been together six months, Holden. You and I—"

I pinch the bridge of my nose. "I never cheated on Christy."

Cat's eyes narrow on me. "Oh. I see what this is. You and Christy aren't really dating. You just need her to clean up your image after Soldier Field. It's a PR stunt."

"It started out that way," I admit, reluctantly. "But Christy and I are together now. For real."

Cat sits up a little straighter. "Well, it would be too bad if the press found out what a liar she is. Faking a relationship to distract the public from the fact that she knowingly represented a fraud? Not a good look."

Dammit. She must have Googled Christy. Not only is my ex jealous, but now she has dirt that could destroy my girlfriend's career.

"She had no idea that Penelope was a fraud," I growl. "Trust me."

"Oh, I believe you." She examines her nails. "But you never know how the media's going to spin a story, right?"

I close my eyes, willing my ex to disappear. No such luck. "What the hell do you want from me, Cat?"

Her tone is firm. All business. "I need the jewelry incident to stay between us."

I run a hand through my hair. "Fine."

"Good." But she doesn't look pleased for long. "So, if

you've been harboring these negative feelings for me all these years, why'd you leave the Sports Illustrated party with me that night?"

I let out a wry laugh. "If you remember, I was going to leave the party with Ava, before you intervened."

"Ava who? I know a few Avas." She averts my gaze.

I roll my eyes, not in the mood to indulge her. She knows exactly who I'm talking about. I was leaning in to kiss this particular Ava when Cat wedged herself between us at the bar. Nevertheless, I spell it out. "Ava Elwood? Top model? Your good friend of many years?"

"She *used* to be," Cat huffs. "But Ava can't be trusted. There's a reason she's been divorced twice and has three broken engagements."

I smirk. "Well, I wasn't planning to marry her, Cat."

"She's a snake, Holden. Remember how she took me under her wing when I was in high school and had just started modeling? She gave me the worst advice, but I took it anyway, because she was older and successful. She said you had to be ruthless if you wanted to make it in our world...so that's what I did. I went to casting calls and spread lies about other models to make them look bad. I flat-out stole jobs from other girls by going straight to the client who booked them and offering to work for less. I was awful—and I'm not proud. But Ava's advice worked, Holden. Before long, I was getting the gigs she wanted, and that's when she started getting jealous."

Cat sighs. "Of course, she never admitted to feeling insecure. But one night, I made the mistake of telling her I was bummed because Dex Oliver turned me down—and what does Ava do? She goes after him herself, all so she can prove that she's hotter than me. The whole time they were dating, she stopped speaking to me. She told people we were never friends, and she hardly knew me. Then he dumped her, and she begged for my forgiveness.

"She's not a good person, Holden. She's even worse than I am. I was doing you a favor, trust me."

"Well, thanks, I guess." I thread my fingers through my hair. "In any case, I shouldn't have gone home with anyone that night. We both know it was a mistake."

"No, we *don't* both know that. When you came back to my place, I thought we were...I don't know, rekindling something. Then you woke up the next morning and said we shouldn't have slept together." She blows out a breath. "I tried to shrug it off, but the truth is, I was hoping you wanted to give our relationship a second chance."

I grit my teeth. "Really, Cat? You seem to be forgetting the fact that you're dating my brother."

"Well, I was trying to make you jealous." She folds her arms over her chest. "Obviously, you don't care."

I don't, and I'm tempted to tell her that, but I don't want to be a complete dick, so I bite my tongue. "Just...please stop stringing him along."

It's not so much that I'm trying to protect Wes. He's an asshole. But I don't like the idea of Cat getting cozy with my family again. Once was enough.

"I'm not stringing him along. I mean, that was the idea when I first approached him, but once we started talking, we clicked." She shrugs. "Plus, he's good in bed. So, if I can't have you, I guess he's the next best thing."

"Jesus." I shake my head. "The last thing Wes needs is a girlfriend who'd rather be with me. He has a giant fucking chip on his shoulder because I'm a pro athlete. Look, you don't need him to launch Siren Serum. Find another investor, and leave my family out of it."

Cat fucking laughs at me. "I know I don't need him, Holden. I have plenty of my own capital, plus investors falling at my feet for the chance to collaborate with me. They know as well as I do that Siren Serum is going to be a huge success. But when Wes told me about the competition, I thought this could be a way for me to make amends for stealing from your mom."

My blood boils. "You know, you really have some nerve vying for my grandmother's money and trying to convince me that it's an act of charity. If you really want to make amends, why don't you just write a check to my family's foundation and call it a day?"

"That would look suspicious, Holden," she argues. "I'm trying to make amends without incriminating myself, *obviously*."

I roll my eyes. "How very altruistic of you."

Cat frowns. "It was Ava's idea, you know. Stealing the necklaces. She told me to invest in new headshots with a well-known photographer, but they were so damn expensive. And my parents couldn't afford it, because my dad had gambled away all our money—"

"What? I didn't know your dad had a gambling problem. How come you never told me?" It feels like another small betrayal. Yet another secret my high school girlfriend kept from me.

"My mom begged me not to tell anyone. She wanted to keep up appearances."

I only nod.

"The truth is, stealing from Margot was the first of many bad decisions I've made, and I know I can't pin all the blame on

Ava. But I was young and impressionable when I met her, so you have to take that into account. And I'm trying to turn over a new leaf now. I'm not perfect, but I'm not a heartless villain either."

"I never said you were heartless, Cat." At least not out loud.

"Yeah, well, that's how you're making me feel." She stands and walks toward me, her words more shrill with every step. "Do you know how hard it is to hear that the night we spent together after the Sports Illustrated party meant nothing to you?"

"Cat, please. Keep it down," I say through clenched teeth.

"We've always had great chemistry, Holden," she continues, ignoring my plea. Then she sits down next to me, forcing me to face her before she goes on. "You may not have feelings for me anymore, but don't pretend you didn't want to go home with me that night. You fucked the hell out of me, and you liked it. I know you remember—it was only six weeks ago."

Her voice is piercing, and I rise to my feet, desperate for space. I need to end this conversation, and fast. But how? There's no reasoning with Cat when she's upset. She doesn't care that I was drunk and grieving. She only cares about herself.

Maybe if I apologize, she'll cool down. "Look, I'm so sorry—"

Behind me, I hear a sob.

Fuck!

I was so focused on getting Cat to quiet down that I forgot to keep an eye on the entryway. But I know that sob belongs to Christy before I even spin around. When I do, all I see is her beautiful red hair flying over her shoulders as she runs off.

My panicked gaze lands back on Cat. "Did you know she was standing there?"

Her eyes are wide, and she appears to be as stunned as I am. "No, I was looking at you. I didn't see her, I promise."

I believe Cat, but what does it matter, anyway? That won't make Christy feel better. "I need to go after her."

My ex nods. "Yeah. Okay."

I jog out of the fitness center and catch up to Christy on the path back to the bungalow. She doesn't stop when I call her name, so I reach out for her hand. "Baby, please. Don't run away from me."

"Why *her*?" Christy turns to me, her beautiful face splotchy, her gorgeous eyes wet with tears. "Why is it *always* her?"

I don't understand. "What do you mean?"

"I have no clue what kind of twisted game you two are playing, but I don't want to be involved—and I bet Wes doesn't either. I knew something was off when she asked me how long you and I had been dating. And the look in your eye when I told you I said six months? You fucking panicked." She wriggles out of my grip and storms away again.

"Please, just give me a chance to explain," I beg. "You're not being fair."

She stops dead in her tracks and scoffs. "*I'm* not being fair? You're the one who didn't play fair, Holden! You made me fall for you! You made me feel like what we had was real—"

"It *is* real. You know it is." I drag a hand down my face. "Fuck...I've never felt this way about anyone in my entire life."

"Then maybe you should've told me that you *just* slept with Caterina Fucking Hart, when we're all basically living together, and it's obvious she still wants you!"

"Look, Cat and I dated in high school," I blurt out, before Christy walks away again. "We broke up and went our separate ways. I didn't talk to her for almost twenty years. Then, six weeks ago, I was in New York for a Sports Illustrated party. I told Grandma I was in town and wanted to see her for dinner. That's when she finally told me she was sick."

I'm talking so fast, I can barely catch my breath. "She'd known for months...she had a live-in nurse...and I was completely oblivious. It wrecked me to see her that way. So thin. So frail. I went straight from her apartment to the party, and I was in bad fucking shape."

I heave a sigh. "I drank more than I should have that night and made a decision I regret. I told Cat as much the next morning, and she acted like it was no big deal. Turns out, she was upset. And when you told her we'd been dating for six months, she thought I'd cheated on you, so I had to set the record straight."

I take a tentative step toward Christy, worried she'll run again, but she stays.

"I told her our relationship started off fake, but it's real now," I continue. "That's it. That's the whole truth, Red. I don't have feelings for Cat. I have feelings for you."

"Then why didn't you just tell me from the beginning?" she pleads. "You know how I feel about being kept in the dark. You saw, firsthand, how triggered I was when I found out my mom and Jenna were keeping a secret from me. And you know how messed up I am from Kyle cheating on me. The least you could've done is tell me you have a history with the most gorgeous woman on the planet."

"Christy, *you* are the most gorgeous woman on the planet." I try to put my hands around her, but she pushes me away.

"Stop it." Her voice is cold. "You're full of shit."

My heart fucking breaks. This morning she radiated confidence, and now it's gone, just like that.

"See, baby? That's exactly why I didn't want to tell you. You were feeling so insecure about your body. Then Cat showed up, and you stopped eating. I was worried about you, and I didn't want to make matters worse."

"Because you thought I wouldn't be able to get the image of you fucking Caterina Hart's perfect body out of my mind?" She swallows a sob. "Well, maybe you're right."

She can hardly look at me, and I've never hated myself more. "You have no idea how sorry I am for hurting you. Tell me how I can fix this."

"I just need some space." She wipes a tear from her beautiful, freckled cheek. "I'm too upset right now, and if we keep talking about this, nothing good will come of it. Can I have some time alone at the bungalow?"

"Of course, baby."

"I'll let you know when I'm ready for you to come back," she says on a deep exhale.

Her eyes look so fucking sad, and all because of me. I'd do anything to put a smile back on her face. I'm tempted to tell her I love her, but not now. Not like this. She won't believe me, even though it's the only thing I know is true. "Call me if you need anything."

She nods and continues to the bungalow, like she can't get away from me fast enough. I watch until she disappears from view, then I turn and walk away like a damn dog with its tail between its legs. I head toward the fitness center, thinking a workout might help me pass the time while I wait to hear from Christy, but I don't make it through the front doors before the urge to run back to the bungalow almost overtakes me.

I reach into my pocket and pull out my cell phone,

desperate for advice from someone I know is a hell of a lot wiser than I am.

"Hey!" she says brightly on the other end of the line. "Everyone online is obsessed with you and Christy, myself included. Your chemistry is fire! Please tell me this is real, and you're not just acting."

"I've never been much of an actor, Lola."

I can hear her clapping through the phone. "Perfect! Because I just started writing a song about you guys."

"Don't get too excited yet." I heave a sigh. "I'm worried I just fucked it all up."

"Oh, no." She sucks in a breath. "Tell me everything."

Of course, Lola remembers that Cat and I dated in high school, so I catch her up on the rest. She can hardly believe it when I tell her Cat went after Wes to make me jealous, and she's here on the island competing for my grandma's inheritance with him. I don't go into detail about Christy's body issues because it's not my place, but it turns out I don't need to.

"Poor Christy. I can't think of many women who'd want to wear a swimsuit next to The Siren. And then she finds out you dated her for three years *and* slept with her again six weeks ago? I'd feel insecure, too...especially if it seemed like you were trying to hide it from me."

"What do I do, Lo?" I sit on a bench outside the fitness center, upset and exhausted. "Christy told me she needed space, but she doesn't always manage her emotions well, and I hate that she's alone right now. I just want to make sure she's okay. She doesn't have to talk—I'll sit on the lanai and she can ignore me—I just want to be close, in case she needs something."

Lola's silent for several seconds. "That's...really fucking sweet."

"Yeah?"

"I mean, maybe I'm just lonely because I've been hiding out at the cabin, but if You Know Who were to knock on my door and say those words to me, I guarantee you, it would go over well." I can practically see the blush on her cheeks, and it angers me.

"Really, Lo? Mr. *Black and Blue*? You deserve so much better than that guy."

"We spent a whole week at this cabin once. I can't help but miss him, now that I'm back here, Holden," she tries to explain. "We had the best time together."

I pinch the bridge of my nose. "You mean while he was cheating on Emmy Mason?"

"He didn't cheat on her, he ghosted her," Lola corrects me.

"Is that better?"

"Ugh," she groans. "I don't know. Okay, let's get your love life in order first, then we can worry about mine. Go work things out with Christy, so I can sing the song I'm writing at your wedding."

The thought puts a smile on my face. "Thanks, Lo."

I jog back to the bungalow, but no sooner am I at the door with my key in hand, than I hear voices coming from inside. They're muffled at first, but then they get louder. Closer.

"You're drunk," Christy says. "You just downed half a bottle of whiskey. Go sleep it off."

Silence.

"Don't look at me like that," she goes on.

My heart hammers, and my muscles brace.

"How about one kiss for the road? It's nothing Cat and Holden haven't done," I hear my brother say.

My brother?! What the fuck?!

Christy screams when the door flies open and hits the wall with a thud. I grab Wes by his shirt collar and fling him onto the porch. He doesn't fall, but lunges toward me, wasted and clumsy. The next thing I know, he's on the ground, and I don't even remember punching him.

What I do remember is the sound of my shoulder popping...and the searing pain that brings me to my knees.

CHAPTER 21

"Holden!" I scream, rushing to kneel beside him. He's clutching his left shoulder. The arm he used to knock Wes out cold. His pitching arm...

The one his career depends on.

His eyes are squeezed shut and his breathing is ragged. He doesn't answer me, so I try again. "Look at me," I plead, which gets his attention.

"Are you okay, Red?" he rasps.

Despite how hurt I feel, I'm touched by his concern. Here he is, in excruciating pain, and he's prioritizing my well-being over his.

If only he'd been so considerate when Little Miss Sexpot showed up on the island, he'd have spared me the humiliation of finding out about their recent history the way I did. The mere thought of Holden and The Siren in bed together hits me like a gut punch again, but I shake it off.

"I'm fine," I assure him. "I'm more worried about you. Do you need to see a doctor?"

He shakes his head even before the words are out of my mouth. "The pain's easing up. I just need a minute."

He stands from the wooden floorboards and sits on the hand-carved porch swing, cradling his left arm against his body. It's so strange seeing him this way. Holden McBride, ace pitcher and MVP, wounded and vulnerable, like a bird with a broken wing.

My mind flits back to before he left for the fitness center. He said his shoulder felt tight because he hasn't been keeping up with his workouts and stretching. But I can't help but wonder, now, if there's more to the story. Why else would that punch he threw drive him to his knees?

My brow furrows with concern. "Can I get you some ice?"

He shoots me a smile that makes my knees weak. He must be relieved that I'm not cursing him out, or insisting he leave. "Not right now, baby. Come sit with me."

Just as I settle in next to him, Wes lets out a weak groan. Holden and I both watch as he attempts to lift a hand to his head, but gives up and lets his arm fall back down with a thud.

When I meet Holden's gaze, his jaw is clenched. "Did he touch you?"

"No." I shake my head. "He didn't. I promise."

Holden nods but his muscles stay tense. Even injured, he looks ready to strike again, if necessary.

For the sake of his shoulder, I hope it doesn't come to that.

"Tell me what happened." His tone is still gruff, every word peppered with disdain for his brother.

I blow out a breath. "When I got back to the bungalow, I was..."

Sobbing. I couldn't see through my tears.

"Distracted," I decide to say instead. Holden's upset

enough as it is, and I don't want to make him feel even worse. "I must've forgotten to lock the door. I went to sit on the lanai, and not ten minutes later, I heard noises coming from the kitchenette. Cabinets shutting. Glasses clinking. I assumed it was you. And well, it wasn't."

"What did he want?" Holden's still watching Wes, who mumbles something unintelligible but doesn't move.

"To talk to you. I told him you weren't here, and he said he'd wait," I explain.

I'm sure Wes knew I didn't want him to stay. My cheeks were streaked with tears, my eyes red. Unsmiling and arms crossed over my chest, I stood there, willing him to leave, but he didn't care. He stalked around like he owned the place—which I suppose he does, being a McBride. This estate is a second home to him, just like it is to Holden. I couldn't very well kick him out, could I?

"Then, he poured an obscene amount of whiskey into a tumbler," I go on, "and downed it like it was Gatorade. I asked him if he was okay, and that's when he told me he overheard you talking to Lola on the phone."

"Fuck," Holden mutters.

"Yeah. Now he knows he's Caterina's consolation prize, and she'd rather be with you." My throat tightens with the threat of a sob, but I choke it back. "And that whiskey did *not* take the edge off his anger. Every minute he had to wait for you made him more enraged. At one point, he slammed his fist on the counter, which rattled me, so I told him to go sleep it off. He agreed, but when we were by the door...well, I'm guessing you heard what he asked me for."

The memory of Wes towering over me, his hand braced on the wall above my head, makes me shudder. His mouth was so close to mine, I could almost taste the whiskey on his breath. He was seconds away from kissing me when I shook my head no.

"I told him to stop, and I'd like to think he would have, if you hadn't burst through the door at that exact moment. He's just so much bigger than I am," I add. "That's why I was scared."

"I'm so fucking sorry, Red." Holden's nostrils flare. "This is all my fault."

I look down at my lap. "Yeah. You should probably be a bit more strategic about where you hold private conversations."

He winces, and I'm not sure if it's because his shoulder hurts, or because of what I just said. It's a catty comment, but I can't help it. Overhearing the one and only Caterina Hart say that the man I'm in love with "fucked the hell out of her and liked it" made me feel sick to my stomach. Especially since it happened only six weeks ago. Every time the thought crosses my mind, another wave of nausea hits me.

Of all the women in the world, Holden has to have a history with the very same supermodel whose photos I caught my ex jerking off to. You have to admit, it's ironic.

It's like the Universe is testing me. Or giving me the finger. I'm not sure which. All I know is that my self-esteem has plummeted again, after being at an all-time high. When I woke up this morning, I felt more confident in my body than ever, and I knew I had Holden to thank for that. After he left for the fitness center, I missed him so much, I decided to keep him company, after all. I'm my own boss, and I've never taken more than a long weekend away from work. Why not enjoy every minute with Holden while we're here?

Why not tell him how happy he makes me?

I was about to, when I overheard him talking to Cat. I didn't catch the whole conversation, but I heard more than enough.

"You...mother...fucker..." Wes lifts his fingers to his cheekbone, then grimaces. The skin around his left eye has begun to swell. He pants as he props himself up on one elbow.

Holden jumps to his feet, wild-eyed. I follow suit.

"Please," I whisper to him, so Wes can't hear. My gaze travels from Holden's face to the arm he's still holding tight against his body. "Don't do anything that'll land you on a surgeon's table, okay?"

Holden lets out a low growl of dissatisfaction as Wes makes it onto his feet, moving with caution. I don't think he's in any shape to defend himself against Holden's wrath, so if there's any sense at all in that whiskey-laden brain of his, he'll leave.

"I'm going to give you thirty seconds to get the fuck off this porch," Holden says. In response, Wes rolls the one eye that isn't circled by tender, swollen flesh. "And if you don't want to end up in the hospital," he adds, "keep your distance from my girlfriend."

By some miracle, Wes ambles his way off the porch and down the path leading to the guesthouse without further incident. When he's out of sight, I heave a sigh of relief.

Holden pulls his phone out of his pocket and stares at the screen for several seconds before telling me what's on his mind. "Under normal circumstances, I'd call our security team to make sure he gets back to the guesthouse safely. He's drunk, and he was just unconscious...he might wander into the ocean. But after the stunt he just pulled with you, I'm not so sure I care."

"You should call them," I urge with a nod. "He's still your brother."

I can't say I feel bad for Wes, seeing as he's such a colossal jerk. But while he was here chugging whiskey, he aired a few of his childhood grievances and, to be honest, I could relate. Just like I grew up in the shadow of my prettier, more popular big sister, Wes always felt second best to Holden. Caterina's admission confirmed his biggest fear. It doesn't excuse the fact that he tried to kiss me, but I do understand what drove him to drink.

Holden leads me to sit on the porch swing again. As he makes the call to security, he puts his arm around me, and my mind becomes a maelstrom of mixed emotions.

It feels so good to rest my body against his. It wasn't long ago that we were tangled up in our bedsheets, naked. We didn't just fuck today—we made love. It was like we picked up where we left off last night on the beach, when he stroked my hair and told me to look into his eyes while he made me come. It was my first time feeling so emotionally connected during sex, and I relished it.

In bed today, every touch, every glance, every whisper was charged with the same heartfelt passion. It was so intense that the last orgasm Holden gave me ended with me bursting into tears. Happy tears. That's never happened to me before.

Not even an hour later, I heard Caterina tell Holden that they've always had great chemistry, and I came crashing down from cloud nine.

"Look, I know I messed up," Holden says to me after the security team assures him they have eyes on Wes. "But if it makes any difference at all, I thought you'd have an easier time hearing about me and Cat after leaving the island, when you didn't have to see her every day. I knew you were feeling insecure around her, and I was trying to be considerate of your feelings."

My gut tightens. "So, I work up the courage to be vulnerable with you...and in return, you treat me like a child who can't handle the truth?"

Come to think of it, that's what my mom and Jenna did, too, when they decided not to tell me about Tim Shaker right away. The fact that the most important people in my life think I'm weak is my worst nightmare.

"Not to mention that *everyone* here knew about your history with Caterina except me," I go on. "Do you know how humiliating that is? I mean, did your parents and Wes assume I knew? Or did you rope them into hiding it from me, too?"

Holden squints his eyes shut for a moment, as if the thought's too painful to bear. "I didn't ask anyone to hide it from you, baby. I just didn't think it through. In a million years, I never would've expected Cat to show up here, and when she did, I panicked. I didn't know what to say to her; I didn't know what to say to you." He stops and wipes his brow, his gaze faraway. "I think it all goes back to..."

"What?"

"Years ago, I told Abby something that upset her, and we nearly lost her because of it." His breath hitches.

"What do you mean?" I rest my hand on his thigh. "What happened?"

It takes him a moment to respond. "When Abby was a senior in high school, she started dating a junior that I played baseball with. I always thought he was a prick, but she said he was 'different' with her." Holden rolls his eyes. "Anyway, they'd been together five or six months when I overheard him in the dugout, bragging about how he'd banged a college freshman the night before. He didn't realize I was there because I'd shown up late that day. Fucking asshole."

I take his hand in mine, and he continues.

"I was so pissed, I turned around, went back home, and told Abby. She said she didn't believe me. But that night, she helped herself to our dad's whiskey, then took his Porsche for a joyride. When my father realized that his daughter and his car were missing, I told him I might have upset her with the news about her boyfriend. About twenty minutes later, the hospital called."

He runs a hand through his hair. "She'd totaled the car. By some miracle she walked away with only minor injuries, but she looked like hell. She had cuts and bruises everywhere."

I frown. "You must have been so scared."

"I was shaken for weeks. My parents recovered much more quickly. Their biggest concern, after finding out that Abby would be okay, was avoiding a scandal. They decided to keep her home for a month, until her bruises and cuts were healed. They spun a story that she'd been offered a special internship at a consulting firm in Paris, but she was in her bedroom the entire time. And my dad blamed it all on me. He said I nearly killed her, and I should've kept my mouth shut."

My forehead creases. "That's absurd. It wasn't your fault. And to top it off, you were a kid. It was cruel of him to put that burden on you."

"Well, my dad's never been known to be kind." Holden blows out a breath. "He also told me to keep my distance from Abby, if I knew what was good for me."

"Does she know that?" My mind travels back to my conversation with her at the pool house the other day. She seemed so sad about her strained relationship with Holden. Has this all been a misunderstanding?

He shrugs. "It doesn't matter. She hated me for what I did. All those days she was stuck at home, she wouldn't so much as look me in the eye. Things haven't been the same between us since."

My heart sinks.

"Look, I'm not saying any of this to get sympathy," he goes on. "I just want you to understand why I was afraid to upset you. But I promise to be an open book from now on."

A hint of a smile forms on my lips. "I do like open books."

"I know you do." He winks at me, then brings my hand to his mouth and kisses it. "I promise to do better, Red. I'm still learning how to navigate relationships. Most of mine have been superficial. Those women cared way more about my name and my bank account than anything else. The truth is, baby...you might be my first real girlfriend."

Girlfriend. It's the first time he's called me that without an audience, and my head spins. Not because I doubt his feelings for me, although I'll admit that was my initial reaction after overhearing his conversation with Cat. But now that he's explained why he was afraid to tell me about their history, I can't help but wonder if I'm up to the task of being his girlfriend. Holden McBride will always have women falling at his feet. He's rich, famous, and so fucking handsome. He needs to be with someone who's confident enough not to wilt every time a woman bats her eyelashes at him.

I am not that woman yet. But I want to be.

God, I want to be.

"What's wrong?" Holden asks when I'm silent.

I'm tempted to say, "Nothing." Being vulnerable with Holden feels scarier now, since it's backfired on me once. But he promised to be an open book, and I need to show him the same courtesy.

"You put off telling me about your history with Caterina because of my body insecurities," I begin. "And I can't really blame you. For better or worse, I dumped my issues onto you—"

"Christy, you confided in me. It wasn't a burden. It was a privilege," he says with an earnest yet smoldering gaze.

Dammit, Holden, do you have to be so goddamn irresistible?

I let out a lengthy sigh. "Well, thank you for seeing it that way. But regardless, I can't very well share my baggage and expect you not to carry it in some way or another."

"Does that..." His eyes light up the slightest bit. "Does that mean you forgive me?"

I nod, but my lip quivers.

Holden's forehead creases, dissatisfied with my answer. "But?"

My eyes well up.

"Talk to me, Red," he urges.

"I was a fool to think that an entire lifetime of insecurity could disappear in four days," I cry. "Even if those four days were full of amazing sex with a man who makes me feel more beautiful than I ever have."

Holden squeezes my hand. "So it'll take more time. I can wait."

"But what if—" I wipe my cheeks. "What if it never happens? What if I always feel like..."

He shakes his head, encouraging me to continue. "Like what?"

You know those nightmares where you're on stage, naked,

in front of a crowd of your biggest critics? That's how vulnerable I feel.

But I answer him anyway. "Like you could do better than me."

Holden winces.

My gut clenches. "Is it your shoulder? Are you in pain?"

"No, baby." His brow furrows. "It just really hurts to hear you talk about yourself like that."

My sobs come on stronger. "I'm so fucked up, Holden."

He puts his good arm around me and draws me to rest my head on his chest. "We're all fucked up in our own way."

"But what if my brand of fucked up makes us incompatible? You can't be with someone who's going to fall apart whenever a gorgeous woman pays you attention."

Holden's tone is teasing yet gentle. "Nice try, baby."

"Nice try?" I look up from his chest, where I've shed so many tears, his shirt is wet.

"You're trying to walk off, but the game's far from over," he declares.

I can't help but smile at the baseball analogy.

"I'm not going to let you give up that easily." He strokes my hair. "Like you said, it's only been four days. Just be patient with yourself, okay? Can you do that?"

I take a deep breath. "Okay."

He presses his lips to my tearstained cheek, then brushes his mouth against mine. It's not the sort of urgent kiss that begs for more. It's a tender one that demands nothing in return.

If it were only me and Holden in this private little bungalow for the rest of time, I know I'd be okay. But we're having dinner with his family at the main house tonight. And directly afterward, we'll board the private jet, bound for the library gala in New York City. A city I love with all my heart, but can't quite separate from the scars of my last relationship.

It's my first time returning to the scene of the crime. But this time, I won't be able to hide from my feelings in cozy bookstores and rainy-day cafes, the way I used to when I lived there. As Holden McBride's date to a star-studded gala, I'll be in the spotlight and under the microscope. And if I'm going to pass muster, I'll have to play the role of the woman I want to be: Comfortable in my body. Unbothered by the beauties who flirt with my date. Confident that I'm the one who belongs on his arm.

It's a tall order for someone whose self-esteem is as fractured as mine.

And as much as it breaks my heart to admit it...I'm afraid I don't have it in me to succeed.

CHAPTER 22

Holden

After packing for New York and changing into dinner attire, I take two minutes alone in the bathroom to panic.

Holy fucking shit, my shoulder.

I must have torn something when I punched Wes. Or maybe there was already a tear, and I made it worse. Who knows. What I do know is, it hurts like hell, and I'm completely and utterly fucked. I couldn't toss a slow pitch to Maisie or Matt right now if I tried.

I'm no doctor, but I'm also no stranger to shoulder pain, and I don't see how any amount of rehabbing could fix the damage I just did. Elisia's an expert physical therapist, but she's no magician. Odds are, I need surgery, and I'll be out of commission for months.

If there's ever a time for me to be on the injured list, this is *not* it. My contract is up at the end of this season, and if the Starlings don't offer me an extension, I'll become a free agent. But who's going to want a sidelined player with a streaking scandal to his name? Not to mention I'm thirty-six, which is practically ancient in my profession. Most pitchers would have retired by now.

The only thing I have working in my favor is that I'm not most pitchers. I've won the Cy Young Award for best pitching in the National League four times. I've also been named MVP twice, despite the fact that pitchers are far less likely to earn the title than position players. Will that be enough to buy me one more season?

I cannot fucking go out like this—with my final act as a Major League player being the stunt I pulled at Soldier Field. I'll be remembered for how my career ended, and the eighteen years that came before that day won't mean a thing. How will I sleep at night, knowing that I could've been a legend, but I threw it all away because of my poor judgment and worse coping skills? I don't know if I'd ever manage to redeem myself.

Unless...

Maybe Racing Hearts is the answer. Is this potential new career another posthumous gift from my grandmother? Did she not only send me Christy, but write the terms of her will so I'd have something meaningful to devote myself to when pitching's no longer an option? Because she worried how I'd manage without her and without baseball?

It'd be nice if you won that competition, she said to me in my dream.

Or maybe it was more than a dream. A dearly departed grandmother returning to help her bereft grandson is just the kind of ludicrous thought a desperate man might cling to...but I need to believe my luck will change. The only woman who loved me like a mother is gone. The only girlfriend I've ever adored might leave me, too. The only career I've ever known is hanging by a thread, like my fucking shoulder. The only money

I have after donating most of mine to charity isn't enough to fund Racing Hearts.

I need to win this competition.

If only I hadn't just knocked my brother out cold.

If only I weren't on my way to a family dinner where my parents are bound to find out...and then what?

Will they tell the board I should be disqualified? I can't see them rallying behind me, regardless of the fact that Wes tried to kiss my girlfriend. He'll call it a misunderstanding, or say it never happened, and they'll believe him. Because, of course, his neanderthal brother punched him for no reason.

Fuck. Fuck. Fuck. Fuck. Fuck.

Time's up—I can't hide in here forever. I have to get through this dinner at the main house so I can take Christy to New York and show her the time of her life. Whatever's wrong with my shoulder can wait until after the gala. Christy loves that library so much, she once dreamed of getting married there. I will not ruin this for her.

I take a deep breath and open the bathroom door. Christy's seated on our bed, wearing a cobalt-blue dress and looking drop-dead gorgeous as usual, but nervous, too. She looks up at me. "This dinner is going to be a shitshow."

I chuckle. "Yes, but not in the way you think. If there's one thing the McBrides are good at, it's putting on a performance. 'The world is always watching,' my mother likes to say. I expect a lot of veiled insults and criticism through gritted teeth, but there won't be any yelling, I guarantee you. Even Wes will be on his best behavior, because our parents will be there." With a heavy heart, I walk up to her and take her hand in mine. "I think he knows better than to even look in your direction, but if you feel at all uncomfortable—"

"I'll be fine," she assures me. "But do you really think he's going to show up drunk, and with a black eye?"

I run my fingers through my hair. "You'd be surprised. Like I said, the McBrides excel at keeping up appearances." I take her other hand and help her off the bed. "Come on, let's get this over with so we can get you to the library, where you belong."

Her smile makes me lightheaded.

We're ten minutes late when we arrive at the main house. I probably allowed too much time for my panic spiral before we left the bungalow, but better there than here. If I still have a chance at winning this competition, I need to be on my best behavior tonight as well, which means no big emotional displays —angry, anxious, or otherwise. It's not the McBride way.

Hand in hand, Christy and I step onto the lanai, where my family's having cocktails. Cat's nowhere in sight. It would be such a fucking relief if she sat this one out, but I won't hold my breath. I do see Wes seated on the couch, talking to Alistair. My brother's wearing sunglasses, though the sun's already set and there's barely any light to speak of, except for the afterglow. I'm guessing he's already told our parents I hit him. I'm sure I'll be getting an earful about it soon enough.

But when my mom greets us, it's not with the air of a woman seeking justice for her golden child. At least not that I can tell, given all the cosmetic enhancements she's had done.

"Oh, hello, dears!" my mom coos with a martini in hand. I have a feeling it's not her first drink, judging by the gleam in her eye and the spring in her step. She kisses Christy on the cheek first, then me. "How kind of you to join us," she says in my ear, a passive-aggressive dig because we're late.

And so it begins.

"Christin*a*," my mother emphasizes, finally letting go of *Christine*, but eager to let us know she considers the extra syllable a chore. (Never mind that we've told her a dozen times to call her Christy.) "I hear that Holden is whisking you away to New York tonight."

She must know because I booked the jet. I certainly didn't go out of my way to tell her. I'm sure she has many opinions about me and Christy playing hooky for a day, none of which I'm remotely interested in. "We'll be back before the board announces their decision on Tuesday afternoon," I tell her.

My mother still shakes her head. "It's such a pity. I scheduled a photographer for tomorrow morning. Didn't you see family photos in the itinerary, Holden?"

"Must have missed it," I lie.

"Well, I do hope you enjoy your trip," she snarls, her lips pursed. "What's the occasion?"

Christy looks up at me, smiling. "Holden's taking me to the library gala. I'm so excited."

"Well, I'm sure you are, dear, being a literary agent and all." My mother takes another sip of her drink. "It's a good thing Holden can rely on you to carry the conversation at the dinner table. It's an intellectual crowd; I can't imagine anyone will want to talk about sports all night."

I watch as Christy's face flushes red, her jaw tightens, and her eyes narrow on Margot McBride. My girlfriend is fucking pissed.

It's so hot. And heartwarming. I take her hand in mine and kiss it. "You're right, Mom," I say, my eyes on Christy. "I'm the luckiest man in the world."

"Well, you're certainly luckier than Wesley," my mother

replies without missing a beat. "Did you hear what happened to him?"

My heart picks up speed. Is this the part where she tells us he was knocked out by some "uneducated boor," then lets her gaze linger on me just long enough to make it clear she knows who the boor is?

When I don't answer, Christy clears her throat. "What happened?"

Margot takes another drink. "He was at the fitness center doing overhead presses, lost his grip on the dumbbell, and it hit him square in the eye. Can you believe it?"

Not really. It's even harder to believe that my brother didn't throw me under the bus. Is it possible he actually grew a conscience and feels badly for making a pass at Christy?

"Thankfully, he let Cat put some of her Siren Serum on it, and it's already looking much better," my mother continues with the kind of beaming smile I didn't know she was capable of. "Isn't that remarkable?"

I heave a sigh. "It's something, alright." So, not only does Siren Serum fight thigh dimples, now it's some sort of magic cure-all?

Fuck my life.

"It's a true testament to the product's potential," Mom goes on. "Even your great-uncle Alistair is impressed. I guess you could say it's the silver lining to Wes injuring himself. Now we can all see, firsthand, how impressive the serum is."

Next to me, Christy threads her fingers through mine in a show of solidarity. Or sympathy. With Alistair in my corner, Racing Hearts stood a chance, but now? Looks like by punching Wes, I knocked my own dream out of the running. And my brother didn't even have to snitch.

My mom, meanwhile, rests her hand on my fucked-up shoulder, adding insult to injury. "Oh, I hope you won't be too disappointed if you don't win the competition, Holden. You really did try your best, and I'm sure it wasn't easy, given your lack of schooling."

Christy squeezes my palm so hard, her hand trembles, a clear sign that her anger at my mother has reached a boiling point. I turn to see her with flared nostrils and wild eyes, chewing her lip to keep from chewing out my mom.

God, I love you, Christy Andersen.

"Well, I'm going to go fetch your father," Margot continues. "He's been on a business call for an hour and seems to have forgotten that we have guests. Anyway, please help yourselves to drinks and appetizers." She turns to my girlfriend and eyes her from head to toe. "And be sure to try the fried coconut shrimp, Christin*a*. I hear it's delightful."

"Mom—" I begin, but Christy elbows me.

"You know, I think I will, Margot, thank you," she says with a mischievous glint in her eye. "Your son and I had quite a marathon workout today, and I'm famished."

My mom adjusts her diamond necklace. If she were wearing pearls, I daresay she'd clutch them. "Of course you did," she responds with a sneer before turning on her heel and sauntering away to find my father.

"I'm sorry." Christy faces me, her fists clenched. "I tried to bite my tongue, but...that woman really grinds my gears, Holden."

I chuckle. "No need to apologize, baby. She was asking for it."

"And the way she belittled your proposal like that?" Christy fumes. "The nerve of her, implying that you should give up on

Racing Hearts and walk away, when the board hasn't even decided yet."

I blow out a breath. "Maybe she's right. I mean, Cat has the board members in her pocket. Zoe idolizes her. Dan can't take his eyes off her. And if what my mother says is true, and even Alistair's impressed with the serum, what chance do I have?"

Christy's shoulders slump.

"It's just my luck," I go on with a wry laugh. "I give my brother a black eye, and all it does is prove how effective Siren Serum is."

My girlfriend raises an eyebrow, wheels turning. "But what are the odds that Caterina and Wes will still want to collaborate if they're broken up? I can't imagine their relationship will last, now that he knows she'd rather be with you. And she didn't come to dinner tonight. Maybe she left and took Siren Serum with her. Maybe he's wearing sunglasses to hide his tears."

"I don't know, baby." I scratch my forehead. "When you're as calculating as Wes and Cat, business relationships tend to take priority over romantic ones. They could hate each other's guts and still work together if the financial reward is enticing enough. And in this case, it seems like it might be."

Christy frowns. "Okay. Let's say, for the sake of argument, that you don't win the competition. That doesn't have to be the end of your dream. You could still fund Racing Hearts yourself, couldn't you?" She shrugs. "I mean, maybe you'd scale back a bit without your grandmother's money, or maybe Dex would put up the rest, depending on how involved he wants to be. Either way, you have options."

She's assuming I'm not an idiot who donated most of my money to charity. If I told Dex Oliver how much I have in my savings account, I bet he'd laugh in my face. There's no way I'll be able to honor my grandmother's legacy the way I want to, unless I win this competition. And, let's face it, the odds are not in my favor.

"But I'm not giving up yet, and neither should you," Christy quickly adds, perhaps picking up on my distress. "The board wouldn't be doing their job if they didn't consider what Grandma Evelyn would have wanted. And in that respect, you make a much more compelling case than Wes."

"Speak of the devil," I mutter as I catch sight of my brother walking toward us. I wrap my arm tight around my girlfriend's waist and pull her flush against me.

"I come in peace," Wes says, hands raised. It looks like he's sobered up a bit in the two hours since we last saw him. He smells like coffee and mint instead of whiskey, now. "I assume Mom told you what happened to me in the weight room?"

"Yeah." I narrow my eyes at him, still unsure of his intentions. "Sounds like quite the freak accident."

"Consider it my apology." He sounds more sincere than I'm used to, and when he turns to my girlfriend, his tone softens further. "I'm sorry, Christy. I drank too much, and I wasn't thinking clearly. It won't happen again."

"It certainly won't," I warn him.

"I appreciate the apology." Christy's tone is a hell of a lot more diplomatic than mine. "It's a pleasant surprise, if I'm being honest."

Wes runs a hand through his hair. "Yeah, well...I told Cat how I really got this black eye, and she insisted I come here to apologize. She called me an asshole with a chip on my shoulder, and she's right. I made a move on you because I knew it would hurt Holden. It's obvious how much he cares about you."

Christy looks up at me, and I press my lips to her forehead, confirming how much I do, in fact, care about her. When she smiles, the tension in my jaw eases.

"Cat also thinks I'm only dating her to provoke him," Wes nods at me, "and I guess she has a point there, too. It could've been any woman saying she wanted my brother over me, and I would've been just as pissed off."

"So, you two broke up?" Christy asks, a hopeful gleam in her eye.

"Not exactly." My brother grins. "I think we just leveled the playing field. We both got into this relationship for the wrong reasons, but the sex is too good to call it quits. So we're going to start from scratch."

"Great," Christy replies with a half-hearted smile.

"Plus, if we break up now, she might take Siren Serum to another investor, and that would be a travesty. She's really onto something with this shit. Take a look," he says, raising his sunglasses.

I can't hide my surprise. "What the fuck? The swelling's practically gone."

"I'll be damned," Christy mutters.

"I know." Wes smiles, then slides the sunglasses down his forehead. "Well, Cat's waiting for me at the guesthouse, so I'm going to head back. She thought it would be best if she didn't come to dinner tonight, under the circumstances."

Hmm. That's awfully considerate of her. And, come to think of it, why is my wily brother being so nice? Maybe Cat confessed to him that she stole Mom's jewelry, then convinced him not to piss me off, so I don't rat her out. Divulging her secret to my family would certainly be an easy way for me to take Siren Serum out of the running and guarantee a win for Racing Hearts.

But I'm not the type to play dirty when the stakes are this high. I need to earn this money fair and square. Not to mention, I can't very well let my family go into business with a jewelry thief. If the truth about Cat comes out, my mom will be livid that I didn't say anything. I promised my ex I wouldn't, though. And if I don't keep my word, she'll tell the press about my fake relationship, further damaging Christy's reputation. That's not a risk I'm willing to take.

My girlfriend nods as Wes waves goodbye and walks away.

"Are you okay?" I ask her when he's out of earshot. It couldn't have been easy for her to hear my brother admit he used her as a pawn in our sibling rivalry. Much less to hear him talk so much about Cat—a woman she feels so threatened by. I draw Christy in for a hug, ignoring the sting in my left shoulder when I squeeze her tight.

"I think that went well, all things considered." When she steps back, she grins, but it's perfunctory. There's no joy in her eyes, which worries me. I know I can't expect her to recover from today's events so quickly, but what Christy said earlier scared me.

What if I always feel like you could do better than me?

Or, what if she decides she can do better than a washed-up baseball player who didn't go to college?

"I heard you guys are leaving tonight," my sister Abby says, appearing from behind Christy. "Mom's pissed."

I can't help but smile. "I know. We're missing family pictures."

Abby rolls her eyes. "Lucky."

Christy and I both chuckle, and Abby's typically hard expression softens. "I guess we'll have to say goodbye after dinner," she adds. "The kids and I are heading back to New

York tomorrow night. They have a violin performance at school this week."

"That's too bad," Christy says, brow furrowed. "We'll miss you."

The words come out of her mouth so easily. Words I've wanted to say to Abby for years, but they always catch in my throat, since Dad's stern warning years ago.

I look over my shoulder and see Maisie and Matt playing with Zoe on the opposite end of the lanai. Maisie's braiding her teenaged cousin's hair, while Matt plays a hand-clapping game with her. My heart sinks. If history's any indication, I'll see my niece and nephew once more over the holidays, and that'll be it for an entire year.

"Kiddos!" Abby calls out. "Come here."

Her command is met with resistance at first, until Maisie and Matt look up and see me standing with their mom. Right away, they come running over.

"Uncle Holden won't be around tomorrow, so you'll have to say goodbye to him tonight." When her kids start pouting, Abby goes on. "I know you're sad, but we'll see him soon for Christmas in Connecticut, okay?"

Matt scowls. "Christmas isn't *that* soon."

"Uncle Holden, can I sit next to you at dinner?" Maisie pleads, jumping up and down.

My heart swells. "Of course you can."

"Hey, no fair!" Matt whines. "I want to sit next to him, too!"

"I think that can be arranged." Christy winks at Matt. "How about Uncle Holden sits between you and Maisie, and I sit next to your mom? I'd love to get to know her better."

Her suggestion gets her a high-five from my nephew and a

rare smile from Abby. Rare around me, at least. She's all smiles when her husband Wyatt's around. And now Christy. Could my girlfriend be the bridge that brings Abby and me closer again?

Not if my girlfriend leaves me.

My sister looks down at her watch. "Alright, I think cocktail hour's just about done. Shall we head into the dining room? I'm hungry, and Alistair just polished off the last of the coconut shrimp."

"Darn," Christy says, shooting me a genuine smile this time. "I promised your mother I'd try them."

With the kids at my side, I follow my girlfriend and sister into the main house as they chat like old friends. Watching them laugh together, I get the distinct feeling that I'm teetering on the edge of happiness. And depending on which way the wind blows, I might get everything I've ever wished for. The woman of my dreams. A family of our own. A mended relationship with my sister. A fulfilling career beyond baseball. A legacy that would make my grandmother proud.

I could live the life that's almost within my reach.

Or, I could blink and end up with nothing.

Christy

The ten-hour trip to New York in the McBride family's private jet is, of course, the most luxurious travel experience of my life. Physically and emotionally exhausted, Holden and I sleep through most of the overnight flight. But the moments we're awake are nice. He reads my copy of *The Great Gatsby*, and I continue the psychological thriller I started by the pool the other day. It's the perfect book for me right now: so fast-paced, I almost forget about my romance woes, both personal and professional. It's a relief, because the insecurities triggered by the news of Caterina and Holden have made the sting of losing *Edison's Love* to another agent even more painful. I've never felt more inadequate.

The McBrides' chauffeur is waiting for us when we deplane, and he drives us to The Plaza, where Holden booked a suite. It's a perfect fall day in New York. We drop off our bags, and Holden suggests we go for a walk in Central Park. I'm still worried about his shoulder and wonder if we should stay at the hotel so he can ice it again, like he did before our flight. But he insists he's fine. Maybe he hopes to minimize the tension of being in this romantic penthouse suite together, while I try to figure out if I'm capable of being the woman he needs.

He holds my hand on our stroll but puts no pressure on me to perform—even when passersby snap pictures with their cell phones. There are no passionate lip-locks this time. Not for the purpose of giving spectators a show, or otherwise. I know he's offering me the space I need, and I appreciate it. But the lack of kisses makes me long for the bliss of yesterday morning, before I was lured to the fitness center by The Siren's song.

Under different circumstances, this might have been one of the best days of my life. A walk around Central Park on a gorgeous autumn day. A stay at The Plaza, including a visit to their salon to get my hair and makeup done. A night at the New York Public Library with the man of my dreams.

But there's a dark cloud hanging over me that I just can't shake.

The last time I felt this down on myself was when Kyle cheated on me with Tessa. That's the beautiful doctor he met at work. When I walked in on them having sex on our couch, she apologized to me profusely, then burst into tears. Lucky for her, she'd kept her dress on and was able to make a quick exit. Although she did leave behind her underwear, which I later found on my fucking coffee table. But the worst part was that Kyle ran after her.

My self-esteem was in the gutter, and yet, I didn't blame myself the way I do now. Kyle was a narcissist. The way he treated me was cruel. Holden, on the other hand, is proving himself to be the best man I've ever met. If I lose him, it'll be my own damn fault for letting my insecurities win.

By the time I'm at the salon, hair freshly done and waiting for the makeup artist to finish with her current client, I'm so angry at myself that I decide to pull out my phone and read the latest news about me and Holden—along with the comments. It's self-destructive, I know. I'm sure I'll see something I don't like. Unfortunately, I feel like I deserve exactly that.

It doesn't take long for me to find *manhattanmarathonman*, whose sentiments are almost identical to the handful of other critics who've chimed in about my appearance.

manhattanmarathonman
Damn. She's getting bigger by the minute.
manhattanmarathonman
I figured he would have moved on to someone hotter by now.
manhattanmarathonman
I guess Holden McBride likes his women thick.

I hold it together while I get my makeup done, but I know the only way to save myself from bursting into tears and ruining it with mascara streaks is to talk to a friend. You'd think I'd have plenty to choose from, back in the city where I spent an entire decade of my life. But the only friends I had here were the ones from my job at Hanover Literary. Friends like Frances, whom I now realize is more of a work acquaintance, considering she hasn't called or texted me once to ask about my relationship with Holden.

I suppose Kyle had such complete control over our routine that it didn't leave me much time to socialize outside of work. Luckily, when I moved to Chicago for my fresh start, Jenna's friends welcomed me into their group with open arms. There's sweet Vanessa, the social worker, who's always happy to lend a listening ear. And hilarious Sam, of course, who provides the comic relief, but always comes through with emotional support when needed. Since she's also single, I'm curious to hear her take on my current situation.

But I need a private place where I can bare my soul to her, and Holden's in our suite, taking a shower and getting ready for the gala. I ask the concierge for help, and he leads me to a quiet conference room, where I dial Sam's number.

While I wait for her to pick up the phone, I decide I'm going to tell her everything. From the extraordinary sex I'm having with Holden and the feelings we share; to the way I found out about him and Caterina; to the reason The Siren triggers me so much. I'll confess that my self-esteem is even shittier than she and Jenna realize.

If I'm capable of being vulnerable with Holden, I should be able to confide in my best friend, right?

For some reason, the idea still makes me feel sick. This is why I haven't been to therapy. I can barely stand the thought of divulging my deepest secrets to a friend, much less a stranger. I guess there's something different about Holden that puts me at ease. But he can only handle so much, right? He thinks my admissions are a privilege now, but I bet my insecurities will get old fast, and I don't want to drive him away. He's my lover, not my therapist.

Shit. What if I'm honest with Sam and she tells me I need to see a therapist? Sam is persistent. She won't rest until I go.

Beads of sweat form on my palms.

"You must have a sixth sense," Sam says when she answers my call. She lets out a nervous laugh, which isn't like her at all. She's typically so cool and calm.

My brow furrows. "Hey—are you alright?"

"I was just, um, wishing you were here. And then you called."

I've never heard Sam's voice shake before. Something's wrong. I think back to our last phone conversation, when she told me she was making lifestyle changes. She said she'd explain when I got home, which worried me, even though she promised she was okay. What if she lied?

Her next words come out before I can form my own. "Can I tell you a big secret absolutely no one knows? Not even my family?"

"Of course." I brace myself.

Sam sighs. "I've decided to do IVF. By myself. I picked a donor, and I'm starting hormone shots tonight. I'm nervous, but I'm so excited, Christy."

My eyes go wide. I'm stunned.

"I've been thinking about it nonstop for the last two years," she goes on to explain. "Since I turned thirty. With every passing month, the urge got stronger. I love my career. I'm happy being single. But something's missing."

I smile. "You want to be a mom."

"I really do," she admits. "I know there'll be people who question my choice to do this without a partner. My family included. My mom is so traditional, she'll probably have a heart attack. But I don't long to be a wife the way I long to be a mother. So, why wait to find a man I can tolerate parenting with, when I can do it on my own?"

I've never met Sam's mom, but I know she was born and raised in Lebanon, and she and Sam have very different views on what being a successful woman looks like. To her mother, it's being married with children and taking on the role of matriarch. To Sam—it's not. Her version of happiness is being an independent woman who excels in her career and beds whomever she wants.

"Speaking of men, aren't you dating someone?" *Sleeping with* someone is probably a more accurate description, but she knows what I mean.

"I was. He's not interested in the whole IVF journey, and I can't blame him. I guess I'd better dust off my vibrators, because I probably won't be getting laid for a while." Her tone is lighthearted.

"I'm so happy for you, Sam. And I'm honored you shared this news with me. I promise I'll be by your side for whatever you need, okay? I'll come to appointments with you, pick up prescriptions. Just say the word, and I'm there."

"I love you," she says with an uncharacteristic sniffle.

"I love you back."

"Wait, don't hang up yet," Sam pleads. "Tell me about you! How are things going with McHottie?"

Well, I can't very well tell her now, I reason. *Sam's got enough on her plate. I don't want to burden her with my neuroses.*

I let out a breath, relieved I can leave my emotions bottled up inside, even though I'm sure they'll come back to haunt me. They always do.

"I'm great," I lie. "Things are going great."

I step back into the penthouse suite, and the view of Central Park from the panoramic windows takes my breath away, even though it's not my first time seeing it. When Holden and I first checked in, I stood speechless for a minute, admiring the vibrant green treetops, speckled with the first hints of autumn yellow.

Then Holden walks out of our bedroom, and I'm even more awestruck. What could be more stunning than the view from the penthouse suite at The Plaza?

Holden McBride in a tux.

Good lord, my heart.

"Wow," he says to me, eyes wide. My hair is in an elaborate updo that I'd never attempt on my own: a loose braid wrapped around the side of my head and swept into an intricate low bun. The stylist made good use of my waves, leaving wispy tendrils to frame my face for a soft, romantic look. And I have to admit, I feel glamorous in the Old Hollywood makeup I asked for. Winged liner on my eyes, a lengthening mascara, and glowing skin, with a peachy sheen on my cheeks. And, of course, my signature velvety red lipstick. I'm not even wearing my dress yet, but Holden's cheeks are flushed. That's rare for him.

"Fuck, you're beautiful," he says, running his hand over his head.

"Thank you." I believe him. For now. Why can't the feeling last? My confidence is so hot and cold, it gives me whiplash.

I kiss him lightly, so as not to ruin my lipstick. He doesn't hide how happy that small gesture makes him. Smiling, he pulls me in for a hug. "Thank you for coming with me."

But when he unwraps his arms from around my waist, he flinches.

"Holden, your shoulder—"

"I'm fine," he insists.

"You're lying," I insist back. "You've been moving gingerly since you punched Wes. Something's wrong. We should go get it looked at."

"And miss the gala? No way. I'm not going to have you sitting in a hospital waiting room all night. If it's still bothering me when we get back to Maui, I'll have someone check it out there. I promise." His eyes beg me to relent.

I blow out a dissatisfied breath. "Fine."

"Good," he says, before kissing the top of my head. Then he reaches into his pocket. "Now...do you happen to know how to tie a bowtie? I don't want to put more strain on my shoulder. Getting into this jacket was hard enough."

"You're in luck," I say, taking it from him and lifting his shirt collar.

"Dr. Fuckface never learned to do it himself?" Holden rolls his eyes as I drape the elegant black satin around his neck.

I stifle a smile and cross the right end over the left, then loop the fabric to form a bow. "He's been demoted from TGI Friday to Dr. Fuckface?"

"I think it serves him right," Holden says.

I don't disagree. But as I step back to check my work, I can't help but worry that Holden's so resentful of Kyle because he's tired of carrying the baggage of that relationship with me.

After I'm satisfied with his bowtie, I take my turn getting dressed. I wear a deep-red velvet gown with cap sleeves and a sweetheart neckline. It skims my hips, then falls to the floor with a subtle flare. Underneath it, I have on shapewear, so I don't have to worry about sucking in my stomach all night. I wish I didn't need it, but such is life. Well, *my* life.

My heels are a matching velvety crimson that peek out from the hem only slightly with each step. And the final touch is the purple silk orchid Holden gave me, which I clip behind my left ear. I love the way it completes my outfit.

Even more so, I love the man who gave it to me.

He practically melts when he sees me. His eyes glisten as he holds out his good elbow for me to hook my arm around. Before we leave, he stops me in front of the mirror in the foyer.

"Don't tell me we don't look good together, baby," he rasps.

I gaze at our reflection and grin. We look like movie stars. "I can't."

My high remains when the McBride chauffeur drops us off at our Fifth Avenue destination, and especially when I walk toward the elegant marble steps of my favorite place in the world. The New York Public Library. The stone lions that guard the entrance seem to wink at me as I approach them on Holden's arm. The camera clicks don't bother me at all.

And when we step through the magnificent brass doors into Astor Hall for cocktail hour, I've never been happier in my life. There are gorgeous women everywhere, but Holden only has eyes for me. He doesn't miss an opportunity to introduce me to the steady stream of partygoers who are eager to catch his ear—some of whom are famous celebrities and well-known authors I can't believe I'm meeting.

"This is my girlfriend, Christy Andersen," he says with a proud smile and a hand wrapped tight around my waist.

I'm practically giddy. How could I not be, when he makes me feel so adored? This night is going so much better than I expected. Maybe I do have what it takes to be Holden's girlfriend.

About an hour later, we walk down the sweeping marble staircases for dinner under the dome. The entire room is aglow with candles as we stroll hand in hand to our table.

When we find our seats, I lean to whisper in his ear. "I'm having the best night."

Smiling, he squeezes my hand. "That's all I want, baby."

But the joy on his face disappears in an instant when another guest comes up behind him and slaps his left shoulder a few times. "Good to see you, McBride."

Holden forces a grin as he looks up to meet the man's gaze, but he's already moving on to the next table. When he's past us, Holden winces.

Worry flutters in my gut. "Oh no, you're in pain. What can I do?"

My date takes a deep breath, his features relaxing. "Tell people to slap my right shoulder instead of my left?"

"Your pitching arm is not a laughing matter." I sigh, my forehead creased.

"I'm fine, Red. I promise." As another couple sits across from us, Holden unfolds his napkin and puts it in his lap. "Now, let's enjoy dinner so I can get you out on that dance floor."

I agree, despite myself, and after every seat at our table has been filled and hellos have been exchanged, a mouthwatering meal of beef Wellington is served. Holden and I eat, and drink, and laugh, and he is every bit the conversationalist I knew he would be. If only his she-devil of a mother were here to see him discuss Hemingway and Faulkner.

God, he's so sexy. I thought his dirty mouth was hot, but this is even better. How and when did he have time to read all these books when he went straight from high school to playing professional baseball?

I'll wait to ask him when we're alone, and I don't have to hide how turned on I am by his nerdy talk.

When the seated program and dinner conclude, a popular New York DJ takes the stage, inviting guests to the dance floor. With the help of uplighting and pop music, the vibe turns from elegant and chic to fun and festive. It's the wedding reception I always wanted, and I'm hit with a wave of longing for the dream I gave up long ago. Even more so when the first slow song of the evening is announced, and my devastatingly handsome date asks me to dance.

The mood is tender and romantic as Etta James's classic love ballad "At Last" begins to play. It's my first slow dance with Holden McBride...a starting pitcher I used to ogle from the bleachers at Wrigley Field. Now, he's pressed against me, larger than life, after stealing my heart and sweeping me off my feet.

"This is a dream come true," I say, when our arms are wrapped around each other and we're swaying to the music. "And I don't just mean the library."

He presses his mouth next to my ear. "I want to make every one of your dreams come true, Christy Andersen. You deserve all of that and more."

My pulse races as he brings his lips to mine for a kiss that gives rise to raucous applause. As cameras flash around us, Holden dips me to the whoops and cheers of the crowd. When I'm upright again, I throw my arms around his neck and hug him.

But his heart is racing much too fast. I feel the rapid thump against my cheek. I look up and see that his jaw is clenched, and there's sweat on his brow. He sways with me anyway, until our spectators turn back to their own dance partners.

"Your shoulder?" I mouth.

He nods, the color draining from his face.

"That's it. We're going to the hospital." I take his hand and try to lead him off the dance floor, but he doesn't budge.

"The party's not over yet, Red."

"Holden, you've given me everything I could ask for

tonight. But there's one last thing I need, and that's for you to trust me. You promised me you'd be an open book, and that includes being honest about your arm. It's worse than you've been letting on, isn't it."

He looks down at his shoes. "Yes."

My heart sinks.

"The truth is, my shoulder's been acting up for months." He blows out a defeated breath. "And when I punched Wes, I heard something snap."

"Then we're leaving," I say.

His jaw clenches, but this time, he follows me.

Once we're off the dance floor, he pulls out his phone to alert the chauffeur, who picks us up outside the library ten minutes later. I'm relieved when Holden directs him to take us to New York Presbyterian. Not only because it's an excellent hospital, but because my ex-boyfriend doesn't work there. He's been at Mount Sinai since he graduated from medical school.

In the car, Holden texts his agent and asks him to alert the hospital's orthopedic staff that we're on our way. When we arrive, we're ushered through a private entrance, and Holden goes directly to an exam room. The perks of being an MLB player. Within fifteen minutes, Holden gets an X-ray, which rules out a fracture. Twenty minutes later, they've whisked him away for an MRI.

I'm in the radiology waiting area scrolling through my phone, when I hear footsteps coming my way. I look up, eager for an update about Holden, but the nurse is here to collect a different patient's family member.

I play a word game to pass the time. I'm so immersed in it that I hardly notice there's someone walking toward me until they're standing directly in front of me. His brown shoes are unfamiliar, as are his khaki pants and button-down shirt, but the name on his white coat is unmistakable.

When my gaze lands on his face, I freeze.

"I thought I might find you here," he says.

My gasp is audible.

Amused by my reaction, he sits down next to me with the same smug look that's haunted my nightmares ever since we broke up two years ago. You'd think the fact that I caught him cheating on me would've knocked him off his high horse, but no. I guess there's no humbling Dr. Kyle Walton. He leans back in the chair with his legs spread so far apart, I have to shift to the opposite side of my seat so we're not touching.

"I just heard over at the nurses' station that Holden McBride was admitted, and I figured you'd be with him," Kyle tells me. "Don't worry, he's in good hands. The Chief of Radiology is going to review his MRI."

I'm so thrown off by his casual tone, all I can do is nod. This is the first time we've seen each other since he moved out of our apartment. Why is he acting like we're old chums with no bad blood between us?

"You know, Christy...when I heard the news about the two of you dating, I honestly couldn't believe it." He blows out a laugh.

Then his gaze falls right to my midsection.

"Tell me the truth," he goes on, nudging me with his elbow, as if I didn't hate him with every fiber of my being. "It's a publicity stunt, right? I mean, let's face it, you're not his usual type. The guy's practically famous for dating supermodels."

He sounds just like manhattanmarathonman.

My stomach churns. I thought I'd dismissed the idea that

the troll and my ex were one and the same, but now I'm not so sure.

Should I confront him? Kyle's not a very good liar. If he's hiding something, he won't look me in the eye, and then I'll know. That's how I sensed he was cheating long before I walked in on him and Tessa.

But questioning my ex is a lot easier said than done. This unexpected reunion has me so flustered, I struggle for words. Sharp-tongued, quick-on-her-feet Christy must have left the building. She's probably back at the library, having another cocktail and wondering how she might sneak away from the main event to see some of the rare books on display.

Ugh, she's so lucky. Meanwhile, I'm stuck here with my abominable ex, trying to remember how to speak.

"Are you, um...have you been, um...*trolling* me online?" I finally stammer.

Kyle looks me dead in the eye. "You're not serious."

Dammit. Now I wish I'd never asked. "Well, I—"

"That's hilarious," he says on a long exhale. "Look, Christy, I know our breakup was tough on you. But um, I moved on...a long time ago. And I think it would behoove you to do the same."

Only Kyle would use the word "behoove" in everyday conversation. *Pretentious fucking prick.*

This is supposed to be the part where I tell him that he's a sorry excuse for a man. That I don't know why I let him manipulate me for as long as I did. That the only part of our relationship I'm not over is the damage he did to my self-esteem.

Instead, I just sit here. Frozen.

I hate this version of myself. The woman I was with Kyle. The woman I've become again, now that he's seated next to me.

So unsure of herself. So meek. But what were the chances I'd breeze through a conversation with the man of my nightmares today, anyway? I was already trying to recover from one blow to my self-esteem in the form of Caterina Hart, and now this? The Universe has a twisted sense of humor. Of all the hospitals in New York, why does my ex have to be at this one?

I guess I may as well ask him, since I can't find it in myself to give him a piece of my mind. Before I speak, I clear my throat for the first time all day. I was starting to think my nervous tic had disappeared, but I guess that's only around Holden. It makes sense, given how comfortable I am with him. When I turn to face my ex, my voice sounds as uneasy as I feel. "What are you even doing here, Kyle?"

"I work here." He runs a relaxed hand through his hair. "Tessa and I thought it would be best if I changed hospitals. I mean, she's an ER resident, so I wasn't her direct supervisor, but we worked together often enough that we didn't want to ruffle any feathers."

Tessa. The way she ran out of our apartment in tears that day, I figured she didn't know he was cheating on me. That he'd told her we were broken up. I didn't think she'd take him back, given how upset she was. My surprise is evident in my tone. "Oh. So, you and Tessa—"

"We're together. Yes." He heaves a sigh. "She broke things off initially, but a few weeks later, she found out she was pregnant."

"Oh my god." My eyes go wide. "You have a child?"

He nods. "He's seventeen months old. Tessa and I got married at City Hall three weeks before he was born." Kyle's brows knit together. "So, you're telling me you really didn't know? About the wedding or the baby?"

I shake my head. "How would I have known? We don't have mutual friends. I'm not in touch with your family—"

"Honestly, I figured you would've Googled me sometime in the last two years." He pushes his wire-rimmed glasses up his nose. "You can find out anything online if you're curious enough."

This time, I'm the one who spurts out a laugh. "You're kidding, right?"

A sheepish flush colors Kyle's otherwise pale face. Finally, the power imbalance shifts just enough for me to find my footing in this conversation. I jump at the opportunity. "Listen, if you think I've been pining over you since we broke up, you're sorely mistaken. And, quite frankly, not as smart as you think you are."

He looks down at his shoes.

"Our relationship was toxic," I go on. "You micromanaged everything I ate, guilt-tripped me if I ever skipped a run—"

Kyle rolls his eyes. "Oh, god, not you, too."

I raise an eyebrow.

"You sound just like Tessa. All I did was offer to make her a workout plan to lose the baby weight, and she insisted I sleep on the couch last night." He rubs his neck and winces. "She called me a misogynist."

I crack a smile. "I kinda like her now."

"Oh, come on, Christy." He wipes his brow. "Give me a break, will you? I mean, fine, my behavior at the end of our relationship was less than ideal—"

"Less than ideal? Wow. Don't be *too* hard on yourself, Kyle." My voice drips with sarcasm.

"But we were together for seven years before that," he goes on. "It wasn't all bad. You said you loved me."

I purse my lips. "You said you loved me, too."

Kyle shrugs. "And?"

"That wasn't love. I know that now." My cheeks flush, and a smile blooms on my face at the thought of Holden.

My ex scoffs. "You're joking."

"What's so hard to believe, Kyle?" I'm beaming now. "That I'm in love with Holden McBride? Or that he feels the same way about me?"

Down the hall, too far away to hear us, Holden catches my eye and grins at me. I've never been happier to see him. He's like my knight in shining armor, here to save me from Dr. Frankenstein.

"There she is." The sound of his voice as he approaches fills my heart with joy. I jump up from my seat, and he picks up his pace to reach me. When he does, he kisses me with so much passion, you'd think we'd been separated for months, not minutes.

"How did it go?" I ask him.

"We should have the results in the next thirty minutes or so." He tucks a wavy tendril behind my ear. "I missed you."

"I missed you more." I look behind me to see Kyle on his feet now, too. His wide-eyed shock at my very real kiss with Holden is almost comical.

So is Holden's sneer when he reads the name on my ex's white coat.

"Baby," my boyfriend says to me, with an eye still on Kyle. "Would you mind getting me a Gatorade, or something? I'm parched."

I bite a smile. This is the first time I've ever seen Dr. Walton appear intimidated, but I certainly understand why. Physically, Holden bests him in every single way. He's taller. Bigger.

Hotter. I used to think my ex was so handsome, but I guess my tastes have changed.

Maybe Sam is right about Kyle. He does kind of look like a breadstick.

I have to purse my lips to keep from laughing. "Sure. I'll be right back with your drink," I tell Holden.

"Thanks, Red." He winks at me. "Oh, and take your time."

CHAPTER 24

Holden

Well, I'll be damned. If it isn't Dr. Fuckface, in the flesh. The asshole I've been daydreaming about sucker-punching for a week straight.

And he looks like he's about to piss himself.

I guess when you're used to being the bully, and a bigger, stronger man bearing a grudge comes along, you start to question your life choices.

It's fun making him sweat. But the truth is, even if my shoulder were in perfect condition, I wouldn't knock the guy out, like I did Wes. That was different. My brother made a pass at my woman and absolutely had it coming. Not to mention, we also have a long history of despising each other.

Although I'll admit I've fantasized about beating Christy's ex to a pulp, I'm not the kind of guy to throw a punch unless I have to. Dr. Fuckface doesn't need to know that, though.

"Let's have a seat," I say, enjoying the way his eyes widen as I crack each one of my knuckles. When he's sitting next to me, I cross my arms over my chest, flexing every muscle. "I take it you know who I am?"

He swallows. "Of course. You're Holden McBride."

"Yes." I heave a sigh. "But more importantly, Kyle—I'm the man who's going to marry Christy Andersen."

"Oh." He blinks at me for several seconds. "I, um, didn't realize the two of you were engaged."

"Well, we aren't yet," I admit. "But we will be."

I'm not going to waste my time explaining to TGI Friday that my dead grandmother told me so in a dream. Call me crazy, but he doesn't strike me as a romantic.

"So, what that means, Kyle," I continue, "is that you messed with the wrong woman. Because when you mess with my wife, you mess with me."

His fingers shake as he sputters. "Look, Holden—um, I mean, Mr. McBride—it was never my intention to—"

"Shut up, Kyle."

"Yup. Okay." He nods, his cheeks reddening. "You got it."

"You tore my wife's self-esteem to shreds, leaving me to pick up the pieces and make her whole again," I go on. "Now, I am more than happy to do that, because it's a fucking privilege showing that woman how gorgeous she is..."

Kyle stares at his shoes.

"But what I need you to know, is that your issues with her body are a reflection on you. Christy was always perfect. She was never the problem. *You* were." I wait for him to meet my gaze. "Got it?"

He pulls his shirt collar away from his neck. "Yes."

"Good. Now, get out of my face."

I've never seen anyone walk away so fast.

When he's about to pass the nurses' station, I stop him. "Oh, and Kyle? One more thing."

He turns around, eyes filled with dread.

I smirk. "I know we can't all be genetically blessed...but just because you have a little prick doesn't mean you need to act like one."

When the nurses start giggling behind him, I swear Kyle's lip quivers before he dashes down the hallway, out of sight.

"God, that was fun," I say to no one in particular.

A few minutes later, Christy comes back with a lemon-lime Gatorade.

I smile. It's my favorite flavor, and I didn't even have to tell her. "Thank you, baby."

"Where's Kyle? You didn't kill him, did you?" she jokes when she sits next to me.

"Nah. But I definitely killed his chances of scoring with any of those nurses over there."

She laughs. "What did you say?"

I fill her in on most of the conversation—except the part where I called her my wife. I don't need to put that kind of pressure on her now, when she's questioning whether she can even be my girlfriend. But one day, I'll tell her just how long I've known we were meant to be.

I know I will.

When I'm done regaling her with the story of how I put Dr. Fuckface in his place, Christy grins. "Thank you for defending my honor."

"Always." I kiss her like we're the only two people in the room.

Unfortunately, we're not. After a minute, someone nearby clears their throat. "Mr. McBride?"

I look up to see a nurse with flushed cheeks.

"I'm sorry to interrupt," she says. "But the doctor is ready for you."

I take Christy's hand in mine. "Will you come with me?"

She nods with a tender look in her eye. "Of course."

As we follow the nurse down a maze of hallways, I try to convince myself this isn't the end of my baseball career. My hammering heart doesn't buy it. Neither does the ache in my shoulder, which seems to get worse with every step. Christy squeezes my damp palm to comfort me, but her forehead's creased, and she looks almost as nervous as I feel.

When we step into the doctor's office, the look on his face does nothing to alleviate my anxiety.

"Well...I wish I had better news," he says.

Fuck.

"Holden?"

Christy stands next to me at the window, her cheeks streaked with tears. I'm not sure when she started crying. Was it when the Chief of Radiology explained the MRI results? Or after we met with the orthopedic surgeon? Or was it just now, when we were taken to a private suite, so I can process the news before I have to be out in public again? I don't know. The past hour has been a blur.

"Holden?" Christy's voice quivers when she tries to get my attention again.

"I'm sorry, baby." I shake my head, trying to clear the mental fog I'm lost in. "Are you okay?"

"Yes, but...your phone is ringing."

"Oh." I reach into my pocket. "It's Russell. My agent. I don't think I can...I don't think I have it in me to—"

She swallows her tears. "Do you want me to talk to him?"

My brows draw together. "Would you?"

Christy takes the phone from my hand and walks to the opposite side of the room, but I can still hear her, of course. I stare at the TV screen mounted on the wall in an attempt to distract myself. Unfortunately, most of her words come through anyway. And even though the information isn't new to me, it hits just as hard.

"Severe tear in his labrum."

"No way it'll heal on its own."

"Recovery from surgery will be long—and unpredictable."

"Most pitchers his age don't come back from this."

My contract is up this season. There's no fucking way the Starlings will give me an extension if I have at least a year of post-op recovery ahead of me, with no guarantee that I'll ever return to my previous form. The shoulder's the most complex joint in the body, and the labrum is tough to repair. A severe tear is basically a career death sentence for a thirty-six-year-old pitcher.

I close my eyes and take in a ragged breath. Before I know it, Christy's handing me back my phone.

"Russell wants you to know he's here for whatever you need. He says we can hold off on telling anyone until you meet with the team surgeon when we get back home."

"Thank you, baby." I pull her close to me. With my arms wrapped around her waist and my head resting against hers, she can't see my lips curl up in a smile.

She said we.

We can hold off on telling anyone about my shoulder until *we* get back home.

Maybe I'm reading too much into her words, but they make

me feel less alone. And I need that small shred of hope right now, when my entire life is falling to pieces.

God, I'm so fucking glad Christy's here.

All I want to do right now is show her how grateful I am. And I think I know just the thing to put a smile back on that beautiful face. Plus, I don't see the point in staying here and stewing over something I can't control. I have pain meds and a sling to help me manage, for the time being. The sling is optional, luckily. If I wear it in public now, my injury will make headlines. Better to keep it under wraps until after I've met with the team surgeon in Chicago, and the Starlings issue an official statement.

I lift my hand to wipe the tears she just shed for me and my career. "Let's get out of here, Red. I don't want the night to end like this. The gala's over, but I do happen to have access to the second-best library in Manhattan."

Her eyes light up. "A library?"

I grin. "Come on."

I've already been discharged, so Christy and I walk straight out of the hospital to our waiting car, and I tell the driver to drop us off at Central Park West and 74th.

It's not until we step into the building's lobby that my girlfriend guesses where I'm taking her.

"This is where Grandma Evelyn lived," she says.

I nod with a wistful smile.

The doorman stands at attention when he greets me. "Mr. McBride. Nice to see you."

I chuckle. "Derrick, we've been over this. Please call me Holden."

"Very well, sir," he answers right away. "I mean, Holden."

"And this is my girlfriend, Christy."

She holds out her hand. "It's a pleasure to meet you, Derrick."

"The pleasure's mine." He turns back to me. "The staff were all so sorry to hear about your grandmother. She was our favorite resident..." He looks around to make sure the coast is clear. "By a mile."

"She was something special, alright," I agree. "Have a good evening, Derrick."

"Good evening, sir. I mean, Holden."

I lead Christy into the elevator that goes up to the penthouse. When the doors open to the elegant foyer, her eyes widen. I hang back and watch as she takes slow, savoring steps across the marble floor to the pedestal table, which still boasts fresh flowers, even though Grandma's been gone for over a week. Christy leans forward to smell them with closed eyes and a smile. In her red velvet dress and heels, with her gorgeous auburn hair swept up and the purple orchid behind her ear, she's so stunning I almost forget that my career's over. Her classic beauty fits in perfectly against the backdrop of this timeless prewar apartment I love so much. It's like she was meant to be here.

I follow her to the living room, which spans the entire width of the building. It looks exactly the way it did before my grandmother got sick. There's no hospice bed, with the neat stack of books she kept nearby for comfort. No glasses of water waiting to be drunk with her pills. The weight of grief is gone, at least in theory. I can almost see nine-year-old me, sitting across from my grandmother at her card table while we played gin rummy.

It's so fucking strange being in this room without her.

"Are you alright?" Christy places her hand on my chest and looks up at me with a furrowed brow.

I kiss her freckled cheek. "Let me show you the library."

The look on my girlfriend's face when she sees the floor-to-ceiling built-in bookshelves is worth every bit of sadness I feel being back here.

She starts near the windows and sweeps her hand over rows and rows of leather-bound classics and first editions. At one point, she stops and chooses a book to smell. It's so goddamn adorable, I can't help but chuckle.

She looks up at me with flushed cheeks and a grin. "I'm a nerd. I know."

I walk over to her and wrap my good arm around her waist. "I think it's sexy as hell. Which book have you got there?"

"*A Farewell to Arms*. You know, this was the novel that inspired Haley Quinlan to write *Edison's Love*? It's a loose retelling, of course. She wrote it because she wanted to change the original ending." Christy frowns, and I think I know what's weighing on her mind.

"I'm so sorry she didn't sign with you." My forehead creases. "She doesn't know what she's missing."

My girlfriend sighs. "I keep watching her social media pages to see if she's announced which agent she chose. When I got her rejection letter, I was sure she'd picked my biggest competitor, Colin Finch. But Haley hasn't posted anything yet. It's a little strange. Most authors are so eager to share the news."

"Do you think she's having second thoughts?"

She shrugs. "It's wishful thinking."

"Sometimes wishes come true, Red. Maybe all Haley needs

is a little nudge." I nod toward the novel she's clutching to her chest. "Do you have her address?"

"Yes."

"Send her the book, then. It's a first edition, and we have multiple copies. Tell her there are no hard feelings, and you'll always enjoy *Edison's Love*. Especially after your boyfriend recreated that beach scene and gave you the best sex of your life."

Christy giggles.

I wink at her. "Okay, don't tell her that last part."

She shakes her head. "It's so kind of you to offer, but I couldn't possibly take this book. It's part of your grandmother's library—"

"Actually, it's my library, now."

"What?"

I nod. "Grandma Evelyn left me this apartment. Abby got the Connecticut estate because Maisie and Matt love to run around the back lawn. And Wes inherited the Hamptons house."

Christy looks at the sweeping bookshelves again. "So all of this is yours? You have a lot of reading to do," she jokes.

I half-smile, looking forward to her reaction when I tell her the truth. "Not as much as you think. When I signed with the Starlings after high school, Grandma insisted I spend my off-seasons reading. Whenever I came to visit, she'd send me home with a box of books. I've made my way through a fair number of these."

"You know, I had a sneaking suspicion when I overheard you talking to your neighbor about *The Sound and the Fury* at the dinner table tonight." Her cheeks flush.

I pull her closer to me. "I bet you liked that."

She bites her red lip. "You have no idea."

"Maybe you can show me when we get back to the hotel."

"I'd be happy to." She glances at my arm. "As long as we don't do anything to aggravate your shoulder."

I follow her gaze. "You know, for a split second I almost forgot? The pain meds must be kicking in. But you're right, we'll have to be careful. Think you can be gentle with me, Red?"

Her mouth quirks up. "After the way you've been worshipping my body all week? I can be anything you need me to be."

The light in her eyes warms me. How any man could witness this smile and not want to move mountains to make her happy is beyond me. But I'll gladly take the win.

I kiss her. "You're the most beautiful woman I've ever laid eyes on. You know that, Christy?"

She chuckles. "Are you sure that's not the pain medicine talking?"

"Very."

"Well, thank you." She lifts her palm to my cheek. "And not just for the compliment. For tonight. For bringing me here."

"Of course, baby."

I look around the library my grandmother loved, and I can practically feel her spirit in the room. When I was three, she'd sit in the leather armchair in the corner, pull me onto her lap, and read me nursery rhymes.

A wave of grief almost drowns me.

"I feel like I know her a little bit more now." My girlfriend smiles, admiring the book in her hands. "I think we would have gotten along well."

She would have loved you, is what I want to tell Christy but can't. How do I stand in my grandmother's favorite place and talk about her without sobbing? Even now, my throat burns with the threat of tears.

I've been holding them back since the day she died. But with the news of my shoulder, and this being the almost-certain end of my career, I don't know how much longer I can keep a lid on my grief.

If I had Racing Hearts to pour my energy into, maybe I would come out of this in one piece. Stronger, even. But the odds of me winning this competition are slimmer than ever.

Then there's Christy. She's the only good thing in my life right now, and I might lose her, too, if she lets her insecurities get the best of her.

How will I—

What will I—

"Holden?" Christy's gaze is full of concern.

A desperate cry escapes me, the likes of which I've never heard come from my throat. My cheeks burn with the sting of hot tears, finally escaping the confines of my eyes. I sob so hard my body shakes, and every inhale feels like a struggle.

"Oh, Holden," Christy says, her own eyes glistening. She sets her book down and wraps her arms around me, rubbing my back. After several seconds, she pulls away, but takes my hand. "You're too tall for me to comfort you like this. Follow me."

She sits against the bookshelves and I sink down next to her and cry on her shoulder, just like she's cried on mine.

"This is good," she whispers. "You needed this."

If it were any other woman, I'd be mortified. But not with Christy. I don't feel a shred of judgment coming from her. No rush for me to pull myself together. She doesn't force me to talk about my feelings. She just runs her fingers through my hair and lets me cry until I run out of tears.

"Fuck," I say on a deep exhale after my last whimper. For as much as I dreaded crying, I have to admit, the relief I feel is worth it.

Christy wipes the tears from my cheeks with her thumbs. "Better?"

I nod.

"Is this the first time you've cried this week?

"It's the first time since Abby's accident, I think." I scratch my forehead. "I was sixteen, and I burst into tears in the hospital waiting room. My parents quietly scolded me for crying like a baby and making a scene."

I feel Christy's body tense where I'm leaning against her. She's angry. "I'm sorry, Holden, but your parents fucking suck."

I sit up and thread my fingers through hers with a smile. "You're not wrong."

"You can cry on my shoulder anytime," she tells me.

But what if you leave me?

"I know things seems dire now," she goes on, "but don't forget you have Racing Hearts. Like I said last night, whether you win this competition or not, you'll see it through."

I can't help but laugh at the irony. "About that..."

Christy tilts her head, confused.

"Remember when we first met at the bar, and I told you I hate being a McBride and everything that comes along with it?"

She nods.

"Well, I hate it so much, I gave away most of my money to set myself apart from my family."

There's a hint of amusement in her eyes that matches my wry smile. "You did what?"

"The McBrides only see dollar signs," I explain. "Even their charitable efforts are for show. They donate for the recognition, that's all. I didn't want to be like them. When I started making money, I saved enough to buy a home and live comfortably, then I chose several organizations to support and began making monthly donations. Anonymously."

"You're the highest-paid pitcher in the league," she says, astounded.

"I am."

"So, you're telling me you've donated...I don't know, hundreds of millions of dollars to various charities over the past two decades, and no one knows?"

"Not even my grandma."

Christy throws her head back and laughs.

There's nothing left to do but join her. "I'm an idiot, aren't I."

"No." She takes my face in her hands and kisses me. "You're an even better human being than I thought."

My heart swells. I showed Christy who I really am, and she likes me more for it. Loves me, even. That's what it feels like, the way she's looking at me.

"You are the definition of selfless, Holden McBride," she says. "Maybe to a fault."

I blow out a breath. "No kidding. That's why I need to win this competition, baby. I don't have enough money to fund Racing Hearts without it. And seeing as this shoulder injury will more than likely end my career, I can't count on another Major League check."

"I get it." She gives me a determined nod. "And we're going to figure this out."

She said *we* again. I crack a smile.

Christy tilts her head, confused by my reaction. "What?"

"You said *we* again," I explain. "You said it after you spoke to Russell, too. You said *we* could wait until *we* get home to tell anyone about my shoulder. I don't know...maybe I'm reading too much into one little word, but it makes me feel good. It makes me feel like—"

"Like we're in this together?" She squeezes my hand.

I nod.

"We are." She kisses me again.

"But what if..."

My heart pumps faster than it did at the hospital, when the orthopedist said I'd need surgery. Because now, I'm terrified I'll lose something far more important than my career. Some*one* far more important. The first woman I've ever truly loved. The only one I ever want to love.

The one my grandmother brought into my life, when I needed a shoulder to cry on. With each passing day, I believe it more and more.

Still, I have to ask Christy the question I dread. "What if you decide you can't be with me?"

She shakes her head. "I'm not going anywhere."

"But just yesterday, you said—"

"I know what I said." She looks down at our interlaced fingers. "That you can't be with someone who falls apart every time a pretty woman bats her eyelashes at you. Like that nurse in the radiology waiting area."

"She did?" I have no clue what Christy's talking about. "Which nurse?"

My girlfriend smiles. "It doesn't matter."

"Good. So, it didn't bother you, then?"

She huffs a laugh. "No, it definitely bothered me. But you know what bothers me more? Letting my insecurities keep me from being with the best man I've ever met."

I kiss her smile, relief flooding my body. "How'd you come to that conclusion so fast?"

"There's nothing like a run-in with your insufferable ex-boyfriend to put your current relationship in perspective." She heaves a sigh before she goes on.

"When I first saw Kyle tonight, I wanted to tell him off, but I couldn't. The moment he sat next to me, my self-esteem plummeted again." She looks down at her shoes. "Eventually, I recovered and found just enough confidence to say my piece. And that was thanks to you."

When her eyes meet mine again, they're wet with tears. "You cared enough to want to help me heal, Holden, and I am infinitely grateful to you for that. You started me on this journey...but the burden's on me to continue it. I can't rely on you to make me feel confident. I'll probably never fully heal unless I do the work myself. So...I've decided to see a therapist."

"Really, Red?"

She nods. "While you were talking to Kyle, I sent an email to Jenna's therapist asking for a referral. And I copied my sister on it, too, so she makes sure I follow through. It won't be easy, because the idea of being vulnerable with a stranger scares me shitless. But you make me want to be my best self, Holden. You're worth doing the scary things for."

Fuck, I love you. "You have no idea how much that means to me, baby."

Sure enough, tears fall down my face again. Christy's, too. For several minutes, we cry and kiss.

Afterward, my girlfriend takes a tissue out of her purse and wipes my cheeks, then hers. "Alright, McBride. We laughed. We cried. Now it's time to put our game faces on, go back to Maui, and win this competition."

I grin. "And how do you suggest we do that?"

She shakes her head. "I have no fucking clue. But I will tell you this—we're not going down without a fight."

CHAPTER 25
Christy

Holden and I didn't take advantage of our romantic suite at The Plaza the way we'd planned. After we left his grandmother's apartment, we were exhausted, both physically and mentally. It must have been all the crying we did, sitting against the bookshelves in her library. When we got back to our hotel room, I helped him out of his tux and into his sling. Then I showered, and by the time I'd finished, Holden was passed out on the bed. He looked uncomfortable, propped up by half a dozen pillows. But at least he was getting some rest.

Our wake-up call from the concierge came only a few hours later, and it wasn't long before we were boarding the private jet bound for Maui. Running on fumes, we both fell asleep as soon as the plane took off.

All of that to say, we're back at the bungalow now, and neither of us is tired. It's noon local time, and we have nowhere to be until 3:00 p.m., which is when the board will reconvene to announce their decision. Per Margot's itinerary, the McBrides are enjoying a spa day at a five-star resort until then, but Holden agreed with me that time alone would be far more relaxing. He's stressed, of course—he has every reason to be, with the future of his career being so uncertain, and the board's announcement looming.

I wish there were something I could say to make him feel better, but I'm as worried as he is. If Alistair, Zoe, and Dan spent even a minute considering what Grandma Evelyn would have wanted, Racing Hearts should be the clear winner. I just don't trust them to make the right decision. When I told Holden we're not going down without a fight, I meant it. If Siren Serum wins, I'll put my agenting skills to use and try my best to negotiate a deal. Two hundred million dollars isn't chump change. What if the McBride brothers split the bequest, and everyone goes home happy?

There's no guarantee anyone will listen to me, of course, which is why my mind is spinning. And since I don't want to lie to Holden and say we've got this in the bag, the best I can do right now is make him forget his troubles.

After I'm done freshening up in the bathroom, I find him sitting on the edge of our bungalow bed with a furrowed brow. I walk over to him and step between his thighs. "You look a little warm in this sweatshirt. Let me help you take it off."

When he responds with an eager grin, I slowly unzip the hoodie he threw on over his bare chest this morning, because it was easier on his shoulder than wriggling into a T-shirt. I peel it off his body, taking extra caution with his injured arm. He watches every move I make with a gaze so hungry, I'm certain he'd have me pinned to the bed right now, if that movement weren't guaranteed to cause him searing pain.

"Let's put on your sling, so I don't have to worry about you making any sudden movements," I suggest with a teasing grin.

He swallows. "Good idea."

I grab the sling from his carry-on bag in the corner of the room. I'm grateful I paid close attention when the orthopedist demonstrated how to put it on, because it's not exactly intuitive. After I get started, Holden guides me by telling me how tight to pull the straps. All the while, I enjoy the way he can't take his eyes off my cleavage. By the time I'm finished, he's hard as a rock. I can tell, thanks to the gray sweatpants he's wearing.

"Perfect," I say, once the sling is secure. "Now, sit back and relax while I have my way with you."

"Yes, ma'am." Holden swings his legs onto the bed and shifts himself with one hand so he's sitting up against the headboard.

I adjust the pillows behind his back, making sure he's supported. "Comfy?"

"Very."

"Good. Now it's my turn to get undressed." Standing at Holden's side, I strip off the joggers and V-neck T-shirt I wore on our flight, then slide off my undies.

"You're so goddamn pretty, baby," he says, his gaze between my legs.

"I'm also very wet."

"Ugh," he groans. "This is torture. You better get your sexy ass over here before I tear my other shoulder reaching for you."

With his jaw clenched and his abs braced, he reminds me of a wild animal stalking its prey. His urge to pounce is so powerful, he's practically vibrating. I know I'm not making things any easier by drawing this out. But his extraordinary desire is like a drug to me, and I'm enjoying the high. Besides, I'll make it up to him.

"Good things come to those who wait," I tease while unclasping my bra. I pull the straps down my shoulders, one by one, letting the lace-trimmed satin slowly slip down my breasts before falling to the floor.

"Fuck...me..." he sighs out, running his good hand through his hair.

"Oh, believe me, I intend to." I wink at him, then prop my knee onto the bed, bringing the other one up and over his lap to straddle him. "I'm going to fuck your brains out, Holden McBride."

He kisses me, cupping one breast and circling my eager nipple with his thumb. "You might want to take off my pants first," he jokes when his lips are parted from mine.

I shake my head. "Not yet. You're wearing *gray sweatpants*, Holden. Do you know what goes through my mind when you have these on? The things I want to do to you?"

Without waiting for his answer, I rub my clit against his thinly cloaked erection.

"Baby," he rasps as I arch my back and tilt my hips for maximum friction. "I can feel how warm and wet you are. You're dripping through the fabric."

"This is what bad boys in gray sweatpants get."

"Then I'll wear these every fucking day for the rest of my life."

In response, I ride him faster, grinding my wet slit in circles over his enormous bulge.

"Goddammit, woman," he says through panting breaths, "how the hell do you roll your hips like that?"

Flattered, I bring my fingertip to my mouth, considering his question, but I don't stop moving. "Hmm. Maybe yoga?"

Holden's blue-gray eyes are drunk with pleasure. "Let me

take over with my fingers, or something. I haven't fucked you in forty-eight hours, and this feels too damn good right now."

"What's wrong with that? You deserve to feel good." I reach back to cup his balls through his sweatpants and give them a little tug.

"Oh my god, Christy...*fuck!*" Holden shudders beneath me, his eyes squeezed shut, his guttural groan long and lingering.

Wait a minute. Did he just...

"Did you just—"

"Come in my damn pants like a horny teenager?" He drags a hand over his stubble. "Yeah."

My hand flies to my mouth. "Oh my god."

"Baby, I'm so sorry," he sputters. "I just...I can't really move my body with this sling on, so I was completely at your mercy... and I tried to distract myself by thinking about baseball, but your gorgeous tits were bouncing in my face, and those damn hips of yours, Red... I didn't stand a chance."

A giggle escapes me.

"I've been so afraid this would happen with you." He frowns. "What a nightmare."

"A nightmare? Are you kidding?! This is the sexiest thing that's ever happened to me!" I exclaim.

His forehead creases. "Huh?"

"Do you know how incredible it makes me feel, knowing that you're so turned on by my body that you came from me *dry humping* you?" I squeal.

"There was nothing dry about it, baby," he teases. "That perfect pussy of yours soaked through my pants."

I chuckle. "In any case, you made my day. And I hope you don't feel like you have to be some marathon sex machine just to please me. You've already given me the best orgasms of my life, and sex is a two-way street. I enjoy making you feel good. Trust me."

My words bring about an earnest look in his eyes. "You're one in a million, you know that?"

"I could say the same about you."

His fingers travel up my thigh, landing on my swollen clit. "Fuck, I wish I could taste you right now. Make you come in my mouth. Maybe if I kneel at the foot of the bed—"

"Oh, I'm not done with you yet," I inform him. "I said I was going to fuck your brains out, and I'm a woman of my word."

Holden chuckles. "As much as I applaud your integrity, I'm pretty sure that ship has sailed. Unless you want to wait twenty to thirty minutes."

"I don't mind. In the meantime, though, let me clean you up."

"You want to, um—oh." Holden watches with an excited grin as I pull off his now-infamous gray sweatpants, ball them up, and toss them to the floor. Fully undressed, he relaxes onto the pillows behind his back.

"No wonder this outfit had me so hot and bothered," I tell him. "You weren't wearing anything under your sweatshirt *or* your pants."

"You know I'm not the biggest fan of clothes, Red. I enjoy being naked. I think you do too, now."

"With you? Definitely." Kneeling beside him on the bed, I take my mouth to the chiseled lines of his lower abs and lick the evidence of his orgasm.

When I swallow, he wipes his brow. "Do you know how fucking hot you are...lapping up my cum like a good girl?"

I let out a little moan, his words setting off a pulsing desire between my thighs.

"Why don't you touch yourself while you finish cleaning my mess," he says, sensing my aching need. "You can have your first orgasm on your fingers, and the second one on my cock."

Desperate for relief, I do as he says. I didn't think I'd ever feel comfortable pleasuring myself in front of anyone, but I guess I shouldn't be surprised that it's different with Holden. Everything's different with Holden. I get to be myself with him and never have to worry about him judging me. It's the biggest turn-on of all.

I rub my middle finger in circles over my clit while my tongue moves to his dick. It isn't hard, but it isn't quite soft either. I put the tip in my mouth and suck him clean. I'm about to come when I feel him stiffen between my lips.

My eyes light up. "Are you ready for me? So soon?"

"I didn't think it was possible." He chuckles. "Then, you started touching yourself, and I'm pretty sure my cock got jealous. I need to be inside you, baby."

I straddle him again, then realize I'm forgetting something. "Oh, wait. Do we need a condom?"

He must be intrigued by my choice of words, because his eyebrow rises. "Do we?"

I tilt my head. "Well...I'm on the pill. And disease-free. I got tested at my last doctor's appointment, and you're the only person I've been with since."

"You're the only person I've been with since my last test, too," he says with a grin.

For a split second, I find myself wondering if Caterina was the last woman he slept with before me. Then I realize I don't really care. How can I, when he's looking at me like I'm his entire world?

"I don't want to use a condom," I confess.

"Neither do I, baby." But there's a look on his face I can't quite discern.

"Are you sure?"

"Fuck, yes." He laughs. "Of course I am. The thing is, though…"

"What?"

"This'll be my first time not using one," he admits with a sheepish grin.

My heart swells. "Really? Ever?"

He nods. "I started having sex young. Didn't want to risk a teen pregnancy. Then in my twenties…well, you know what my reputation was." He flushes, embarrassed. "There were many women, but very few real feelings involved. I could tell they only wanted me for my body, or my career, or my money. I know it's a cynical way of looking at things, but a McBride baby would set them up for life. So, when they told me they were on the pill, I didn't trust them." He heaves a sigh, an earnest smile appearing on his impossibly handsome face. "But I trust you."

I grin back at him. "I trust you, too."

Holden gives me a kiss that's short and sweet.

"When I walked into O'Reilly's the night we met," I go on, "my plan was to drink until I forgot all about Penelope Dwyer and the ones who betrayed my trust before her. And I mean everyone—down to the blind date who'd stood me up the day before."

"Moron," Holden declares. "But also, thank god."

My lip quirks up for a second before I continue. "I didn't think I'd ever be able to trust again. I didn't see the point in letting down my guard. I'd been played too many times. And then you came along." My smile returns. "Who would have thought that the pitcher I loved to hate would be such a game-changer?"

His smile gives me butterflies. "Was that a pun, Red?"

I bite a grin. "Maybe."

His gorgeous eyes gleam with something bigger than joy. For a moment, he's quiet, but his gaze tells me everything I need to know. He doesn't have to say it out loud. I can hear it in the silence.

It's still too soon to exchange I love you's. But we will, one day. I know it. This might sound crazy, but Holden's grandmother told me so in a dream.

Last night, I lay in bed thinking about how he'd cried on my shoulder in her library. I was so happy he'd been comfortable being vulnerable with me. As I dozed off, I pictured the scene in my mind's eye, and suddenly there she was—Grandma Evelyn—sitting next to me as I comforted her grandson. She looked just as she did in the old family photo I found in the bathroom vanity, on my first night in the bungalow with Holden.

In my dream, she said she couldn't stay long, but she wanted to thank me.

"For what?" I asked.

Her smile was ethereal. "For being here, Christy. And for loving him."

"I haven't told him how I feel yet," I confessed. "I want to, but I'm still trying to process it, myself. I just can't understand how I fell so hard, so fast. It's not like me at all."

She looked at me with a twinkle in her eye. "That's what happens when your love story is written in the stars."

Written in the stars.

I woke up reeling. I'd said those words before. Years ago, to Jenna. We were waxing philosophical about relationships, and I said, "I want to think that love can be written in the stars." I still do.

It's as if Grandma Evelyn read my mind. Maybe that's not so unlikely, given I was dreaming, and she was just a figment of my subconscious.

Right?

I wonder what Holden would think if I told him his grandmother visited me in a dream? Something tells me he'd believe it.

But for now, I take my palms to his stubble and kiss him with the passion of a woman who knows she's found the man she's meant to be with.

In return, Holden plunges his tongue into my mouth and grips my ass with one hand, drawing me as close to him as possible. When he parts his lips from mine, he moves them up the length of my neck, making me shiver. "Fuck me, Red," he whispers in my ear. "I need to know what you feel like without a condom. Nothing between us...just your tight, wet pussy wrapped around my cock."

I nod, lifting my hips so I can guide him inside me.

"Remember, it's my first time, so be gentle," he teases.

When I sink down onto him, he sucks in a breath. "Holy shit. You're heaven, baby."

My heart flutters. "Thank you for making me your first."

"My only," he says.

We've had plenty of great sex already, but this level of bliss is unparalleled. I've never felt closer to anyone in my life. Not physically. Definitely not emotionally. It's such a fucking turn-on. The stream of dirty words coming out of Holden's mouth tells me he feels the same way. One more filthy comment about how pretty I'm going to look with his cum dripping down my thigh, and I'm convinced I'm going to climax. But it's the nerdy talk he surprises me with next that sends me over the edge.

Suffice it to say, I'll never think of *Lady Chatterley's Lover* the same way again.

Rocked by the explosiveness of my orgasm, Holden joins me seconds later, then brings his forehead to my chest with a sigh. "Fuck, that was incredible."

"Yes, it was," I agree, stroking his hair.

He looks up at me. "Baby, you just gave me the world...but I need to ask you for one more thing."

I tilt my head, curious. "What's that?"

"I've been daydreaming about motorboating these titties since the first time I kissed you."

I giggle. "Knock yourself out."

CHAPTER 26

Christy

Holden and I walk into the conference room ten minutes early, and we're still the last to arrive.

"Well, look who's here. Finally." Mrs. McBride's barely detectable smirk spikes my blood pressure. We're not even late, but of course she wouldn't dare miss an opportunity to greet us with a passive-aggressive jab.

That's Margot Fucking McBride for you. My future mother-in-law, if the ghost of Grandma Evelyn is to be believed. Maybe Abby's husband, Wyatt, has the right idea not showing up to these insufferable family functions. But the McBrides aren't cruel to their daughter the way they are to Holden. How could I send him into this viper den alone?

As we approach the table, I'm hit with a medley of tantalizing tropical scents, which I assume can be attributed to luxurious massage oils. Everyone is fresh-faced and glowing from their spa treatments. Even Great-Uncle Alistair looks more relaxed than I've seen him. Is it merely the hours of pampering that has him looking so serene? Or did he sleep well last night, knowing that the board made the right decision? The decision that honors Grandma Evelyn's legacy.

One can only hope.

Sitting on either side of Alistair, his granddaughter and Dan appear calm as well. Zoe barely looks up when I take the seat next to her. She's busy on Instagram, uploading a selfie she took with Caterina at the spa. The two beauties look thick as thieves.

Oh god. Just what Holden needs. An impressionable, young board member who thinks she's The Siren's bestie.

Speaking of the supermodel, she and Wes are seated directly across from me and Holden, avoiding our gazes. Wes's eye looks completely healed, by the way, no doubt thanks to Siren Serum.

Fuck. Fuck. Fuck. Fuck. Fuck.

Caterina's listening to Margot complain about the "idiot" spa employee who double-booked the aesthetician and made the McBride matriarch wait a whole ten minutes for her Champagne and Caviar Facial (*is that really a thing?*). Cat, for her part, seems distracted—fiddling with her bracelets and shifting in her seat—but maybe she isn't interested in bad-mouthing the resort staff the way Margot is.

Then there's Mr. McBride, who's reclined in his chair, reading *The New York Times*. Next to him, Abby catches my gaze and waves at me.

Wait a minute. What's Abby doing here?

"I thought you were flying home for the kids' violin performance," I say with a grin.

"Maisie and Matt begged me to stay. They haven't gotten enough of their favorite uncle yet," Abby explains, with a nod toward Holden.

If Wes overheard his sister, he doesn't seem to care. Holden, for his part, is ecstatic, despite the beads of sweat on his brow. His smile makes my hammering heart slow the slightest bit.

But I'm still nervous as hell.

Alistair takes a quick glance around the table. "Looks like we're all here, so let's get started."

My stomach flips. I turn to my boyfriend again, whose leg is shaking. He also looks pained. While the medication's helping, the sling seems crucial for his overall comfort. The problem is, he won't wear it here, because he doesn't think this crowd can keep his injury a secret until the Starlings issue a statement. I can't say I blame him.

When Alistair folds his hands in his lap and opens his mouth to speak, I feel like I'm going to throw up.

"After taking both proposals into careful consideration," he begins, "Daniel, Zoe, and I have—"

"Wait!" Caterina blurts out.

Everyone's attention shifts to The Siren, who jumps from her seat and walks swiftly to the head of the table. But when she gets there, she's speechless. Her hands are shaking, and the blood's drained from her face.

Alistair's voice is laced with concern. "Ms. Hart, are you quite alright?"

The supermodel looks down, past her chic, tailored pantsuit, to her stiletto heels. Then she glances at Wes, who's stone-faced, but gives her a nod that seems to relax her a bit.

"I'm fine, thank you," she breathes out. "But I have an announcement to make. Wes and I have decided to take Siren Serum out of the race. Well, *I* decided. But Wes agreed to support me, regardless of the choice I made."

"So...that means Racing Hearts wins," Abby declares with a smile on her face.

"By *default*," Mrs. McBride emphasizes. "It's hardly a victory."

Holden heaves a frustrated sigh. A win is a win, but I know how much he wanted to earn this money fair and square.

"Why on earth would you back out now, Cat?" Mrs. McBride asks, looking crestfallen and, once again, making no effort to conceal whose side she's on. "I was so looking forward to collaborating with you, dear."

The model's lip quivers. "Me, too, Margot. I've always really liked you."

Ugh. Why?

"And that makes this all the more difficult for me to say. But I can't live with the guilt anymore." Caterina's eyes shoot to Holden, whose suspicious gaze is narrowed on his ex.

What the hell is going on here?

"When Holden and I were dating, back in high school, I made a decision that I regret to this day. I, um..." The Siren inhales deeply, fiddling with her bracelets again. "I stole some of your necklaces, Margot."

There are several gasps around the room, including my own. Everyone but Wes and Holden looks stunned. I can't help but wonder how long they've known.

Margot's jaw drops. "I don't...I don't understand."

"My parents wouldn't give me money to book headshots with a top photographer who charged three times more than anyone else," Caterina says. "So, I stole your necklaces and sold them to pay for the pictures. That photographer made me famous, which means...my entire career can be owed to a misdeed."

"A crime, you mean?" Mrs. McBride's voice is stern, and her

gaze even more so when she turns to her son. "Did you know about this, Holden?"

"I begged him not to tell," Caterina jumps in. "But when I showed up here to compete for his grandmother's money, Holden was upset, of course. Then I explained that I was trying to make amends by sharing Siren Serum's success with your family."

"What an absurd idea," Mr. McBride huffs, *The New York Times* still open on his lap. "You could have made a donation to our family foundation, if you felt so badly."

Caterina's shoulders slump. "Yeah, that's what Holden said. It took me a couple of days, but I realized he's right. I was trying to make amends without arousing suspicion, which kind of misses the point. I'm so sorry for what I did, and I wish I could get those necklaces back. I tried to trace them years ago, and I wasn't successful. But I promise to pay any amount you see fit. I want to turn over a new leaf. I'm going to launch Siren Serum on my own, and I want this to be a fresh start for me." She turns to Wes. "For us."

"Us?" Abby raises a skeptical eyebrow.

The supermodel smiles at her boyfriend. "Wes has agreed to be my sole investor."

Abby shakes her head. "So, what I'm hearing is, you're *not* really doing this alone, and you're still using McBride money to fund your company."

Caterina purses her lips. "Well, yes. But not your grandmother's money. *That* should go to Holden. I think Grandma Evelyn would have loved Racing Hearts," she tells my boyfriend before turning to her own. "And Wes is eager to invest, right, honey?"

The younger McBride brother gives an earnest nod.

"He believes in Siren Serum wholeheartedly," Caterina goes on to tell Abby. "I mean, look at his eye! You can't tell he was punched at all."

"*Punched?*" Margot gasps. "You said you dropped a dumbbell, Wesley!"

Caterina winces. "Oops. I did *not* mean to say that."

"Let me guess who punched you." The McBride matriarch turns from her golden boy to the black sheep of the family.

Holden's jaw clenches. "Wes made a move on Christy. He gave me no choice."

"I had too much to drink that night, and I apologized to them both," Wes tells his mother. "We've moved on."

Mr. McBride chuckles into his newspaper. "Ah, to be young again."

"Holden, I did not raise you to throw punches like some barbarian," Margot huffs.

Holden smirks and shakes his head. I think that's going to be the end of it, but then my boyfriend leans forward in his seat. "You're right, Mom. But only because you didn't raise me at all. Grandma did."

It's the first time I've heard Holden stand up to his mother...and dare I say, he has never looked hotter.

Margot rolls her eyes. "Is that why you chose to conceal the fact that Caterina stole from me? Because I was such a disappointing mother?"

I mean, it's not a bad reason.

"Jesus Christ!" Abby exclaims. "When will you ever lay off him, Mom? I mean, Cat just admitted she stole your jewelry, and you're mad at *Holden*? Give me a fucking break."

So much for the McBrides not yelling. But Abby's cut from a different cloth, like my boyfriend. That's why I like her. And

I'm sure it's why Holden's always wished they were closer. I look up at him, and he's grinning at her, his eyes full of gratitude.

Margot gives her daughter a dismissive wave. "Oh, not you, too."

Mr. McBride doesn't look up from his newspaper. "You should have told us, Holden."

My boyfriend sneers. "Sorry, Dad. It's kinda hard to keep track of when I'm supposed to be honest, and when I'm supposed to keep my mouth shut."

His father challenges him with an equally contemptuous gaze, but says nothing.

Margot looks at her husband. "What is he talking about, Julian?"

"Nothing," he grunts in return.

"It's not nothing." Holden's gaze stays fixed on his dad. "You blamed me for Abby's car wreck."

Abby gasps.

"Oh, *that*," Margot says, as if the accident couldn't be more trivial. "It was years ago. Why must we dredge up the past?"

Holden ignores her, eyes still on his father. "You said I should've kept my mouth shut about Abby's cheating boyfriend. And you told me to keep my distance from her, if I knew what was good for me."

"Oh my god, Dad!" Abby's hands fly to her mouth, and her face reddens. "So, not only did you blame a child for an accident that *wasn't* his fault...you destroyed his relationship with his big sister? It wasn't enough that you pitted Holden and Wes against each other—"

Julian scoffs. "I did no such thing."

Abby's eyes go wide. "Are you kidding? You wanted Holden

to be an academic, like Wes. You wanted Wes to be athletic, like Holden. And look at Wes now! You gave him such a massive inferiority complex, he looks like Thor—"

Wes smiles. "Well, thank you."

His sister sighs. "That was not meant to be a compliment. You haven't eaten a carb your entire adult life! And you used to love bread. Remember that summer you spent making sourdough with our nanny? I mean, I still think about that olive loaf. It was fucking good."

"*So* fucking good," Holden agrees.

"Stop depriving yourself, Wesley," Abby urges. "It's no wonder you act like such an ass all the time. You're probably just hungry."

Wes's childish pout looks comically out of place on his chiseled features. "Am not."

"Abigail, that's quite enough," Margot insists, avoiding her daughter's angry gaze. "Leave Wesley alone."

Abby's laugh is ironic. "Of course you come to his rescue. You've always favored Wes, and you made me hate him for it. You're no better than Dad."

Silence hangs heavy in the room.

"You know, it makes perfect sense that you two would want your children to despise each other," Abby goes on. "You hoped we'd be so preoccupied with our sibling rivalry that we wouldn't notice what shitty parents you are. Well, guess what? Your plan backfired."

Abby stands, slinging her purse over her shoulder. "I'm outta here. And don't plan on seeing me and the kids at Thanksgiving. We're going to celebrate with Wyatt's family this year."

Before she walks away, her gaze travels to a tray of gourmet chocolate chip macadamia nut cookies sitting untouched on the table. "And by the way—what is the fucking point of ordering dessert if no one's going to eat it?"

My thoughts exactly!

Abby grabs two cookies, takes a bite out of one, and gives the other to Wes. "It's delicious. Enjoy."

Wes stares at the baked good—an old friend turned foe— for several seconds before surrendering. "Fuck it." He tastes a piece and groans, then breaks off a chunk for Caterina. "You have to try this, babe."

"But...I'll bloat." She grimaces.

Wes shrugs. "We'll bloat together."

His girlfriend smiles and opens her mouth for Wes to feed her. When she's done enjoying the morsel, they kiss.

I don't know that I'll ever be their biggest fan, but I have to say...Wes and The Siren are pretty cute together.

On her way out, Abby stops next to me and Holden. "Do you guys want to have dinner with me and the kids at the guesthouse tonight?"

I can't contain my smile. Neither can my boyfriend when he replies. "Absolutely."

Abby kisses the top of his head, then mine. "See you later."

Mr. McBride folds his newspaper and stands. "Well, I think I've had enough family time for today. To those of you who had to sit here and listen to my ungrateful children air their grievances, please accept my apologies. I suppose this is what happens when you spoil your kids rotten."

Before he leaves, he turns to Caterina. "As for you, dear—"

She flushes.

"The necklaces were insured, so there's no need to write us a check. As far as I'm concerned, your apology is amends enough." On that note, he exits the room.

Margot shrugs. "Honestly, I can't even remember which necklaces we're talking about."

Holden drags a hand down his face.

Alistair breaks the ensuing awkward silence with a wry smile. "Well, Ms. Hart. I'm glad you got that off your chest. But as far as this competition goes, your withdrawal changes nothing."

Caterina's brow furrows. "Oh. So, you're saying that…"

"Racing Hearts was the winner by unanimous decision, yes." The old man grins at Holden.

"Alistair!" Margot exclaims. "Why on earth didn't you tell us before? You could've spared us a lot of trouble."

Alistair's voice is stern. "You had that trouble coming, Margot. You and Julian, both. You remind me of my parents. All they cared about was money and status."

Margot sinks back in her seat like a sullen child.

"Congratulations, Holden," his great-uncle continues. "While Siren Serum is both remarkably and *inexplicably* effective, at the end of the day, it's a product. Racing Hearts is much more than that. It's a legacy."

"It's what your grandma would've wanted," Zoe adds.

Dan nods. "I grew up playing baseball, and I would've loved to have access to a program like Racing Hearts. It's a great initiative, Holden."

I throw my arms around my boyfriend. "You did it."

"*We* did it," he says, reminding me of our team effort with Charlie. "This is our win." Then he gives me a smoldering kiss that makes me forget his mom's in the room.

Unfortunately, she's quick to remind me. "I see you haven't had your fill of my son yet, Christin*a*?"

Actually, he filled me up about an hour ago, you raging—

Mrs. McBride sighs. "Well, I'm sure it won't be long now. I mean, let's face it, dear. You're an unlikely pair. An athlete and a scholar? Sooner or later, you'll get bored and move on."

"You're wrong," I blurt out before I can think twice. "Look, I'm going to be completely honest with you, Margot. My relationship with Holden began as a PR stunt."

"Called it!" Wes says with a mouthful of cookie.

"But I fell for him in a matter of days," I go on. "Your son is the most thoughtful, caring, generous person I've ever met. Not to mention, smart. And if you can't see that, then you're the one who needs educating."

I glance at Holden and see him smiling at me before I turn back to his mom. "He's the entire package. The only thing he lacked when I met him was trust. But what else would you expect from a man whose own mother never cared enough to know him? And, let me tell you, Margot, you're really missing out. Because getting to know Holden is the best thing that's ever happened to me."

When I turn to my boyfriend, his eyes are glistening. "What did I do to deserve you?" he asks.

I reach for his hand. "All you had to do was be yourself."

"Well, I've taken quite enough abuse for one day," Margot declares, standing up. "My nerves are shot. I'm going back to the spa."

After she stomps out, there's a rumbling of murmurs around the room.

"Let's get out of here," Holden whispers to me. "I need some time in my sling."

I nod. Considering how heated this meeting ended up being, it's a miracle Holden didn't inadvertently wave his arm in a moment of passion. The pain would've been too unbearable to hide.

"Abby's right about the cookies," he says. "Let's take some back to the bungalow, so they don't go to waste."

With an eager grin, I grab a handful, just as Dan comes up to Holden.

"Congrats again, man," he says. Then he slaps Holden's left shoulder—hard.

"Holy shit!" My boyfriend groans, clutching his arm.

Dan's face pales. "Oh my god! Are you alright? Did I hurt you?"

"It's not you," Holden says, wincing.

He turns to me and shakes his head with an ironic smile, his features relaxing slightly as the searing pain begins to dull. "What's one more piece of dirty laundry, when we've already aired so much?"

He turns to address the room. "I have a shoulder injury."

"Fuck," Wes mutters. "Is it because—"

Holden shakes his head. "It started long before I knocked you out. But throwing the punch made it worse, and I'll need surgery. Nobody knows right now, except for my agent, so I need everyone to keep this quiet until I meet with the team doctor and the Starlings issue a statement. Can I trust you all to do that?"

I look at the remaining faces around the room, all nodding enthusiastically. Their foreheads are creased with genuine concern. Without Holden's parents here, I realize the rest of the McBrides might not be so bad.

Then there's Caterina, whose gratitude toward Holden is

written all over her face. "You covered for me all those years ago, and I owe you big time. We won't say a word," she tells him, hooking her arm around her boyfriend's.

"I grew up on the North Side of Chicago, and I'm a huge Starlings fan," Dan chimes in. Your secret's safe with me."

"Thanks, everyone," Holden says. "Appreciate it."

After wishing my boyfriend well, Alistair, Zoe, and Dan exit the conference room next, leaving only four of us.

"Wes and I are flying to Paris tonight for my next photoshoot," Caterina says, "so, I guess this is goodbye. I'm so glad everything worked out...with Racing Hearts...and with you guys." She turns to me. "You're perfect for each other. It's easy to see."

"That's sweet, thanks," I tell her. "I was thinking the same about you and Wes."

"Really?" The model's forehead creases. "I can't imagine what you must think of me after hearing my confession about the jewelry..."

"Actually, I think you're pretty brave," I say. It's true.

"I'm proud of you for being honest," Holden tells his ex.

"Thanks, guys," she says, her cheeks flushed. Then she turns to Wes. "We should probably start packing."

"Congrats, bro," he says, shaking Holden's good hand. "Well-deserved."

"Who the fuck are you, and where's my jackass of a brother?" Holden jokes.

Wes shrugs, smiling at Caterina. "What can I say? This woman brings out the best in me."

"Aww, honey." The Siren gives him a peck.

"All of that shit Abby said was true," Wes goes on to tell Holden. "Dad's the one I should resent, not you. I'll try to be less of a dick from now on. She may have had a point about me being hungry, too. That cookie hit the spot."

Holden chuckles. "Take care, guys."

When it's just the two of us, I take a big bite of one of the cookies in my hand. It's even sweeter than I imagined. Maybe it's because I can rest easy now, knowing that Holden's career is far from over. Even if he never returns as the Starlings' star pitcher, he'll still continue to shine through Racing Hearts.

"How's it taste?" Holden asks, grinning when I lick chocolate off my lips.

I smile back. "It tastes like victory."

CHAPTER 27

Holden

Two hours later, Christy and I leave our bungalow for the guesthouse where Abby's staying with my niece and nephew. As we walk hand in hand through the warm evening air, I'm still just as stunned by Racing Hearts' victory as when Great-Uncle Alistair made the announcement. The fact that he also took the opportunity to scold my mom before the meeting adjourned was the icing on the cake.

I'll admit, I walked into that conference room with low expectations. I figured I'd already gotten as lucky as I was going to get today. After all, I'd just had the most intense sex of my life with the woman of my dreams. Granted, I did come all over myself first, which I still can't say I'm proud of. But I'd happily do it again just to see Christy's face light up the way it did. She's still glowing, although I know it isn't only from the self-esteem boost. She's as ecstatic about Racing Hearts as I am. It's just one of the reasons I'm crazy about her.

As soon as I knock on the guesthouse door, Christy and I hear squeals and eager footsteps heading our way. It's a good thing Abby greets us before Maisie and Matt, because the kids are so excited, they look like they want to tackle me. Under any other circumstances, I'd be game but, given my injury, I'm not in the best shape for roughhousing.

"Oh my god!" Abby exclaims when she sees my sling. Then she stretches her arms out wide to block her children's escape from the doorway. "Maisie, Matt—stay back. Uncle Holden hurt himself."

"What happened?" Abby says, then lowers her voice so the kids can't hear. "You didn't punch Dad, too, did you?"

I laugh. "No. This is from the, um, incident with Wes the other day." My niece and nephew look up at me with furrowed brows, so I kneel down to meet their gazes. "I'll be fine, guys, I promise. I just can't play ball tonight, but I *can* play cards. Have you heard of a game called gin rummy?"

The kids shake their heads.

"Well, I happen to be an expert, so I can teach you. Just like your great-grandma taught me when I was around your age." I wink at them.

"I get to go first!" Matt yells.

"No fair! You always go first!" Maisie screams.

Abby rolls her eyes as she turns back to her kids. "No fighting! Go to the kitchen and pour two glasses of lemonade for our guests, okay? And don't forget to clean up any spills."

My niece and nephew practically trip over each other, racing to see who can get to the fridge fastest.

"Good. Now, I can properly welcome you both," Abby says, throwing her arms around Christy first. Watching them hug brings a tear to my eye, and not for the first time today. I nearly started bawling when my girlfriend stood up to my mom earlier, in the conference room. I swear, I've been more emotional the past two days than I have my entire adult life.

It's not a bad thing. It's fucking great, actually. This must be what happens when you find true love. Your heart just cracks wide open.

My sister moves over to me and wraps one arm around my good shoulder. "So happy you're here."

We follow her inside, and no sooner do we cross the threshold than I hear someone jogging down the stairs. I look around, confused. The kids are both in the kitchen—and, besides, the footsteps sound like they belong to a man. But Wes is busy packing for his trip to Paris with Cat. And I can't imagine Abby would invite Dad, tonight of all nights. So who else could it be?

When a familiar face comes into view, I'm stunned. It's a face I haven't seen in years and wasn't expecting to see anytime soon. But it's a pleasant surprise.

My mouth quirks up as I reach for the mystery man's hand. "Hey bro, long time no see! This is my girlfriend, Christy… Christy, this is Abby's husband, Wyatt."

"So nice to meet you," she says with that warm smile of hers that could put anyone at ease. It's the one she offers to most people she first meets. Even my parents, before they quickly proved themselves to be assholes.

"Guess the cat's out of the bag," Abby says with a chuckle. "Wyatt's been here the whole time. If Mom and Dad know, they haven't let on."

"The in-laws and I have a pretty mutual loathing of each other," Wyatt explains to Christy with a wry grin.

"Can't say I'm shocked," my girlfriend replies. Then her gaze lands on me and Abby. "No offense, McBrides."

"None taken," my sister and I say in unison.

"What's with the sling?" Wyatt asks. "You okay, brother?"

Now that the kids are out of earshot, I go into more detail. "Truth is, I have a torn labrum, and I need to go under the knife. As far as my career goes, everything's up in the air."

"Oh, Holden…" Abby's eyes glisten.

"It's okay," I assure her. "After you left the conference room, Alistair announced that the board unanimously voted for Racing Hearts. I won fair and square, and now I get to honor Grandma the way I hoped. It doesn't get much better than that."

"She'd be so proud," my sister says, swallowing her tears.

"Happy for you, man. That's incredible," Wyatt adds.

"Thanks, bro." I huff a laugh. "I still can't believe you're here. Exactly how many Maui trips have you been on where we were none the wiser?"

He looks to his wife. "What is this, Abs, my fourth?" When she nods, Wyatt turns back to me. "I provide the comic relief when your sister comes back from the main house looking murderous."

Abby smirks. "And it's a damn good thing he was here today."

"My wife filled me in on the gory details," Wyatt says, his brow furrowed. "But setting aside my rage toward Julian for a second, I'm thrilled you and Abs cleared the air. I've always liked you, man. I could tell you weren't like the rest of the McBrides the moment we met."

"That's the best compliment I could ask for," I reply.

"I feel the same way about Abby. These two are cut from the same cloth," Christy chimes in, nodding toward me and my sister.

"Jury's still out on Wes," I joke. "But that cookie did seem to help."

"It's the same strategy I use when Maisie and Matt are crabby," Abby explains. "And Wes has always been a bit of an overgrown child, so…"

We all laugh.

"I think there might be hope for him yet," Christy muses, which is mighty generous of her, given the terrible first impression he made.

But then again, I made a terrible first impression on her, too. And look at us now.

"You guys are too cute," Abby says when she sees the lovestruck way I'm gazing at my girlfriend. "I hate to separate you, Christy, but do you mind if I borrow my brother for a few minutes? We'll just be in the kitchen. You and Wyatt can swap war stories about Margot and Julian, if you want."

Christy's eyes light up. "Sounds fun."

She and Wyatt head into the living room, and I follow Abby. The kids are nowhere in sight, but I hear giggles coming from the playroom downstairs.

My sister shakes her head at the two nearly empty glasses on the counter. "Looks like Maisie and Matt drank the lemonade I asked them to pour for you."

I grin. "Par for the course, right?"

Abby rolls her eyes with a wry chuckle. Then her gaze turns wistful. "I missed you so much, Holden. That's why I brought you in here. I've been wanting to tell you for years."

I pull her into a one-armed hug. "I missed you too, Abs," I say. "So much."

"I don't think I'll ever forgive Dad," she says when she steps back. "But I'm also so mad at myself. I should've talked to you when I got home from the hospital. Asked if you were okay. You must have been so scared—"

"Abby, you didn't need to do that—"

"Yes, I did. I'm the older sibling. I should've reached out. I should've asked you why you weren't speaking to me. I was just so...embarrassed. I couldn't believe I'd done something so stupid. I figured you wanted nothing to do with me. That's why I left you alone."

"I thought you were mad at me," I admit.

She takes my hand. "You did nothing wrong, Holden. I'm glad you told me that Jeremy cheated."

"Fucking Jeremy. That piece of shit." My anger reignites, as though it happened yesterday. Although, I will say it's a huge relief to hear Abby say she never blamed me.

"You know, Jeremy's a partner at Wyatt's law firm? He's in the Chicago office, though, and he's a litigator, so they never interact, thank god. I mean, I'm over it, but Wyatt hates everyone who's ever wronged me." She smiles. "Kinda like you, it seems."

I heave a sigh. "Chicago, huh? Well, that asshole better hope he never runs into me, because I'll be happy to give him a piece of my mind. Just ask Christy's ex."

"I've never seen you like this over a woman," my sister says, her eyes gleaming. "Is this it? Is she the one?"

"I sure as hell hope so." Grandma wouldn't lead me astray.

"I do, too. You should bring her to New York for Thanksgiving. I'd love to have you over with Wyatt's family. You remember them, right? From the wedding? They're cool. Nothing like our parents."

My heart swells. "That sounds great."

"Maisie and Matt are going to be so happy," my sister says, her lip quivering. When a tear falls from her cheek, she wipes it away, her cheeks flushed with embarrassment. "Ugh, I'm sorry."

"For crying? Don't be."

"But it's not the McBride way," Abby says, her voice laced with sarcasm.

"Fuck that," I tell her. "I finally cried over Grandma last night, and my tears haven't stopped flowing since. It feels amazing. You should try it."

She shakes her head. "I can't. Not now. We're about to have dinner and—" Abby struggles to swallow her tears. "Dammit."

"Come here," I say, wrapping an arm around her. "Bring it in."

When my sister returns my hug, the floodgates open. "I love you," she says between sobs.

My own eyes water. "I love you too, Abs."

As she cries, her muscles relax against me, the tension in her body melting away. Eventually, her tears stop, and she heaves a sigh. When she steps back, she's smiling.

"Feels good, right?" I ask.

"It feels fucking amazing. And Wyatt'll be thrilled. He's tired of being the emotional one."

We both laugh.

"Thank you, Holden."

I nod, grinning. "Anytime."

Abby wipes her eyes. "We should probably head back out there. You hungry? There are appetizers in the living room."

I follow Abby out of the kitchen to see Christy and Wyatt sharing a well-deserved laugh at my parents' expense. At the same time, Maisie and Matt bound upstairs and race over to me, wrapping their little arms around my legs.

"Be careful not to knock Uncle Holden over," Abby warns them. "We don't want to make his shoulder worse."

"I'm good, thanks," I reply, chuckling at the idea that my

pint-sized niece and nephew could topple my 6'4" frame. Then Christy catches my gaze and gives me a grin that makes me unsteady, and for a second, I think I might actually lose my balance. Luckily, Maisie and Matt let go of my legs, lured by the tray of pizza bites and mini corn dogs on the coffee table. With full mouths and proud smiles, they announce that their mom let them pick the appetizers for our dinner party. And when I tell you I'm as excited about their choices as they are, I'm not lying.

But before I dig in, I take a moment to soak up the scene. I watch my girlfriend fitting in perfectly with Abby, Wyatt, and the kids. *This* is the kind of family gathering I want more of. This is the kind of life I've always craved. Love, laughter, warmth, connection. And the redheaded beauty who makes my knees weak with just her smile. If I'm lucky, she'll be by my side for many more moments like this one. Thanksgiving dinner in New York. Christmas in Connecticut. And a new year full of surprises.

Maybe one day I'll bring her back to the Honeymoon Bungalow for our *actual* honeymoon. And, when she's ready, we can start working on giving Maisie and Matt a couple of cousins to play with. As I take my seat on the couch next to Christy, I can almost see my future playing out before my eyes.

And fuck if it's not everything I ever wanted.

"Mini corn dog?" Christy asks, holding one up for me.

Rather than take the stick from her hand, I take an eager bite, almost nipping her fingers, and my niece and nephew burst into giggles. When Christy joins them, my damn heart melts.

Who would've thought I could be this happy with my pitching arm in a sling.

CHAPTER 28

Christy

NOVEMBER 2012

Two *Months Later...*

I wake up to the sound of something crashing onto the kitchen floor.

"Holden?" I sit up in bed and rub the sleep from my eyes.

"I'm good, baby," he assures me. "Stay right where you, are, I'll be there in a minute. Or three."

I fluff up my pillows as I eagerly await my boyfriend. Then another loud clattering ensues, followed by Holden muttering obscenities.

I bite my lip. "Are you sure I can't help?"

"I got this, Red, I promise. It's your birthday, and you deserve to relax. Just give me five more minutes," he says. "Ten, max."

"Take your time." I reach for the glass of water on my nightstand. Well, it's Holden's nightstand, technically. This is his house. But I've been living here for two months—since he had his shoulder surgery, mere days after we got back from Maui.

The procedure went well. That's the good news. The bad

news is that the Starlings didn't extend Holden's contract. But he honestly didn't expect them to. A thirty-six-year-old pitcher recovering from labrum surgery is a risky investment, to say the least. Holden accepted the news with grace, and the team promised they'd reevaluate things when he's further along in his recovery. The Starlings didn't make it to the postseason without their ace pitcher this year, and I'm sure they'd love nothing more than to have him back.

At least we know that, if they don't extend an offer, it won't be because of his reputation. Holden's public image has never been better, especially after our outing to a Bears game last month.

It was his first appearance at a sporting event since the Starlings announced his injury, and his first time back at Soldier Field since the infamous streaking stunt. Holden's agent Russell came up with the idea, and it was genius: go back to the scene of the crime, but fully clothed, and looking wholesome in a Racing Hearts sweatshirt to match your girlfriend's.

In case that weren't attention-grabbing enough, Russell arranged for the Bears' production team to air a short promo video for Racing Hearts, featuring soundbites by Holden and Dex. When the montage appeared on the jumbotron before kickoff, the stadium erupted in cheers. So many fans posted about it online, in fact, that the news of Racing Hearts went viral. This time, Holden was thrilled to make headlines, and he's counting the days until the program launches next year.

In the meantime, he's working tirelessly in physical therapy to retrain his shoulder to move. He's in the early stages of healing, and his mobility is very limited, which is why I'm still staying with him. But I get the sense he enjoys having me here. And the feeling's definitely mutual.

After checking emails on my cell, I notice that I have one new voicemail from a number I don't recognize. Intrigued, I hit play.

"Hi Christy, this is Haley Quinlan. I'm sorry it's taken me so long to thank you for the incredible gift you sent me. I went into early labor at thirty weeks, and it's been a long road. But my daughter's finally home, and we've been settling into a routine. Anyway, I'm rambling...probably from lack of sleep, but...will you call me? Okay, thanks. Bye."

I shouldn't get my hopes up. It's been two whole months since Haley told me she'd chosen a different agent. Granted, she still hasn't announced her pick, but that's probably the last thing on her mind, given her daughter's early arrival.

Nevertheless, my heart races as I dial her back.

Haley answers right away, sounding nervous. "Christy, hi! I wasn't sure you'd call. Thank you so much for the gift. I've always wanted a first edition of *A Farewell to Arms*. It's like you read my mind."

"Of course. I thought of you the moment I saw it," I tell her. "And congratulations on the new baby. I'm sorry you had a rough start."

"Thank you," she sighs. "You know, it's been such a whirlwind, I never actually ended up signing with an agent? I decided to put *Edison's Love* on the back burner until my daughter was out of the NICU...and I only started querying again last week."

"Well, you've had so much on your plate," I say, trying my best not to get excited.

"Look, I'm going to be completely honest," Haley says. "I turned you down too quickly, and all because I didn't want to be associated with Penelope Dwyer. But you were far and away my first choice, Christy, and I regret my decision."

I catch my reflection in the mirror across from the bed. I'm beaming.

"I was just going to suck it up and live with my mistake," she goes on, "but then you sent that lovely gift and said there were no hard feelings. So I thought, what's the harm in reaching out, especially since..."

"Since?"

"Well, I don't want to put any pressure on you," she begins. "But Colin Finch extended an offer a few days ago, and I haven't responded yet. He's getting antsy."

I swallow a laugh. Of course Colin's getting antsy. He's notoriously stingy with offers and isn't used to being turned down. Especially recently. His client roster has grown quite a bit since Penelope tarnished my image, and I doubt it's a coincidence. Haley can't be the only author who didn't want their name attached to my scandal. For weeks, I hardly got any submissions, and every author I extended an offer to ended up choosing Colin.

Until now, it seems.

"Christy, is there any chance you would still consider representing me and *Edison's Love*?" Haley asks.

I can practically see her biting her nails, so I answer right away. "Today's my birthday, and this is the best gift I could ask for, Haley. Yes. I would love to represent you."

After making plans to chat later in the week, I hang up the phone, so giddy I squeal. I think it's safe to say my luck is starting to change. It doesn't hurt that wily Penelope recently announced she's self-publishing a memoir called *Loving Dr. Liar*. It's a tell-all account of how she rose to fame by fooling the masses...including one of the top literary agents in the business. As far as apologies go, it left a lot to be desired. But in any case, my professional reputation no longer seems to be in jeopardy, as evidenced by the volume of submissions I've been receiving. And the fact that the author-who-got-away came back to me.

To think, just two months ago, I was so jaded about love that I'd nearly sworn off all things romance. Now, not only am I representing the genre's next big name, I'm in the best relationship of my life. Holden and I haven't exchanged I love you's yet, but I'm not worried. I feel it every time he looks at me.

It would be kinda nice if he told me on my birthday, though.

That's what I'm thinking when my boyfriend walks into the room. Naked. With a breakfast tray balanced on one hand, and a blue ribbon tied around his dick.

I laugh so hard, tears stream down my face, and I forget all about love confessions and Haley Quinlan, for the moment.

"Happy birthday to you," he sings, making his way over to me. He sets the tray down on the bed, then takes his place beside me.

"You're hard," I say, staring at his penis.

"What can I say? Thirty-one looks good on you, baby. Plus, I'm always hard around you," he reminds me.

It's true. Holden excels at a lot of things, but making me feel beautiful, sexy, and oh-so-desired are at the top of the list. Every woman should be so lucky to have a partner who worships her body the way he does mine. In fact, that's my birthday wish this year: that all the ladies who need a Holden in their lives find one.

In the two months we've been together, I already feel leaps

and bounds better about myself. Of course, my self-esteem and body image issues still lurk in the shadows. There are moments I still can't believe the hottest man I've ever laid eyes on wants *me*. But that's what therapy is for.

I've been going for six weeks now, and the waves of insecurity are definitely fewer and farther between. My therapist also confirmed that my anger responses are normal, just like Holden said. Now, I don't worry about being judged when I'm pissed off. The only person who'd judge me is my father, who's as uninvolved in my life as ever. My therapist is helping me come to terms with that, as well. She's warm and easy to talk to. I got over my dread of being vulnerable with a stranger much quicker than I anticipated.

And it's all thanks to Holden McBride, the cocksure athlete who tore down my walls.

"So, what am I supposed to put my mouth around first?" I tease. "You, or this croissant?"

He pulls the sheet over his erection. "Eat first. I know how much you hate cold eggs."

I crinkle my nose. "I do. And these look delicious. I can't believe you did all this for me. You haven't even been out of your sling for two weeks."

"Don't worry, I only used my right arm. Hence the crashing sounds you heard. I got it done, though, and believe me, you deserve it, baby. You've been waiting on me hand and foot during my recovery."

"Well, you're my favorite patient," I tell him, which earns me a kiss.

"And you're my favorite doctor." He grabs his own croissant from the tray and takes a bite.

I giggle. "That's only because I give you head."

"The *best* head of my entire life," he corrects me.

"Well, your blue-ribbon penis deserves it. I'm guessing you chose that color on purpose, right?" I dig a fork into my perfectly scrambled eggs.

His half-smile is mischievous. "I don't know, baby. Would you say I have an award-worthy cock?"

"You already know my answer," I say when I'm done chewing. "In fact, I was so distracted by your hard-on that I forgot to tell you the amazing news! Haley Quinlan called to thank me for the first edition I sent, and..."

I love the way his eyes light up with excitement. "*And?*"

"She wants me to rep her. She never signed with anyone else." My gaze turns wistful. "She said it was always me."

"Of course it was, Red." He beams. "I knew she'd come to her senses."

"Thank you." I press a light kiss onto his recovering shoulder.

"Look at you, racking up new clients. What is this, three authors already this week? And a meeting with Lola in the books?" Holden winks at me. "Welcome back."

It still feels surreal. A few days after Holden's surgery, he FaceTimed Lola so he could introduce us. I'll admit, I was starstruck at first. I mean, Lola Piper is larger than life. But once we got to chatting and I realized how down-to-earth she is, I nearly forgot I was talking to the biggest pop star on the planet. I could even see the two of us being friends.

I can't wait to meet her in person. Lola's officially out of hiding now, and as part of her comeback, she's performing pop-up shows around the country. Needless to say, Pipettes everywhere are in a tizzy, seeing as they have no clue where their favorite singer will turn up next. Typically, I would fall into this category, but I happen to be one of the privileged few who knows that Lola will be in Chicago next week. While she's in town, she wants to take me to lunch to discuss the vision she has for her memoir.

"I gotta say, though," Holden goes on, "now that Haley's signing with you, I'm afraid my birthday gift doesn't compare."

My eyes widen. "Breakfast in bed and a blue-ribbon cock? What could be better than that?"

Holden laughs. "This isn't your birthday present, baby. You know you can have my dick whenever you want. And the eggs aren't my best work. I haven't mastered whisking with my right hand."

I chuckle. "Don't be so hard on yourself. They're delicious. And this is already hands-down the best birthday I've ever had." It's true. Just waking up next to Holden was enough. "But I am curious to see what else you have up your sleeve."

"Well, you'll have to wait until after dinner tonight. We're still on, right?" His smile is playful. "You haven't overbooked yourself with client meetings, now that you're in such high demand?"

"And miss the fish and chips special at the pub where we first met?" I scoff. "Not on your life."

"Good." My boyfriend leans back into his pillows. "Arnie would be heartbroken if we didn't show up. Well, if *you* didn't show up. I wonder how long it'll take for me to win him over..."

I chuckle. Holden and I have been back to O'Reilly's a few times in the past couple of months, but the old bartender still greets my boyfriend with a scowl.

"It's got to be any day now," I assure him. "I mean, who could possibly resist your charm?"

Holden looks at me with hearts in his eyes.

CHAPTER 29

Christy

When Holden and I walk into O'Reilly's at 7:00 p.m., the lights are turned off. The delectable scent of golden-fried batter hangs in the air, but there's no one in sight. The door closes behind us, and all I hear is silence.

I turn back to Holden. "Bummer. They must have closed early."

My heart sinks, but more so for Holden. He was so excited to celebrate my birthday at the bar where we first met.

"Fuck. I'm sorry, baby. We'll have to come back next week." In the dim glow coming from a streetlamp outside the windows, I see Holden scratch his forehead. "Your favorite sushi restaurant isn't too far from here... Or we could try the new Italian place that Jenna and Charlie were raving about. What are you in the mood for?"

"Honestly, I'm up for any—"

"Surprise!"

My hand flies to my mouth as the pub lights flicker on, and

a slew of familiar faces pop up from where they were crouching behind the bar. As they clap and cheer for me, the first single off of Lola's latest album starts playing over the speakers.

I turn back to see Holden with a beaming smile. "Happy birthday, baby."

Before I can reply, my sister runs up and throws her arms around me. "I have a feeling this is going to be your best year yet," she whispers, trying to contain a squeal. Jenna hasn't stopped fantasizing about my wedding since the day Holden came over to pitch his fake-dating scheme.

"This was all his idea, by the way. I mean, he reached out to me for help with the guest list, but that's it." Jenna nudges me. "Sounds like husband material, wouldn't you say?"

"I just hope you're not so busy planning my wedding that you've forgotten about your own," I tease.

"Actually...I have exciting news!"

"Is it about the house in Tuscany? I know you've been anxious for an update from the contractor."

She nods. "Charlie and I talked to him today, and the renovations should be complete by August. So, we've decided to go full steam ahead and have our wedding there next fall!"

I squeeze my sister's hand. "I'm so happy for you. You'll have the Tuscan wedding you've been dreaming of."

She leans in to whisper to me again. "We could make it a double, if you and your beau are interested."

I roll my eyes, laughing, just as Charlie briefly turns from his conversation with his best pal, Holden, to give me a hug.

"Happy birthday, sis," he says.

I smile, delighted that he and my boyfriend get along so well. "Thanks, Charlie."

"I want a hug, too!" My mom wraps her arms around me

next, followed by Tim Shaker, who, it turns out, is one hell of a guy.

As promised, Jenna waited until I got back from Maui to meet him. When my mom opened the door to the apartment they now share, Tim greeted me with just as much warmth and enthusiasm as he did his own daughter. I figured he'd spend most of the afternoon getting to know Jenna, but he was equally curious about me. He even gave me the same bear hug my sister got when we said goodbye.

I'd been so threatened by the idea that Mom, Tim, and Jenna would get together without me—and I couldn't have blamed them if they had. But it's been two months since we met, and that hasn't happened once. Jenna, Mom, and I are still as close as ever, and Tim is a welcome addition to the mix. Every other week, my mom and Tim have me and Jenna and our significant others over for dinner. It's the kind of family gathering I've always dreamed of. And all it took was a shocking paternity revelation to make it happen.

When Mom and Tim move on to greet my boyfriend, Jenna turns back to me. "I told Holden not to bother inviting Michael," she says, speaking of the man who raised us. She stopped calling him "Dad" as soon as she found out about Tim and, frankly, I don't blame her. "I hope that's okay," she continues. "I figured you wouldn't want him here, even if he did come. Which is a big *if*, knowing him."

"You figured right. I haven't heard from him in months." I shrug. "Honestly, I think Tim cares more about me than Michael Andersen."

"Tim cares about you just as much as he does me, and I'm not just saying that," Jenna insists. "You feel it too, don't you?"

I nod, a smile playing on my lips. "Yeah. I really do."

"It's part of what I love about him. And you've seen how happy he makes Mom." Jenna wipes a tear from her eye. "He's a good man. The kind of father we always deserved. And I'm happy to share him with you."

"I love you," I say, throwing my arms around her.

"I love you more."

"May I cut in?"

I look up to see yet another impossibly handsome man to add to the growing collection here tonight. It's Dex Oliver, along with his leading lady, Sunny.

"I can't believe you guys drove all the way from Beachwood!" I exclaim, after we all exchange hugs and Jenna joins Mom and Tim at the bar. "Are you and Holden going to discuss Racing Hearts while you're in town?"

"That's the plan," my boyfriend chimes in, shaking Dex's hand. "Good to meet you in person, man. Really looking forward to working together."

As the two men continue chatting, I turn to Sunny. I swear, the woman gets more gorgeous every time I see her. She has that beautiful pregnant glow, of course, but it's more than that. She's living her best life, and it shows. Being married to her childhood sweetheart looks good on her. So does being a bestselling author.

"How's my favorite romance writer?" I ask.

"Fantastic. I just finished writing Book Three, can you believe it?" She heaves a happy sigh.

I shake my head. "You're a writing machine. I don't know how you do it."

"Truthfully...I don't sleep as much as I should. Dex has been on my case to get more rest, and he's right. But now that my third book is with my editor, I can relax a bit before this little guy comes along." She rubs her belly.

"Little *guy*? So..."

"It's a boy." Sunny beams. "We're so excited. Well, Dex and I are excited. Stella's still too young to understand what being a big sister means."

"How is that little sweetie?"

"She's great. She's with Dex's parents this weekend. They invited my mom and Luis over for dinner tonight, too. I'm sure Stella's getting spoiled rotten."

I smile. "Sounds like she's living the dream."

"How are my two favorite girls?" a voice behind me says. Sam swoops in, enveloping me and Sunny in a hug.

"I've missed you so much!" Sunny squeals. She and Sam went to college together and have been close friends for over a decade. But now that Sunny's back in Beachwood, they don't see each other nearly as often as they'd like.

"Ditto," Sam says, admiring her friend's belly. "Look at you, mama. Such a MILF."

"Thanks." Sunny laughs. Then a silence settles over us, and judging by the concern in her eyes, I'm sure she's thinking the same thing I am.

Sam completed her first cycle of IVF last month, and the pregnancy test came back negative. The doctor told her there was no cause for concern at this stage. But Sam was heartbroken. I was with her when the nurse called. Afterward, she cried in my lap for an hour.

Since then, she's been reluctant to talk about the process. Before the negative pregnancy test, she was an open book and didn't hesitate to reach out for emotional support. Now, she's more guarded. But I get it.

"It's okay," Sam says with a wistful laugh. "We don't have to ignore the elephant in the room. You can ask me how I'm doing."

"How are you doing?" Sunny and I ask in unison.

Sam nods. "Hopeful. Nervous. Hormonal as fuck, because I'm in the middle of my second round of shots."

I rest my hand on her shoulder. "You know we're here for whatever you need, right?"

"I do," she says, smiling. "And I appreciate it."

"Look who I found," Jenna says, joining us with her best friend, Vanessa, in tow. This is the first time I've seen her since she gave birth to her baby boy, Lucas, two months ago.

"Happy birthday, Christy! I'm so sorry I'm late. My son decided he wanted an extra-long feeding tonight." She rolls her eyes, laughing.

"He knew Mommy was trying to party without him, that's why," Jenna teases.

"Is Lucas with his dad?" I ask when I don't see Vanessa's husband, Asher.

She nods. "He took one for the team. But he's sorry to miss the party and wants you to have a shot for him."

"Done." I grin, then turn to Sunny. "You remember Vanessa, right?"

"Yes, of course. We met at Jenna's art show last year." She turns to Vanessa. "Congrats on the new baby. I'm having a boy, too. You'll have to give me some pointers. I'm scared he's going to pee on me."

"Oh, he will," Vanessa says, chuckling. "Trust me."

I glance at Sam, who gives me a nod, letting me know she's okay. As Sunny and Vanessa continue chatting, I pull her in for a tight squeeze. When I step back, she winces.

My forehead creases. "You okay?"

"It's all the estrogen," she explains. "My tits are so damn sore. They look phenomenal though, I gotta say. Not that anyone's going to see them but me. Even if I found a man who didn't mind that I was going through IVF, I wouldn't want him to touch me. I feel like I've had a lobotomy. For the first time in my life I have zero interest in dick. It's so fucking weird."

I laugh. "I love you."

Sam blows me a kiss to avoid another painful hug. "Love you."

"Alright, who's hungry for fish and chips?" Holden bellows to the crowd. His question is met with raucous applause.

As my friends and family disperse to the bar, where good old Arnie is serving up his special, my amazing boyfriend turns to me.

"Abby and Wyatt wished they could be here, too, but they're in Napa for a friend's wedding. They're really looking forward to having us for Thanksgiving, though. Abby pre-ordered every flavor pie at Magnolia Bakery."

"Oh my god, yum. I can't wait." I wrap my arms around his waist. "And thank you so much for this gift, Holden. No one's ever planned a surprise party for me before."

He chuckles. "You're welcome, baby. But this isn't your birthday present."

My eyebrows rise in disbelief. "There's more?"

"Just you wait." He kisses the top of my head, and I get butterflies. In the far corner of the room, a group of about half a dozen partygoers cheer when Arnie turns on the TVs. I crane my neck to get a better look, but I can't quite place them. "Who *are* those people?"

Holden grins. "I asked my pal Arnie to invite every regular

who was here the night we met. I wanted to recreate the atmosphere. With a few small tweaks."

"That's sweet. Was Arnie happy to do it?"

"Not even a little bit."

I look over at the bar to see the man in question glaring at my boyfriend. But when I wave at the old man, he beams at me.

I giggle and turn to the table of regulars. I was so worked up that night, I didn't pay much attention to the other bargoers, but I do recognize the Lola Piper fan who posted that first viral video of me and Holden. I was livid when I saw it, but look where that video got me.

"Her name's Diane, but you may remember her from her YouTube channel as PiperFan4Ever. We should thank her," Holden says, reading my mind.

When we approach Diane, she's as pleasant as ever. Probably because she isn't drunk this time. At least, not yet.

"Diane, you hard-launched our relationship before we even had one," I tell her with a laugh. "But if it weren't for you, I'm not sure Holden and I would've seen each other again. How can we ever thank you?"

"Oh, no need to thank me. I'm a romance reader, and I've been hooked on your love story," she tells me. "You've got main character energy, honey. And I'm happy you found your happy ending."

Main character energy. It's what I've been trying to cultivate for years. And well, if Diane sees it, who am I to argue?

We spend the rest of the night eating and drinking with family, friends, and our handful of new acquaintances, all while listening to Lola Piper's greatest hits play over the sound system. As a tried-and-true Pipette, I know every word by heart, of course. Or, I thought I did…until I hear Lola's signature voice paired with an unfamiliar melody.

"Why have I never heard this song before?" I ask Holden, perplexed. We're sitting at the bar, in the same seats we chose the night we first met.

He tilts his head. "You haven't? I have. Listen closely…I think you'll recognize the lyrics."

I strain to hear Lola's words over the low hum in the room.

Lip-lock, shell shock, the chemistry was rare

Right off the bat, the way I fell, like stardust in the air

Red lips, red hair, I couldn't help but stare

Oh, maybe we can win this game—

Baby, if we play fair

I turn to Holden, my hands shaking. "Oh my god. Did Lola write this song…about *us*?"

He smiles. "You can ask her yourself, when she's done singing."

With wide eyes, I follow his gaze to the kitchen door, which swings open, as if on cue. My jaw drops as soon as I see her pink hair. Singing into a mic, live and in person, is none other than the pop princess herself, Lola Piper. Along with two security guards, who take their places on either side of the room.

The crowd in the bar goes wild, and everyone jumps to their feet, ready to dance.

"Who else knew about this?" I ask Holden, my eyes welling up as I see the excited faces behind me.

"Well, I know how big a fan Jenna is, and I was afraid she'd have a heart attack, so I told her first," Holden begins.

I laugh. "Good call."

"And I told Diane, too. She's the president of Lola's fan

club, so I figured she'd need to mentally prepare herself. I also needed her to sign a contract agreeing not to post videos of Lola's performance, since this song hasn't been released yet."

"Another good call."

"But I thought this would be a great way to thank PiperFan4Ever for posting the video that changed my life."

I choke down a sob. "Oh, Holden..."

He kisses me.

After Lola's done singing, she runs straight over to me and wraps me in the tightest hug of my life. "Happy birthday, Christy! Did you like the song?"

"Did I—are you kidding?" I stammer. "I *loved* it!"

She breathes a sigh of relief, as if she had anything to worry about. "Oh, good. I'm calling it 'If We Play Fair.'"

"That has a nice ring to it," Holden says.

"It's perfect," I agree. "Thank you so much, Lola."

"Thank *you* for the inspiration," she says to me and Holden. "I'm going to sign some autographs and take some selfies, and then I gotta run. My manager booked a surprise show at a bar in River North. But I'll see you next week!" Lola smiles and kisses both me and Holden on the cheek.

"Now, *that* was the best birthday present I could ever hope for," I tell Holden with a giddy grin.

"That wasn't your birthday present either, baby." He laughs, clearly enjoying this little game.

I shake my head, smiling. "You're something else, Holden McBride. And I am so lucky."

"I'm the lucky one," he says, sitting on his barstool and pulling me to stand between his legs. As usual, his gaze tells me what I already know. But this time, he says the words out loud. "I love you, baby."

I burst into tears and bury my head in his neck. I've imagined this moment so many times, but nothing prepared me for the rush of overwhelming joy I'd feel.

He presses his lips against my ear. "I've loved you for a really long time."

"Me, too," I say, after catching my breath. I take a step back so I can look him in the eye. "I love you, Holden. You're my favorite fucking person on the planet."

He laughs. "Ditto, Red. You're the woman I've been waiting for my entire goddamn life."

His words render me speechless. I knew he loved me, but to hear just how much...

All I can do is kiss him. The crowd around Lola gives us ample time.

"Can I tell you something?" I ask when I pull away.

"Anything."

"This might sound crazy, but...after you took me to Grandma Evelyn's apartment, I had this really vivid dream about her. She said that you and I were meant to be. 'Written in the stars,' actually. She used the exact same words I'd said years ago, when I was telling Jenna about the kind of love I wanted. It had to have been a manifestation of my subconscious...but it felt so real."

Holden's eyes fill with tears and his lip quivers.

"I didn't tell you at the time, because we hadn't said 'I love you' yet, but now that we have, I wanted you to know. I thought you might like the idea that Grandma Evelyn's rooting for us. Even if it was just a dream."

"I do. You have no idea how much." Now, Holden starts to cry. I wrap my arms around him.

It's the first time he's cried over his grandmother in weeks.

Inspired by the work I've been doing in therapy, Holden asked his doctor for a referral for grief counseling. He's been going for a month, and it's helping a lot. But the first thing he learned is that grief isn't linear. Sometimes a wave hits, and all you can do is ride it out. Like now.

After a minute, he wipes his eyes. "Jesus. Who knew falling in love would turn me into such a sap."

"I like this side of you," I admit.

"I don't hate it either, to be honest. I'll cry all day in the privacy of my home, but in public, I need to at least try to keep up appearances," he tells me.

"And why is that?"

He tucks a strand of hair behind my ear. "Well, how am I supposed to intimidate assholes like Kyle if they know I'm a big softie at heart?"

"Kyle who?" I'm kidding, of course, but he hasn't crossed my mind once since Holden and I left the hospital that night.

My boyfriend smiles.

"Alright, everyone, Lola has to leave, so if you haven't gotten a picture, now's the time," one of her security guards announces.

Holden and I watch as the pop star takes a few more selfies, then walks toward the door. When she gets there, she turns and blows kisses at me and Holden. "Talk soon," she mouths.

Before she leaves, her eyes travel to one of the televisions over the bar, and a flicker of sadness washes over her face. I look up, curious, and see the actor Grady Brooks being interviewed on an entertainment news show. With his jet-black hair and ocean-blue eyes, he's hot as hell. But he's a notorious asshole. My sister met him through Dex, and—trust me—he's nothing but trouble.

I wonder if he and Lola have a history. Holden did say she has terrible taste in men.

I look to the door again, but the pop singer's gone.

When I turn back, Mom and Tim are making their way over to say goodbye to me and Holden. Our remaining guests leave shortly thereafter.

"Ready to go home?" my boyfriend asks.

I nod, my heart swelling. Even though my apartment is closer, his place feels more like home to me now.

As soon as we're through the front door, he takes my hand and leads me to the bedroom. "Are you ready for your birthday present?"

I blink at him. "I thought saying 'I love you' was my birthday present."

A laugh escapes him. "Baby, have you ever gotten an actual birthday present? They usually come in gift bags? Or little boxes, wrapped in paper?"

My face flushes as I giggle. "Well, yes, of course. But...I don't know, it's different this year. I already feel like the luckiest girl in the world. I don't need presents. Being loved by you is gift enough."

"That's the sweetest fucking thing I've ever heard," Holden says before his mouth meets mine. When we pull apart, he nods toward the dresser. "But just to be clear...what I'm hearing you say is that you *don't* want the gift sitting right there?"

My eyes light up when I see the elegantly wrapped box. "Well, since you went to the trouble, I suppose the least I can do is open it..."

Holden chuckles as he picks up the present and hands it to me. "Happy birthday, baby."

I peel off the tape and unwrap the gorgeous navy paper to

find a shimmering silver box. Inside is a stunning pendant necklace. I take it out to get a closer look at the sparkly gold medallion, decorated with a diamond-studded moon and stars. "Oh my god, Holden. This is so beautiful."

"Check out the back," he says, his voice cracking. When I look up, his cheeks are streaked with tears.

I turn the pendant over and see that it's engraved. My heart pounds as soon as I read the words. Even more so when I say them aloud. "'Sometimes love is written in the stars.'"

He nods.

"I don't understand." I shake my head. "How did—"

"Grandma Evelyn visits me in my dreams, too," he rasps. "The last time was a month ago. She told me exactly what to get you for your birthday. And she insisted I wait until the end of the night to give it to you."

My breath hitches. "Until after I told you about my dream."

"It packed a bigger punch this way." His smile is wistful.

I blow out a laugh. "It sure did."

"You came into my life at the exact right time." He puts an arm around my waist. "I always suspected it was more than coincidence, but now I know for sure. Christy Andersen, the smart, feisty, sexy-as-fuck literary agent, and Holden McBride, the cocky ace pitcher with a hopelessly dirty mouth—"

"And a heart of gold," I add.

"—were meant to be. And, seeing as we're written in the stars," he goes on, "I have a pitch for you, Red."

I raise an eyebrow. "I'm intrigued."

"I think you should move in with me," he says. "And, in exchange, I will give you toe-curling orgasms with my blue-ribbon dick, whenever the hell you please."

"Hmm." I flash him a playful grin as I pretend to mull over

his offer. "Will you make me scrambled eggs whenever I please, too?"

The gleam in his blue-gray eyes makes my heart flutter. "I think that can be arranged."

"Holden McBride," I say, reaching out my hand. "You've got yourself a deal."

Holden

Ten *Months Later...*

It's a perfect day for baseball at Wrigley Field. Seventy degrees and partly sunny. Low humidity and a light breeze blowing in. These are the days I used to live for. After a year away from the Friendly Confines, it feels damn good to be back.

I'm also nervous as fuck.

"Looking good, Number Twenty-Four," Christy says, eyeing me from head to toe.

"Speak for yourself, Red." I can't help but ogle my wife, who's wearing a fitted version of my jersey over a tank top and shorts.

Well, she's not my wife *yet*. But she will be. I told Kyle I was going to marry his ex-girlfriend, and I meant it.

The truth is, I had planned to ask her months ago. Then I looked into booking the New York Public Library for our wedding. Christy once dreamed of getting married there, and I want to make all her wishes come true—even the ones she gave up. Unfortunately, she was right about the price tag. Not only does it cost a fortune to get married there, I don't have near enough saved up. That's why I haven't asked her yet.

"How does your shoulder feel?" Christy asks with a slight crinkle in her brow.

"Want me to show you?" I pick her up off the floor of the tunnel behind the dugout and press her back against the cool, concrete wall. She wraps her legs around my waist, like the good girl I know she is. Then I give her the kind of kiss that elicits her little moan I love so much.

"We're going to get caught," she teases with a devious smile on her pretty red lips.

I huff a laugh. "It's a miracle we haven't yet."

A year into our relationship, Christy and I still can't get enough of each other. I knew this woman was wild the first time she straddled my lap and screwed me senseless. But the longer we're together, the more uninhibited she gets. She says she owes it to me for making her feel like a goddess, but I think she's selling herself short. Her commitment to therapy has also been a game-changer. Christy's more comfortable and confident in her body than ever, which has made her even more adventurous in *and* out of the bedroom. For the sake of our professional reputations, I'll take most of the details to my grave. But I will say that our last time flying in the private jet ranks miles higher than the rest.

Of course, this isn't the place for those kinds of shenanigans...at least, not minutes before first pitch. My teammates are only feet away, in the dugout, so I put Christy down. Typically, players' significant others don't watch from here, but today's an exception. I'm about to step out on the mound for the first time since last September. It was days after I'd streaked across Soldier Field. Christy and I had just negotiated our fake-dating deal because my career was in crisis, and all I could think about was how badly I wanted to kiss her.

It's hard to believe how much has changed since then. And I'm not only talking about all the mind-blowing sex and late-night talks we have. The parts of our lives that were on shaky ground last year are stronger than ever now. It's like the stars aligned when Christy and I met, and everything started falling into place.

My girlfriend's career is in rock-solid shape, for one thing. When word got out that megastar Lola Piper had signed with her, Christy began getting more query letters from authors than she could keep up with. And because the idea that she might overlook the next Hemingway kept her up at night, she hired two literary agents to help with the load. That's how Christy Andersen & Associates was born. Seven months in, business is booming.

In addition to Christy's professional success, we've also enjoyed quality time with both of our families. Not the deadbeat members, of course. Christy's dad and my parents are barely in the picture. But you know what? Good riddance. The Andersen women are living their best lives, and so are the men who love them. Our Sunday dinners together have become a highlight of my week. What Michael, Margot, and Julian lack in warmth, Ingrid and Tim have in spades. It's ironic that Tim, who has no parenting experience to speak of, is more of a father figure to me and Christy than our own dads.

Then, there's my relationship with my sister, which has never been better. In the ten months since Christy and I had Thanksgiving dinner in Manhattan, we've seen Abby, Wyatt, and the kids six times, including today. Yes, they're here, sitting in the VIP seats behind home plate, eager to cheer me on. Abby and Christy have become so close, they talk almost daily. And don't get me started on how Maisie and Matt have been calling my girlfriend "Aunt Christy" since we said goodbye in Maui. Another woman might have buckled under that kind of pressure, but Christy was tickled pink. It's obvious she adores our niece and nephew as much as I do.

Finally, I'd be remiss not to mention Wes. If you'd told me last year that my brother would marry Caterina Hart *and* become a much better man for it, I never would've believed you. But it's true. Wes and Cat eloped six months ago, while in Rio de Janeiro for a Siren Serum photoshoot. I'll admit, I was pretty sure working together would be the end of their romantic relationship. Turns out, they make a great team, and Cat's commitment to being a better person seems to have rubbed off on my brother. As the only McBride sibling who dabbles in real estate, he helped me find the perfect facility to house Racing Hearts: an old fitness center with outdoor space, not far from Wrigley Field. Although it needed renovating, starting from scratch with new construction would've added an extra year or two to our launch schedule. Thanks to Wes, Racing Hearts is opening its doors to the public tomorrow.

Which is why I'm here.

From the tunnel, Christy and I hear the Lola Piper song Dex and I chose to open our promotional video, which means it's showtime. With a giddy grin, Christy takes my hand and leads me up the steps to the dugout, so we can see the jumbotron.

The intro music fades, and my voice echoes throughout the stadium over a montage of pictures of me playing baseball over the years. As a kid in Little League. A middle schooler who'd just made the travel team. And a teenager who'd just turned down an Ivy League education to pursue his passion.

I don't regret my decision. Not one bit. I wouldn't be the man Christy fell in love with if I'd chosen otherwise. Everything worked out the way it was meant to. I'm reminded of that every time I see the starry pendant my girlfriend wears daily.

When a clip of me explaining the mission of Racing Hearts appears on the screen, the deafening roar of applause gives me goosebumps. As far as the eye can see, fans are wearing branded hats that Dex and I ordered for the occasion. It's a dream come true, after all the hard work we put in over the past twelve months. I'm already choked up, and this isn't even our opening day. Something tells me I'll be bawling when the first group of kids comes through the doors after we cut the ribbon tomorrow morning.

Yup, it's been one year since my heart cracked open, and I'm still a sap.

After the video introduction wraps, the announcer's voice booms over the speakers. "Starlings fans, we have a very special guest this afternoon. Former pitcher Holden McBride has returned to Wrigley Field to celebrate the launch of his charitable organization, Racing Hearts—a sports program designed to support the mental health needs of children and adolescents. Let's give him a warm welcome as he makes his way back to the mound to throw today's ceremonial first pitch."

"Have fun." My girlfriend gives me a quick peck, and my old coach throws me a ball, a wistful smile on his face. The news of my retirement hit him hard, particularly since my recovery from surgery went better than expected, and my doctor cleared me to play. The Starlings even reached out about negotiating a one-year contract. The fact that I chose not to was a shock to everyone but Christy and Dex, who've seen firsthand how fulfilled I am by Racing Hearts.

This is a new chapter of my life, and one I'm excited to pour my energy into. If I were pitching, I wouldn't have time to be as hands-on with this organization as I'd like. I don't want to run this program from behind a desk, responding to emails in the middle of the night because it's the first chance I've had all day to read them. I want to be inside our facility, working with the kids, teaming up with our therapists, and making sure we're meeting our full potential.

My decision to retire from baseball was made even easier by the fact that Christy and I are both eager to start a family. When that happens, I don't want to be on the road, missing out on first words and first steps. I want to be nap-trapped and covered in spit-up, the way a new dad should be.

All of that to say, this is my last hurrah at Wrigley Field—at least, until they invite me back for an anniversary or other celebration. As I walk to the mound for probably the thousandth time since I signed with the Starlings, my heart hammers, though not for the same old reasons. It's not like anyone here expects a retired pitcher to throw a hundred-mile-an-hour fastball, especially after a relatively recent shoulder surgery.

But that's not why I'm nervous.

In fact, tossing the ball feels great, and the crowd goes wild for me. Everyone's on their feet, and I can tell by their grins that it's not only about the pitch I threw. It's about Racing Hearts. It's about the man I've proven myself to be. At least now, I don't have to worry about the legacy I'll leave behind. No one's looking at me and seeing the jackass who streaked across Soldier Field. They're seeing the man my grandmother knew I could be. The one who's loved by a woman as incredible as Christy.

A year ago, I didn't think I deserved her. Now, I know better.

I meet the catcher at home plate and we shake hands. Then I wave goodbye to the fans and head toward the dugout, where the team photographer takes a few pictures of me and my old teammates for social media and posterity.

And when it's just me and Christy in the tunnel again, I let her kiss me and tell me how proud she is before I drop down to one knee.

This is why I felt anxious walking out to the mound. And why my hands are shaking now. I mean, I know she's going to say yes, but—

Fuck. Is it possible she'll say no?

"Oh my god!" The moment Christy gasps, my fears are put to rest. She's ecstatic. I thought I'd seen all of her happy faces, but this one takes the cake.

"Baby, I spent the better part of this past year unable to move my left arm, and it was the best goddamn year of my life," I say. "That's all you."

She bites a smile, her lips quivering.

"You are my first love. My only love. I've been calling you my wife in my head for a whole damn year now," I admit.

Her eyes go wide as she giggles. "You have?"

I nod. Then I pull the ring box from my pocket and open it for her to see. Her eyes glisten, which makes me teary, of course.

"All that's left is to make it official," I go on. "So, what do you say, Red? Will you marry me?"

Christy wipes her eyes. "Hell yes, I'll marry you!"

My heart's still racing as I put the ring on her finger. When I stand, she jumps into my arms and peppers me with kisses.

"Thank god." I blow out a breath. "I was nervous as fuck."

She laughs. "You didn't actually think I'd say no, did you?"

I tilt my head. "Well, I didn't want to be cocky and assume."

"Oh, how things have changed," she teases.

I put my bride-to-be on the ground. "Well, now that that's settled...you haven't made any plans for Valentine's Day yet, have you?"

Her brow furrows, but there's a twinkle in her eye. "No..."

"Good. How would you like to get married at the New York Public Library that day?"

"What?" Christy's jaw drops. "But how? It's so expensive, and we don't have enough saved up."

I sigh, a wry grin forming on my lips. "Don't I know it. I was going to ask you to marry me months ago, but I wanted to figure out how to give you the wedding of your dreams first."

"Holden, I don't need all of that," Christy insists. "I'd be happy marrying you at a chapel in Vegas."

"I know, and that's part of the reason I love you so damn much." I lean down to kiss her. "It's why Abby loves you, too. She's been asking me for months why I haven't proposed yet, and I finally told her the truth about how I'd donated most of my money to charity and couldn't afford the wedding of your dreams. That's when she offered to pay for the venue."

Christy shakes her head. "No, it's too much. We can't possibly accept."

"That's exactly what I said. Even when she told me how much she has saved up from working on Wall Street, before the kids were born, I still said no. But Abby's stubborn. So, she reached out to Wes."

My fiancée chuckles. "Well, Wes is so head over heels in love, I'm sure *he* said yes."

I nod. "They're going in on it together, as our wedding gift. I promised I'd pay them back when Racing Hearts starts generating revenue. They said they don't give a shit, because they just want us to be happy. You know I'm not going to cave that easily, but that's my own problem to work out with my siblings. As for the venue, it's booked. If you're interested, that is."

"Are you kidding?" Christy swallows a squeal. "Getting married at the New York Public Library on Valentine's Day? It's so romantic, I might swoon."

"Don't worry, baby." I grip her waist. "I've got you."

"You always have, Holden," she replies, tucking her gorgeous hair behind her ear. "Your devotion to me has been unwavering since we met. I mean, you dipped me with a bum shoulder and didn't let me fall, even though you were in excruciating pain."

"Oh, yeah," I say, remembering our first and only dance at the library gala. "I owe you a do-over at our wedding. And, now that I'm healed, you can fly into my arms like Baby in *Dirty Dancing*, if you want."

She throws her head back, laughing. "Let's not do anything that'll land you in the hospital again."

"It'll still be the best day of my life, because I got to marry you."

"Ditto," she says. "I love you, Husband."

My heart swells. "I love you, Wife."

My wife. Just five more months until it's official.

That night, Christy and I celebrate with our families at O'Reilly's. Jenna practically keels over when we share the news.

I couldn't tell her beforehand, because I knew she'd be so excited, she'd have a hard time not spilling the beans. But Ingrid knew. I asked for her blessing, and she was thrilled to give it to me. As for good old Arnie, well...when he sees the ring on Christy's finger, he smiles at me for the first time ever. Twenty bucks says by this time next year, he and I are best friends.

The next morning, I get an email from the Starlings' PR manager with a picture the team photographer snapped of my proposal. He must have been lurking around a corner of the tunnel, out of sight. I don't mind. The picture is epic. It's the moment I put the ring on Christy's finger, but she isn't even looking at it.

She's looking at me.

In the body of the message, the PR manager asks for permission to post the photo on social media. Since Christy and I have already shouted the news of our engagement from every rooftop, we agree.

And, wouldn't you know it, an hour later, we've gone viral again. But, this time, it's the headline I've been hoping for since we agreed to play pretend:

"Love at First Pitch: Holden McBride and Christy Andersen are Endgame."

I never could have written this story if it weren't for my husband, Dominique. For one thing, he's entirely responsible for my love of baseball. Before he came along, I'd been to Wrigley Field maybe three times—and only for the promise of a perfect Chicago hot dog (hold the ketchup). But Dominique, a lifelong Cubs fan and baseball player through high school, worried our relationship wouldn't make it past the regular season if I didn't at least tolerate the sport. So, on several lazy Sunday afternoons in front of the TV, he explained the rules to me. And, wouldn't you know it? I fell hard—almost as hard as Holden fell for Christy. Ten years later, I'm enthusiastically attending Cubs conventions and publishing my first baseball romance.

Of course, that's not the only reason I have my husband to thank for this book. If it weren't for you, Dominique, I wouldn't know the kind of love that feels as natural as breathing. Nor would I understand the magnetic pull that Christy and Holden experienced from the start. When I wrote the scene where she cries on his shoulder in the ocean on their first night in Maui, I teared up. That's when I knew Christy had found her husband. The man who would support her unconditionally, the way you support me.

Then there's my book coach and editor, Emily Colin. Your

enthusiasm for this novel helped me knock it out of the park (pun intended, as always). I am more grateful for you with every chapter I write. You've helped me grow in ways I never thought possible. I wasn't sure I'd be able to pull off an enemies-to-lovers, fake dating romance, with all its infinite layers, but here we are—and I have you to thank. I can't wait to see where this journey takes us next.

To my kiddos, who inspired the characters of Maisie and Matt, I'm so excited to see where your love of softball and baseball takes you. Watching you two out on the field, bats in hand, is one of the greatest joys of my life. You both made the travel team this year, and I'm so proud. And to my mom, who competes with my husband for the title of Nathalie's Biggest Fan, thank you so much for your support. I hope you weren't too offended by Holden's dirty mouth.

To my beta readers, Abigail, Dominique, Elisia, and Parissa; and to my street team, Ana, Abigail, Ashley, Elisia, and Shelley, your support means the world to me. Thank you for reading, reviewing, and helping me spread the word about the Dramatic Hearts Club. You are the ultimate cheer squad.

To my friends, who are as excited about this chapter of my life as I am—Jenn Bush, Aurea Chambers, Emily Giger, Amy Goff, Sarah Imberman, Puja Kapadia, Jane Kenyon, and Mia Lewisman—I love you all so much. Thank you for providing the laughs, caffeine, and power walks to help me slay (as our kids would say) this year of little sleep.

Last, but certainly not least, a huge thank you to my readers. I'm so happy you found me. I started writing the Dramatic Hearts Club series because I hoped it would help people feel less alone. After working as a therapist for fifteen years, I'm keenly aware that everyone is fighting some sort of battle. Unfortunately, Christy's personal struggles aren't unique, and she might be my most relatable character yet. If you identified with any part of her story, I hope her journey helped you heal. And I hope you know how beautiful you are.

About the Author

Nathalie Theodore is the IPPY award-winning, Amazon bestselling author of *If the Stars Align*, *If My Wishes Came True*, and *If We Play Fair*, the first three novels in her Dramatic Hearts Club series. A lawyer-turned-therapist and novelist, she writes love stories that dive deep into the psychology of her characters, using her background in mental health to create beautifully flawed, true-to-life protagonists. In addition to writing, she enjoys spending time with her family in their hometown of Chicago. More often than not, you'll find her at a coffee shop, a bookstore, or a baseball game.

CONNECT WITH ME ON SOCIAL MEDIA

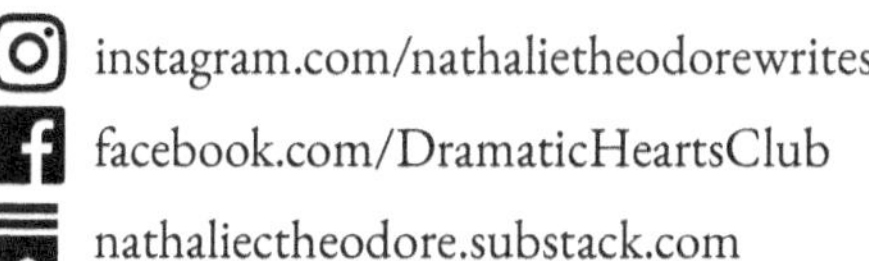

instagram.com/nathalietheodorewrites

facebook.com/DramaticHeartsClub

nathaliectheodore.substack.com

If the Stars Align

A standalone friends-to-lovers romance that spans a decade

(Sunny & Dex)

If My Wishes Came True

A standalone love-at-first-sight romance with a plot twist

(Jenna & Charlie)

If We Play Fair

A standalone enemies-to-lovers fake-dating baseball romance

(Christy & Holden)

SCAN THE QR CODE TO READ MORE

Thank You!

As an independent author, your support means the world to me. If you enjoyed *If We Play Fair*, please consider leaving a review on Goodreads or your preferred bookseller's site. Not only does your thoughtful feedback make my day, it helps put my books in more readers' hands.

Want more Christy and Holden?

If you're anything like me, you're not ready to part ways with this pair of soulmates. Scan the QR code on the left for a *Bonus Epilogue* and find out what happens when Christy and Holden take a whirlwind trip to Paris—with Caterina and Wes.

Join the Dramatic Hearts Club

Scan the QR code on the right to join my newsletter for exclusive first looks and bonus content.

BONUS EPILOGUE

NEWSLETTER